Beggar's
FLIP

BENNY LAWRENCE

Mindancer Press
Bedazzled Ink Publishing Company • Fairfield, California

978-1-949290-29-5 paperback

Cover Design
by

Mindancer Press
a division of
Bedazzled Ink Publishing Company
Fairfield, California
http://mindancerpress.bedazzledink.com

This is for all of you who asked for it.
You have only yourselves to blame.

PROLOGUE

THE SIXTH TIME that the Lady Melitta sent me down the stairs, I realized what should have been obvious to begin with: It was going to be a real bitch of a day.

It had begun the night before, as most bad days do. One of my many daily tasks as Melitta's handmaid was to bring my lady her supper tray, and I'd dropped it, sending all its contents crashing down onto the carpet. Wine. Gravy. Custard. A particularly greasy duck. It wasn't *exactly* an accident and Melitta knew it, but she didn't get as angry as I'd expected. I think she was distracted by something more pressing. Maybe she had crabs, or a raging infection. I can only hope.

She thrashed me, of course, but it was a routine kind of thrashing. Her heart wasn't really in it. I'd become a bit of a connoisseur of thrashings, in the years I had spent as Melitta's servant, and this one didn't come close to ranking in the top twenty on the all-time scale. And yet, for some reason, I lost my head in the middle of it, and I bit her hand.

Why? Damned if I know why. I was sixteen years old then, and my moods went up and down like a bucket in a well. I was unpredictable even to myself.

It was, I say in all modesty, a hell of a bite. I got my teeth into the fleshy part of the palm, below the little finger, and clamped down until my teeth nearly met. If I'd had a few more seconds, then I probably could have taken a whole chunk off. But Melitta—I'll say this much for her—Melitta knew how to stay calm under pressure. Instead of squawking and flailing uselessly, she snatched up a stick of firewood and smashed blows against the side of my head until I had to let go.

And after that, things got unpleasant.

It went on so long, and I made so many noises, that we woke up my father on the floor below. My father, Lord Iason, always was a light sleeper—I think it was because of his lifelong terror of assassins—but my howls that night could have woken a corpse.

Once awake, my father trailed up the stairs, peeked through the door, and cleared his throat uncomfortably. Which may not sound like much, but it was rare for him to go so far. Though it might have been coincidence, Melitta dropped her stick of firewood, and then me, a few seconds later. She paced back and forth across the room—quick, impatient, furious steps—then threw herself into her chair. Her fingernails drummed on the arm.

She wasn't supposed to do anything that would put my life at risk. My father needed me too badly, for a reason that was never ever mentioned or discussed. But Melitta probably spent half her time daydreaming about some kind of fatal accident.

When she finally spoke, it was a hiss, like seething water. "Get out of my sight."

I checked the floor, to be sure that I wasn't leaving any teeth on it, and then scrabbled backwards out of the door. My father had ghosted away by that point. He always tried to avoid getting involved. Such a shy, sensitive man.

I collapsed onto my straw mat outside Melitta's door and wrapped my blanket around me. We were a month into winter, and there was a white tracery of frost over the flagstones.

Just as I was beginning my post-thrashing ritual (catch breath, rub bruises, curse a lot), Melitta's door crashed open. She stormed out in her robe, a violet whirlwind. In one swift, vicious motion, she snatched my blanket away from me, and then stormed back into her room. The door smashed shut again.

For some time, I didn't do anything—didn't curl up or hug my knees to keep myself warm. I just stared at the opposite wall and hated her, hated her, hated her. Nothing else in the universe seemed more vivid or more real.

It was my breath that eventually caught my attention, the way it misted out in front of me. That's when I realized that I was shivering hard, my muscles jerking in something close to convulsions. It was bitter, bitter cold. My feet were bare, and already they looked bloodless and chalky blue.

How the hell, I wondered dully, was I supposed to sleep?

That was a stupid question, because of course I wasn't supposed to sleep. I was supposed to pass a miserable night out on the bare landing and transform by morning into a quivering little rabbit who wouldn't even dare to raise her eyes from the floor in my lady's presence.

Unlikely. But it's hard to predict your own breaking point, it really is. You can hold out through a lengthy beating, and then dissolve in snivelling tears when your shirt gets torn.

A thought popped into my head, and I almost laughed. Right that moment, right that *second*, my half-sister Ariadne would be getting ready for bed, a couple of turns down the spiral stairway from where I was sitting. Servants would have put warming pans between her sheets and aired out her pillows. Fluffed her coverlets, which were filled—I shit you not—with swan feathers.

Our evenings couldn't be more different. But then, she was Melitta's daughter. *My* mother, now dead, had been a servant who wasn't fast or lucky enough to stay out of my father's way. Apparently that was important, for some reason that I'd never really understood.

I managed that night by wrapping my straw mat around me like a stiff pancake. It kept some of my body heat in. Even so, there were times when I could feel my heart laboring, thudding with slow, painful jolts, as if my blood had grown too thick to flow through my veins. When that happened, I would get up and race up and down the stairs until my lungs burned.

The problem was that running made me sweat, and sweating made me colder. As night inched towards dawn, I stopped trying to sleep. I walked around and around and around the landing, with my arms inside my tunic, hugged against me, and I could only hope that my footsteps were keeping Melitta awake.

Whether it was that or something else, I don't think that my lady slept well. When she rang the bell at daybreak to summon me into her room, it had a particularly impatient sound to it: *Ting! Ting! Ting!*

She was out of bed when I entered the room, sitting stiffly in an armchair by the low-burning fire. I bowed my head and waited.

Melitta inspected me. Not that I was looking at her face—I was studying the toes of her slippers, face downcast—but still, I could tell. I could tell whether Melitta was smiling or frowning from the way the hairs on the back of my neck prickled.

"What are you waiting for?" she snapped, with sudden irritation. "Move."

MELITTA'S CHAMBER WAS at the top of the tower keep, so waiting on her involved an awful lot of climbing up and down. Melitta first took me as her handmaid when I was eight, and back then, it only took a trip or two up and down the stairs to bring me to the point of collapse. By the time I was sixteen, I was a lot tougher, but the work still took its toll.

As always, the first job of the morning was to carry Melitta's slop-pail down to the yard and empty it. Then I carried up her breakfast tray. That much I did by sheer reflex. Shuffling along half-asleep, I almost didn't notice how much I was hurting. Almost.

I was hungry, too, though it hardly seems worthwhile to mention it. I was always hungry back then. The scraping ache in my stomach was like the feel of stone underfoot. Just one of the bastard facts of living.

Melitta watched me narrowly as I put the tray down, but she said nothing—just drew her chair up to the table and waved for me to keep going.

Another trip down the tower stairs to fetch firewood, and another for a bucket of water. By then I was really struggling. My legs felt almost liquid, trembling beneath me, and my heart pounded so hard that I saw stars.

It was a vast relief when I reached the top floor. As I filled the washbasin, Melitta stared out of the window. She had already finished her breakfast. My lady was always, always trying to slim down, and so she ate very little in the morning: a hard rusk dipped in wine, and perhaps a few raisins or olives. Stupid, if you asked me. She was always starving by the time supper came, and would gobble something like two roast fowl and a pile of honey cakes, giving herself terrible heartburn. Which made her just a peach to deal with.

Her voice bored into me, all of a sudden. "Did you bring up enough wood?"

"Yes, my lady," I said, instead of the answer I wanted to give, which was *Of course I did, you stupid bitch.*

"It doesn't look like enough." Idly, she picked up a split chunk of ash wood, as if to inspect it.

"It'll last until supper. My lady."

"I don't think so."

Melitta was stronger than she looked. She gave a quick flick of the wrist, and the chunk of wood sailed backwards, in a graceful arc, straight out of the tower window.

I must have been a little light-headed by then, because I just stood there stupidly for the few seconds it took for the wood to reach the ground. There was a distant *thump* when it landed in the courtyard. Melitta didn't even look to see where it hit.

"No," she went on, picking up a log in each hand. "I don't think it's enough wood at all." Two more jerks, and those logs went out the window as well. "Not nearly enough." Two more logs followed. "You're going to have to learn, Gwyneth, that I won't tolerate shirking." Two more. "You're going to have to learn to work." Two more. "Without complaint." Two more. "Without question."

That emptied the woodbin, and she dusted off her hands. "More wood. Get moving."

I looked her in the face then. This was absolutely forbidden, but if I hadn't done it, I think I would have howled or thrown a boot. Melitta's pupils were black and blown wide, as if she was in the grip of terrible anger or terrible excitement. She expected me to crack—to scream or to fight, to resist somehow—and when that happened, she would resume what she had been doing the night before, exactly where she left off.

She didn't need to wait for me to crack, could have started the beating whenever she wanted. But she preferred it when I gave her an excuse. It scored her a point in some elaborate game that she played with Iason, on days when he wasn't ignoring her.

I bowed, too late, and backed out of the door. I wasn't going to win this, but damned if I was going to let her have any fun.

IT WAS SHEER hatred that got me down the stairs that time and back up with my armload of firewood. I didn't bother to lower my eyes when I shuffled back into my lady's room. She glared at me and I glared right back. We were too angry, both of us, to observe any of the niceties—too angry, even, to talk in sentences longer than one word.

"Wood," I announced unceremoniously and dumped it in the middle of the carpet.

Melitta's eyes swept down to the logs, the bark dust and mites scattered over her rug, and then back up to me. Her voice rasped as she ordered, "Water."

"Water," I repeated and snatched up the bucket next to the door. "Water," I muttered, and headed down the stairs again.

The anger was good; it pumped adrenaline through me, and that kept me going for a while. I clattered down six flights of steps at top speed, the empty bucket banging against my knees. All too soon, though, the last of my energy went out of me in one great *whoosh*. My aching legs buckled, and I sat down on the steps.

I went through my mental checklist: exhausted? Yes. In pain? Yes. Hungry? Hell yes.

In short, a real bitch of a day. Such days are common, when you work for a real bitch of a queen. But you never really get used to them. I never did, anyway.

It wasn't safe to sit still for too long. I got up and headed down the stairs again, more slowly, while I weighed my options. There were only two. I could slip away and look for a place to hide and rest. If I was very lucky, I could scrounge something to eat and maybe even take a nap. But sooner or later, someone would find me and turn me back over to Melitta and then . . . well. I flexed my shoulders and felt the pain roll through me, like one of the great foam-capped waves I'd seen in the distance through Melitta's window. I couldn't handle another thrashing so soon.

Maybe that left me with only one option: to do what I was told, for as long as my limbs kept obeying me. Simple—but not easy. Melitta could keep me going up and down the stairs all day, if the fancy took her. She wouldn't even have to speak. She would only have to raise and lower one finger, over and over and over.

I filled my bucket at the courtyard well and lugged it back to the base of the tower. If I had gone straight up, without hesitating or thinking about it, maybe I could have made it, but I didn't go straight up. I looked far above me, to the cornice that crowned the top tower window, and all of my muscles screeched in unison: *Not a chance.*

I stood there for quite some time.

And then I heard it: a gleeful, high-pitched titter.

It seemed vastly unfair that somebody—*anybody*—was in the mood to laugh when I was so miserable. Still, it was a distraction, and that was something.

The sound was coming from the stables, to my right. I abandoned the bucket of water by the stairs and slipped through the half-door into the steamy, straw-and-dung-smelling warmth of the stalls.

I didn't understand right away what I was seeing. All I could make out at first was some vast mound of frills, quivering away in an empty stall. Best I can describe, it looked like a vast levitating plate of dessert. As my eyes adjusted to the gloom, I realized it was a woman, leaning back against the wall, with her wide skirts flipped up over her head.

There was only one person in the castle who wore that kind of ridiculous frilly gown. It was my half-sister, the Lady Ariadne, heir to the house of Bain, ruler-to-be of the island of Bero.

There was no need for Ariadne to wear all those piles of lace. She had, after all, just turned seventeen—the celebrations went on for days and even I was given a cup of wine. She was old enough to order her own clothing, and all the seamstresses in the palace jumped four feet in the air when she walked by. Yet she refused to trade her frilly frocks for something that made her look her age.

I asked her once why the hell she didn't dress like a grown-up. She said, "Because I like to know something other people don't."

"What's that? How to shimmy around a ballroom wearing ten petticoats?"

"I know that I have a brain, and nobody else does, except for you. People look at me, see mounds of pink fabric, and think, 'Aha! Girl! Must be stupid.' It's like camouflage."

Maybe it was like camouflage, but not when she was backed up against a stable wall, tittering, with her skirts flung over her shoulder.

Then I saw what was making my sister squeal. There was a woman there with her, a lean brown woman, whipcord thin. She was one of the servants in the castle bakery—I'd seen her in the kitchen when fetching

Melitta's meals. She was about the same age as Ariadne and I, and she didn't say much but she had an interesting kind of face.

Now she had my sister backed up against the stable wall. She was moving rhythmically, in time to Ariadne's squeals, her hand buried somewhere I didn't want to see.

If it had been any noblewoman other than Ariadne standing there with her skirts over her head, I might have been worried about the kitchen girl. But I trusted Ariadne not to force this on someone who didn't want it. And besides, there was all the giggling. However things had gotten to this point, they were both of them having a *very* good time.

Well. Good for them, I guessed. But it wasn't going to happen for me, and now I'd wasted three precious minutes that weren't mine to waste. My lady Melitta was up in the tower counting the seconds until I returned with her damn washwater, and she'd make me pay for every last one. I started backing towards the door, keeping as quiet as I could.

Two steps away from the open air, my foot slipped and I went flying. The floor rushed up to meet me and I crashed heavily on my side.

For just an instant, I was too stunned and hurt to move. Then I was hit by a wave of total, all-consuming fury. Did the entire universe hate me today? Couldn't I *ever* catch a break? I clawed my way to my feet and stalked out to the yard in a red-hot haze.

"Wait," called a voice from behind me. "*Wait!*"

I nearly howled in frustration, but instead I stopped and turned around.

Ariadne whisked out of the stable, knotting her sash back into place around her gown. At the sight of my face, her eyes snapped wide, so I must have been looking worse than usual.

"Gwyneth, what on earth happened to you?" she asked.

There were so many sarcastic things that I could have said in reply, I couldn't even pick one.

"My mother," Ariadne said a second later, answering her own question. "Gods on high, I'm going to strangle that woman one day."

She always said that. Lately, it had begun to piss me off.

"Why are you out here?" I asked. "Don't you have to get back to your . . . thing?"

Ariadne waved that away. "She went back to the kitchens. Anyway, that's not important. Are you bleeding?"

"I don't know. *No,* Ariadne, don't check. There's no time. I have to get back to your mother. She's waiting for water."

"You're hauling water up the stairs?"

"Well, I considered *throwing* water up the stairs, but I decided against it in the end. Because that would be stupid."

She ignored my sarcasm, as usual. "Gwyn, you're shaking like a leaf. How are you going to carry a bucket up a hundred steps?"

"I'm going to imagine what your mother will do to me if I don't."

That was the honest answer, but I should have known better, because it brought on Ariadne's heroic side. Her nostrils flared and she stood so straight that she seemed six inches taller.

She said, "Where's the bucket? I'll carry it for you."

This was a typical Ariadne plan. Generous and giving—and totally impractical.

"You can't carry it for me," I said tightly. "What if Melitta sees you doing my work? What do you think will happen? We shouldn't even be talking right now. It's broad daylight!"

Officially, I wasn't supposed to talk to anyone but my lady Melitta. Ariadne was most definitely off limits. And though Ariadne rarely got into trouble, that could change very quickly if she was found hobnobbing with the bastard brat. There didn't seem to be anyone watching us in the courtyard, but it was never safe to assume that. Our father Iason was so paranoid that he posted spies everywhere from the breweries to the brothels.

"You're right," Ariadne said, after half-a-second's thought. "Hang on a minute. I'll get someone to help."

She turned, skirts swishing, but I caught her elbow. "I can't wait, Ariadne. I've already been down here too long."

"So I'll hurry." She detached herself from me. "Wait. *Please* wait."

She bustled away so fast that the dust of the stable yard swirled around her. I began to follow, but just then, a scullery boy staggered into the yard with an armload of dirty pots from breakfast. I had to retreat to a safe distance and pretend that I was picking a splinter from the bottom of my foot.

While I did that, I tiredly reviewed the conversation in my head. Ariadne had been kind and caring. I'd been a bit of a bitch. That had been happening a lot lately, and I wasn't sure how to fix it.

Ariadne was the one bright streak in the grey grime of my life. For the past eight miserable years, her loyalty to me had never wavered. She visited me as often as she could, to listen to my complaints and bind my cuts, to teach me and comfort me.

You might think it strange that she went to all the trouble—but that was just the way she was. They could tell her all they liked that peasants were born with stunted brains and could only learn lessons taught with a whip. All that kind of thing rolled straight off of her, like water from a duck's back. The two of us were sisters, and that was what mattered to her.

Apparently, it mattered enough that she was willing to cut short a very nice escapade with a kitchen girl for my sake.

So why, why, *why* did I snap at her every time she tried to be nice?

But then again, why *shouldn't* she be nice? She'd had breakfast. If I'd slept on swan feathers the night before and woken up to hot buttered crumpets, then I might be in a mood to help the downtrodden myself. And that was the thing. Grateful as I was to Ariadne, I was sick of being grateful. Sick of my neediness. Sick of never having anything to give her in return.

And as a minute passed, and then another and then another, my fuzzy feelings towards Ariadne disappeared. I needed to go, I needed to go right away, and she was nowhere in sight. Maybe the kitchen girl had caught up with her in some dark passage.

I was trying to scrape together enough energy to start up the stairs when a tall shape jogged across the yard—a man in the hardened leather jerkin of a castle guard.

I backed away. Force of habit. Child servants, girls and boys both, know not to be caught alone with a soldier. But I'd seen this man around before, and I didn't have the sense that he was dangerous. With his hunched posture and his too-ready smile, he looked like the kind of person who would say "Sorry!" if you kicked him in the shin.

He didn't meet my eyes as he neared me. He just stooped and grabbed the bucket. Then he loped up the tower stairs, taking them two at a time, as water sloshed over the bucket's rim.

I didn't know how Ariadne had found him or what she had told him. Probably very little. When you were the heir of the most powerful lord in Kila, you didn't have to explain yourself very often. Like her mother Melitta, Ariadne could get her meaning across with a finger snap.

As I headed up the stairs behind him, a question started to throb away in my brain like a headache. It was an old and stale question, and it was something I tried not to think about, but I couldn't always help myself, especially when I was tired.

Why couldn't Ariadne get me what I really needed?

Why did she have to stop at bringing me bread and teaching me arithmetic? Why couldn't she tell her mother to find a different hobby? Why couldn't she persuade our father to send me back to work in the kitchens, where I could scrub pots or peel potatoes in peace? And if that didn't work, why couldn't she get me away from here? There had to be a ship that would take me as a passenger, if she stomped her foot hard enough and often enough.

I tried not to think about this because there *were* reasons, and I sort of understood them. Ariadne's authority had hard limits. She could boss the servants around the citadel all she liked, but security was our father's domain, and not even the heir to the house of Bain could get someone in or out of the walls who hadn't been cleared by the gate guards. She had no money of her own—even her jewellery was locked away in the treasury at night—so she couldn't offer bribes.

As for trying to convince her parents of the errors of their ways . . . well, that was laughable. Once Lord Iason had made his mind up about something, you would have to use a sledge hammer to get him to change it. And there was no way of changing Melitta at all, short of assassination. In her seventeen years of life, I don't think that Ariadne had ever managed to persuade her parents to do anything they didn't want to do. In a way, she was at their mercy just as much as I was.

Yes, in a way. A well-fed, well-treated, well-educated kind of way. Maybe my sister had her own problems but it was damn hard to believe it on a day like this.

Though my progress was slow and stumbling, I was close to the tower's top. Three more turns of the staircase to go. As I paused for breath, the soldier who had helped me came loping down the steps.

"I left the bucket around the next bend," he said, but without stopping. He had his eyes lowered so he wouldn't see me.

For some reason—maybe because I was tired of feeling ungrateful, on top of everything else—I said, "Wait."

He jolted to a halt, staring at me as though I'd suddenly dropped down from the ceiling, and there was something in his face that was close to panic.

"Thank you," I said. "I mean it."

He ducked his head, as if to tell me that it had been his pleasure, but it really hadn't been and we both knew that. It would not be a good thing for a castle guard to be seen bounding up the steps towards the Lady Melitta's room. His career might not survive that discovery. *He* might not survive that discovery.

He should have left then, but for some reason he lingered, studying my face. The lump in his throat bobbed as he swallowed.

"I'm Whytock," he told me in a hoarse whisper. "Maybe some time I can help you again."

He gave another awkward nod, and the next second he was flying down the stairs, out of the tower, and away from danger.

I kept going up, step by step, retrieving the bucket from the landing where Whytock had left it. Why had he bothered to help, I wondered. Was he sorry for me? Or was he trying to get in Ariadne's good books, hoping for rewards when she eventually came to power? Maybe it was simpler than that—maybe he just wanted to get in my skirts. Or Ariadne's skirts, for that matter.

That was the problem with accepting gifts. There were always strings attached. Hell, even Ariadne would expect my life-long friendship in return for everything she'd done for me. There were days when I couldn't even figure out what I felt for her. Was it actual love, or just the fawning devotion of a hound towards a person who happened not to be holding a whip?

I'm embarrassed to admit this, but I was still deep in thought when I opened Melitta's door. I hadn't done something so stupid in years, but I was beyond tired by then. There was a grey film in front of my vision and I couldn't feel my own feet.

And that is why, when I lugged the bucket of water into my lady's chamber, I didn't see the stick of firewood which she had strategically placed in front of the door.

As a booby-trap, it was pretty weak. Melitta had probably done it as an afterthought, without any high expectations. She must have been pleasantly surprised when I barked both ankles on the log, flew headlong, and smashed into her carpet face-first.

After the first shock, I found I was lying in a spreading wet patch. The bucket rolled on its side, empty.

"My, my," came my lady's voice, syrup-sweet and low. "I suppose I'll be needing some more water, won't I?"

Well, I lost it right about then. I think that's understandable, but my timing was rotten. I should have kept it together until I was on my feet again. It's hard to fight when you're lying flat on your face.

Somehow I managed to grab the bucket and sling it at Melitta, but it struck her only a glancing blow, and that's as far as I got. She pounced, grabbing me by my hair—her favourite handhold. She wrenched it hard, forcing my head back, and then wrapped my long braid twice around her fist to make sure I couldn't go anywhere. She half-dragged and half-led me across the room, her hand held so low that I had to clamber after her on all fours.

Then she was leaning close into me and her breath was in my face. Sour wine and raisins. The veins in her eyes were inflamed. I knew she would cry soon. She always did.

"You're a rather stupid girl," she said. "Did you know that?"

I looked her straight in the eyes, because no matter what I did or didn't do, this day would not be getting any better. "You're a heartless bitch. So I guess we're even."

She jerked on my braid. "Keep dreaming. I'll just keep waking you up."

Her hand was almost gentle when it wrapped around my wrist and guided my arm behind my back, but then came the upward jerk.

Several seconds before I felt it, I heard the bone snap.

I ALMOST CLAWED my way out of sleep, wrenching myself upright. Phantom pain was shooting through my right arm. I clasped it, bent it, wiggled my fingers, rolled it from side to side. There was no deformity, no bleeding, no break. Just the familiar throb-throb-throb. That arm hadn't been the same since the day, six years before, when my lady Melitta broke it to teach me a lesson about dreams and waking.

I sat still for some time, as my heartbeat slowed. I wasn't certain what was real and what wasn't until I touched my wrist and found my garrotte tied around it, the braided sinew coiled loosely. Then I knew.

Melitta was dead. My father was dead. Whytock, the sheepish palace guard, had replaced my father as lord of the island of Bero, posing as my father's long-lost cousin. By all accounts, he was doing pretty well.

I wasn't in the castle where I grew up. I wasn't sleeping on a straw mat outside Melitta's bedchamber, or at the foot of her bed, or locked inside the stone closet in her room. I was on a beach two hundred leagues away, under a tent made of an old foresail.

The most brutal war in living memory was ripping apart the islands of Kila, and I was trying to do something about that.

And a pirate queen was asleep beside me.

I couldn't see my mistress's face—the canvas above us blocked the moonlight—but I could feel the easy pulse of her breathing. Good. At least one of us could keep dreaming a little longer.

I sat up, careful not to wake her, and slipped into my tunic. Then I groped my way out of the tent, into the chilly night air.

PART ONE

THE COST OF DOING BUSINESS

CHAPTER ONE

Darren, formerly of the House of Torasan (Pirate Queen)

I WOKE UP as soon as Lynn woke up, of course.

If you've ever had your slave girl kidnapped from you by a couple of brutal sadists, then you know that the experience is not good for your beauty sleep. It had been five months since we rescued Lynn from the island of Bero, and, in all that time, I hadn't slept through my watch below. Five or six times a night, I woke halfway and poked around on the bunk beside me to make sure Lynn was still there.

I never slept through her nightmares anymore.

After the tent flap swung shut behind Lynn, I scooted carefully over and peered through a crack. She was trudging barefoot through the sand, towards the shoreline.

We had spent the day scrubbing the *Banshee*'s hull. Careening is a long job and not an enjoyable one, unless, for some reason, you have some special fondness for barnacles. Lynn had been on the jump from dawn to dusk, and I knew she was exhausted. But I also knew she wouldn't come back to bed for hours, if she came back at all.

I don't learn from my mistakes the first time I make them. I don't even learn from my mistakes the seventeenth time I make them. But somewhere around the thirty-second go-around, I start to get wise. And after two years with Lynn, I was finally figuring out how to act when she had a bad dream. She didn't like being crowded too closely, but she would lapse into gloom if I just left her alone. That meant that I had to be patient.

I am not remotely patient.

I let the tent flap fall shut again, took a deep breath, and began to count to one thousand. I'd had to do this far too often since the day of the escape.

HERE'S THE THING about being a pirate queen: It's damn hard to take a vacation.

Five of us escaped from Bero: Lynn, her sister Ariadne, my first mate Regon, my bosun Latoya, and me. We were not in good shape as we began the journey south. Lynn had just spent twelve days as the Lady Melitta's punching bag, taking pummelling after pummelling as Melitta tried to break her of the habit of independent thought. Regon and Latoya and I were better off, but we'd suffered quite a few knocks and scrapes in our various feats of derring-do. Ariadne wasn't injured, but she *had* just killed her mother and been banished from her homeland, so I think it fair to say that she wasn't at her best.

The wounds didn't seem to matter that much in the first flush of our victory, when we boarded the *Badger* and set sail. But the euphoria wore off fast. It was cold, and we weren't dressed for it. Regon had a lump the size of an apple on the side of his head. Ariadne puked her guts out the first time she tasted salt beef.

The sea was choppy and our little boat leaked like a sieve, and the sailor in me was screaming that we ought to head for shore. But I refused to give the order, because I could see the colour grow stronger in Lynn's cheeks the farther away we sailed from Bero.

Somehow we managed to hold the boat together and keep it on top of the waves. It was mainly thanks to Regon, who came from ten generations of sailors and was himself (I firmly believed) part duck. It still took a series of minor miracles, and for a very very short time, I rediscovered the habit of prayer.

It took us two weeks to limp our way to the hidden harbour on the mainland, with Lynn and Regon and Latoya and I working watch and watch about the whole time. When we rounded the cove and saw the *Banshee* at anchor, with my red-and-black banner rippling from the masthead, I got a touch emotional. If you really want to know, I cried just a tiny little bit.

While I did that, Lynn stood by and rubbed my back. I almost stopped her. Considering everything that had happened, it seemed perverse that I was the one crying and she was the one soothing. But then, Lynn liked being the strong one. Maybe I could best comfort her by letting her comfort me.

At last, I dashed the tears from my eyes and tried to think of something tough and piratical to say. "They better have taken good care of my ship."

I DIDN'T GET the chance to inspect my ship right away. My entire crew charged me as soon as I swung on deck, all of them flailing various body parts and screaming like—well—like banshees.

There was Teek, the helmsman, and Corto, the quartermaster. There was Jess, who had been my lover what seemed like a couple of lifetimes ago, and Holly, her wife. Holly was very fond of Lynn, and now she looked like she didn't know whether to hug me for bringing her back or strangle me for losing her in the first place.

And then there was Spinner, the young sailmaker whom I'd sort of left in charge while I was away. He seemed ready to give up the title of pirate king, judging from the way he dashed towards me and all but hurled my cutlass back into my hand.

I raised the blade high, roaring at the top of my lungs, and drew Lynn tight towards me with my other arm. My sailors cheered so loudly that I felt a prickling at the corners of my eyes and knew that I would collapse into sobs then and there if I didn't get things back under control. So I called them all puking scuts and dirty sonsabitches and damned them to hell and back, and they cheered at that even louder. And though Lynn was exhausted, the purple circles under each of her eyes as deep as bruises, she smiled, too.

LYNN SAID THAT she would cook that night, and everyone in earshot said like *hell* she would cook that night. Jess and Holly, our resident landsmen, took over. They rolled up their sleeves, rowed to shore, and set to work wreaking havoc on the local population of chickens. When they rowed back a few hours later, their boat was groaning with a load of roast fowl, loaves of bread, plump red cheeses, slabs of honeycomb, and a whole bucket of cream.

It was a ridiculously lavish feast. I thought I should protest, tell Jess and Holly that they didn't need to waste so much food on us, but Jess's hard eyes warned me that she wasn't going to listen. I gave up and piled my trencher so high that I had to use both hands to heft it.

We all stuffed ourselves until the stars came out. Half the crew got drunk off their faces and danced in the torchlight; the other half sat back, lost in silent dreams. I nursed my third cup of wine and watched Lynn. She and Ariadne were leaning on the gunwale, staring out to sea, their heads almost touching as they talked about whatever sisters talk about. Every so often, I heard them laugh: Lynn low and soft, Ariadne quick and bright.

Jess was watching the two of them as well, but unlike me, she was frowning.

"Why did they dye Lynn's hair?" she asked, out of nowhere.

I had taken aside the people who mattered—Jess, Holly, Spinner, Teek—and told them a very little about what had happened back on Bero. Enough for them to understand why Lynn had been taken. Not enough for them to understand all the finer points. It was only natural for Jess to ask about Lynn's hair. It was usually as pale as flax, but Melitta had dyed it an unhealthy liver brown. It didn't suit her.

"I don't know why they did it," I said. "Probably because Lord Iason was blond, and Ariadne, too. They must have been trying to hide the family resemblance."

Jess snorted. "Lynn doesn't look *anything* like Ariadne."

"She does so. You can tell that they're sisters. Ariadne's just . . ."

I weighed my words. Ariadne was taller and bustier, her hair was thicker, her lips were fuller . . . Lynn was short, bony, and boyish, flat where Ariadne had curves.

"Ariadne looks healthier," I admitted. "And yet I've got no interest in her whatsoever, and Lynn leaves me a puddle on the floor. Does that make me a bad person?"

"Yes. You're a pervert."

I glared. "That wasn't what you were supposed to say."

"Then why did you bother to ask? *I'm* not one of your adoring followers. *I'm* not going to blow smoke up your behind just so that you can feel better about yourself." Jess took a long slow swallow of wine. "Is that why our relationship didn't last? Were you secretly pining for a scrawny little woman in a skimpy little tunic who would call you 'Mistress' and kneel at your feet?"

"Apparently, our relationship didn't last because you think that I'm a pervert."

"Stop being so sensitive."

"Stop calling me a pervert. I didn't plan to end up with Lynn—it just happened. And don't even pretend that I'm exploiting her. I can't make Lynn do anything that she doesn't want to do. I wouldn't even know where to start."

Jess sighed. "I know."

"Good."

"You're still a pervert."

"Oh, shut up."

She smiled crookedly, but the lines of worry in her face didn't smooth away. "I have a proposal for you, Darren."

"I'm not going to marry you. I'm over that phase of my life."

"Save the sarcasm." Jess nodded towards Lynn. "She's wounded, you know."

I grimaced. Things were getting serious. "She's a lot better than she was. Her ribs have knitted some and she doesn't hunch over when she walks."

Jess shook her head. "That's not what I mean. Lynn's wounded somewhere deep." She paused. "I don't know if she's really going to heal."

This was uncomfortably close to what I had been thinking myself, but I wasn't going to let it be true.

"She'll heal," I said, with as much conviction as I could muster. "She needs time."

Jess cocked an eyebrow. "Let's see if I've got this straight. Lynn's mother was murdered when she was eight. Lynn's stepmother took her as a servant and tormented her for the rest of her childhood. Lynn's father didn't give a damn for her as a person, but he did plan to use her as a brood sow and force her to bear his grandchildren. This because five-day fever withered up his testicles and left his trueborn daughter as barren as a piece of toast. These were the people who kidnapped Lynn from you. These were the people who had their way with her for a couple of weeks. And the end result was, when you found her, she was cowering in a closet, too whipped to even tell you she was there. Darren, she needs more than time if she's going to heal!"

As usual, I could have done without the lecture, but Jess did care for Lynn, in her own pushy mother-knows-best kind of way. If she wanted to help, so much the better. I forced down my defensiveness. "What did you have in mind?"

"I think the two of you should come back to the valley with Holly and me. Don't look at me that way. I'm not asking you to give up piracy for good. I tried to keep you away from the ocean once, and it didn't work out so well. But the valley is a good place for healing. It's quiet, and it's safe. No need to risk your lives or battle barbarians every other day. And now that the harvest's over, there isn't too much work to be done. The two of you can take it slow for a while. Read a few books, milk a few cows, eat too much and . . . Darren. Are you listening to me?"

"Of course I am."

"You're *not*. You're just waiting for the chance to say 'No.'"

"I'm not," I said. (I was, of course I was.)

She threw her hands up in exasperation. "Why won't you at least consider it?"

"I will consider it. All right? I will ask Lynn. But she won't want to come."

"Why *not*?"

A few months earlier, I wouldn't have known the answer to this question. Now, as I watched Lynn leaning on the gunwale, the moonlight touching her bare shoulders, it seemed all too obvious.

"Because," I said, as if I'd known it for years. "She loves the sea even more than I do."

NOW, JESS HAD the soul of a drill sergeant combined with a granite cliff, so she didn't give up her master plan just like *that*. Instead, she cornered Lynn later that night and made her pitch, about the peace and quiet in the valley, about reading books and eating too much and healing. And cows. Lynn heard her out, and then said, "No, thank you" with cheerful finality.

Jess's lips were a tight line. "I worry about you."

"Do you?" Lynn said lightly. "*I* worry about shellfish."

" . . . why shellfish?"

"Because nobody else ever worries about shellfish. Whereas people worry about *me* all the time. Which saves me the bother of doing it for myself."

Then, without even needing to look, she reached back and took my hand. "We're leaving tomorrow. Aren't we, Mistress?"

And I shrugged, because, apparently, we were.

So we did. The *Banshee* sailed the next day. We left Jess and Holly behind on the mainland, to return to their peace and quiet and books and bovines. Lynn was still so mottled with bruises and scratches that she looked like a piebald cat, but without a pause for breath, she took up her old place in the ship's routine: standing watches, conducting daily inspections, listening for murmurs of discontent from the crew, managing the supplies, plotting our course, planning strategy, boiling stew.

Even after everything Lynn had been through, she wouldn't slow down. She couldn't, I suppose. You can't sail out onto the high seas with a war raging all around you and *sort of* be a pirate. Less than two days after we left the harbour, we encountered our first post-Bero crisis: the House of Jiras, short on oarsmen for its war galleys, had started to kidnap entire villages at a time. So we gathered up six ships of my fleet, all of us flying my storm petrel banner, and sallied off to cause trouble. When that was done, there was the famine in the southern islands, and then the outbreak of plague, and the cannibals in the west, and . . . well, we kept busy.

Lynn's hair grew out pale gold, and when I trimmed her hair into its usual short cut, all traces of the ugly dye vanished. The bruises faded. She started to breathe more easily, walk without that trace of a limp. Her mind was as sharp as ever, her senses as keen. She could outthink a warlord cross-eyed and dead drunk and pummel me at koro with only half her mind on the game.

She was so much herself—her tricky, conniving, slightly ruthless self— that for days at a time, I could make myself believe that she really was all right. And then something would happen. She'd wake up screaming, ripping gashes in her arms with her own fingernails. Or she wouldn't sleep at all for a week.

Once, after a particularly bad night, I spent some time kicking a couple of empty barrels into splinters, pretending that they were Iason and Melitta. It didn't really help, but that wasn't surprising. I'd already killed the real Iason and Melitta and even *that* didn't make me feel much better.

Latoya happened on me when I was staring glumly at what was left of the barrels. "You can't fix her yourself," she told me. "Just be patient."

It was good advice, I knew, but patient I am not.

"FIVE HUNDRED AND *one*, five hundred and *two*, five hundred and . . . You know what? Screw this."

Abandoning the count, I pushed open the tent flap and stalked out onto the beach in search of Lynn. The sand crunched beneath my feet like damp sugar. I sniffed the air. Wet. We were in the southern part of the islands, where I had grown up, and where it rained for most of the year, with a hurricane or a blizzard now and then for variety.

Lynn was sitting near the waterline, pale in the wan moonlight, her legs drawn up, her arms wrapped around them. Despite the damp and the chill, she wore nothing but one of her thin tunics. It was slicked against her body like wet paper. She had to be freezing.

Most of my crewmen were asleep in a single great tent made of the *Banshee's* mainsail. But it was Regon and Latoya's watch, and those two were huddled together on an upturned longboat next to our campfire, passing a bottle back and forth. I ambled towards them, casually, as if I just wanted to ask some question about the weather.

Both of them showed surprise when I got close.

"Lynn's over there," Regon said, pointing.

"I *know* where she is." I shoved his hand down. "Stop it. You'll give me away."

"What do you mean?"

"I'm trying to be smooth. Subtle. I'm pretending not to know that she's upset. Oh, stop that," I snapped, as they exchanged weary glances. "I can be smooth, you know. I can be smooth like a bandit. A smooth bandit."

"Captain," Regon said gently. "Remember how Lynn has frighteningly good hearing?"

"So what?"

Regon pointed again towards the spot where Lynn sat by the waterline. She didn't turn her head, but she raised her hand and gave a little wave.

Crap and *crap* and crap again. It's a real challenge to keep secrets from a girl who can hear a whisper from twenty yards away.

I tried to recover some dignity by snarling something incomprehensible at Regon and Latoya. They didn't seem fazed. Latoya just saluted me with the bottle as I went.

I walked slowly, descending the slope of the beach. Lynn's head cocked to the side when I neared her, but she still didn't turn. Her sleeveless tunic left bare the angry red lines that formed a criss-cross pattern on her shoulders and back. Fresh scars. Gifts from Melitta. I didn't know what kind of weapon had inflicted those blows, but it must have been something heavy. Five months after Bero, they still hadn't faded.

"Hey," I said.

"Hey," Lynn echoed. "Just so you know, I don't want to be touched right now."

"Understood. I kind of figured. It's cold out here. Want my coat?"

"Thanks. No."

I laid it down on the sand beside her, in case she changed her mind, and then sat down myself, leaving a clear six inches between us. For some time, we watched the breakers roll in.

It startled me when she finally spoke. "To answer your question, I don't really remember what my mother was like."

"What are you talking about—oh. *Oh.* Do you always wait five months before answering a question?"

She half-smiled. "Only if it's important."

I dimly remembered asking Lynn about her mother while we were dashing around in the cellars beneath Iason's castle. We got interrupted by half of an army before she could answer, and, somehow, we'd never come back to the topic in the time since.

"You know what's stupid?" Lynn asked. "Ariadne remembers my mother better than I do."

"Really?"

"Really. I don't even remember what she looked like, not really. Red hair, I think. Freckles."

"Didn't you live with her until you were eight? In the castle kitchens?"

"I remember the kitchens. Or the colour of the kitchens, anyway. Orange bake ovens and saffron in the festival cakes. Russet apples, yellow pears. Copper kettles. And the smells. Venison and butter and cumin and cinnamon. I remember all that. But my mother . . . She was always just *there,* so I guess I never paid any attention to her."

"Oh, Lynn."

"Stop that. No being maudlin. That's the rule. We've discussed it." She was quiet a while longer, then said, "I hate the cold."

"My coat's right there."

"No."

"You're hardly wearing anything. It makes me colder just looking at you."

"So don't look. Look up instead. There's a ring around the moon tonight, see it?"

I squinted up through one eye. The ring was pale frosty blue, which did nothing to make me feel warmer.

Trying to be casual about it, I asked, "Do you want to tell me what you dreamed?"

I wasn't touching Lynn, but I still felt her shrug. "You know what I dreamed. I dreamed that I was back with Melitta."

"I mean, details."

"What do the details matter? I dreamed that she hit me. I dreamed that it hurt."

"It seemed like a bad one."

"I dreamed that she hit me a lot. I dreamed that it hurt a lot. I'm not trying to be coy, Darren, I just don't know what else there is to say."

"You could tell me exactly what Melitta did to you while you were growing up. If you wanted to, I mean."

"Can't you just imagine it for yourself? It's nothing you haven't seen before."

Somehow, her offhand tone made it all worse. "Lynn, what they did to you was disgusting!"

She was drawing in the sand with her forefinger: a cup, a sword, a wiggly-tailed fish. "It wasn't fun, no. It also wasn't anything out of the ordinary. I was a small helpless person. Small helpless people get hurt, every day and everywhere. There are child servants in every wealthy house in Kila. And what about the kids who end up on the ships? Remember where you found Spinner?"

I raked up a handful of sand, and let it slip through my fingers. "I remember."

"And there are too many other examples to count," Lynn went on. "Walk into a neighbourhood tavern, put on a blindfold, and throw a bread roll. Chances are, it'll bounce off the forehead of someone whose childhood was just as crap as mine. That's the kind of world we live in."

I wanted to argue—but there swum up in my mind, unbidden, the image of a long-ago child with wide eyes like a startled fawn. The servant girl who used to wait on me and my siblings when I was growing up on Torasan Isle. My sisters and brothers used to slap her around mercilessly when we were children. They were born noble, so they practised mistreating peasants the same way that kittens practise chasing mice. And—no use in pretending otherwise—I landed a few hard slaps on that girl over the years. Why? Probably just so I would fit in. I shook my head, banishing the memory.

"All right, so it wasn't special," I said doggedly. "It still matters. Everybody's pain matters. No one deserves to be treated the way you were treated. Isn't that the whole reason why we're doing this?"

She looked back at me. "Doing what?"

I gave a little wave around the beach, to indicate the guard pickets, the tents holding my sleeping crew, the row of torches stuck into the sand, and my flagship, its newly-scraped hull reflecting the firelight and star glow. "Saving Kila. Being pirates."

"I thought we were being pirates because you had no hope of getting an honest job." She picked up my heavy embroidered coat and drew it over her lap like a blanket. "I think I'm about ready to be touched now."

"You sure?"

"No, I'm only saying so to trick you . . . of course I'm sure, twit. Come here."

I snaked an arm around her and counted five under my breath. She didn't throw things or try to beat me away during that time, so I pulled her back against my chest. She spread the coat over us both, and I tried to rub some heat into her arms, but I might as well have been rubbing two icicles.

"All right, that's it," I said. "You're coming back to the tent."

She glanced over her shoulder, eyebrows arched. "Is that an order, Mistress?"

So she *was* feeling better. Good. "Damn right it's an order, girl. You need your sleep. I fully intend to work you into the ground tomorrow."

"Oh. Spiffy. What are we doing? Wait, don't tell me. Burying treasure."

"Well, don't sound all excited or anything."

"I was plenty excited the first time we did it. But honestly, Mistress— once you've seen one huge chest crammed full of gold, you've seen them all. If you want to hold my interest, you could—"

"I'm not going to sit naked in a chest of gold again. I told you, that was a one-time-only kind of adventure."

"Pity. It suited you."

"It chafed, darling."

"Wimp."

As we walked to our tent, we were both soaking wet from the damp sand and spray. It was blue cold, the kind of cold that sinks so deep into your bones that you don't stop shivering for hours.

So why had Lynn gone outside wearing nothing but one of her holy-*crap*-that's-short tunics? Was she hardened to cold, after a childhood spent in threadbare clothing? Or maybe she was afraid to wear anything that might blunt the edge of her senses. Lynn had always been hyper-aware of her surroundings, almost animal-like in the way she could detect danger. Maybe that came in part from her reluctance to put layers of cloth or leather between herself and the world. She didn't even wear shoes, unless we were walking over razor coral or hot rocks. Even then, I had to beg.

Wounds in the mind, scars in the mind. No way for me to check whether they'd scabbed over or were still bleeding.

I circled her with one arm as we walked. Absent-mindedly, she stroked icy fingertips along my cheek.

"I'm going to be fine," she said.

"I know."

"No, you don't know . . . but you'll see. You're being so patient with me, Darren. Don't think I haven't noticed. But you may have to be patient for a while longer."

"I can be patient for as long as it takes," I said, and did my best to mean it.

CHAPTER TWO

Lynn

THE NEXT MORNING, Darren "left me in charge of the camp" while she went off with two treasure chests to play buccaneer. Really, she hoped that I would catch up on my sleep while she was gone. Normally, I wouldn't have let her get away with that kind of nonsense, but she was so worried about me and trying so hard to hide it that I decided to give her a break.

I did go down to the beach to see them off. The chest of gold was loaded onto a wooden sledge, hauled along by six sailors. Behind them strode Latoya, who carried a second chest, this one empty. Darren followed, balancing the shovels on her shoulder.

We'd started to bury money a few months earlier. I wasn't really comfortable with this, didn't like leaving chests of treasure lying around on various beaches, but with Darren's fleet growing richer by the month, we had to do something with the loot. The only other option was to keep it aboard, and that would never do. If word got out that every one of Darren's ships was stuffed with gold up to the rafters, then not even the pirate queen's mighty reputation would be enough to keep the sea-wolves at bay.

So we buried it, but I insisted on taking precautions. Some of the stashes were hidden under heaps of seabird guano. Others were lodged under rocks beneath the tideline, in places where the current could suck you down unless you knew exactly where to put your feet. Sometimes we sunk a deep shaft for the chest of gold, filled in the hole halfway, and then put an empty chest on top, as a blind. Scavengers who found the empty chest almost never dug any deeper. People are so quick to give up.

With the treasure party gone, I settled down to real work. First came a tour of the sentry posts. Darren had done this already, first thing in the morning, but some added caution was in order, since we were in the southwest part of Kila.

The southwest was the domain of Lord Stribos of Torasan, Darren's father. That was a problem because ever since Stribos exiled Darren, the two of them had not been on the best of terms. By that, I mean that Stribos had hired a number of mercenaries to go after Darren and try to chop her into tiny bits. It had been a while since he sent the last bunch, but with horrible fathers, you could never be too careful. That much I knew from personal experience.

All the sentries were at their stations and alert. The water was rippled glass, the horizon broken only by a ship's silhouette. That was the *Sod Off*, one of Darren's smaller vessels, which was anchored in the bay, standing guard while the flagship was beached. No sign of danger, no hint of an approaching storm, not so much as the puffiest little cloud overhead.

The next job on my list was something that Darren called "taking the pulse of the crew," and I just called "snooping." It involved drifting around between sailors, listening to their conversations, but more than that, listening to what they *weren't* saying. You had to be alive to the meanings hidden in a shift of stance, a fidget, the downward flicker of an eye.

A ship at sea is a little world, with its own wars and alliances and fashions and fads, its own culture and climate. A good captain knows that world so thoroughly that she can read the moods of her men like the wind and weather. A good captain knows that Sal can't eat the salt pork because his teeth are wobbly in his gums, and that Gurny is so homesick that he blubbers in his hammock when he thinks no one can hear him. If two sailors start taking their pleasure with each other of an evening, a good captain knows what it means to each of them and how long it's likely to last. A good captain knows whose toes are aching and who eats too much, who sings below-decks and who can't stand music, who wanks on the foretop and what he thinks about when he's doing it.

The smallest things become important when you're on board a ship. When you're at sea—that is, when you're trapped in a wet wooden crate with seventy or so other people—you're never alone. You eat and work and sleep and fight with someone at each elbow, and if you are secretly longing to step on Sal's face and stuff Gurny's hammock up his nostrils, then life gets very difficult very quickly.

A good captain can track grumbling and bitterness to the source and roust them out before they grow into something worse. A bad captain understands none of this and acts surprised and almost offended when a mutiny suddenly erupts.

That morning, I learned that half the crew of the *Banshee* was snubbing Deriak because they thought he was swiping rum from the galley. I had my doubts, but never mind—*they* all believed it, and that could be enough to get Deriak bumped off the side of the ship some foggy night. We would transfer him to another ship, a smaller one, and warn its captain to keep an eye on the booze.

It was late morning by the time I was finished making the rounds. Time to think about feeding the crew. The day before, while most of us were careening the *Banshee*, a few sailors had scoured the coast for fresh food, but came up empty-handed. That meant the meal was made up mainly of salt beef, a large lump of which had been soaking in brine overnight. I shredded it and boiled it for a couple of hours until it was almost soft enough to chew, and thickened the resulting mess with crumbled biscuit.

It's impossible to make anything from salt beef which tastes genuinely *good,* but the stew was, at least, recognizable as food. The sailors made no complaints as they lined up at the pot with their tin pannikins. But they were sailors, and sailors don't complain if you give them rat for dinner, as long as you double their rum ration for the day. We had someone else on the *Banshee* who was a little bit pickier about her diet, and she didn't show up to eat.

It was no big surprise, but I wasn't about to ignore it, either. I filled a bowl with stew and went looking for my sister.

I FOUND ARIADNE a few minutes' walk away from the campsite, at the line where trees met sand.

She didn't look anything like the ornamental princess who had joined us on the *Banshee* a few months before. Gone were the long gowns and petticoats and corkscrew curls, replaced by the same woollen shirt and trousers that most of the sailors wore. Her hair was braided and pinned around her head in a neat flaxen crown. Her face was bare of paint and powder, but between the wind and the weather, her cheeks were always vivid pink.

"What are you doing?" I asked when I reached her. It was a pointless question in a way because I could see what she was doing—she was ripping up handfuls of a long, spotted grass. But damned if I knew why.

She shook dirt from the grass's hanging roots, and glared at them angrily. "Scurvy grass."

"That's scurvy grass?" I'd heard of the stuff. It was supposed to be good for bleeding gums.

Ariadne wiped her face, leaving a muddy trail. Her mouth looked pinched. "I don't know whether it's scurvy grass. I *think* it's scurvy grass, but I've only ever seen drawings. For all I know it could be 'looks like scurvy grass but is actually poisonous as all hell' grass. And since I don't know whether it's scurvy grass, this whole exercise of picking it is pretty pointless. Which is why I'm pissed."

She threw away the handful of grass. Then she sat down with a bump in the sand. Then she screeched at the top of her lungs, "*Balls!*"

I squatted down next to her. "What's going on? Are you and Latoya on the outs?"

"No! Well, yes, but that's just part of it. Lynn, I've got a bone to pick with you. You never warned me that women are insane."

I raised an eyebrow. "If you couldn't figure that out for yourself, then women might not be your thing."

"That's occurred to me." She rubbed dirt from her hands, pondering. "Maybe I should give the other side another try. Regon's available, isn't he?"

"Yes, and you could do a lot worse. But what's going on? You and Latoya were all over each other until a couple of weeks ago. Which of you is being the asshole?"

"Neither of us. Not really. Everything is just so . . ." She made vague, grabby hand gestures at nothing in particular. "I swear, marriage was never this complicated. Not that I miss Gerard, but at least he was low-maintenance. Two tugs in the right spot, and he was done for the night. Now there are all of these conversations, and feelings, and more conversations . . . honestly, it's a full time job."

And Latoya already had one of those. She was the bosun of the *Banshee*, which officially meant that she was in charge of the deck crew, and unofficially meant that she solved most of our problems while everyone else was screaming and running in circles. Invading barbarians? Call Latoya. Dry rot in the captain's cabin? Latoya again. Mast snapped in half? Call Latoya, tell her to bring a hammer. Raging flood? Call Latoya, tell her to bring a bucket. No doubt that cut into the time that she had available for romance. I made a mental note to try and adjust her workload.

"I won't interrogate you if you're sick of talking," I said. "But you've got to eat."

Ariadne's eyes flicked to the bowl of stew I was holding. She swallowed hard and jerked several more handfuls of the spotted grass out of the ground. When she spoke, it was in the same soft, self-damning tone that Darren always used when she thought that she had disappointed me. "I can't eat that stuff, Lynn. I'm sorry. I just can't."

My sister was having trouble adjusting to ship's biscuits and salt beef after a lifetime of roast peacock and sweet almond cakes. Of course, if she got hungry enough, the problem would disappear, but I was holding that in reserve as a last resort option.

I abandoned the stew, found the handful of sugary lumps that I'd been carrying in my cleanest pocket, held them out.

Ariadne studied them warily. "What are these?"

"Figs. Pretty dry, but still good. Try them."

She narrowed her eyes in suspicion. "Is the rest of the crew getting dried figs?"

I briefly considered lying, decided against it. "No. These are from Darren's private stash. Don't worry, she won't mind. It'll save her from having to fret about whether she deserves a private stash of food in the first place."

"I don't want special treatment!"

"Yes, you do. You just don't want to want it."

She flounced. "Well, I don't need it."

"You kind of need it. You haven't eaten all day."

"I'll survive."

Why were all the women in my life so stubborn? "All right, you'll survive. But why suffer? What's the point?"

"I'm not pulling my weight."

She said it very abruptly, blurting out the words before she could change her mind. I leaned back on my haunches and closed my eyes. It was going to be one of *those* conversations.

"I'm not, am I?" she asked. "I'm not doing any work on the ship that's worth the cost of my keep."

"What do you expect of yourself?" I asked, feeling tired. "It's only been five months since you came aboard. There's a learning curve."

"There's no learning curve when it comes to swabbing down the deck, and I can't even do *that*."

Fact. She'd only tried it once. A few minutes in, she fell down and started wheezing. She had to nap in the shade for half an hour before she recovered enough to speak. Latoya finished the job for her. Embarrassed, I looked in the other direction.

She was in full flood now. "You do three times the amount of work that I do, and you're half my size, and you hardly ever sleep! How the hell do you handle it?"

I couldn't help it—I had to laugh. "I've been working since I was five."

"You were a house servant!"

"Exactly. If you're a servant in a noble house, you work every minute that you're not unconscious. Compared to that, the work I do shipside is peanuts. Tiny little peanuts."

She flounced again. "You're not making me feel any better."

"Just take the damn figs, would you?" I rattled them in front of her. "When we were kids, you spent half of your life bringing me food. Consider this payback."

She rolled her eyes, but she took the figs.

"Besides," I said, once she was eating. "You're our surgeon, remember? You'll pull your weight once we have injuries on board."

"Oh gods," she said thickly, through a mouthful of fruit. "I'm no surgeon. I don't think you realize how little I actually know."

"You know more than the rest of us." That, at least, was true. After all the years that Ariadne had spent tending my various injuries, she could split a broken toe or wrap a cut while half-asleep. "The important thing is that you're willing to learn. You're new to all of this. Let yourself grow into it."

Still chewing, she upturned her face to the noon sun. "Lords of the deep preserve us, Lynn. When little squirts like you are the only ones talking sense, then the world truly is in trouble."

I grinned, would have responded, but a whistle split the air, coming from the direction of our sentries on the beach. Instantly, I hopped to my feet.

"What does that one mean?" Ariadne asked, getting up herself. "I don't know all the signals yet."

"Short-short-long, long-short. A ship's heading in, but it's not a warship, not an attack, and it hasn't noticed us yet."

"Not an emergency, then?"

Maybe not, but I hadn't survived as long as I had by toying around with dangerous things like optimism.

I WAS THE first to reach the lookout who had given the warning, and he answered my question before I had a chance to ask it.

"Small dinghy," he said. "Looks like it's being washed in on the tide."

I squinted at the little boat, bobbling aimlessly as it made its way to shore. The oars were missing, and the sail was ripped to rags. "Unmanned?"

"Not quite." The lookout pointed.

It was hard to make out, but I saw it—a white hand and arm flopping against the dinghy's bleached white wood. A corpse, I thought, until the fingers clenched into a fist.

"Get your kit!" I called back to Ariadne, who was panting up towards us. She nodded and changed direction. As she sprinted off, I yelled for Darren's first mate. "Regon!"

He was already wading into the waist-high water, his strong, stocky body fighting the breakers. The lookout followed him, and then two other sailors. I shifted my weight from foot to foot, wanting to help, but knowing that I was of limited use in the hauling-heavy-things-around department.

The four of them together managed to manoeuvre the boat close to shore. Regon hoisted a weakly moving body from the boat into his arms, sloshed to dry land with it, and laid it in the sand.

I saw the wounds first: a deep one slashing across the torso, another in the gut, gaping so wide that there was a shiny gleam of entrails. Ariadne ran up with an armload of rags and set to work plugging the holes.

Then I saw the victim's face, and my heart flipped over. Was this *Darren*? There were a few seconds of raw, desperate panic before my vision cleared. It was a man, a whole head taller than my pirate. Still, he had Darren's lean, hawkish features, her shaggy dark hair. They looked too much alike for it to be coincidence.

I glanced up. "Regon?"

He knew what I was asking. Squatting down beside me, he explored the remains of the man's shredded clothing with his fingers. "Black tunic, silver piping. Lord Stribos's colours. And the hawk's head emblem. Yes. He's a noble. House of Torasan."

I swore under my breath. "Darren's brother, then."

"Or a cousin or an uncle, at least. I don't recognize him."

"I do." That was Spinner, behind me. He must have been repairing a sail, because he still had a lump of beeswax clasped in one fist, gripping it so tightly that ribbons of warm wax curled out between his fingers. "That's Lord Alek."

"Alek?" I brushed hair from my eyes. "You mean, the one who—?"

"Yep."

Worse and worse. "Regon, get the *Banshee* afloat. His wounds are fresh, so there are probably warships nearby. I don't want company coming while we're still landlocked."

"I've already given the orders," Regon said. "But it's nice to know you agree."

"And Spinner," I said. "Maybe . . . maybe you should go."

Spinner rocked back on his heels. "Why? You think I'm panicking? He's not going to beat any cabin boys any time soon."

"No, but somebody has to tell my mistress that he's here. That might as well be you. No reason for you to stick around unless you want to kick him in the head few times while he's unconscious."

"Tempting," Spinner said tightly. He shoved the wad of wax into his pocket. "But I like to think I'm a bigger man than that. I'll get the captain."

Ariadne had Alek's wrist now, checking his pulse, and she looked grim. "Better tell Darren to hurry, if she wants to say goodbye."

OVER THE NEXT few minutes, Ariadne and I did what little we could for Alek. The seawater washing over his wounds had kept them clean, but it had also kept the blood from clotting, so the gashes still oozed pink-red. We bandaged the cuts, and dribbled some fresh water between his parted lips, but we were just going through the motions. He had lost so much blood already that his skin was bluish-white, like the underbelly of a fish, and that was something that we couldn't repair.

I wished that I hadn't sent Spinner after Darren. Alek was going to die whether she was around to watch or not, and what difference would it make whether she spoke to him one last time? Darren had been cast out by her family, and while Alek may not have made that decision, I doubted that he'd taken any heroic stand in her defence. And once Darren was exiled, her ties to the House of Torasan were—at least officially—severed. She was clanless, orphaned, with a place on the social hierarchy just above mine as a runaway servant, and slightly below that of a naked mole rat. If Darren came racing up to comfort her brother in his last moments, he might just spit in her face.

"How does Spinner know this man?" Ariadne asked suddenly.

I glanced up. "Alek is Darren's brother, a Torasan noble . . ."

"I got that much, thank you."

"Spinner first went to sea as a ship's boy, when he was about ten. Alek was his captain."

My sister hissed and pulled a bandage tight with more force than strictly necessary. "*Don't* tell me, *let* me guess. Alek made his life miserable."

"I don't think it was anything personal, or calculated. Just offhand cruelty. But offhand cruelty is enough if you're a skinny kid with a terrible stutter who gets seasick every time you smell salt. Spinner went through hell until he ended up on one of Darren's ships."

"How did that happen?"

"He stowed away. *Dammit.* This man's waking up."

Alek's limbs jerked and twitched. His breath rattled in his chest.

"Broken ribs," Ariadne said. "A lot of them. He's had a bad day."

He probably deserved it, I wanted to say, but I bit the words back and yelled, in no particular direction, "*Mistress, hurry!*"

Footsteps. The slushy sound of someone trying to run through soft sand. Darren appeared, loose-limbed, flailing, floundering through the dunes. She reached us seconds later, threw herself down by her brother and gasped, "Alek!"

Now here's the thing: she *sounded* worried, and her face was drawn, as though she was under horrible strain, but it didn't seem all that sincere to me. She was like an actor in a melodrama, playing a grieving woman.

His rolling eyes focused on her, and there was a flash of recognition. He licked his lips with a tongue like leather and croaked, "Darren."

"It's me," she said, in between gulps of air. "Gods, Alek. Is there anything I can do for you?"

He stared at her, pulse ticking faster and faster as if he was wrestling with himself. Then he lunged and grabbed her by the shoulders.

"*Warn . . . our . . . father.*" The voice was raspy and grating, but the words were clear enough. "*Warn . . . him . . .*"

He fell back after he got that far, exhausted. Darren grabbed his hand and squeezed it. "Warn our father about what?"

Alek took a deep breath and gave a strangled sob of pain. That was his broken ribs, I figured—with each breath he took, he was tearing his own organs apart.

"Ambush," he whispered. "Three warships . . . in the Refulon Strait. We were betrayed . . . Darren . . . our father has to know—"

"I'll tell him," she promised. "I'll tell him, Alek. Tell me who betrayed you. I'll tell our father."

Another wave of pain wracked him. His entire body went into a spasm, his chest jerking.

Darren caught his wrists and held them tightly. "Alek, *who*?"

More desperate breaths. "Traitor . . . one of us . . . it was one of our own. Betrayed us. Backstabber . . . you have to . . . not much time. Darren. Darren, it was my—"

The words were cut off by Alek's own moan of anguish. His body jerked again, and again. Bloody foam dribbled between his lips and down his chin.

Darren waited, gripping his hands. For a while, she tried asking questions. First about the traitor, and then, when that failed to rouse him, about their father, about his wife, about his home. But Alek was beyond talking now.

In stories, wounded people pass out once the pain gets intense. In real life, it's a little bit different. Alek was conscious—more or less—for over an hour, gouging trenches in the sand as he kicked and writhed. Sometimes he screamed in agony; sometimes he cried. All that weary time, Darren sat beside him, sometimes touching his hand, sometimes trying to talk, sometimes just staring dumbly.

Finally, Alek reached the deep stage of suffering: too exhausted to scream any longer, but not too exhausted to hurt. He lay still, sunken eyes fixed on the sky, seeing nothing, and Darren rose shakily to her feet.

"I'll be right back," she whispered, and headed for the nearest set of bushes at a run. The sound of retching wafted back to us.

But we didn't dwell on that. Latoya had come to join us at some point during the festivities. The moment Darren was out of sight, she turned to me, one eyebrow arched up questioningly. I nodded my agreement.

Latoya stooped down beside Alek and cracked her knuckles. I couldn't see what she was doing down there; her broad back blocked my view. There was just the tiniest rustle and a soft little *click,* and then no more sound of tortured breathing. Latoya was about as good at killing as she was at everything else.

Ariadne couldn't conceal her sigh of relief. She pushed down Alek's eyelids firmly, as if closing a terrible book. "That's that, I guess."

Of course, it wasn't.

CHAPTER THREE

Darren, formerly of the House of Torasan (Pirate Queen)

THEY GAVE ME space for the rest of the day.

Regon and Lynn took charge as my crew launched the *Banshee* and loaded the stores. I barely noticed any of it. The hours slipped by blurrily, until, at twilight, I found myself sitting on my bunk and staring at my own hands.

I tried saying the words to myself, as if I was prodding a bruise. "My brother is dead."

Nothing. Not even a flicker of pain. Weren't you supposed to feel something when your brother died?

Then again. Alek was my second-oldest brother, ten years my senior. We hadn't spent much time together while we were growing up. Young nobles are sent to sea to captain the merchant ships as soon as they're old enough to stand a chance of surviving the experience. Alek was given his first command and went away just as I was getting old enough to toddle around and notice things. Shortly after Alek was summoned home to take charge of my father's army, I was sent on my own maiden voyage. It would be an understatement to say that we weren't close. For most of my childhood, I didn't say anything to him more meaningful than "Pass the salt."

I did have one vivid memory involving Alek, though it wasn't one I especially relished. It involved the night when I began to live the glamorous life of a noble in exile—the night when I was banished from Torasan Isle.

YOU'VE PROBABLY HEARD the story, or at least bits and pieces of it, so I don't need to go over every detail. What happened, briefly, was this: I invited Jess to visit my father's court.

That was, to say the least, a bad move. Jess was a beekeeper and a midwife, a peasant from her tanned face to her muddy boots. Life at court, with all its intrigues and pretensions, alternately bored and repulsed her, and she wasn't very diplomatic about it.

I should have expected that, and I think I did, really. But Jess and I were together back then—these being the days before *she* decided I was a pervert, and *I* decided that a life spent with her in peaceful agricultural pursuits would drive me barking mad. An invitation to my family home, even though I knew the visit would be a disaster, seemed like an offering worthy of my love. Or something stupid like that. I was young then—too young to realize that things aren't always worth doing just because they're painful and difficult.

Whatever. I invited Jess to Torasan Isle. It was a disaster. She spent all her time sneering at the nobles, with their lace-trimmed shirts and their velvet pantaloons, and they spent their time sneering right back at her.

Even the nights were bad. Being a peasant, Jess didn't rate a guest room. She was supposed to sleep on a reed mat in the Great Hall with the servants and the tradesmen, and I didn't have the balls to protest. So, every evening, she would bed down dutifully among the commoners. Once the castle was asleep, I would sneak out, fetch her from the Great Hall, and smuggle her back to my own quarters. We would spend the night lying a foot apart in the billowy plushness of my feather bed, both of us staring, glum and wakeful, at the ceiling.

It came to a head after we'd been there a week. An ambassador had just arrived from eastern Tavar. My father hated Tavarenes, but he liked Tavarene gold and Taverene rubies, so he ordered up a welcome feast and wrenched a smile onto his face.

I was seated at the high table for the feast, of course, but they put Jess somewhere well below the fourth salt, so far down the hall that I could barely even see her, let alone speak to her. I caught a glimpse of her every now and then, but mostly I just sat hunched over my roast boar and apple cake, scowling at the food instead of eating it.

All around me churned the hubbub of tipsy nobles enjoying themselves. Two of my brothers were playing their favourite dinnertime game: balance a ripe fig on top of a wine bottle, and slash it in half with a rapier swipe. My father had pulled a young serving girl onto his lap, and was whispering in her ear, as he held her chin tightly between two fat fingers. A few ladies-in-waiting were clustered together, and their laughter was like the shrieks of parrots.

I sneaked a look towards Jess for the thousandth time and found that she had pushed her bench back from the table. She was staring, arms folded, at the drunken scene before her, her expression so foul that she could have been contemplating rotten meat.

Why did I do what I did next? Why did I push my own chair back from the table and stomp down the steps to join Jess? It was one of the pivotal moments in my life, so you'd think I would remember it better. Fact is, I really don't know what I was thinking. Probably I wasn't thinking *much*. I'd put back more than one goblet of Torasan's famous cherry wine that evening, and usually just a swallow of the stuff was enough to make me slide happily under the table.

I stomped down the whole length of the hall, rigid with self-consciousness. People were staring already. When I reached Jess, I thrust out one hand. "Dance with me," I ordered gruffly.

Jess had her eyebrows raised high. "Is this a good idea?"

"No. Come on."

"Oh dear," she muttered. She took my hand, but very gingerly, so I would know that she was acting against her better judgment.

Feeling worse by the moment, I led Jess into the centre of the floor. Some wit among the musicians struck up a slow dance tune, and the others followed. I don't know what happened to those musicians in the aftermath of my little display of defiance. They were probably whipped, at the very least. Maybe a couple of them lost a finger or two.

"Darren," Jess said warningly. There was a parental note in her tone, as if she was speaking to a child playing with a live coal. She always did think of me that way.

"Just dance," I said, desperate now, and already aware that I'd made a terrible mistake. Dancing had never been one of my special talents, but it had been years since I'd even tried it. I'd spent almost a decade away from court, stopping at the Isle for only a few days here, a few days there, to pay my respects to my father and take his orders. I couldn't remember any of the steps that I had memorized so painfully while I was growing up. I wasn't even sure which of us was going to lead.

More than ever, I wanted to retreat back to my chair, but it simply wasn't an option. I grabbed Jess's right hand and slapped it on the small of my back, and then pulled her in towards me. Together we executed just about the clumsiest dance in the history of our nation. It was kind of a back-and-forth shuffle and then we did a little twirly thing that didn't go anywhere.

At least the absurdity of the situation had Jess amused. She laughed helplessly and tossed her hair back from her face.

In spite of everything, it wasn't lost on me how beautiful she was, amber hair aflame in the light of the torches. Her long tunic was only woollen homespun dyed with nut hulls, but it caught the contours of her body, riding her breasts and hips. She was a vision, and she was my lover, and for some reason she hadn't abandoned me in the middle of the dance floor, so I did what seemed appropriate. I leaned in to kiss her.

Now, that kiss has become sort of famous in recent years. I think there are a couple of ballads on the subject, even. So I'm sorry to be a spoil sport, but I cannot tell a lie. That was the single worst kiss of my life. Jess was still laughing when I leaned forwards, so my lips squashed against her bared teeth, and our foreheads bonked together, and she was so confused that she sneezed on me.

Afterwards, there was silence all around us—even the musicians had stopped playing. But I thought, or imagined, that I could hear my father's breathing, loud and furious.

Jess groaned in my ear. "Oh, Darren, no. Darren, you did not just do that."

"Please do shut up," I muttered. My eyes were closed tight and I planned for them to remain that way.

A deep sigh, and then her hand found mine and squeezed. "Come on. Let's get out of here."

SOMEHOW, WE FOUND our way out of the Great Hall and back to my quarters. Jess had to steer me. Left on my own, I kept bumping into walls.

When we reached my room, I collapsed into an armchair and sat there clutching my head. Jess packed our bags, slipping a few small but valuable items of bric-a-brac in among the clothes.

"Darren," she said, as she squashed an armful of stockings into an overfull pocket. "We had a gentle little agreement that you weren't going to do this kind of thing anymore."

"Do what kind of thing?" I mumbled into my hands.

"Radical things. Dramatic, radical, spur-of-the-moment things. We agreed that you weren't going to do anything dramatic anymore without talking it over with me first. We discussed it. At some length. I think we even put something in writing. Is any of this sounding familiar?"

I scrubbed at my face, hoping that if I scrubbed hard enough, the world would right itself. "Could you hold it in for a while? If I'm still alive in six hours, I promise, you can yell at me all you want."

Jess softened just a bit, coming near enough to pat my hand. "Your father isn't going to execute you over one not-very-good kiss."

"You don't know that and neither do I."

She made a sound of exasperation. "Then why are we still in this room?"

"What are you saying?" I tried, and failed, to keep the panic out of my tone. "Are you telling me that I should just *run?*"

"Well, I don't claim to be a great military mind, but isn't it traditional to run away when people are trying to kill you?"

She had a point and yet . . . I stared down blankly at my court clothes: a black doublet studded with agates, soft black half-boots, and pearl-grey hose. From my belt hung a silver dagger with the hawk's-head crest, marking me as a captain who bore arms for Lord Stribos of Torasan.

"Jess, if I leave the Isle without being dismissed by my father, that's treason."

"Yes. But sticking around until he has a chance to pass sentence is *stupid.* Wouldn't you say?"

I breathed hard, stricken. "But where am I supposed to go?"

"Back to the valley with me, of course. Back to my place. It's a little premature, but I'm not about to abandon you in the wilderness. You're going to have to learn to pick up after yourself, though. No more leaving your boots in the middle of the floor and your trousers draped over the kitchen table and your shirts every damn where. I'm going to be very strict about that, Darren."

It was gentle teasing, meant to make me feel better, but it did not have that effect. I barely understood the words she was saying. All I heard was this: *Everything you have ever known is over.*

I swallowed, again and again. There was a lump in my throat that wouldn't go down.

It's easy to do something reckless and heroic, when you're in the moment and getting carried away. It's especially easy if you have a few stiff snorts of cherry wine in you. What's hard is holding onto those heroic feelings in the months and years that follow, as the cost becomes clear. Only the best of us can deal with the consequences of our sacrifices without coming to regret them.

Tested by that measure, I am not heroic. Not even vaguely. As I stared at Jess, and panic rose in me hot as vomit, all I wanted to do was start the day over again and erase that life-changing kiss.

That's when a heavy fist hammered at the door.

I didn't know whether to scream, fight, cry, or roll over and play dead. In the end, I rose about halfway out of my chair. My silver knife slapped against my thigh with the motion—I wondered wildly if I would have the guts to stab whomever tried to arrest me. And only then did it occur to me to worry about Jess. If I was in danger, what in hell was my father going to do to *her*?

I reached for my knife hilt, but the door swung open and Alek stood behind it, clad in full scale mail.

Alek had been sort of crap as a merchant captain—so I'd heard—but he was gifted in the area of swinging heavy metal objects around and making people dead. Since it was wartime, there was a market for that particular talent. As the war raged on, my father had come to depend on Alek more and more, and liked to keep him close.

Alek was just the man that my father would trust with a very dirty job. And now my heart really did begin to hammer, because he had a naked sword in one fist.

I thrust Jess behind me and raised my silver knife. As I did that, I remembered, belatedly, that it was a ceremonial weapon, as dull as a knitting needle.

Alek just shook his head. "That's the problem with you, Darren. You never know when to stop."

His arm moved and I flinched, but he only rammed his sword back into its sheath and held out the scroll.

I hadn't noticed it before. The sword had been occupying all my attention, as you can imagine. But as soon as I focused, I knew what it was. A banishment scroll is supposed to be conspicuous, with its red wrapping and seals of black wax. Time was, they marked exiles with a bloody slash across each cheek, and a smear of black tar across the back of the neck. The scroll is the modern, civilized alternative.

"You have three days," Alek said. "Don't waste them."

Mechanically, I took the scroll from him. I had to. During my three days of grace, I would have to show the scroll to any Kilan—noble, peasant, or slave—who asked to see it. If I didn't have the scroll at the ready when questioned, or if I was still in Kila when my grace period ran out, then anyone who found me could deal with me as they liked, the options limited only by their creativity. A lot of exiles get stoned to death, or hanged. Sometimes raped first, sometimes not. I've heard of one who was crushed by a red-hot wheel. I've heard of one who was held prisoner for months in a wicker hutch, like a rabbit, before she was sold to a whorehouse in Jiras. I gripped the scroll hard, crushing the paper wrapping.

Alek should have left then. There was nothing else he needed to do or say. But, for some reason, he stood there, the expression on his face midway between pity and disappointment.

It was the pity, more than anything, that helped me find my tongue. "Our father is a fool. He doesn't have so many captains that he can afford to throw them away. Banishing me is like dropping money down a well. He'll regret it."

Alek splayed his fingers wide, as if he was letting something drop between them. "That's not your concern any more, is it?"

No, it wasn't, and if I was a stronger woman I would have just marched from the room at that point, while making a suitably rude hand gesture. But the words slipped out. "Did anyone speak for me, Alek? Did you?"

There was a flash of annoyance in his grey-blue eyes—eyes that were so like my own that they could have been mirrors.

"Just answer me!"

He sighed, loud and long. "Did you have to slow-dance with a woman in front of the fucking Tavarene ambassador? Gods, Darren, what possessed you? Nobody would have stopped you from having your bit on the side, but you have to know where to draw the line. If you'd been discrete, we would have had options. As it was, what choice did our father have? You know that there's a cost of doing business. Sometimes you have to write things off."

For the first time, Jess spoke up. "Will you go now, please?"

Somehow, just with those five words, she managed to communicate that Alek was sexually unattractive to people of all genders and had a member the size of a lima bean.

I honestly thought that Alek was going to hit her—one fist did clench. But he mastered himself and turned away.

When he reached the door, he dipped his hand into his pocket and came out with a small leather pouch. It clinked when he set it down on a nearby table.

He didn't speak again, but he did look back. Once. Then he was gone, and the door swung softly shut behind him.

Jess and I were left there, surrounded by my clothes-press and my writing-desk, my chairs and linen chest. A soft breeze streamed through the open window. It was all perfectly normal, except for the crumpled scroll clutched in my fist.

Jess, ever the pragmatist, went at once to the leather pouch Alek had left behind and poured the coins into her palm.

"Copper," she said. "But better than nothing. We might have to bribe someone to get passage off of the Isle."

She slung her leather satchel over one arm and hefted my bundle onto her shoulder. "Come along, sweetheart. It's time to be somewhere else. And—quite frankly—I don't think you're losing much. Once you have a chance to think it over, you'll realize that this is the best thing ever to happen to you."

THAT HAD BEEN five years before. And that was the last time I saw Alek, until he washed up mostly dead on the beach. It was the last time I had seen any of my siblings, come to think of it.

Now, on the day of Alek's death, I leaned back against the bulkhead of my cabin, and tried to picture my sisters and brothers. Most of us in the House of Torasan had high cheekbones, slightly hooked noses, and hair as coarse as a horse's mane. It made it hard to remember the differences between individual faces.

Where were they all now? What with the war, Alek probably wasn't the first of us to die. I hadn't seen my oldest sister Sala since the day before her wedding. (I wasn't allowed to come to the wedding itself. Too many guests, not enough chairs.) Was she still alive? What about Brayan? Or little Jada? When had I even thought about them last?

I was so deep in thought, I didn't notice the footsteps approaching. It jolted me when the cabin door opened and Lynn slipped inside.

"Are we underway?" I asked automatically—and needlessly, because I could feel, through the vibration of the planks, that my ship was in motion.

Lynn didn't bother to answer. "You know, Mistress, I could hear you all the way from the crow's nest."

"I wasn't making any noise."

"Not out loud, but you're thinking too hard. I can hear it. Sounds like grinding teeth. You should give up thinking, you know. You'll live longer. And your ulcer might finally go away."

I felt the sore spot on my stomach, gingerly. It had been there for months, and I was pretty sure that it would stick around, even if I gave up the habit of thinking.

"Give me a break," I said, in my most wounded tone. "My brother just died."

Lynn made a sympathetic kind of noise.

"I'm distraught."

"That can't be fun."

She wasn't buying it. I heaved out a breath, giving up the act.

"Shouldn't I care more?" I asked her, almost in a whisper. "Shouldn't I feel something more than I do?"

Lynn crossed the room to kneel at my feet—a quick, practised, graceful gesture—and began to unlace my boots. "We're not the same, you and I."

"What's that supposed to mean?" I leaned back on my elbows to give her space to work.

"I don't see the point in trying to feel anything other than what you're actually feeling. Seems like a waste of time to me. But as I said, we're not the same." She worked the first boot free and laid it on the deck beside her. "What was he like? Alek, I mean."

"He . . . was . . . well . . ." What came to mind was "Tall," but that wasn't much of a eulogy. I made an effort. "He was my older brother. My father's second son."

Lynn nodded. "Second in the line of succession. He actually had a chance of becoming Lord of Torasan."

"Only if my oldest brother had died childless."

"I take it that your oldest brother didn't die childless."

"Konrad was married on his fifteenth birthday. He fathered his first son before he even had a full beard. By now, he probably has—lord, I don't even know. Seven kids, at least."

Lynn was still working on my second boot—the laces were tangled. "Why didn't your father ever marry *you* off?"

Strange to be talking about something at once so distant and so familiar. "I was the eighth-born, and my mother was my father's third wife. I wouldn't have been entitled to much of a dowry, even if my House were wealthy. And it wasn't. Torasan Isle is mainly rocks and trees and dirt. The most valuable asset that we . . . that *they* have is the salmon fisheries. None of the neighbouring nobles showed much interest in me, so my father kept me on the merchant boats. I was more useful to him that way. But I'm sure he would have found someone for me in the end."

He would have, too. Because that was the most important of all commandments if you were born a noblewoman in Kila: multiply, multiply, multiply. Bear children, and still more children, to serve your husband and your noble father, to expand their realms and magnify their wealth, to captain their ships and die in their wars, to safeguard their bloodlines, to grant them life eternal. *Bollocks.* My skin itched at the thought. Lynn had narrowly escaped a life as a brood sow, but maybe the same could be said for me.

Lynn set the second boot aside. "What was it like? To grow up with that many sisters and brothers?"

"It was . . . I don't know. Normal? Noisy? We all shared a room—like a long hall, with beds lining either side. It smelt of milk, and pitch from the torches. It had a huge fireplace, with an iron grille at the front so we couldn't fall into it. And a washbasin made of pink marble. And a stairway at the back, down to the shore of a calm little bay where we all learned to sail. We told ghost stories at night, and the small ones would squeak and hide in each other's beds. The older ones would sit up late, reading or working by candlelight. It was . . ."

All of a sudden, there was a hard lump of pressure in my chest that wouldn't let me breathe. I didn't get nostalgic very often. When I thought of Torasan Isle, I mostly remembered the fakery and nastiness of life at court, all of the etiquette and fuss. I never missed *that* crap. But speaking of my childhood, I could remember a thousand smells and thoughts and feelings connected with life on the Isle, and each one was tugging at me like a tiny kite string. Overlaying all of them was that one inescapable fact: I could never, never go back.

Lynn rested her crossed arms on top of my knees, looking up at me gravely. "You're homesick."

"It's not home." Her head was right there, so I stroked it. "It hasn't been home for a good long time now. I'm not one of them anymore."

"Your father has been going out of his way to make that clear, hasn't he?"

"By the time he sent the fourth assassin, I had pretty much figured it out, yes."

Lynn sighed. "Fathers."

"Fathers," I agreed. "Is there a reason that you're still sitting on the floor?"

"I'm comfortable." She closed her eyes, bowing her head just slightly as I stroked the back of her neck. "So, O my mistress. Since we agree that your father is ten degrees of arse, why are you going to bother to give him Alek's warning?"

"Who says I am?"

"Mistress? If you'd decided *not* to warn your father? You would have begun to agonize about it by now. Loudly."

Every now and then, I used to wonder what it would be like to have a slave girl who couldn't read my mind. It would have made it a lot easier to get away with certain things.

"All right, I'm going to warn my father about the traitor. But not for his stupid sake. It was Alek's last request, that's why. Besides, if someone's trying to kill my father, the rest of my family might get caught in the crossfire. And I'm not quite pissed off enough to wish that on them."

Lynn opened one eye and squinted up at me. "There's a good chance that Alek was murdered by someone in your family, you know. What with all that talk about *traitor* and *one of us.*"

"Hell, there's more than a good chance. I would call that a solid working theory. And my money's on Konrad. I wouldn't put it past my father to have Konrad strangled so that Alek could take the throne. Maybe Konrad decided to strike first. But there's nothing I can do about it, right? I'll send Alek's body home. I'll write to my father and let him know what Alek said. And then I'll sit back . . ."

". . . and pretend that you don't care what happens next. Fooling no one, by the way."

I gave her my best frosty look. "Will you please come to bed? I'm starting to feel neglected."

"Well, we can't have that." She eased up next to me. "What do you want me in the bed for? Are we sleeping, or are you doing unspeakable things to me?"

Good question. "It would be nice if we could combine the two. Fact is, I'm exhausted. I don't know if I could manage any unspeakable things. Maybe something mildly impolite, if I exerted myself."

"We'll save the ravishing for another time, then. For now—roll over onto your stomach, Mistress."

I did, with a shiver of pleasurable anticipation. Then gasped, as fingertips began to probe into the exact parts of my back where they could accomplish the most. Lynn knew all my muscles and nerves the way a minstrel knows the strings of his lute, and with effortless strokes, she began to take me apart and put me back together again. It was the extraordinarily good kind of pain, and it made me realize that I wasn't nearly as exhausted as I had believed.

"That offer of unspeakable things," I murmured into the blanket. "Is that off the table?"

"Oh, Mistress." I couldn't see her smile, but I could hear it. "As if I could stop you from taking what you want from me."

Why do words like that make my blood run twice as hot? Why do they make my heart skip three beats, and then start to pound harder than ever? Why do they send electricity crackling through my veins, as power surges into my every muscle? I don't know. But they do, every time.

It was *wrong,* I knew, with everything that had happened that day, but for once, I didn't care. I pulled Lynn down and flipped my body on top of hers, pinning her with my full weight. As my hands closed around Lynn's wrists and guided them up over her head, the last thing on my mind was apologising for the way I was feeling.

CHAPTER FOUR

Lynn

DARREN WAS YAWNING when we went up on deck the next morning, and Regon smiled tolerantly as he fell into step beside us. "No need to ask what you were doing last night."

On an ordinary day, Darren might have blushed at that. But I had put in some good hard work on her the night before—and a little bit in the morning, as well—and that had done wonders for her ego. Instead of stammering out something like an apology to her first mate, Darren gave him a dirty look. "I was saving the country, as usual."

He rolled his eyes. "Right. Well, captain, I'll give you this. You two are surprisingly quiet when you're saving the country. I didn't even hear any squeaking."

Darren jerked a thumb at me. "Lynn's a pillow-biter."

"Captain, you don't have a pillow."

"No, but I have an arm." Darren pushed up her sleeve, exposing a row of teeth marks. "Same theory."

Then her tone turned businesslike. "Where's my brother?"

Alek's body lay on the quarterdeck, wrapped in clean white canvas. Ariadne and I had done a quick amateurish embalming job the day before, cutting out the bits that would start rotting first and packing the gaps with coarse salt. With luck, the body would be more or less intact when it arrived at Torasan Isle after its three-day journey, but it was not going to look very pretty.

It would have been smarter and easier to wrap the body in a hammock, tie a good-sized rock to the feet and tip it overboard. Nobody had mentioned that option. Nobles get buried on land, in their family tombs, so that they can mingle with their own kind in the hereafter. I might have tried to persuade Darren to break with tradition, if it hadn't been for one thing: Spinner would be buried at sea when his own time came, and Alek didn't deserve to share the water with him.

Darren knelt over the corpse, and she stayed there for an awfully long time. I didn't know what she was doing—praying, maybe—but Regon and I stood well back to give her space.

It was one of those blinding blue mornings that you sometimes get down south, though the pale sun didn't have any heat in it. I hadn't slept much, so I felt glassy and not-quite-there as I massaged a sore spot on my shoulder. Darren wasn't the only one who got bitten when the two of us were fooling around. She was the only one who complained about it, that was all.

Without warning, Regon spat over the rail. His saddle-brown face was flushed with anger, which almost never happened. Regon was so even-tempered that he wouldn't cuss you out even if you stole his last clean shirt. (I did that, a couple of times.)

"Out with it," I said. "Come on."

Regon stared at Alek's corpse, disgust thick on his face. "The captain hasn't forgotten what that son of a whore did to Spinner, has she?"

Ah. That made sense. Regon was a gentle person, but he had his limits, and when people messed with Spinner, the top just about blew off of his head.

"She hasn't forgotten," I said. "But you have to understand. It's not Alek she's mourning—it's her childhood. It's a long hall that smells of milk, and a washbasin of pink marble, and ghost stories at night, and everything else that she's lost. Besides—Alek was her brother, even if he was a thug, and he *was* murdered."

He snorted. "The captain murdered *your* father, and *you* didn't go all gooey."

"Well, no, but I'm very special and magnificent."

I scanned the deck. "Where's Spinner? It's not his watch below, is it?"

"I sent him down. If the captain's going to blubber over that stinking dog, Spinner doesn't need to see it." He spat a second time, hard and with feeling. "I can't bear this, Lynn. I'm going below. If the captain asks—"

"If the captain asks where you are, I'll tell her that you ate some bad fish and are puking with mighty abandon." I waved a hand. "Go."

He didn't answer—just stomped down the steps to the hold, arms rigid at his sides.

I watched him leave, brain buzzing. There was a sweetness in Regon's protectiveness towards Spinner—always had been—and it was tempting to think that the sweetness could become something more. But I knew better. Regon liked the ladies, and Spinner, like me, was too practical to spend his life pining after impossible things.

Still. Regon was too good a man to waste. Maybe I should throw him at Ariadne after all, if she and Latoya couldn't work things out. Regon liked breasts, Ariadne had two of them—relationships have been built on less.

Darren straightened up, rubbing her eyes with one sleeve, and snapped
her fingers blindly in my general direction. Obediently, I trotted up to the
quarterdeck. "Mistress?"

"Signal to Flint," she said, naming the captain of the *Sod Off*. The
harshness of her voice almost concealed the fact that she was close to
tears, but not quite. "I'm ready for them to come and take Alek."

"I'll signal," I said, and waited for more.

She sniffed and groped for her handkerchief. "That letter I wrote to my
father—it's pretty terse. Maybe I should add another page."

"You shouldn't. Not unless you're going to write BUGGER OFF over
and over and over, and then wrap the paper around a dead fish. And that's
not your style. Anything else?"

"I'm thinking of lending Flint some of our men."

"Why?"

"Because he's going to have to give my father bad news. If worst comes
to worst, he ought to be able to defend himself."

"Flint will only have the one ship. If worst comes to worst, he won't be
able to defend himself no matter how many men you lend him."

"Still," Darren said doggedly. "He'll be a little safer if we beef up his
crew."

He'd be a *lot* safer if Darren didn't send him off on corpse delivery detail
in the first place. Sometimes, though, Darren got so stuck on something
that even I couldn't change her mind.

"Flint's no fool," I said. "Give him space and let him work. It won't
help if you clutter up the *Sod Off* with a bunch of spare sailors he doesn't
even know."

"Maybe," she admitted grudgingly. "I know what, though. I'll lend
him—"

"You're not lending him Latoya."

"Why not?"

"Because we run crying to her every time we have a problem, and it's
messing with her love life, and I'm starting to feel a little bad about that.
No. You're not lending him Latoya. I'm going to make sure she gets a few
days off, even if it kills me."

"What if it kills Flint? I know I've been relying on Latoya too much,
I'll make it up to her, but I need her now. I can't send a ship to Torasan Isle
unless it's equipped to deal with a little rough-and-tumble and she's the
best bruiser we have. She's going."

"But—"

"End of story. My decision. Me am boss."

She said this in her gruffest, sternest, most piratical voice, the one she
used when she was explaining to callow young recruits that they would

jump when she hollered or by *god* she'd know the reason why. I wasn't a callow young recruit and it took more than a few gruff words to make *me* hop, but still I sighed, and surrendered.

"All right, Darren," I said.

Darren, I said, not *Mistress,* and that was so she would know why I was giving in. Not because she was the pirate queen, not because she was the senior partner, not because she was being an ass and throwing her weight around—but because her brother had died the day before. Also, I could tell from the tightness along her jaw and cheek that she had a headache. Again.

Piracy has its points, but it's bad for your health.

"All right," I repeated, more softly. "I'll tell Latoya and see that she gets to the *Sod Off.*"

Darren nodded, but she looked apologetic, now that she had won. "Your sister is going to kill me, isn't she?"

NOT QUITE, BUT it was a near thing. Ariadne went chalk white when she heard the news, except for two brilliant red splodges on her neck.

"You want Latoya to go *where*?" she asked, in a voice like thorns and razors.

Darren still looked sheepish. "I just want—"

"You. Just. Want. Darren, for the love of sainted trout! When your father finds out that Alek was murdered, he's going to take a swing at everyone in reach. Isn't he? *Isn't he?*"

"But that's why—"

"That's why you want my woman to be within swinging distance? I know you're jealous of her good looks, but that's still mighty cold."

"Ariadne."

"Don't you 'Ariadne' me!" My sister puffed out an angry breath of air. "You listen here, pirate queen. Everyone else seems to be tiptoeing around this, so I'll give it to you straight. Your brother was a brutal dipshit. We're all happy he's dead. He's not worth mourning. And you have no right to send Latoya into danger, just so that you can feel better about the whole thing. He's dead. Throw his body over the side, get drunk, write a sad poem and move the hell on."

Darren had been standing in a hangdog kind of posture, shoulders slumped. But now she drew herself up to her full height, and lifted her chin. It wasn't a fighting stance. This was how an aristocrat looked when she had suffered a terrible insult.

In the chilliest of tones, she said, "Lady, you forget yourself."

"Oh, do I?" Ariadne snapped back. Almost unconsciously, she too drew herself upwards, mirroring Darren's pose. "Let me remind you of something, so there won't be any confusion: You're not *my* mistress, and you're not *my* queen."

"You are on my ship. You stay on my ship, you submit to my authority."

"I'm on your ship so I can be with my sister. That's all. You have no authority over me. You never did. You never will. Stop pretending otherwise or you'll only embarrass yourself."

Both their faces had frozen into stiff, haughty masks, with their eyes narrowed and their lips curled as though there was a bad smell in the room. (Which I suppose there *was*, but if you live on board a ship, you have to learn to get used to that sort of thing.) I don't think either of them knew how ridiculous they looked, nor would it have done any good if I'd told them. They were, both of them, obeying the call of something deeper, impulses ingrained in them before they'd even learned to walk.

Almost unconsciously, I exchanged a glance with Latoya, who was silently stuffing her kitbag. We both rolled our eyes.

"I don't have any authority, do I?" Darren asked. "So I suppose you'll be taking over as captain in the future?"

"Why not?" Ariadne asked tartly. "I know how to stomp around the deck, drink too much, and cuddle with Lynn. Those seem to be the main job requirements."

"Splendid. Then I can take over your responsibilities. What were they again? Eating, sleeping, whining, and sarcasm?"

This was stupid and would only get stupider. I jerked my head towards the companionway, Latoya nodded, and we both climbed from the forecastle.

Once we were out on deck, with the gull cries drowning out the argument, I asked, "Would you rather not go?"

She shrugged as she tied her kitbag shut. "Captain wants me to go."

"Give me a couple of hours alone with her, and the captain won't remember *what* she wanted you to do. Or what year it is. Or what her name is. Or what anyone else's name is. Or whether she has feet."

"I wouldn't ask you to do that."

"You didn't ask. And I wouldn't exactly be suffering during the operation."

She slung her kitbag over her shoulder. "There's no need. But walk with me."

She headed for the longboats at the ship's stern, with a quick, swinging stride that forced me to trot to keep up.

"Hang on," I said. "You're not going to leave without speaking to my sister, are you?"

"That was the plan."

"I hate that plan." I got in front of her and walked backwards so I could keep her face in view. "That plan is crap. Come on. Say something to her. It doesn't have to be well thought out. Start with one syllable and go from there."

Latoya shrugged. "I've never been much for goodbyes. Besides. I don't know what to say to her when she's like this."

"Like what?"

"You know what. When she's a *lady*." Latoya shot me a quick, searching look. "She's not like you, your sister."

"No," I agreed, without needing to think about it. "You're lucky. She's the nice one."

"Maybe. But you're the adult. Ariadne—she has some growing up to do. Doesn't even know who she is yet. It'll be good for her to have some space to do her thinking."

Latoya slung her kitbag into a longboat and fiddled with the oars. Without any change of tone, she asked, "Why is she pulling away from me?"

This was getting dangerous. "I'm not the one you should ask."

"I know. Asking anyway. As a favour to me, Lynn—please."

It was hard to ignore that appeal, considering how many times Latoya had saved Darren's life. (Seventeen, if you count the time when she explained to Darren that you shouldn't eat dragon fish even if you're *sure* that you didn't puncture the poison bladder. And I do count that.)

"I'd just be guessing . . ."

"But . . . ?"

"But . . . you might be too *whole* for her."

Latoya raised an eyebrow. I grimaced and stared down at her hands—brown hands roughened with callous and criss-crossed with scars. Those hands, with equal ease, could break a man's neck or carve an apple into a swan, make a rope fast or calm a frightened horse.

"Like I said, it's just a guess," I said. "But Ariadne finds things easiest to love when they're half-broken. When she was a child, she could have spent all her time sitting on satin pillows and playing koro with dice made of diamonds, but she wasn't interested. Her favourite things were dolls without heads, and three-legged cats, and mangy horses . . ."

I faltered, but Latoya understood, and finished the thought. "And you."

"And me. Granted, I've caused a lot more trouble for her than any of those three-legged cats did. Well, except for Marvin. He was a bad cat, Marvin was. But it's the same kind of idea. She likes to be needed. She needs it."

"So you think I'm not broken enough to keep her happy."

"Doesn't make much sense, does it?"

"No. But fuck me running, you might just be right." She sniffed the freshening breeze. "I should go."

She hesitated, and then, more softly, "Keep an eye on her. Nobody falls in love with broken things unless they're a little cracked themselves."

I PERCHED ON the rail to see her off. The longboat was a big, cranky craft, and it took four normal sailors to row it, but Latoya, with an oar in each hand, fairly lifted it out of the water. She reached the *Sod Off* in about eight and a half seconds, climbed the rope ladder in easy swinging jerks, and gave me a last wave as she pulled herself over the gunwale.

As I crossed the deck, I was thinking about Darren's breakfast—both about cooking it, and about the shenanigans that I might have to pull to get it into her. When she was distracted, Darren would forget that she had a body, much less that it had needs of its own. Sometimes, even when I put a plate in front of her, she didn't notice it until I shoved her face down into the porridge.

Then I heard Ariadne again, screeching from the forecastle, loud and shrill even through the wood planking. "Oh, don't pretend that you saved her, Darren. You don't even *know* her."

"Who *is* her saviour then?" Darren asked, her voice as nasty as I'd ever heard it. "You?"

"Look, you stupid bloody pirate, I know better than to think that Lynn needs a saviour! I—oh, don't you tell me to be quiet—"

Their voices went down to a muted grumble, but it was only a few seconds before Ariadne was yelling again. "It's pathetic! You think that Lynn is your big success story? You don't get to take credit for Lynn. You didn't save her—she saved herself, and she saved you too because she had some time to kill and why not? And she lets you pretend that you're in charge so that your fragile self-esteem won't crack. And you know what I think? I think she's settling for you until she can find someone who can actually keep up with her. When all of this is over, you'll be the woman who got her started. That's all."

Well, shit. I was getting ready to sprint to someone's rescue—whose rescue, I wasn't quite sure—when I heard Darren reply, her words measured and venomous. "Right now, Lynn still thinks that you're the good angel of her childhood. But when she gets her head right, she'll figure out that you stood by for seventeen years, watching her get tortured and starved. You'll say that you helped her—and maybe you did—but you sure as hell didn't stick out your neck. And you know what that tells me? Shut up, I'm talking. Even if you liked Lynn, even if you loved her, she didn't mean dick to you. Not compared to your position, your title, your *real* family, and your *real life*. She didn't. Mean. Dick."

A sharp intake of breath from Ariadne. "How dare you?"

"Face facts, princess. Maybe you're right—maybe Lynn will move on from me someday. But by the time that happens, you'll just be a slightly brighter part of a bad, bad memory."

Someone softly touched my elbow, and my hand flashed to my knife. I had it halfway out of its sheath before I recognized Regon.

"What do you reckon?" he asked, eyebrows bobbing. "Should we pull them apart, or just grab a pump and hose them down until they start to squelch?"

"Neither," I said. I was a little light-headed—it could have been the lack of sleep, the argument, the sudden shock, choose your weapon—and I grabbed Regon's arm to steady myself. "I should have known this would happen eventually."

Regon gave an affirmative kind of grunt. "I've seen this kind of dick-measuring contest before. Hard to avoid it, when you put two nobles on one boat."

"Well, they'll have to sort it out for themselves, because I'm not going to give up either of those two. And I will *not* spend the rest of my life playing monkey in the middle."

He nodded, but still asked, "What if they strangle each other before one of them gets smart?"

"They'll figure it out," I said fiercely. "If those two can't figure it out, then I don't know what hope there is for Kila."

I just felt so terribly tired. The war had gone on so long already, and Darren and I had been fighting for years, and had we even begun to make headway? We could ferry a thousand starving children to a place of peace and plenty, and a million more hungry mouths would gape open. We could cut down a thousand murderous raiders, and a million more would rip bloody sabres from their scabbards. I might be able to draw the line and call it quits sometime, when I couldn't take it anymore, but Darren wouldn't. Darren couldn't. And how long could I keep her alive in the centre of the firestorm?

And hell, say that we won. Say that it all went exactly according to plan, and we managed to end the war and unite the islands and put my sister on the long-vacant throne of the High Lord. Wouldn't there still be small children who had to carry heavy buckets up and down tower stairs every day, and who got the crap beaten out of them if they took too long?

When you have, for whatever idiotic reason, made it your mission to save your country, there are bound to be times like this, when your energy drains out of you all at once. At such moments, you wonder why you would ever bother, and you're tempted to crawl back into bed and sleep for a solid month. For a second, I looked longingly at the hatch that led to the captain's cabin.

Just for a second, though. Maybe servants have an advantage when it comes to dealing with moments when nothing seems worthwhile. Every servant knows that the work has to get done, no matter how you feel.

I sighed, and refocused.

"I'll be in the galley, if anyone asks," I told Regon. "My mistress needs her breakfast."

CHAPTER FIVE

Darren, formerly of the House of Torasan (Pirate Queen)

AFTER THAT DAY, Ariadne and I were barely on speaking terms. We stepped carefully around each other if we met on the companionway, and only went to the galley when the other wasn't there. If we *had* to look each other in the face, we maintained expressions of weary indifference, as if the other was just too tedious to be borne.

All right, you don't need to tell me, it wasn't my finest hour.

Lynn told us conversationally that we were both being idiots, and then left it alone. Regon wasn't nearly as restrained. First chance he got, he cornered me on the maindeck, and gave me a look that suggested he'd caught me eating babies or using puppies as bedroom slippers. "Word to the wise, captain: if you want to stay in good with a girl, then you have to stay in good with her sister. It's just a law of life."

"But she's a spoiled brat!"

"And you're a fluffy kitten, are you?" He snorted. "Fix it before someone gets hurt."

I thought of a really snappy retort to that—half an hour later. I considered tracking Regon down to deliver it, but even I could tell that was a bit pathetic.

For a whole ten minutes, I thought about apologising to Ariadne. Then I thought about how she'd called me a stuck-up, self-obsessed megalomaniac, and suggested that I could only get off if I was looking at my own face in a mirror all the while. Then I decided that *she* could apologise first.

So I ignored her, with what I liked to think of as cold dignity, and got back to work.

We should have been heading north by then, away from my father's sphere of influence. Just a few months before, he'd sent an assassin after me who looked about sixteen. She posed as a refugee and sat sobbing on the shore while my crew drove raiders from a burned-out village. When I came near enough to pat her on the shoulder, she flung herself into my arms, sobbed some more, and then, without changing expression, she lunged for my throat with a saw-edged blade. I managed to catch her wrist, but even so, I took a nasty slash in the shoulder before Latoya could reach me. The wound didn't hurt nearly as much as the tongue-lashing that I caught from Latoya after the fact. As she reminded me fifty-six times in succession, I knew better than to assume a woman couldn't be dangerous.

I also knew better than to spend too much time paddling around in my father's domain . . . but somehow I couldn't make myself give the order to change course. I knew this southern stretch of ocean better than I knew the alphabet, after all those years spent on my father's merchant ships. Every time I saw a landmark, I went almost drunk with memory. There was the yellow sand of the Tavarene coast. There was the islet with the purple oyster beds. And there was the reef where, at the age of fourteen, I very nearly sunk the first ship I ever commanded. I'm going to save myself a little embarrassment by not telling you the whole story. Suffice to say, if you insist on sailing at night *and* taking the rudder yourself, you should at least be sober.

Gods, I'd been an idiot. Still, I felt some inexpressible tenderness, thinking of that first command. My ship back then was a balky, ugly old scow, over-generously named the *Glory of the Isles*. Her sails were heavily patched and she had so many leaks that she could have been usefully employed as a sieve for boiled asparagus, but she was *mine*. That was the first time I encountered the magic that's a ship at sea, a mass of wood and metal that can take you anywhere. Ships stink, and unless you stick close to land, the food is worse than what you'd get in prison. Still, if you want my opinion, they're better than wings.

Then, too, there was the heady joy of being in charge for the first time in my life. No older siblings to thump me on the head and stuff worms down the front of my shirt. No tutors to whip me with bunches of reeds when I made an mistake in a geometry problem. Just a crew of ten sailors who did their best to pretend that I knew what I was doing.

Whenever I gave a particularly stupid order, Teek the helmsman would tug his forelock and say of *course,* captain, of *course.* Then he'd quietly do the opposite and never mention it again.

Regon had been there too: a dark, stocky youth with a cautious smile. Though he was three years older than I was, he'd served as my cabin boy, bringing me my morning porridge and my evening wine, blacking my boots and washing my shirts every other month. I pretended to accept all this as my rightful due, but the truth was, I was a little bit in awe of him. He'd been at sea since age seven. He could climb the rigging like a set of stairs, set the sails as neatly as a maid could thread a needle, and he never stumbled in the dark of the hold. He positively *liked* the taste of salt beef.

Meanwhile I was pretending to understand what it meant when someone yelled out, *"Heave her to!"* I was always tempted to respond, "Make it three, and you've got a deal!"

Gods of hell, it had been so long ago.

A week after Alek's death, when we still hadn't headed north, my excuses were getting increasingly threadbare. *I think we should sail around that completely random patch of ocean for a while*—that was the kind of thing I was coming up with. No one broke out in open revolt, but Lynn's tone of voice became more and more exasperated with each *Yes, Mistress.*

I wasn't sleeping well, either. Every time I sunk deep enough to dream, the same words went thudding through me: *Traitor—one of us—one of our own—betrayed us—backstabber. Darren, not much time, Darren, Darren, it was my—*

I would wake dry-lipped and shaky, and find it impossible to get back to sleep. Instead, I'd watch Lynn sweating and shaking in her own nightmares, and wonder why I couldn't save either of us.

All in all, it was a good thing that the Tavarene ambassadors showed up then.

"THEY WANT YOU to help them negotiate a peace," Lynn said, amused. "I think I should tell them how you and Ariadne have been plotting each other's deaths all week."

"Go ahead. Just make it clear that she's the evil aggressor and I'm simply defending myself."

"You're looking at me like you expect a *yes, Mistress,* and lover, it isn't going to happen."

A word about Tavar. It's not part of Kila, of course. It's on the mainland, removed from the isles, and it wasn't a player in the Kilan war. But violence is like a liquid, in the way it spreads, and stains, and spills. With every lord in Kila busily trying to slaughter his neighbours, it was no surprise that some of our friends in the south were getting in on the act.

Two Tavarene villages had spent the past several years locked in a small but brutal conflict of their own. Now, with many of their young men dead, and many of their women abducted or sold, and their cattle butchered, and their date palms burned, they'd become sick of the whole mess.

It's always a hopeful sign when two warring parties agree to come to the bargaining table, but it's a mistake to hope too much. Peace talks can, and do, break down over the stupidest things. Accidental insults, for example, or strange signs that someone takes as a portent, like a two-headed calf or a shooting star. Sometimes the talks go on for so long that no one has the energy to continue. And there are always war profiteers—weapon sellers, slave merchants and the like—pulling puppet strings behind the scenes.

So it's a good idea to call in some neutral third party who will keep the talks moving forward. That's why the village chieftains called me.

This was what I needed: something that would keep me in the south, but keep me too busy to fret. I threw myself into the job, and Lynn followed suit. We both needed the distraction.

It would have been a great help to have Latoya there, but even without her, we had two Tavarene sailors on board. We began by questioning them mercilessly about the customs on the coast: how the locals dressed, acted, thought, and spoke. Then, when we reached the warring villages, we dispatched the crew of the *Banshee* to fan out and comb the area. They inspected buildings, counted crop fields, and struck up conversations with every Tavarene they could find, asking about their problems and their fears.

The chieftains of the warring villages asked me to dinner. I accepted and, as if it was an afterthought, offered my own slave girl to serve at table. All through the evening, as the headmen and I sprawled on couches padded with leopard hides, Lynn went back and forth between us, filling wine cups and passing platters of pomegranates and dates. She wore the briefest of white linen tunics, with copper anklets and bangles, and the chieftains looked at her the way you would look at an elaborate table decoration. They gave her a single appreciative glance, and then ignored her.

While the chieftains and I were talking about the war and cows and millet fields and trade and temples and mining rights and date palms, Lynn glided invisibly from couch to couch, noticing all manner of tiny details that you or I would never see. She knew it every time that the headmen changed expression, changed position, fidgeted, or began to breathe faster. With those signs as a guide, she was able to follow their thoughts throughout our conversation. She knew what made them nervous and what made them bored, what issues mattered to them and which were throwaways.

The chieftains both drank heavily. Lynn pretended to fill my cup every time she filled theirs, but, in fact, I made one cup of palm wine last the whole evening. When the chieftains began to slur and ramble, Lynn slipped from the tent and Ariadne slipped inside to replace her. Nobody appeared to notice that the blond serving girl had suddenly gained a hand's breadth of height and an extra stone of weight. The chieftains just yelled for more drink and Ariadne went to serve them, rolling her eyes.

As soon as Lynn was free of the tent, she tracked down the chieftains' luggage and rifled through it, taking note of every detail that might give a clue to their personalities. Then she met up with my crewmen and heard their reports. Spinner had done the best—he'd found a loom-house and spent the better part of two days with a bunch of weavers. Weaving is one of those things that keep about one percent of your brain busy, so weavers keep up an endless flow of chatter as they work. You might think it strange that they would talk freely when there was a strange man standing nearby listening in, but Spinner, like Lynn, had a gift for blending into the scenery. Don't ask me how he managed it. Maybe he held a potted plant in front of his face. I'm not good at that kind of thing myself and I don't understand the people who are.

Eventually, the feast ended and the chieftains staggered off to bed. I retreated to my tent and Lynn briefed me, summarizing all the information my crew had managed to glean, as well as everything that she'd learned or guessed during dinner. Then, with Regon and Spinner and Ariadne, we held a council of war—actually, not a council of war. A council of not-war, I suppose. We hashed out a plan for the arbitration, guessing what problems would come up and deciding how I would respond to each of them. It went on long into the night and we only broke it off when we were too tired to see.

Ariadne and I managed to maintain a sort of chilly politeness during the meeting. I'd included her mainly so that Lynn wouldn't glare at me, but if I'm going to be honest about it, she came up with more good ideas than I did. It made sense, as I realized when I really thought about it. As my father's eighth child, I had always been destined for the merchant ships, so my schooling had focused on navigation, mathematics, and languages. Ariadne, as Iason's heir, had been trained in politics and diplomacy from the cradle. But—going for complete honesty again—it still irked me to be out-thought by someone so . . . girly.

Ariadne's diplomatic education wasn't the only thing that gave her an edge, though. She and Latoya had been together five months, and during that time, she'd absorbed a lot of information about her lover's homeland. I guess that all those times that she and Latoya snuck away together to "talk," some talking actually did go on.

The peace talks began the next day. We started in the late afternoon, to give the chieftains a fighting chance to recover from the effects of far too much wine. I sat in state on a throne made of boxes, doing my best to look profound and wise while my palms were so damp with anxiety that I had to wipe them on my trousers every other minute.

Meanwhile, Lynn lounged at my feet on a red beaded cushion. She kept a vacant stare on her face, as if she was an ornament or a pet, but all the while her brain whirred mightily. As I strove to keep the talks going, she sent me signals by tapping my ankle. One tap for *yes, go on*; two for *no, stop*; three for *change the subject*; four for *not yet*. A hard squeeze meant, *Hold everything and give them booze.*

I'm talking a lot about tricks and gimmicks, and don't you underestimate tricks and gimmicks—they help. But it was still damn hard work, as peacemaking always is, and it was the chieftains doing almost all of it.

They were the ones who had to do all the imagining and the forgiving on behalf of their two peoples, and the effort of it made the sweat stand out in beads all over their faces. We talked until we all wanted to murder each other, took a pause for breath, and talked again. During the breaks, while she was passing out refreshments, Lynn gauged the chieftains' levels of fatigue and frustration. Then she'd come back to kneel at my feet, and she gave me hints in whispers, her eyes fixed on the deckboards, while I pretended to sharpen my dagger.

My biggest fear during all this was that one of the chieftains would offer to buy Lynn from me, at which point I would be forced to shatter the truce by dealing out bloody death to him and to anyone who came between us. When one of the chieftains (name of Ano) drew me aside, I was sure that the time had come. But all he did was to give me a long lecture on the need to respect all women, no matter their station in life. He strongly suggested that I buy Lynn some decent clothing and stop petting her like a cat. This conversation left me hideously embarrassed, as you can imagine, but Lynn found it hilarious and had to force down her snickers.

It took a week, but we got there in the end, tying the final knot on the string of red-and-blue beads that set out the exact amount of reparations to be exchanged. As soon as the knot drew tight, Regon waved a blue flag at the villagers waiting ashore, and the coast erupted with cheers. The sounds brought on a shuddering in me, halfway tears and halfway laughter. I grabbed Lynn around the chest, pulled her back against me, rested my chin on the top of her head, and squeezed hard.

I didn't hear her sigh, but I felt it. "You did good, Mistress," she murmured. "You did good."

I'm not pretending that I stormed down on Tavar and stopped a war all on my lonesome. But still, when the *Banshee* set sail, the women of the villages were preparing to plant the millet fields, for the first time in almost two years.

So you see, it's not as if there's *nothing* we can do.

LYNN AND I celebrated on our own that night. Guess how.

After an hour, we lay sweat-slicked and panting on our hard bunk. I was feeling so languidly good that Lynn had to elbow me twice before I remembered, and reached down to untie her wrists and ankles. Once loose, she rolled over on top of me and nipped my lower lip. "You know what I've been thinking?"

I propped my head up on my arm. "I'm sure you'll tell me before I have to use harsh interrogation techniques."

Not that I would have minded. Harsh interrogation techniques, under the right circumstances and in the right company, can be quite delightful.

"There's an old legend in southern Kila," Lynn said. "It's about a holy leader. Someone destined to rise from the mists and pacify the islands and put an end to war and strife and unite heaven and earth. Latoya told me about it. Have you heard it before?"

"The story of the Master of Storms. Yes, I've heard it."

She nipped again. "I think you should own that story. That could be you. 'Master of Storms' would be a nice addition to your list of titles. Don't make faces. I'm serious."

I coughed, embarrassed on her behalf. "Did you listen to the whole story?"

"Of course."

"Then you know that, according to legend, the Master of Storms will be a ten-year-old boy who can shoot lightning from his fingertips. And I think he's supposed to be able to talk to dolphins? Can't swear to that last part. It's been a while since I've heard it."

"So?"

"Huh?"

"Who cares? Ten-year-old boy who can shoot lightning from his fingertips, adult woman who looks good in leather—what's the difference? People around here want a saviour, and there's no pre-pubescent dolphin talker in sight. They can't afford to get picky."

"Lynn."

"Look, if you're all that worried about it, we'll find some dolphins and you can exchange some chit-chat with them. I don't know what to do about the lightning thing. I guess I could embroider thunderclouds all over your coat."

I puffed out an exasperated breath. "Lynn, I'm not the Master of Storms!"

"You might as well be," she said reasonably. "Nobody else is."

"Why are you even bringing this up? So far as I know, you don't believe in prophecies."

"And there you are wrong, O my mistress. I believe whole-heartedly in the power of prophecies to make people do things that they wouldn't do otherwise. You're a good woman, you're a gifted leader—and yet there are morons a-plenty in the world who don't think that's enough of a reason to follow you. Make no mistake, those same morons will fall over each other to butcher people under your flag, if they believe that some prehistoric lunatic once predicted that you'd show up one day to throw lightning bolts. It's stupid, but there it is."

Lynn rolled off the bunk and rummaged for her tunic. I felt strange and prickly as I watched her get dressed. "So you want to lie to people."

"I want the war to end. Don't you?"

She bent over me, dropped a glancing kiss on my cheek, and headed for the door. "Don't wait up."

"Why?" I sat upright, trying not to whine. "Where are you going?"

"To find Ariadne. Haven't seen her much in the past week or so."

No, she hadn't, since she'd spent the past week sitting on a cushion at my feet. But she hadn't been spending much quality time with *me,* either. Didn't "mistress" outrank "sister"?

"You know, Darren," Lynn said, pausing at the door. "I said that I wasn't going to interfere—and I'm not—but don't you think that this whole blood feud thing is getting a bit ridiculous?"

I SPENT A good part of the next day stomping up and down my cabin, trying to make up my mind. I had this horrible feeling that if I approached Ariadne to make peace, I was going to have to do a lot of apologizing and looking humble, neither of which are my specialities. On the other hand, I had an equally horrible feeling that I wasn't going to be able to wait her out. I was a hot-headed pirate, she was an ice princess—she had the advantage when it came to waiting.

So I yelled a few bad words and stomped up to the deck to get it over with.

It was the forenoon watch and half my men should have been sleeping, but there was a milling crowd of sailors on deck, clustered in a ring around something I couldn't see. There were roars of encouragement and the clink of coins changing hands, and eventually I figured it out. Iason's daughters were playing koro again.

Koro, the Game of Kings, is played in every noble house in Kila. We played a great deal of it back on Torasan Isle, because of the weather. On the Isle, the sun shone, on average, one day a month and the rest of the time it was raining, hailing, snowing, or all three, so we had to find ways to amuse ourselves indoors.

While I was growing up, I fancied myself a pretty good player. I was far better than my brother Alek, I'll tell you *that* for free. But I hadn't a hope in hell when matched up against Lynn or Ariadne. Lynn had been teaching my crew how to play—Spinner, in particular, showed promise— but Ariadne was the only one who could really push her.

My sailors liked to watch the two of them fighting it out. It gave them something to bet on that was a little bit more interesting than those other classic shipboard games, "How many maggots will I find in my biscuit?" and "Which seagull is going to take a crap first"?

I shouldered my way through the circle and squinted. There they were, the princess and the slave, blond heads together as they sat cross-legged on the deck, bent over the dice. Ariadne was winning, it looked like, but not by much.

Ariadne threw the dice and scanned them through narrowed eyes. "I'll bid. Full moon rising."

"Buyout," Lynn offered. "Twenty if you stop here, fifteen on the next throw."

"Oh, you wish."

Ariadne won that round, but bid royal five on her next throw and didn't make it. Then Lynn got busy, her eyes serene and deadly as she moved in for the kill. She made a hundred points in a single round, closing the gap between their scores to almost nothing, then made two cautious but solid plays that pushed her into the lead. Ariadne had the last turn, but an unlucky roll of the dice left her unable to recover and before she could say "Aw, *screw* it," all Lynn's backers were collecting their winnings.

Ariadne, lips pursed, glared at Lynn and rattled the dice-cup. "Small annoying person, you're being most inconsiderate. You know perfectly well how much I like to win."

Lynn shrugged. "Then you'd better stop overbidding your throws."

"Look, you, my bidding's just fine. The problem is the dice. These dice are defective."

I snorted in amusement, and Ariadne wheeled on me. "All right, Chuckles, wipe that grin off your face. You think you could do better?"

"I know damn well I can't do better," I said, with perfect honesty. I'd never won a single koro game against either of Iason's daughters . . . unless you count the time when Lynn got a headache in the middle of the game and had to go belowdecks for a nap, and I kept throwing the dice while she was gone and scored five hundred points before she resurfaced. And even *then* it was close.

I'd given up trying to play either of them, just so that I could hang on to the last few tattered shreds of self-respect that I had left. But I was trying to make peace, and peace doesn't happen without pain and sacrifice. I nerved myself.

"I know damn well I can't do better," I repeated. "So what? Let's you and me play, and you can show me how it's done."

Ariadne made a mocking sound, a sort of *chuh*. "Listen, pirate queen. If your past performance is any guide, I would need six years and a marching band to show you how to play koro."

Lynn opened her mouth, ready to intervene. I shook my head at her. She'd been right all along. I was either going to have to learn to live with Ariadne, or kill her in her sleep.

"All right, I'm awful," I said. "So school me. Why don't we play a different game?"

A thought seemed to strike Ariadne. She cocked her head, and her lips curled upwards in a thin, wicked smile. "Did Lynn ever teach you the Beggar's Flip?"

"Oh, don't be a prick," Lynn said. "That's not a game."

Ariadne swept up the dice and rattled them in one hand. "But it'll be funny, won't it? I mean, watching her try to figure it out. How long do you think she'll spend fumbling around despairingly in front of the whole crew before she gives up and begs for the answer?"

I'd really been trying to be meek and agreeable and all, but that made me bristle. "You know what, princess? Before you decide that I'm an idiot, you should try your hand at the kind of mental gymnastics I have to pull off every day. Have you ever determined a ship's latitudinal position? Have you ever calculated a cosine in your head in the middle of a howling gale? Have you—wait. The whole crew?"

Ariadne gestured at our audience. "I think just about everyone's here. Why, are you shy?"

That was not the point, as Lynn and Regon had already realized. Both of them—startled, a little guilty—shot to their feet.

"The entire crew can't be here," I said, starting off low and dangerous and letting the volume rise with each word. "Because I *know* that my sodding *lookouts* would not just abandon their sodding *posts.*"

By then, all the sailors were scrambling away, running to the rails to scan the horizons. I waited for the cries of *All clear,* the signal that no lurking danger had crept up close while we were distracted. I waited five seconds. I waited ten.

Spinner spoke first, his voice a trembling treble. "Shit. I mean—sails, captain. I mean, shit."

AS I SPRINTED for the gunwale, I had my hand outstretched. "Spyglass!"

Someone gave me one, I didn't look to see who, and I clapped it up to my eye. Sails, yes, two of them, and—fuck in a bucket, no wonder Spinner was scared. I knew those ships, sleek and predatory as a shark's fin slicing through the water.

"Corsairs," Regon growled beside me, making it sound like the dirty word it was.

Corsairs: the vultures of the sea, who had preyed on the southern trade routes long before the war began. They'd found it very easy to adapt once everything boiled into chaos. They were human scorpions, more or less, who chewed dajiki root before battle to inflame themselves to a frothing, murderous frenzy. I've heard that after one lump of dajiki root, the screams of your enemies as you cut them down sound like sweet music. I've heard that after two lumps of dajiki root, running a cutlass into another human body is enough to make you . . . well. Finish the sentence yourself, in the interests of delicacy. Corsairs are scum, is what I'm trying to get at.

"Another sail!" Spinner roared, and his voice was pitched higher than usual but there was no other sign that he was practically wetting himself. And that was impressive, since, except for Regon and me, Spinner knew better than anyone what corsairs could do.

Up went the spyglass again. Sure enough, there was one more ship on the horizon: a square red blot.

"That's one of ours," Regon said.

I snapped the spyglass out to its full length. "That's not just any one of ours. That's the *Sod Off*—that's Latoya and Flint!"

"You can tell? For sure? From this distance?"

"It's one of my damn ships, isn't it? Do you ask a mother whether she can recognize all her children?"

The corsairs were wheeling, bearing down on the *Sod Off* like wolves scenting prey. I saw the blot of red veer to the side as Flint tried to change course. It wouldn't be enough to get him clear. He was a fine sailor, my man Flint, but when it came to ship handling, he was no Regon, or Teek.

I watched the corsairs' ships turning, swift and light. It made me ever more aware of the massive weight groaning under my feet.

"We're too far out," I muttered, partly to Regon and partly to myself. "The *Banshee's* too heavy to move well in this miserable wind. I could *fart* harder than it's blowing now."

"Whine, whine, whine," Regon said. "It'll be enough, because it has to be enough. That's all. I'll get the men to stations . . ."

"Yes, and then you can line them up on deck, have them all bend over, and we'll give the farting thing a try, because I don't see how the hell we're going to get this beast moving otherwise."

There was a crackle then, as though something in the sky had torn like paper. And then . . .

I've mentioned what the weather's like down south: violent and changeable. The heavens are constantly on fire, lightning flogging the ozone, the very clouds a-hum with forces that could rip a man apart. And every now and then, the sky tears above you, and something falls through.

The sky came apart. I felt a blow on my back, as if I'd been punched hard just below the neck. That was the rain beginning to fall, solid as a sheet of iron. I gasped, abruptly drenched.

"Here." Lynn was at my side, helping me out of my sodden coat. "You ready? This is your wind, Mistress, so you better make the most of it."

She was right. The sudden, violent squall had brought with it a sudden, violent wind, blowing abaft the beam. So there was still a chance.

"I'll have men aloft!" I roared, wiping water from my eyes. "Lynn, Spinner, up up *up!*"

They raced for the rigging—both of them light and agile, nimble as monkeys on the ropes. Lynn slipped once on the wet lines, but Spinner shot a hand out to steady her, and they made it up to the foretop without disaster.

The *Banshee* was flying, the strong wind hauling her through the waves like a racehorse would pull a child's wagon, in great, bounding leaps. Too fast.

"Captain, we have to reef!" Regon yelled at me, raindrops pounding on his forehead. "At this clip, you'll capsize her!"

"All right, all *right!*" I snapped at him, but already I was distracted by the bigger problem. The *Banshee* was one ship. The corsairs had two. Whichever of them I chose to grapple and board, the other would be left free to go after the *Sod Off*, and Flint's twelve-man crew. Maybe Latoya would be able to even things out a bit, but I still wasn't happy with the odds.

If only I had more of my ships with me! With the *Black Rush* on one flank and the *Destiny* on another, and the *Idiot Kid* lurking by for emergencies, I could have carved through the corsairs without slowing down. Wasn't that why I built a damn fleet in the first place? And here I was, in a single ship, with the *Sod Off* in trouble and my thumb up my arse. How stupid could I possibly . . .

Stop it. I actually slapped myself in the face. I knew better than to get locked inside my own head when there was work to do. Focus—that was what Lynn would tell me. Focus on what you have, not what you don't. I didn't have any extra ships. I did have the *Banshee,* my beautiful *Banshee,* and I loved every plank and peg in her, but still . . . she couldn't turn as swiftly as the smaller corsair vessels, couldn't manoeuvre as easily. She was too large, too heavy, too . . .

Yes. *Heavy.* Use what you have. Yes. Use what you have. Buggering fuck against a spiky tree, that was it.

The *Banshee* surged forwards. All around me was a clutter of sound, the blatting of the rain, creaking of ropes and the barking of orders, as my crew prepared to shorten sail. I raised my voice over all of it, "*Belay that!*"

"Captain?" I couldn't see Regon, but I could hear him bawling in the grey mist.

"Don't shorten sail!" I roared, clambering towards the helm. I'm not one to stumble on board ship, but we were moving so fast, even I had to grab at the lines to stay upright.

"*Captain?*" Regon said, a note of pure panic entering his tone. It wasn't hard to translate: *She's gone off the deep end at last. I always knew this day would come.*

"I need her going full bore!"

"Captain, we'll capsize! The wind's too fast; she'll go straight over!"

"Not *my* ship!" I yelled in no particular direction, shoving the helmsman away from the wheel so I could take his place. "Not *my* beautiful girl!"

I wasn't the best helmsman among my crew, not by a long shot. But at a moment like this, with the *Banshee* ploughing through the water so fast that the planks quivered and groaned, and the wind so hard that we'd tip if someone sneezed in the wrong direction, I needed to be in control of things myself. I needed to feel my ship moving beneath me, responding to my every nudge and gesture, sweet and pliant as a thoroughbred mare, or . . . well . . . Lynn.

On and on the *Banshee* lumbered. Now the masts were creaking painfully, straining as the vicious wind surged against the sails.

"*Captain!*" Regon yelled at me. "We'll lose the mainmast; we *have* to lower sail!"

"She'll manage," I gasped out, fighting to keep my grip on the bucking helm. "I just need another minute."

"Captain!"

Now we were so close to the corsairs' ships that I could count the daggers tucked into their sashes. As I'd expected, they'd split so they could hit the *Sod Off* from both flanks. I chose the vessel to starboard and angled the *Banshee* so she'd strike the smaller ship broadside.

A gust hit hard, and the *Banshee* listed so badly that half the sailors went sliding across the deck. I snarled, but held course.

"*Captain!* What the hell are you playing at? We'll never . . . aw, what's the use." Regon raised his great bullhorn of a voice, which could boom with twice the thunder of a south sea storm. "*All hands, grip and brace!*"

As the *Banshee* reached her target, the whole world slowed for a moment, as if we were going to balance forever at the very tip-top of the wave. I saw a corsair gaping at us, and it seemed as if I had forever to study the wooden toggles on his ragged vest, and the hair bristling in clumps from his nostrils. Then, the world spun back to its normal dizzying pace, and the *Banshee's* side slammed against the corsair sloop. My teeth nearly shattered with the force of the impact, and my vision blurred. At first I didn't know whether I'd wrecked the *Banshee*, or the corsair ship, or just killed all of us.

Then I saw the wet, slick belly of the corsair ship, floating uppermost on the surface of the sea, and I started to breathe again. It had worked. A whack from the heavy *Banshee*, travelling under full sail with the force of the squall behind her, had been enough to make the smaller ship turn turtle. But the force of the blow had also sent us yawing, almost out of control.

"*CUT AWAY SAIL!*"

Regon and I yelled this at almost the same instant, and barely half an instant after that, there came a sound like *flump-flump-flump,* as the heavy folds of the soaking mainsail dropped to the deck. Spinner and Lynn—lords of the deep love 'em both—had known what was needed, and they'd slashed the taut lines as soon as the sloop went over.

With the mainsail gone, the Banshee slowed and righted itself, like a runner taking breath. I spun the wheel once, sending us towards the surviving corsair ship at a more sedate pace.

Regon whistled beneath his breath. "Anyone ever tell you that you're a cheeky bloody bastard?"

"Often. And loudly." I unclenched my hands from the helm and shook out my stiff fingers. "I'm off to play with pointy objects. The ship is yours. See if you can hold her together. And keep Lynn away from the fighting."

"Captain . . ."

"Just do your best, Regon, I don't expect miracles!"

The sea was alive with bobbing heads, the flotsam from the capsized ship. I wondered whether dajiki root helped you to swim.

Meanwhile, Ariadne was clutching the *Banshee's* mainmast for everything she was worth. She had the look of fixed concentration that people get when they're trying not to vomit on their own shoes. The *Banshee* rocked as her grappling hooks sung through the air, and Ariadne gulped desperately.

"Get below, princess," I told her—and that was all the time I had for her. Ripping my cutlass from its sheath, I sprinted for the quarterdeck.

The grappling hooks had done their work, sinking deep into the wooden gunwales of the enemy ship. Now twenty pirates stood straining at the winches, hauling the corsair sloop towards the *Banshee*, closer and closer. Twenty more of my men waited on the quarterdeck, their faces lean and eager.

Corto, the quartermaster, had his foot up on the rail. His cutlass was already drawn, slick and silver in the rain, his main-gauche clasped between his teeth. I've known better sailors than Corto, but in the red hurly-burly of a battle line, with a blade in each hand, he was a whirling devil.

I took my place in the line, on Corto's right. If she'd been on board, Latoya would have been at my other flank, with a length of anchor chain. You don't usually think of bloody destruction when you see a chain, but the thing was easily the most deadly weapon on the *Banshee*. Once Latoya got it going, it ripped skulls apart like melon-rinds and snapped limbs like runner beans.

The two of them, Corto and Latoya, were the best fighters in my fleet. If I'd had fifty more like them, I could have put an end to the war in about forty-two minutes. I didn't have fifty more fighters like them, so I made sure that they both ate very well and I tried not to get in their way when they were working. They would scythe their way through the melee, and I'd trot along behind them, cleaning up.

The winches groaned. The ropes tightened. A wave broke, and the sloop's side slammed into the *Banshee*. Corto leapt, and when his feet hit planking, it was on the enemy ship. He spun into the crush of the corsairs, his blades moving as fast and light as silver scarves in the hands of a dancing girl. I vaulted the gunwale to follow him, hardly feeling the wood under my fingertips, and then the whirlwind took over.

You don't think a series of connected thoughts in mid-battle. I don't, anyway. It's all a bunch of jagged, divided pictures: man with a sword, another man with a sword, bad breath, hairy chest, slashed someone's gut open, rain in my boot, man with a huge pimple *and* a sword, ducked a punch, cut off someone's ear, slipped in gore. Still, at some dim level I knew that they were forcing us back, taking the fight to the *Banshee's* deck. Not good.

I shouted for Corto, with some vague idea of a clever counterattack, but that was a mistake. As he turned towards me, a scar-faced raider with a smile full of broken teeth closed in. One quick slash, and then a spraying arc of blood, the scarlet raw and hideous in the rain. Corto staggered, looking thoughtful, and tipped over sideways, crashing to the deck.

Broken-Tooth was raising his sword for the killing strike when there was a horrible crunching sound. Broken-Tooth's eyes, which had been alight with dajiki-fire, went dark. He crumpled like a rag, and there was Lynn, stooping over the body to retrieve her long knife. She had thrust it in at just the right place, the spot where the base of the skull meets the spine, and he never knew what hit him.

Good so far as it went, but now she was standing there in full view, which was exactly where I didn't want her. Lynn belonged to the kill-them-before-they-see-you school of warfare, and her favourite weapon—the garrotte—wasn't something you could whip out in a duel to deflect a sword strike.

"Get out of here!" I roared at her.

"Gods, you're bossy today," she said absently, trying to wiggle the knife free from Broken-Tooth's spine. "Oh, damn."

"Oh, damn" was Lynn's only comment on the fact that a berserker was bearing down on her with a wicked-looked axe, bloody foam streaming down his jaws as he gibbered and howled. Lynn tugged twice more at her knife, but it was stuck tight. Barehanded, she rose to her full height, all five feet of it.

"I screamed again, ran a corsair through, and kicked the body off my blade. I was trying to chop my way to Lynn through the crush of milling men, but there was just no way. I was seriously considering trying to pole-vault in her direction when I saw her tense herself, raise her fists, and lunge towards the axe-wielding madman.

She was going to punch him. She was going to *punch* him? That would not end well. I'd taught Lynn something about hand-to-hand fighting and there was nothing wrong with her technique, but she didn't have the weight to drive home a blow. The axeman grinned at her, hoisting his weapon overhead.

As my body turned liquid with horror, I saw Lynn's thumbs protruding from her fists, and realized what she had in mind.

Lynn dove in close to the axeman, so close that his breath left flecks of foam on her face, and thrust up with both thumbs. With a wet squelch, they disappeared into his eye sockets. While he was still pawing at his face, yowling, she snatched the dagger from his belt and slashed his throat.

I cut down one more corsair and finally, *finally,* reached her. She was pinned to the deck by the body of the blinded axeman. I yanked him up to let her wriggle free.

"That," I said, "was horrible."

She was wiping her thumbs clean on the axeman's trousers, but at that, she looked up in irritation. "What? Was I supposed to kill him *nicely*?"

"You should have stayed up at the masthead, that's what you should have done, you bloody contrary-minded wench!"

"Yes, yes. I was bad; no biscuit for me. Why are you yelling at me in the middle of a battle?"

"Because I'll yell at you whenever I bloody well choose!"

"Yes, Mistress, but in the interests of us not dying, could you hold it in for a while? At least until the battle's over?"

Right around then came the whining sound of a chain whipping through the air in circles—then the thunder crack of a shattering skull.

Latoya, and her anchor chain, had finally made it to the party.

I cast a look of triumph at Lynn, and she sighed, surrendering.

"Battle's over," she admitted. "Yell away."

THE SQUALL ENDED as quickly as it had begun. Sunlight burned away the grey mist, leaving the horizon clear. Rainwater, murky with blood, drained through the *Banshee's* scuppers.

Regon muttered to himself as he sloshed through puddles. I had to kick him to get his attention. "Where's Flint? I'll want to talk to him."

"Now, Captain?" Regon said plaintively. "We're not exactly ready for guests."

To illustrate his point, he grabbed a corpse by its ankles and upended it over the side of the ship.

"It's just Flint. You don't have to change your shirt."

"That's comforting," he said, picking up a severed arm and pitching it after the body.

"The corsair sloop isn't damaged, Mistress," Lynn said, passing by me and looking none the worse for the vicious scolding she'd just received. "That's another one for your fleet."

"Fine. Have you named it yet?"

"I was thinking *Contrary-Minded Wench*, but it's a work in progress. I'll give it some more thought once I've helped get Corto down below. By the way, Latoya's looking for you."

I could see Latoya already, looming head and shoulders above the rest of my sailors as they cleared the decks. The coil of chain draped over her shoulder was smeared with bits of things that I didn't want to think about. She *had* been busy.

As Latoya neared me, I had the noble intention of giving her something like an apology for sending her away to face my horrible father. That didn't work out. As soon as I got a good look at her—or, more correctly, at what she was carrying—I turned pale and grabbed for her belt.

"Captain. *Captain!*" Latoya held me off with one hand while she unhooked the scroll case from her belt. "There. Take it. And next time, get someone else to carry your mail."

She stomped away, I guess, but I never saw her go. My whole being was focused on the scroll case, a tube of leather one foot long and three inches wide, treated with grease to make it waterproof. A hawk's head was branded into the tight-fitting wooden stopper.

During the thirteen years I'd spent on my father's merchant ships, I constantly had one of those cases at my elbow, filled with despatches and instructions. Just touching one was enough to transport me back to that long-ago time. My fingers shook so hard that I had to use my teeth to pull the stopper.

Inside, there was a single roll of paper. I fumbled to break the seal, but paused. What could my father have to say to me that I would possibly want to read? What with the banishment, and the assassination attempts, and all, he'd kind of forfeited any claim on my affections. So why should I give a red-hot damn? Why didn't I just toss the tube over the *Banshee's* side, collect my slave girl, swagger down to my cabin, and call it a night?

It could be anything, I reminded myself. A death threat. A ransom demand. Hell, a shopping list. There was no sense in making too much of it. But my heart was still pounding at a speed that it usually only reached during lovemaking or war.

Somewhere nearby, Lynn was probably waiting for me to resurface from my haze and get back to work. And I would, I *would*, of course I would—but couldn't I take five seconds away from piracy to remember the life that I used to live, and pretend that I still meant something to the people who used to love me?

I rolled the scroll between my fingers. I broke the wax seal. I flattened it out.

It was a letter. Eight words long, that was all. My distracted eyes first took in the signature at the bottom: *Konrad*. My father's heir. My oldest brother.

Then I read the first line. It said simply, *Our father is dead.*

Below that were several ink-blots, as though Konrad had sat over the paper for some time, collecting his thoughts. Long enough for the pen to drip at least three times.

There was one more sentence below that, in neat, precise handwriting that showed how much thought had gone into the decision.

Please, it said. *Come home.*

PART TWO

BLOOD AND BONE

CHAPTER SIX

Darren, formerly of the House of Torasan (Pirate Queen)

"NOT NOW."

"But Lynn—"

"Later."

"Can't we—"

"We'll talk *later,* Darren." Lynn's voice was apologetic, but firm. "If you think about this, you're going to get lost in your own skull, and that can't happen right now. You're needed. We have to secure the prisoners, tend the wounded, and deal with the dead, in that order. Then we'll have time for family drama and I'll listen to you until my ears bleed—but *not now, Darren.*"

I hissed out a long, long breath. "Fine. I'll help Regon clear the decks."

Lynn paused with the utmost delicacy. "Or . . ."

"Or . . . or I could do something completely different. What's the completely different thing I'm going to be doing?"

"You're going to help Ariadne."

" . . . *or* I could do something even more fun than that, like carving poetry into my thighs with a meat cleaver."

"Sounds intriguing. Let's save it for a special occasion. In the meantime? Help Ariadne."

"But why?" I asked, feeling grouchy and put upon. "I'm useless at doctoring. You know that. Remember that time up near Sohanchi? If Latoya hadn't stopped me, I would have put a tourniquet around that poor man's neck to stop his head from bleeding."

"You don't have to doctor anyone. Just be with my sister while she works. Get her talking and keep her talking. It'll help. She's probably feeling overwhelmed right now."

"And you think I'll be able to calm her down?"

"No . . . but I think you'll be able to piss her off. Ariadne's a bit like you, Mistress. She always does her best work when she's angry."

THE FORECASTLE HAD been sort of transformed into a makeshift surgery. Emphasis on *sort of,* emphasis on *makeshift.* There was a single trestle table, where Corto lay groaning, and a box or two of rags. Wounded men, slumping against the bulkheads or hunching on the deck, took up the rest of the space. The decks themselves were sodden with blood and—well, other things. There were streaks of foulness along the wood, marking the paths where men had been dragged along by their good limbs.

All that was delightful enough. Add a smell that could have been wafting from hell's own crotch, and it was no wonder that Ariadne was starting to crack by the time I got there.

She was using both hands, daubing ineffectually at a gut wound with one and trying to tie a bandage tight with the other. But she found the time to look up at me with burning eyes when I came through the hatch.

"Not one word, Darren," she warned me, voice icy. "Not one, single, solitary word or there will be *consequences*."

I said, "Spinner."

"*That* was a word. Did you think I was kidding? I swear, Darren, I will kill you so hard that—"

"Spinner," I said again, and tapped one of the walking wounded. "Go get him. He can help sort out some of this mess."

Ariadne snarled. "Are you saying I can't handle it?"

Ariadne had a magical way of making irritation bloom in me, like some fast-growing thorn-bush. I glared at her. "I'm saying that *if* you can't handle it, *princess*, you'd better let me know so that I can make other arrangements. My men need care and they can't wait until you've finished with your breakdown."

"Who's going to treat them if I don't do it?" Ariadne wiped her bloody hands on a rag and threw it into an overflowing bucket. "Spinner? Because let me tell you, the only thing Spinner knows about surgery is that it's a bad sign if the patient's head falls off."

"You're exaggerating. He can stitch wounds."

"And what do you think I'm doing right now? Making soup?"

She stalked over to Corto and peeled back one of his eyelids, squinting down at the eye's glassy surface.

I followed her. "You do know that the wound's on his thigh, right?"

"Deep gash in his thigh and another in his forearm. Yes, the gushing blood was my first clue."

"So why are you looking at his face? Are you planning to kiss him better?"

"I gave him opium, smartass. I'm checking to see whether he's good and doped yet." She released his eyelid. "He is. So make yourself useful and cut his trousers away."

De-trousering men is not my area of expertise, but in a pinch, I can manage. I split the seam from waistband to cuff and peeled the cloth back from the wound. It was an ugly sight under there, a mash of blood and ragged flesh. Ariadne began to sort through the mess with her fingers and a long iron needle.

There are few things quite as unpleasant as the sight of someone piecing bits of torn flesh back together, as though they're sewing a meaty sort of quilt. I broke the silence not because I felt like talking, but because I needed the distraction.

"How did you learn to do this, anyway?" I asked. "Surgery isn't one of the typical accomplishments of a noblewoman."

"I read about it," she said, squinting at a wiggly pink thing that I couldn't identify and didn't want to. "And I snuck into the hospice to watch the physicians, too."

"But why?"

"I spent my whole childhood watching my sister getting pounded into raw meat every other day. I had to find *some* way to help."

She hissed in frustration. Corto's raggedly-torn flesh wouldn't close cleanly. There were gaps between her stitches, with pink-red serum leaking out. "He's going to get wound fever."

"That's to be expected."

"Yes . . . but with a wound this deep, he'll get it bad. Wish I had some mouldy bread."

I raised an eyebrow. "I know you're trying to get used to peasant food, but you don't have to go *that* far."

"Don't try to be clever. Twit. I need mouldy bread to put on the wound."

"I'm beginning to have second thoughts about letting you near my sailors."

Ariadne snorted, impatient, and then paused in her work long enough to jerk down the shoulder of her shirt. "See that?"

It was a raised knot of flesh, a circular scar. Ariadne let me get a good look at it before she adjusted her shirt and picked up the needle again. "When I was seven, a spider bit me there. I *hate* spiders, the creepy little bastards, but I was never afraid of them before that. Darren, you can't even imagine. First, it swelled up. That was the overture. It felt so hot that I thought I had a live coal under my skin, and I couldn't touch it without screaming. Then it split across the middle and pus dribbled out—are you covering your ears? *Darren? Why are you covering your ears?*"

Reluctantly, I lowered my hands. "I don't like hearing about pus. Blood is fine. Pus, not so much."

Ariadne rolled her eyes to the ceiling. "How did my sister end up with such a wimp?" She knotted the end of the suture, bit off a trailing end, and threaded the needle again. "Anyway. The spider bite turned into a massive weeping sore. My parents called physicians and they did all the usual things. They bled me, they purged me, they cupped me, they read my horoscope, they rubbed the wound with a moonstone, they dosed me with pomegranate juice and crushed amber—all of that."

I nodded. Those were common treatments, though not everybody could afford them.

"But nothing helped. After about a week, I was fiery with fever and my head ached until I thought it was being squeezed in a vice. I was miserable and I hated the world, so I slipped away from my nurse and went to find my sister. Found her playing in a corner of the kitchen."

"Playing?"

"Yes. Does that sound strange? I suppose it does. This was when her mother was still alive. She did get to play sometimes back then."

I perked up. All the details about Lynn's life in the Time Before Melitta were precious to me, since Lynn didn't remember much and revealed even less. "What was she playing with?"

"Spoons. Wooden spoons. The girl liked spoons, don't ask me why. I guess if you don't own any toys, you work with what you have. I went and plumped down next to her. Hoped that she would cheer me up, at least. But she got one good look at my crusted weeping sore and she shot to her feet and ran away, yelling for her mother to come help."

"Why? Elain wasn't a healer, was she?"

"Elain was a servant from the day she grew big enough lug a bucket down the hall until the day she died. But when you're small, you go through a stage when you think your mother can solve any problem."

I frowned, casting my mind back to my own childhood. "I don't think I went through a stage when I believed my mother could solve any problem."

"Me neither," Ariadne admitted. "Probably had something to do with my mother being an evil hellbeast. Damn. The opium's wearing off."

Corto's pupils were still tiny pinpoints, but his limbs were starting to twitch. Ariadne, annoyed, drummed her fingers on his chest. "I hoped it would last longer. I still have to stitch the gash on his arm."

"Nothing's stopping you."

"Well, no—but he'll kick."

True enough. I considered putting him out again with a quick blow to the back of the skull, but that kind of thing never works out quite as well as one would like. Instead, I unrolled another length of bandage and lashed his wrists and ankles to the legs of the trestle.

He struggled reflexively against the bonds, so I gave his face a little slap to orient him. "Relax, Corto. You spent all day being a hero. Lie still now and bask in the glory."

Sweat prickled on his forehead, though he tried to smile. "You're going to watch the vixen while she cuts on me, right? Make sure that she doesn't slice off anything important?"

"It's a matter of opinion what's important," Ariadne said, snipping off a loose thread with a large pair of shears.

Corto's eyes shot back to me. "Get me off this table."

"I'll watch her," I said, pulling the final knot tight. "Don't worry about it. You just drift. Let yourself tap out, if you can."

I folded a piece of cloth into a wedge and held it towards him. With a groan of resignation, he took it between his teeth and braced himself, pushing back against the trestle as Ariadne cut the sleeve of his shirt away.

The wound there wasn't quite as messy, but the flesh was mangled enough that Ariadne had to do more patchwork. Corto's chest moved faster and faster, and through the cloth that gagged him, he grunted. I watched, deeply grateful that I wasn't the one on the table.

"Anyway," I said, to keep my mind off of it. "You were saying?"

Ariadne looked up. "I was . . . Oh, yes. Lynn ran off screaming for her mother, and in a few seconds, both of them came running back. By then, I'd come over all strange. My head was so light, I thought it was going to lift me off the ground. Well, Elain looked at the sore and she went and fetched a piece of mouldy bread."

"Why did she have a piece of mouldy bread kicking around?"

"You know, I forgot to ask. Maybe she was going to feed it to the chickens, or something. This was properly mouldy bread, too. Looked like a piece of furry blue carpet. Anyway, Elain wanted to put it on my open sore . . ."

"*On* the sore?"

"Yes, and I didn't want to let her and she said . . . I've never forgotten this. When I was little, I visited my sister in the kitchens every chance I got. Usually two or three times a week. And I saw Elain every time . . . we became quite chummy by the end. But she never managed to call me by my name. She was probably afraid—servants often are, when you start to get familiar. Whatever the reason, she never slipped—it was always 'yes, my lady' and 'no, my lady' from her. Except that day. There she was, sitting beside me with a piece of rotting bread, wanting to smear it on my back, and she said, 'Please, Ariadne.' Just that. 'Please, Ariadne.' She was so determined. So I let her do it."

I couldn't imagine this ending well. "What happened?"

"She scraped the mould off the bread, rubbed it on a rag, tied it against the sore, and then she pulled out a pallet and made me take a nap. Lynn lay down next to me and we both fell asleep. That was the only time we ever slept in the same room, I think. And do you know, when I woke up, I felt better. My head didn't feel like it was going to burst, for a change, and the swelling in my shoulder was down. Elain put more mould on it before she sent me upstairs."

"Didn't your parents notice anything?"

"Of course not. My parents never saw me during the day. I was presented to them for ten minutes each evening before they went to supper, and they'd nod at me from across the room and ask whether I was being good for my nurse. They might have noticed the smell, but I didn't smell all that good before Elain rubbed rot on me. The sore was leaking pus, and pus stinks. My nurse did realize that I'd been up to something, because I had ashes and straw all over my frock. So she gave me what she considered to be a spanking. In other words, she patted the air next to my hindquarters and I dutifully shouted, 'Ow! Ow!' But nobody noticed that there was bread mould all over me. The next day, I was feeling so much better that I snuck down to the kitchens and made Elain do the whole thing again. By the next week, there was beautiful new pink flesh over the entire sore. Next month, nothing but a scar."

"But . . . mouldy bread? That makes no sense!"

"It made no sense, but it worked. The cures that the physicians tried made perfect sense, but didn't work. Life is strange, what can I say? But since it *did* work, I plan to smear a lot of mouldy bread on open wounds, and let somebody else worry about the whys and wherefores."

She knotted a last suture, and squinted critically at her work. "There. That's the best I can do."

Somehow, miraculously, all the shreds of flesh on Corto's arm and thigh had been replaced by a few neat lines of stitching. I nodded, impressed in spite of myself. "Not bad. I'll recommend you to my friends."

"Don't have much of a choice, do you?" Ariadne said. But there was new confidence in her movements as she stripped blood from the blades of her shears. "All right. Bring on the next one."

CHAPTER SEVEN

Lynn

IT WAS EASIER to cope while I was moving. So I interrogated prisoners, helped clear and swab the decks, supervised the hoisting of a new sail, cooked up a mess of plum duff, served it, counted the casks of salt beef, and scoured the brass knob at the centre of the helm. When I couldn't think of any other mindless tasks to do up top, I retreated to Darren's cabin, found her second-best pair of boots, and gave them an unnecessarily violent polishing.

It was long after dusk when Darren came in, and she was fairly rippling with smugness, as if she'd made a great discovery.

"You know something?" she asked, as she peeled off her blood-stiffened coat. "Your sister will be a fine surgeon one day, if she isn't hung first."

Had she only just figured that out? I bit back a sarcastic remark, with some effort, and brushed the second-best boots again.

Darren threw herself back on the bunk and scratched her belly. "Report," she ordered.

For a fraction of a second, I was tempted to scream real loud and break something instead, but I shook it off. "Ten prisoners. I made a first stab at a debrief, but they're so jacked up on dajiki root, they thought that I was a pink elephant who was holding them prisoner in the lair of the mushroom king. I'll have Ariadne give them a purge before I talk to them tomorrow. We've got three dead, and I made duff for dinner, and you're getting blood on the bunk, and for the love of flying fuck Darren are you actually going to go back to Torasan Isle?"

Darren froze, all her casual ease evaporating into the atmosphere. I brushed the boots again.

"You don't want me to go?" Darren asked hesitantly.

She was not at her most insightful that day. I brushed the boots once more. If this went on, I was going to wear right through the leather.

Darren sat upright, suddenly wary. "It's a trap, right? That's what you're thinking. If I step onto the Isle, Konrad is going to pop out of a box, shoot me through the eye, skin me, and use me as shoe leather. Is that what you're worried about?"

I was tempted, so very tempted, to say yes. I had to brush the boots three more times before I could force myself to tell the truth.

"It's not a trap," I said. "Your brother wants you back."

"How can you be so sure?"

"Darren. Think. Torasan is a not-very-large house with a not-very-large treasury in the middle of a very, very large war. In the past year, you've become a crazy famous pirate with your own fleet of ships and so much money that you could wipe your arse with silk. Does it really surprise you that your brother suddenly wants to be your best friend?"

Something crumpled in her face. Darren had been hoping, then, that the letter from Konrad had more to do with brotherly love than politics. After everything she'd seen, how could she still be such a hopeless innocent?

"My father never asked me to come home," Darren said, defensive and wilted all at once. "Not even after I started to rake in the cash."

"That's because your father made a big public deal about banishing you, and he probably thought that his testicles would wither and retract into his body if he ever changed his mind. Plus, he spent his entire life pissed drunk, so he probably couldn't form a thought as complicated as *Me want money.*" I paused. "You're not going to go gooey about your father now he's dead, are you?"

Darren shook her head. "Even I have my limits."

"Good. Because that would be a little bit too much, today."

I threw the boots against the wall, first the left, then the right. There was a sort of tightness at the back of my throat which made me wonder whether I might burst out into tears. I never did that in front of Darren, it *never* happened, but I was dog tired, you see. I hadn't gotten enough sleep the night before, or the night before that, or . . . really, I couldn't remember when I'd last slept well. I wrapped my arms around my knees and gripped tight, staring into the corner.

I felt Darren's hand hovering above me before it descended. Reflex took over, and my arm jerked up to protect the side of my head. Instantly, Darren's hand shot away.

I didn't apologise—what was the point?—but I knew I'd upset her by flinching. In the stillness, I heard her swallow, and swallow again.

"I won't go," Darren said abruptly. "Simple as that."

I had to bite my knee hard for almost a minute before I trusted myself enough to answer. "Why does it always have to be about sacrifice with you?"

"It's not a sacrifice."

"You want to see your family, Darren. Do you really think you've managed to keep that a secret?"

"I don't give a damn about my family! I give a damn about you!"

"You can give a damn about both. It's allowed. I won't tell your adoring public."

"Can I come closer?"

"Not yet."

The bunk creaked as she sat down. More silence.

"Good god, Darren, why don't you yell at me?" I asked with a flash of sudden irritation. "You've just been un-disowned and summoned home by the family that you still love, much against your better judgment and mine. You're aching to go and swagger around Torasan Isle waving your shiny cutlass and showing all your stupid relatives how you made good. And here I am pouting and staring at the wall and ruining a perfectly decent pair of your boots. Yell at me already."

"I don't want to yell at you."

"You do."

"I don't."

"You're lying and if you don't stop, then so help me, I will bite you and it won't be in a fun kind of way. You do not need to protect me from you."

"*Fine!*" Darren yelled, and she smacked the bulkhead for emphasis, no doubt raising a bruise that she'd complain about later. "Lynn—listen, Lynn, I am not that bitch Melitta!"

Now I had to look at her. "If there was the slightest confusion about that, do you really think I'd be sitting here?"

"You know what I mean."

"I really don't."

"I mean—oh, bollocks." Scowling, Darren ran her fingers though shaggy hair. It was clotted with sweat and blood, and I made a mental note to end the fight in time to give the pirate queen a bath before bed.

"I'm not going to change," Darren said, starting over. "I'm not going to transform into some rampaging asshole of a noble, just because my family doesn't want me dead anymore. If I visit the Isle and wear a clean shirt and sleep in a real bed for once, I won't become a different person. I'm not going to treat peasants like scum and I'm not going to start whoring with every girl in reach and I'm not going to create my own empire and name it Darrenland. And I'm not going to . . . Lynn, I'm not going to . . ."

She was floundering, so I cut her off. "You're not going to decide I'm subhuman, put me in a cage, and beat me with sticks. Again, Darren, I know. It's not you that I'm worried about."

Darren narrowed her eyes briefly, then widened them. "My family? You're scared of my family? Lynn, you haven't even met my family!"

"Jess has. She gave me the details."

"I don't think you're allowed to listen to anything that my ex-girlfriend says. I'm going to make that a rule. Look, not all of my relatives are evil.

There's my youngest sister, Jada . . . I haven't seen her in years, but she was a good kid. And I have hordes of nieces and nephews. Some of them are tiny, so they're probably all right."

"They're probably adorable. Not that I'll be able to tell. I'm never going to get a good look at them."

"You will if you come to the Isle . . . Hey, easy, easy. If you groan that hard you're going to bust your vocal chords. Did I say something stupid?"

I breathed carefully, trying not to explode. How could she not understand?

"I wouldn't be allowed to look at their faces." It was ridiculous that I had to explain this—like having to warn someone that water can be really quite wet. "Your nieces and nephews are *nobles,* Darren. I would have to keep my eyes fixed on the floor at their feet, and address them as Young Master or Young Miss."

Darren, who had been pacing restlessly up and down, stopped short at that. Her expression twisted, as though she was about to laugh or cry or vomit or all three. "You think I would let them treat you like that? I would never let them treat you like that!"

"They treated Jess like that. And anyway, how would you stop them? Whip out the old cutlass and leave a trail of bodies in your wake? That'd make for a hell of a family reunion."

"I don't give a damn about—"

"Yes, you do—and even if you didn't, what's the point of making a fuss? I'm the bastard brat of a scullery maid. A runaway servant. Under Kilan law, I have no rights. Zero. None. The great houses have spent the last seven years trying to messily exterminate each other, but still, they all agree on *that* much."

"We don't have to tell my family who you really are. I'll say that you're a sickeningly wealthy heiress from a house like—I don't know—Nimian, or Tours. I'll say that you have your own private army and any insult will be met with lethal force."

I could have screamed. "*Darren. Think.* What's the punishment for a commoner who impersonates a noble?"

" . . . oh."

"Yes, oh. It's usually flogging and branding, right? For a first offence. That's what they did on Bero. For repeat offenders, I think it's death by dismembering. You'd know better than me. You're the one who got all that fancy upper-class education."

"*I would never let them hurt you!*"

"And again, you would stop them . . . how? You can't take on the entire aristocracy single-handed."

"Watch me," Darren snarled. She was pacing faster now. "You just fucking watch me!"

"Calm down. Remember your ulcer."

"Fuck my fucking ulcer! Fuck my fucking—"

There was more along these lines, much more. Eventually I had to lead her back to the bunk, sit her down, and rub her shoulders. She slumped there, growling into her hands, until sanity returned.

"Sorry," she mumbled at last. "It just makes me so angry."

I gave her back an extra rub instead of answering. It was nice that she cared, but she shouldn't have needed me to spell it out for her, and anyway, there was no point in getting hysterical.

"You're one woman," I said, once the growling stopped. "You can't bust every noble skull in Kila by yourself, just to protect my dignity. And I wouldn't want you to try. You'd fail. I'd bleed. End of story. That's how things are."

Darren yanked at her hair. "How can you be talking this way? You, of all people?"

"How can I *not* be talking this way, me of all people?"

"Because—damn it, Lynn, you don't lie down and surrender. You find a way around or over or through."

"I try, sure. When I have to. When I have a reason. I have no reason to swan off to Torasan Isle pretending to be a daughter of the House of Tours. What do you expect of me? You want me to risk forty lashes with a cowhide whip, just so I can have the honour of patting your nephews and nieces on the head?"

"That's not . . . I didn't . . . oh, *damn* it! Look, I won't go. Nuts to my family, I just won't go."

"It's up to you," I said, brushing some dried blood from the shoulder of her shirt. "But you know you really should."

LET'S TALK ABOUT Darren for a second. As if we weren't doing that anyway.

When I ran away from Melitta, I was seventeen: a short, skinny kid with no real skills except the ability to take a stubborn stain out of any material, from velvet to chamois. I had no weapon with me, except a kitchen knife that I lost on the first night. I'd never slept out of doors, had never seen a river or touched a living tree, and had only the most general idea about money. That is, I knew that having it was good, so not having it was probably bad.

And there I was, trying to make my way across the islands with a civil war in full bloody swing, in a time when there was a sex-starved soldier behind every tree, a warship in every harbour, and when nobody was happy to see a hungry stranger.

How I survived, I really don't know, except for the obvious: I always did what it took, no matter what it took. Some people can't do that, I'm told, and while I know that must be true, it's not something that I understand in my gut. How can anyone not be willing to do what it takes to keep on breathing?

I'm not going to go into details about that time, the three years that I spent perfecting the business of survival. Some parts were ugly, some parts were very ugly, some were close to being all right. But the whole experience got me thinking.

Thinking about people, mainly—those slippery things. Why are there people who get up in the morning, eat a hearty breakfast, and then spend the day killing, burning, raping, and ravaging? Why do other people sally out to save the downtrodden and protect the weak? Why are there people who do both on alternate days, with a pause every so often to drown a kitten or adopt a puppy?

The answer, as I eventually figured out, is a whole lot simpler and sadder than might be expected: It's just habit. A man can spit naked babies onto a spear and feel no more emotion about it than you feel when you pierce a piece of ham with a fork, as long as he does it for eight hours every day, with a break for lunch. And anyone can develop a murder habit, given the opportunity.

Maybe it's a sign of my own sickness that I can't believe in heroes. Maybe it's part of that brokenness that Ariadne always half-loved and half-feared in me. Fucked if I know. Fact remains, when you get right down to it, people—all people—are hungry, lonely animals. It doesn't matter if they're wearing burlap or velvet, fetters, or rubies. The beast is underneath all the same, and if you want to keep it quiet then you have to keep it fed.

But that doesn't explain Darren.

Darren had flaws, dozens of them. I could list her flaws alphabetically before I'd known her a half a month, from "arrogant" to "zombie-like" (the latter applied only when she was tired). But somehow, Darren didn't let the sheer weight of reality break her spirit, or let habit define the boundaries of the possible. Darren had glared Destiny in its bloodshot eye, and said only: Fuck this shit. Darren got up one morning, ate a hearty breakfast, and then went out to change the world. And that may not be heroism, but in my jaded, cynical book, it's about as close as you can come.

Why did I bind myself in service to this beautiful madwoman? Many reasons, some of which, as you can imagine, stemmed from the desire to get in her pants and have a good old rummage around there. But I could have done that without throwing myself headlong into her crazy crusade.

Nor were my motives unselfish. Hell no. I wasn't out to save my country or the peasantry when I turned Darren into a pirate queen. I did it because I knew one simple thing: If Darren ruled the world, I could be safe.

Imagine, if you can, what it was like for me to be with Darren in the beginning. On a pirate ship, there's no god but the captain and no law but the captain's law. I was what Darren said I was, and I could do whatever she said I could do. And the rest of the world could take a flying leap.

But I think I always knew that we couldn't hide at sea forever. Piracy was a good starting point, but Darren would need to do more if she was going to take the nation. Sooner or later, she would have to deal with the ruling classes—not just fight them, but find allies in their ranks. She'd have to attend banquets, pay off lords, wheedle, flatter, broker deals, sign treaties. When that happened, then she'd start to look a lot less like a pirate and a lot more like a noblewoman. She'd be recovering her place in the world she once belonged to, a world of ballrooms and trade relations and political manoeuvres—a world where I didn't have the right to exist, except as Melitta's *thing*.

Yet, in spite of all that, I couldn't ask Darren to forget about Torasan Isle. She was changing so fast, you see. Already she was so much *more* than she had been when we started. Rescuing damsels and burying treasure was all very well, but Darren had outgrown her pirate boots. She was ready to be a new kind of leader, to fight a different and longer and harder kind of war. And I couldn't, or wouldn't, stop her from doing it, even if it meant that she would outgrow me as well.

Because Darren wasn't the only one who had changed during our time together. And gods help me, now I wanted to save the world, too.

THE NEXT DAY and a half was busy—so busy that Darren and I couldn't continue our conversation in one unbroken block. We had to snatch moments here and there.

"I really should go," Darren told me as we headed to the brig to interrogate the prisoners. "Torasan isn't a rich house, but it has good sailors and good harbours. Konrad could be a valuable ally, if he's serious about making friends."

"I know you should go," I said. "I just can't go with you. That's all."

At that point, Darren was called away to deal with a rowdy corsair, and I was called away to help scrub Corto's wounds with brine, and we didn't see each other again until I was ladling out supper.

"I get that it would be too risky for you to pretend to be a noble," Darren said, holding out her tin plate. "But why can't you just come to Torasan Isle as my slave?"

"I could, I guess." I slopped out a portion of stew. "But I won't."

"It's not that I'm arguing," Darren said half an hour later, when she came to get a second helping. "But why not? You're not exactly shy when it comes to the yes-Mistress thing. When we were in Tavar, you spent practically the entire week on your knees."

"Yes, but that was my choice. I could have taken a time out whenever I wanted. Have an extra biscuit. You missed lunch."

Some hours later, as Darren and I walked the deck together on evening watch, she pointed out, "You never did take a time out in Tavar."

"I never needed to, but it was always an option. It wouldn't be that way on Torasan Isle. I'd have to obey you to keep the skin on my back. That's the difference."

Later, as we lay in our bunk, Darren mumbled into my shoulder, "Does it really make that *much* of a difference?"

It was the kind of question that she only asked when she was already half-asleep, too tired to worry about pissing me off. I stroked her hair, teasing the dark heavy locks. "Yes. It does make that much of a difference."

I didn't bother to explain, because she wasn't asking for an explanation. It just took her a while to accept facts that she didn't like. She had a way of prodding at them over and over, as if reality was a side of roast beef that she was trying to cook medium rare.

But now, at long last, she heaved a sigh of surrender that filled the whole room. "So I'll go to the Isle. And you won't come with me."

"Looks like."

"It'll just be a couple of weeks."

"I know."

"I'll feel lost without you there to steer me, and I'll be useless at everything." She yawned. "And you'll spend the whole time worrying. You probably think I'll get myself killed if I go off to be a hero without any supervision."

She fell asleep then, so I didn't have a chance to point out the obvious: there was no way in hell that I was going to let her go off and be a hero without any supervision. No matter. She really should have known.

"ARIADNE?"

"That is her name, Mistress, yes. People usually don't pronounce it as a despairing screech."

"*Ariadne?*"

"Or a tortured moan."

"Aw, *bugger* it."

"You didn't really think that I would let you go to Torasan Isle without a chaperone, did you?"

"I'm not a helpless infant, Lynn! Just occasionally, just once in a while, you could let me do something on my own."

"There are all kinds of things that I'd let you do on your own. Like weaving a lap rug. Or petting a sheep. Well—a small sheep, anyway. But you're going into a political snake pit instead. So you need backup. So you're taking Ariadne. Now stop screaming before you rupture something."

I hadn't slept at all the night before. After two hours of staring at the ceiling, I'd given up, and spent the rest of the dark watch pacing to and fro on deck, grunting every time Regon tried to make conversation. Brittle with fatigue, I was even less inclined to put up with nonsense than usual.

Darren saw and turned apologetic. "You have to deal with a lot of bullshit from me, don't you?"

"It's an occupational hazard for slave girls. Are you done arguing with me about this?"

"I suppose, but . . ."

"What?"

"Ariadne's not going to be excited about this plan, any more than I am. There could be some pushback."

"Yeah? Give me ten minutes."

It took five. When we began our conversation, Ariadne was annoyed, argumentative, and spoiling for a fight. By the time we finished, she was hushed, penitent, and kept saying things like, "Well, you would know best."

Near the end, she pointed out rather meekly that she didn't have anything to wear. That wasn't a real problem, though. All sailors know how to sew; if they didn't, their clothes would break down into useless salt-crusted rags in a few months. So, although pirates may be rowdy and smelly and drunk half the time, they're exactly the people you need if you want a bunch of tailoring done in a hurry.

We had bales of cloth down in the hold: fine white linen and black silk for trading, and some deep purple velvet we'd been saving to make Spinner a surprise for his birthday. It was all sacrificed to the cause. Ariadne described the latest dress styles and Spinner sketched them on a scrap of canvas, adding a few flourishes of his own. Regon and I cut and fitted linen for drawers, shifts, and petticoats, and turned it over to the sailors for sewing. At one point, we had the whole crew of the *Banshee* sitting cross-legged around the quarterdeck, heads bent, tongues protruding with effort, as they stitched away busily at Ariadne's underwear. Darren, the only person on board ship who couldn't sew for toffee, stomped around the deck making suggestions which we all pretended were helpful.

Spinner basted the seams of Ariadne's gown, while Ariadne embroidered lacy, intricate swoops around the bodice and I handled fiddly bits like hems and buttonholes. We finished the thing off by stitching a row of tiny grey seed pearls all along the neckline.

The result was not a typical ball gown. It was beautifully cut and sewn, but it clung in places that court attire was not supposed to cling and left things exposed to view which nobles were not used to seeing. When Ariadne first tried it on, her eyes went big as dinner plates. She told the crew she loved it. That may have been true, or it may just have been diplomatic. She was, after all, standing in a ring of heavily-armed pirates at the time, all of whom had just dedicated days and days to her lingerie.

At that point, the sailors turned their attention to Darren. She had been announcing to anyone who would listen, and most of the people who wouldn't, that she didn't need no stinking court clothes. She would go to Torasan Isle in her ordinary working gear, and if her family didn't like it, well, they could go pound sand. She kept repeating this in an increasingly loud and panicky tone when the crew converged around her. Regon and Latoya muttered soothingly into Darren's ears as they yanked her arms up, and Spinner whipped a knotted measuring string around her chest.

Darren's court clothes turned out even better than Ariadne's. The black doublet, with its trimming of silver fox fur, was luxurious and stern all at once. There were loose trousers and heavy boots to go with it instead of hose and pointed shoes. The combination gave Darren an almost military air, instead of the butterfly look of most courtiers. Dressed that way, in the Torasan colours, she seemed like a woman with the strength of a whole kingdom behind her, and I could not fucking cope.

I stuck it out for a whole five seconds, while Darren inspected the crisp new sleeves of her doublet. Then I stormed down to the bilges of the ship, stuffed my fist in my mouth, and screamed until my lungs burned.

It was Latoya who found me. She'd spent the past week watching Ariadne flounce around the deck in silk and velvet and pearls while we were getting her dress fitted, so she knew how I was feeling. I tried to push past Latoya, to find somewhere else where I could go on being miserable without interruption, but she clapped one strong hand on my shoulder, hauled me back, and caught me up in a businesslike embrace.

I struggled for a couple of seconds, but then gave in to it. The coarse wool of her sailor's shirt was rough against my face and smelt reassuringly of salt.

Have you ever been hugged by someone about four times your size? I can recommend it. Being surrounded by that much solid warmth and concern makes the world suddenly seem a lot more manageable.

After I'd gotten my head back together, I muttered, "My sister is a moron if she leaves you."

Latoya shrugged, practically lifting me off the deck in the process. "Maybe. But there's been a lot of stupid going around lately."

AND THEN TIME started to slip. One minute, we were all huddled around maps in the captain's cabin, as Darren and Regon argued about the best route to Torasan Isle during rainy season. The next minute, so it seemed, the Isle was a green humpback on the horizon.

The sun was out, for once, when we made port, and the coast was thronged with people. They cheered as the *Banshee* and the *Sod Off* swung into harbour, scarlet sails billowing. When we docked, burly stevedores ran forwards to catch the hawsers.

We'd had warmer welcomes at the Freemarket, but that didn't mean anything. The merchants at the Freemarket would hang up bunting and scatter flowers for a pack of wild wolves, as long as the wolves were prepared to pay for beer at a three hundred percent mark-up. This was something different.

Darren tramped down from the quarterdeck, tugging at her doublet's stiff new collar. "I keep thinking that I'm forgetting something."

"You forgot your knife, your pocket comb, your toothpick, your tinder-box, your coin purse, your spare stockings, and the secret brandy flask that you think I don't know about. I packed them all for you, except for the brandy flask, because seriously, Mistress, you promised."

Darren grimaced. "I don't like going into a dire situation without booze. You know that."

"I don't like you having an ulcer the size of a manta ray. You know *that.*" I reached up and adjusted Darren's collar, flexing the fabric between my fingers until it softened. "And let's try to avoid a dire situation. Can we make that a goal?"

"Look, I'm taking your sister, I'm taking Regon, I'm taking Corto, I'm taking money, and I'm taking a great big sword. I don't know what I can do to make myself safer."

"Corto got sliced halfway to cat meat the other day and he's still healing. You should probably take—"

"I'm not taking Latoya. You're the one who keeps saying that she needs time off. Besides, I want her with you while I'm away."

"I don't need a minder."

"Lynn, you're trembling."

A slanted shadow overhead, and the creaking of ropes: the crew was lowering the gangplank into place. A couple of the ropes were fraying, I noticed. Maybe I'd replace them while Darren was away. *While Darren was away, while Darren was away . . .* I stared at Darren's crimson flag, rippling at the masthead far above: there was her emblem, the black storm-petrel, wings outstretched, which matched the tattoo on my own shoulder. That helped a little. I breathed.

Darren slid two fingers under my chin and tilted my face up towards hers. "Tell me not to go, Lynn. That's all you have to do. Say *don't* or *stay* or . . . it doesn't even have to be a word. Make a random vowel sound. Or just kick me."

Times like that, I wondered how Darren could have even a drop of blood in common with brutes like Alek and Stribos. I swallowed, over and over. My mouth was so dry that my voice came out as a rasp. "Promise me that you'll listen to Ariadne."

"Well, I doubt that she'll let me roll her up in a rug and forget about her."

Irritation swelled in me, swamping the dread. "Darren, I mean it. I want her by your side every minute you're on shore. And you had better not be all, 'Leave it to me, little lady.' You will listen to her and you will take her seriously or for the love of buggery I will sink your damn ship. *Don't* smirk. I *will* do it. I will put your precious *Banshee* a full forty fathoms down, and you can figure out how to be a pirate in a floating chamber pot."

Darren lifted her hands, surrendering. "Fine. Fine. Although if I have her with me every moment, then . . ."

Her voice died, and she flushed deep scarlet. "Lynn, if I keep Ariadne that close to me, then some people are going to think . . . well, they might think . . ."

It was so like Darren to clue into a detail like this at the last possible moment. "They are all going to think that you are screwing her. Every person you meet, without exception, will think that you are screwing her. Why is that a problem?"

"Why is that—Gods! It's a problem because it's not true!"

"You know that, I know that. You really think I give a damn what anyone else believes?"

With a final creak and a bang, the gangplank slid into place. Then came the sound of marching feet. Soldiers, a full dozen of them, each wearing the hawk's-head surcoat of Darren's house, tromped in formation across the harbour. An honour guard, here to bring a Lady of Torasan back home. I crushed my lower lip between my teeth to stop myself from screaming all the foul words I knew.

I had meant to give Darren some last-minute good advice. The usual. *Don't get your feet wet. Scowl whenever you're in public. If anyone accuses you of something, accuse them of something worse, and do it louder.* But she'd heard all that from me before. If she hadn't absorbed it by now, she wasn't going to get it in the last thirty seconds before showtime.

But now, with a jolt, I realized there was something I had completely forgotten to mention. "Quick, one more thing. While you're there, don't tell anyone about me."

"What?"

"Promise. Don't tell anybody that I exist."

"Why?"

"Just promise me. *"*

Two soldiers strode up the gangplank, which bounced under their booted feet. They saluted Regon, who seemed surprised but kind of flattered. I heard a few words being exchanged—*Captain Valens and Captain Milo here to escort her ladyship to Lord Konrad*—before I literally put my hands over my ears.

Darren reached out for me at the same moment that I pulled back.

"I'll see you in two weeks," I said.

"Wait. Don't you want to—?"

"No. If I stay any longer, I'm just going to do something I'll regret."

Ariadne swished up to us, enveloped in the billows of her new black gown. The night before, for the first time in half a year, she had put her hair in pin-curls. Now her face was framed by boinging blond ringlets. Her cheeks were rouged, her lips were reddened, her forehead was powdered, and I couldn't take any more of this.

"Take care of her," I told Ariadne—quickly, before she could say anything. I was already backing away. "Two weeks. I'll see you both."

I put my head down and headed for the forecastle, before the two of them could start with any pointless goodbyes. But I made the mistake of looking back just before I went down below. Darren and Ariadne were at the top of the gangplank, poised like a royal couple on a balcony. Somewhere on shore, a trumpet sounded a long, triumphant blast. Almost unconsciously, Darren offered Ariadne her arm, and Ariadne took it.

Down the gangplank they went, but as the crowd swelled forward to claim them, my thoughts took a different turn. I had missed something. I had missed some microscopic but vital detail, something that had brushed against the surface of my mind for the briefest instant before melting away. I didn't know this in a rational way, I just felt it as a sinking in my guts, as though I was watching something incredibly precious slipping away downstream.

CHAPTER EIGHT

The Lady Darren of the House of Torasan (Pirate Queen)

WE WERE HALFWAY up the path to Torasan Keep when Ariadne's elbow took me in the ribs, the blow so sharp and sudden that I made a noise like a cow being stabbed with a boat hook. (And yes, I know exactly what it sounds like when a cow gets stabbed with a boat hook, and no, you shouldn't ask why.)

"Was that necessary?" I choked.

"Oh, don't be such a baby. I nudged you about six times and you didn't notice. I suppose you were too busy posing for your fans."

"I wasn't posing, I was waving."

"I can wave and talk at the same time. Can't you?"

"I'm putting effort into it. This is quality waving that I've got going on."

The streets were lined, three deep, with cheering villagers. I wasn't dim enough to believe that this was a spontaneous outpouring of patriotism. My brother's troops must have come through town earlier in the day and explained to everyone what was expected of them. Hopefully, the explanation hadn't involved any wooden clubs and bullwhips, but you could never be quite sure.

It was depressing, but dammit, when people are cheering for you, you wave. Anything else just seems rude.

"All right," I told Ariadne, as I got back to waving. "You have my attention."

Ariadne, woman of many gifts, could talk while maintaining a beaming smile for the benefit of the crowd. She did it by kind of spitting the words out between clenched teeth. "What are we trying to accomplish here? What's the goal?"

"Goal? No real goal. We're going to make nice with Konrad, I guess, and see what opportunities come up."

Ariadne's blinding smile didn't waver as she said, "You're a total asshole, aren't you?"

I sighed. "Oh, what *now*?"

"Why torture Lynn by coming here if you don't have something concrete to gain? She was *this* close to breaking down when we left."

"I know."

"Really? You barely looked at her when we were leaving. You didn't even touch her."

"She didn't want me to."

"How could you tell?"

"Couldn't you? Lynn doesn't like to be touched when she's upset—"

"Well, you could have done something to acknowledge her existence. A few words, would that have been out of the question? Would it have killed you to let loose with something wild like, *I love you*? Gods' teeth, Darren, you don't ever seem to say that."

I sighed. My waving hand was getting tired, so I switched to my left. "I've had a lot of women say that they loved me, but you know what? Lynn is the only one who's ever been willing to polish my boots."

Ariadne snorted. "A lot of women? Seriously, Darren, a lot of women?"

Lousy stupid perceptive princess. "Fine. Three women. Well . . . two and a half. My point still stands."

"Your point seems to be that you like women who do your chores."

I glared at her sidelong, to make sure that I was still talking to Ariadne, not Jess. "You know, I don't owe you an explanation, but just so you don't spend the next two weeks feeling superior, I'll illustrate. A couple of years back, the *Banshee* hit a rock and took on a lot of water . . ."

"Another victory for the pirate queen's superior sense of direction?"

"Fuck you, I wasn't steering. Anyway, we were marooned for almost a week while Regon and Latoya rowed a longboat to the nearest town for planks and a shipwright, and it was raining the whole time. I mean steady, bucketing rain. If you stuck out your cupped palm, it was full in a few seconds. We were on this bare stretch of shore, and after two days, we were out of fuel, so no fires, not even for cooking. We ate groats and cold salt pork. Every stitch of cloth on board was sopping wet: blankets, shirts, stockings, everything. When you got up in the morning, you were chilly and soggy and when you crawled to your bunk at night, you were soaking. It was miserable."

"So?"

The crowd thinned out. We had almost reached the guard-towers that flanked the front entrance to the Keep. In minutes, we'd reach the bailey . . . and then, we'd have to confront my family. I'd faced a lot of horrors in my time, but this one, I felt, would top the lot. Patronizing and annoying as Ariadne's interrogation was, I was almost glad that I had it to distract me.

"So," I said, "one morning I woke up and I was just so sick of it all. I could not face rolling out of my sodden bunk and squelching off in my wet boots to a freezing cold breakfast of maggot-ridden meat and icy water. I wanted to pretend to have the plague or something, so I could stay in bed for a week. But I'm the damn captain. So I crawled out from under my damp clammy blanket and I grabbed my clothes . . ."

We were finally beyond the cheering villagers, so I dropped my arm and rubbed sore muscles while I recalled that golden moment.

"And my clothes were dry," I said. "Lynn had spent days hoarding everything she could find that would burn. She chipped wood from the undersides of biscuit boxes and barrels, collected some straw from the middle of packing cases, where the water hadn't seeped in. She managed to get an armful together, just enough for a tiny fire, and she got the galley stove going long enough to dry out a shirt and stockings and trousers. They were dry, and warm, and clean, and they smelled halfway like wood smoke and halfway like heaven. When I pulled them on, I almost . . . cried."

That was not true. In actual fact, when I pulled the dry clothes on, I almost . . . well, did something other than crying. Let's just say that my happiness extended to my pants.

Ariadne did a sort of over-the-shoulder wave to acknowledge the crowds behind us. "If there was a point to that story, Darren, I missed it."

The glow of the memory faded. I scowled a pirate-queen scowl. "Look, you asked me to explain and I'm explaining, but you'll never get it. What do you know about being bone-tired? What do you know about being cold to your marrow? What do you know about the things that you give someone when you haven't got anything to give? Lynn and I, we don't buy each other jewellery and flowers. But I've bled for her, and she's drowned for me. And you want to know why we don't use the words? Lynn doesn't have to *tell* me that she loves me. Lynn doesn't have to *tell* me a thing."

A rough hand clapped me on the shoulder. "Easy there, captain. Don't break the princess on the first day ashore."

I redirected my scowl towards Regon. "If I was trying to break her, she'd have fewer fingers."

Ariadne gave a loud *huh* of contempt. "If I were you, I wouldn't do anything to these fingers without talking it over with Latoya. She's got a very personal interest in keeping these fingers intact."

"Well, well, don't we think a lot of ourselves. Don't give yourself too much credit, princess. Latoya could have anyone she wanted, if she made up her mind to ask. One of these days, she'll figure out exactly how much of a catch she is. When that happens, she'll straighten her back, snap her fingers, and all the single women in Kila will fling their clothes off in unison."

Behind us, somebody coughed, and I wheeled around. "*What?*"

I had not intended my reunion with Konrad to take place while I was yelling obscenities on his front doorstep. It was supposed to be in the throne room, with firelight and trumpets, Konrad dressed in the cloth-of-gold robe that our grandfather brought back from Tavar in his first voyage. I would be serene, a bit distracted, oh so unimpressed, while my hand rested lightly on my cutlass hilt.

But here we were, and I gaped at my oldest brother. He was wearing riding gear rather than court clothes, and his boots were grubby with sawdust. His face didn't have the pale flabby look of a man who spent all his time indoors, groping servant girls and gorging on pastries. Instead, it was tanned and weather-lined. If I'd seen him out of the corner of my eye, I could have mistaken him for myself, at the end of a long day.

I tried to pull myself together, but without warning, my eyes started to leak. I don't remember making any decisions. I just stumbled forwards, and then strong arms were around me, gripping.

It took Konrad and me a second to realize that we were hugging each other. When we did figure it out, we drew back, looked at each other in embarrassed confusion, and then quickly turned the emotional moment into a macho one by pounding hard on each other's backs.

"Pirate queen?" Konrad said, pounding me one more time for good measure. "Really? What happened to the girl who was frightened of puppets?"

The mere mention of puppets made me shudder. I stuttered out a gulpy sort of laugh, wiping my eyes.

"Welcome back," he went on, with a squeeze to my arm. "Welcome home."

THE HOUSE OF Torasan—my house, as I suppose I should say from now on—was a newcomer in Kila. They—we—had ruled our corner of the islands for only three hundred years, while families like Bain and Jiras could trace their lineage back for thirty generations or more. It was my grandfather who built the stone wall that surrounded the courtyard of Torasan Keep, nearly bankrupting the family to do it. Before that, the fortress was defended by nothing but a palisade of mud-caulked logs and a few soldiers who hadn't yet accepted better-paying jobs elsewhere.

And the Keep was the jewel of the Torasan holdings, the crown of the empire. It all went downhill from there. Besides the Keep itself, we had the fishing grounds, a few villages of wattle-and-daub huts, and some meagre farmland that produced the occasional cabbage and a whole lot of bugs. There were mountain steppes where goats grazed and charcoal-burners made their camps. Finally, there was the hill fort built by my great-great-grandfather. He'd meant it to be a bolt-hole, a place to safeguard livestock and children if the Keep came under attack, but it was so far inland that we almost never used it. Not for military purposes, anyway. My older brothers and sisters would go there sometimes when they wanted to spend a few days getting drunk without any nosy adults around to interfere.

Torasan, like most of the smaller houses, had been eager for the war to begin. In fact, Torasan played a part in the assassinations, backstabbings, and general assholery that got the bloodshed started. It was supposed to be this magnificent opportunity, a chance to wipe out the weakest of the noble families and sap the strength of the greatest. All this was supposed to leave vast swathes of land empty and ripe for plundering by the houses that remained after the cull.

How had Torasan coped during the war? The image that comes to mind is that of a bad boy who tries to ride his father's stallion after being told about twenty times to keep away from it. The experience is exhilarating for six seconds at most. After that, he just holds tight and blubbers, wishing he'd never set foot out of the nursery, and wondering, in a dazed sort of way, why his trousers are so wet.

That's what the war was like for me, back when I was still bearing arms for my father: a pretty much constant state of panic. No matter what I was doing—coiling a rope, charting a course, eating a peach—there was a shadow over my mind, a feeling of creeping doom that never really went away. Whenever my father sent me from the Isle on a trading voyage, I couldn't be certain that the Keep would still be standing when I came back. Hell, there were days when I hardly believed that the island itself would be there to greet me.

My father had fun, though. He poured money and ships and men into his damn campaigns the same way he sloshed gravy over his batter cakes. He talked about things like Five Year Plans and The Expansion Of Our Sphere Of Influence, and he wore a sword that he would draw and flourish every now and then, as if he had a clue what to do with it. It was out of character for him, but I guess he enjoyed the break in his normal busy schedule of fondling every backside in reach.

Fortunately, I never had to put up with his antics for very long, because I was never at court for more than a week at once. The time did seem to stretch endlessly when I was sitting through formal dinners, yawning through dances, or enduring business meetings with my father during which he would try, and usually fail, to remember my name. But then it would be over. My silk and velvet would be laid away in a sandalwood chest, with camphor packed into every crevice to keep the vermin away. I'd trudge down to the harbour, hands in my pockets, while the sun rolled into an orange sea and gulls screamed their welcome from the cove. All the fancy fakery of court would disappear, like a whiff of bad perfume, in the first gust of salt breeze. And I would feel like I could manage this thing called life.

Then I'd sail back into the war zones, and the feeling of life-management-ability would vanish pretty quickly.

Had the war been good for Torasan? One word: No. Three words: Really, really no. The Keep hadn't yet burst into flames and fallen into the sea, but that was about the only positive. Month by month and year by year, my father poured men and ships down the drain of his imperial ambitions, and seemed happily oblivious to the fact that we had nothing to show for it. If someone had taken a map and charted out the movements of our troops, all the advances and retreats, then a thick black zig-zag of ink would have formed all around Torasan Isle. For years on end, our men had been surging forward and pulling back, surging forward and pulling back, over the same few yards of land and sea.

"NO TROUBLE GETTING here, I hope? Did you have good weather?"

"Good weather? Ah yes. I have heard tell of this miraculous thing called good weather. One day I hope to see it with my own eyes."

"Ha. Yes. My captains tell me that it's been brutal this year. Tam, bring wine for my lady sister."

Konrad and I were in what had once been my father's study. It had undergone some changes since my father's time. My father was not what you would call a scholar—to be honest, I'm pretty sure he couldn't read—so he used his study as a place to ambush the women who had already learned to avoid his bedchamber. Back then, a ratty old bearskin rug covered the study floor, and it was mottled with stains that none of us wanted to look at or think about very hard. He did leave a few books on his desk, for the look of the thing, but a furry coat of dust built up on their covers over the years.

That was all gone now. The place was scrubbed clean from stone floors to beamed ceiling, the bearskin rug conspicuously absent, wooden surfaces gleaming with beeswax. There were real pens on the desk, with real ink stains which showed that Konrad actually used them, and ledgers and a counting frame. The leather seat of the desk chair had a shiny smudge at the centre, proof that it had spent many hours in close contact with Konrad's rear end.

At the moment, the owner of that rear end was over by the windowsill, raking his hand through his sweaty hair. He hadn't bothered to change out of his riding clothes.

The servant Tam whispered across the floor, soft-footed in calfskin shoes, and passed me a silver goblet. Nervously, I rubbed my hand dry on my trousers before taking the shiny cup between two fingers. Tam made as if to return to his post by the door, but at a gesture from Konrad, he reversed direction and bowed his way out of the room instead.

It had begun to rain, slow steady drops that blattered on the sill. The light through the window was grey and shifting. I moved my weight first to one foot, then to the other.

When Konrad did turn, he gave me a rueful smile. That was very un-lordly of him. We had always been taught to maintain bland expressions, to never give away anything that we could manage to hide.

"Well," Konrad said, without any preamble. "This is awkward, isn't it?"

"That's one word for it, I guess."

"Do you have a better way of describing the situation? I suppose you do. You sailors use the most vibrant language. What would you call it?"

"Um. Fucking awkward?"

"Ah. Yes. Crude, but apt. It would probably be easier to talk if we could go for a stroll, but we can't, I'm afraid. This is the only place in the Keep that's secure enough to talk business."

"Oh, hell. Is talking business a thing that has to happen?"

He smiled, and the skin around his eyes crinkled, as though he smiled a lot. "Alas, my sister, it must. How shall we fortify ourselves for the ordeal? Shall we get drunk? Is that the solution?"

"It's worth a try," I agreed, and took a long draught from the goblet. The flavour hit me like a small explosion. On the Isle, there's only one time of year when the sun can be relied on to shine: late summer, when the fruit ripens on our few wild cherry trees. It doesn't last long, a handful of days, but our cherry wine captures all the warmth and spice of the brief Torasan summer. It's sour-sweet, subtle but fierce, smooth but deadly, and it makes you want to dance and fight and yell and sing all at once. Imagine the first time you were in love, then imagine it juiced, fermented, bottled, and corked. It's pretty much like that. The aftermath is more or less the same, too. Lots of groaning and whining and wondering where your trousers went.

Konrad didn't notice the tears in my eyes, or he pretended not to notice. He looked out the window again. "Why don't we get the worst part out of the way? I'll tell you about Father, you tell me about Alek."

I nodded, swallowed my mouthful of summer, and began.

Telling the story wasn't as bad as it could have been. Konrad already knew the basic outline from my letter to Father, so all I had to do was fill in the bits and pieces. That was plenty bad enough, though. Twice, when I was describing Alek's wounds, my eyes went hot and stinging and I had to look hard at the ceiling to keep things businesslike. For some reason, sitting there in the serene calm of Konrad's study, death seemed much like a much fouler and more terrible thing than it did on an ordinary day.

Konrad listened with eyes half-closed, nodding slowly. When I was finished talking, he ran a finger down the barbs of his quill pen—it was just a goose feather, but it was painted in rings of blue and emerald like a peacock's plume—and launched into an explanation I hadn't asked for.

"Father had this asinine plan," he said. "Yes. Father, an asinine plan. Do your best to conceal your astonishment. He'd been trying for years to get a foothold on Cromm Tuach. The theory was that if he could land troops at the lighthouse, he could take control of—"

"The shipping routes north from the iron smelters. That old fantasy. People keep trying. It never works."

"Really? When did someone last . . . never mind, I'll pick your brain later. Father's idea was to commit most of our ships to an attack from the north, to draw out the Tuach navy, and then send Alek winging around the far end of the battle line. He took the fastest of our war galleys—the *Harrier*, you remember it?"

I winced, and not for show. It really did cause me pain to hear Konrad talk about a glorious beast like the *Harrier* as if she were a thing no different from a wagon or a doorknob. "*Her.* I remember *her.*"

"You sailors and your superstitions."

"It has nothing to do with superstition. Ships are ladies and they deserve respect. You wouldn't refer to your wife as an *it*, would you?"

"To be honest, I speak about my wife as little as possible. It works out better for everyone that way. To return to the point, though, Alek took the *Harrier* around the end of the line with fifty picked men and the best steel we could spare. The plan, Father's plan, called for him to make land, wipe out the undefended garrison, and hold it until we could send reinforcements . . . Darren, why exactly are you groaning? It may not have been an inspired strategy, but considering Father came up with it, it made a surprising amount of sense."

"That's the worst kind of strategy. Plausible enough to get people moving, but nowhere near good enough to bring them home alive. You can't use a strike force to defend a garrison. Fifty men? I wouldn't even try to hold Cromm Tuach without two hundred. Minimum. Even then, I'd probably just buy the beer instead."

"The beer . . . ?"

"Oh. Um. Sorry. It's a silly thing that we came up with . . ." I caught myself just in time, remembering the strange order Lynn had given me just before I left the ship. "I mean, it's something that *I* came up with a few months back. Sort of a thought experiment, a way to check yourself before you do something stupid. When deciding whether to risk life, limb, ships, and sanity in an act of desperate bravery, ask yourself whether you could achieve more for your cause by staying home and buying just a shitload of beer."

His eyebrows went up. "What would you do with the beer? Bribe your enemies to surrender?"

"Sure. Or build morale among your own troops, either one. You'd be surprised how often buying beer is a sound tactical decision. Anyway, you were saying. Father surfaced from his whores and his wine cup long enough to send fifty men to certain death, with our brother lolloping happily in the lead. Did any of them make it back?"

"Four or five, enough to tell us what had happened." Konrad pinched the bridge of his nose. "They didn't even get as far as the coast. The Tuach commander had left part of his fleet in reserve around the far side of the island, where the cliffs hid them. They rammed the *Harrier* as soon as it rounded the point, and that was that. Alek ordered the longboats launched once the *Harrier* began to sink. The survivors who made it back to the Isle lost track of the boat carrying him. I suppose he drifted south, but I don't know why he was alone by the time he reached you."

I frowned. "Alek said they were betrayed. Did you ask the survivors about that? Did they know what he meant?"

"Yes I did, and no they didn't—although they could guess and so can I. Someone must have tipped off the Tuach forces about the sneak attack. Alek must have figured out who the traitor was, though heaven only knows how."

"He would have had a lot of time to think." I'd already tortured myself by picturing Alek's last day alive, the hours he must spent drifting helpless and in agony under a cold sky. Plenty of time to dwell on the lost chances, the if-onlys and the might-have-beens. "What did Father say when he heard that his stupid plan had crashed and burned?"

"He never found out. The same day the *Harrier* left port, right after dinner, Father collapsed, foaming from the mouth and bleeding from the eyes. He never regained consciousness and died that evening. The surgeons called it a sudden apoplexy." Konrad flexed his quill pen slowly between his fingers and let it bounce straight again. "Do you believe in coincidences, my sister?"

"Not when they're this convenient." And for one person, more than anyone else on the planet, the deaths of Alek and my father had been very well timed. "So, did you kill them?"

I expected the temperature in the room to get a bit chilly, but Konrad showed no annoyance or even surprise. Instead, he picked up a mother-of-pearl penknife and set to work whittling his quill to a fine point.

"You know, it's a relief to have someone accuse me to my face," he said. "It gets tiresome, having everyone just stare and speculate. I didn't kill Father and Alek, no, but I understand why it's a popular theory."

I studied him, the steadiness of his hands and the rise and fall of his chest. In my years working as a trader, I'd learned the various signs that mark a liar: rigid shoulders, sweating hands, fast breathing, a flickering look of distress that draws lines of tension across the forehead. Thing is, I learned these signals by rote, as you might learn a prayer or a piece of poetry. When it came to reading the signs on a real flesh-and-blood being, my success rate was pretty dismal.

Now I felt the empty space in the air where Lynn should have been. If she'd been with me, she would have taken in Konrad's every word and gesture while I kept him talking, and by the end of the conversation, she would have distilled him to an essence and learned every piece of him by heart. Instead, she was back on the *Banshee,* prowling around like an angry ghost with nothing to haunt.

"Let's face it, people are right to be suspicious," I said. "You don't seem all that sorry that they're gone."

"I'm not sorry and neither are you. Father was a stupid, selfish, overblown pig of a man, and Alek was his attack dog. Whoever arranged for them to leave the scene early might very well have saved the House of Torasan. When I find out who killed them, I'll have the devil's own trouble figuring out whether to hang him or shake his hand."

"What if he tries to kill you next?"

He smiled grimly. "Well, that would simplify the decision-making process, wouldn't it?"

"Don't count on it. Remember what Alek said: *It was one of us.* Unless he was delirious—which I guess is possible—the traitor is someone in our family. Are you really going to start lopping our siblings' heads off left and right? Because that would put a real strain on the bonds of sisterly love. Who's still here on the Isle, anyway?"

"You want the list? Sala, Vita, and Orienne all left the Isle when they married. You knew that already, I suppose. Gunnar's here. Talon's here. Both of them bear arms for Torasan. Cerys is still on loan to the House of Beaugest. Brayan's dead, pneumonia. Rikki's dead, bled out giving birth for the seventh time—triplets. Fletcher's ship disappeared in a storm last year and no one's holding their breath waiting for him to swim home. Frankly, it's just as well. I know that sounds heartless, but he never got over that little . . . issue . . . of his, and we couldn't afford to pay the hush money any longer."

Clunk, clunk, clunk, and just like that, I'd lost three more siblings. I'd never been close with Fletcher or Rikki, especially not Fletcher. We'd all kept our distance. Because of his . . . issue . . . it was best not to be alone with him if you could help it. But Brayan had been only a year older than me and his bunk was next to mine. I used to wear his old tunics and boots once he outgrew them, and we would sit together at dinnertime on days when we didn't happen to hate each other.

"Let's see, who did I miss?" Konrad tapped on each of his fingertips in turn, counting. "Oh, yes. Jada."

"Jada!" I perked up. "Is she still here?"

"She is. Unfortunately. I had a very nice match lined up for her with Governor Acasa—you remember him? He's not in the line of succession for the House of Mulcar, just a cadet branch, but he has timber rights for a thousand acres of hardwood forest. It would have been a nice little earner for Torasan, if Acasa hadn't pulled out at the last minute."

"That's terrible," I said dutifully, as if it really was a tragedy that my youngest sister hadn't been handed off to some thick-as-a-brick governor's son in exchange for a lower tariff on lumber imports. "Maybe it's better this way, though. Running cargoes isn't a soft job, but some of us prefer it to marriage and baby-making."

Konrad's lips twitched. "Perhaps some of you do. Jada isn't on the ships, though. She hasn't had a command since her maiden tour."

"Hasn't had a . . . what?"

As a statement, "She hasn't had a command since her maiden tour" made approximately as much sense as "I am a fish man, tiddle tiddle tum." My brain almost broke as I tried to figure out what the sweet hell Konrad meant.

"You mean . . . she's only made one voyage? But . . . why? What's wrong with her? Did she lose all her limbs or get bashed on the head or something? If she isn't married and she isn't running cargoes, what *is* she doing?"

"Not much. Let's put it that way." He slammed a ledger shut with an air of finality. "And perhaps we should leave it there. I don't want to bore you too badly with politics on your first day back at home. Tam? Tam, show the Lady Darren to her quarters, if you please."

I knew a dismissal when I heard one, and it irked me, but for some reason, I still bowed to my brother before I left the room.

I DUMPED MY satchel onto the bed, then looked around, marvelling. All this space for me? My cabin back on the *Banshee* would have fitted comfortably into one of the room's three closets, with space left over to accommodate a large goat or a not-too-fussy family of four. There was no glass in the windows, but there were heavy wooden shutters which could be closed against the rain, snow, hail, fist-sized chunks of ice, and various other things that fell from the sky on Torasan Isle. At that moment, a shaft of sunlight had managed to find a path between the rainclouds, washing the pale wood of the furniture in buttery light.

There was even a mirror. I'd never rated a mirror back when I bore arms for Torasan. My father must have figured that it would be a waste of money; my value had nothing to do with my face. I hefted it and gauged the weight of the metal—it was bronze rather than silver and dented on the back, but still, on a good day, I could trade it for a few barrels of tar or a fair-sized bolt of sailcloth.

That being the case, I realized, I really ought to don my pirate pants and steal the thing. It's expensive to be at war with the whole damn world, and though my fleet raked in a lot of cash, we couldn't afford to ignore opportunities. If Lynn found out that I had passed up a chance for a quick easy profit, then she would sigh long-sufferingly and dig out the account books and make some pointed comments about how Latoya almost lost an eye the last time I sent her out to raid a treasure fleet. And she'd be right, I knew that, but . . . hell . . . it's different when you're stealing from your family. I pictured how Konrad's face would look if he caught me sneaking out the back door with the mirror stuffed down the front of my trousers, and made up my mind not to pinch any of the furnishings.

I'd make it up to Lynn somehow. Maybe I'd surrender all sense of dignity and address her as "me proud beauty" in public. That always made her melt.

Anyway, Ariadne commandeered the mirror as soon as I was done with it. She lugged it over to the writing desk, propped it upright, and installed herself at the makeshift vanity table with a collection of bottles and jars. While I bounced on the mattress to test the rope springs, she powdered her face chalky white and traced her veins with hair-thin lines of blue oil. The effect looked every bit as ghastly as you would expect—like a drowned corpse, except that her hair was dry. I thanked a selection of gods, once again, that Lynn never bothered with makeup.

Ariadne's eyes met mine in the mirror. "Stop that."

"Stop what?"

"Oh, don't play innocent. I can feel you quietly judging me back there."

"All right, say I am. You look ridiculous. Do you like dressing up like a doll?"

"Do cooks like their aprons?" Ariadne shot back. "These are my working clothes. That's all." She frowned at her reflection, picked up a rag, and carefully blotted her lips. "So, do you think Konrad killed them?"

"My father and Alek, you mean?" I shrugged. "Buggered if I know. It's been so long since I've seen him, and we were never close . . . If he has any tells, I don't know them. What about you? Do you have a theory?"

"I'm not committing myself this early in the game. I haven't even met the rest of your family yet. For what it's worth, though, I think Konrad means well. And he's certainly determined to keep you happy."

"How do you figure?"

Ariadne looked back over her shoulder. "This is our room."

"So?"

"So, has it escaped your notice that there's only one bed?"

It had. Shouldn't have, but had. I gaped down at the mattress—it seemed very narrow all of a sudden—and heat surged up my neck to pool in my cheeks. It was exactly the feeling I'd experienced at age fifteen when the dairymaid from the village finally admitted that, in spite of what she'd been telling me, not all girls liked to kiss other girls on the mouth.

Ariadne laughed. "Didn't you realize what people would think?"

"Of course I did," I said with dignity. "I mean, I knew that people would jump to the wrong conclusions. I just didn't expect Konrad to jump so enthusiastically and quickly."

"He's sort of desperate, I think." One of the makeup jars seemed to be worrying Ariadne; she scowled as she poked at its contents with a mink-fur brush. After a few pokes, she gave up, pushed it away, and drew a new jar towards her. "I didn't like the look of the people down in the village, did you?"

"They're just people, princess. They may be commoners, but that doesn't mean they're dangerous. Regon and Spinner were both born in that town . . ."

She slammed down the jar so hard that it spat out a cough of white powder. "Darren, how does someone as terminally dense as you put on her own boots in the morning? I mean that the villagers aren't well. Did you see their skin? Pale as bad cheese, flaking around the eyes and lips. Half the children had rashes and running sores. That's chronic hunger. They're not starving, but they're living on the brink. Torasan Isle is one bad harvest away from famine."

" . . . oh." That sick feeling of shame was not going to go away any time soon. "And you think Konrad called me here because he wants me to . . . do what? Distribute some sandwiches?"

"Who knows? If he's smart, he'll ask you to wipe the corsairs out of his waters, to give the fishing fleets a chance. If he's stupid, he might want you to conquer some other islands for him so he can have even more subjects to starve. When he tells you what his plan is, we'll see whether he's any different from your father. In the meantime, I have an invitation to spend the afternoon with Konrad's wife. We are to have what she describes, rather horribly, as a 'nice girly chat.' Also music. Did you know that she can play the lute?"

"Err . . . I know that she thinks she can. Bring something that you can stuff into your ears." I scowled down at the bed. "I guess I'm sleeping on the floor tonight."

"Don't go into your martyr routine. We'll flip a coin for it. Actually, I suppose we'll have to draw straws. I don't see any beds in here for Regon and Corto."

"Konrad will probably have someone put down pallets for them in the hall."

She flashed me a look that could have stripped the paint off a barn. "The hell he will. I am *done* with people sleeping on pallets out in the hall. The four of us will take turns with the bed and we'll draw straws to see who gets it first. Although," she added thoughtfully, "Regon and I could probably fit on the mattress together, if we really tried."

The woman was just impossible. "Oh, no you don't, princess. If you're going to break Latoya's heart, you do it to her face and you do it clean. You don't get to test the waters with Regon first."

"You think you can stop me?"

"I think your sister can."

"My sister's not here." Ariadne adjusted one last curl and, apparently satisfied, pushed back her stool. "I might as well make the most of the opportunity."

Regon walked in and slung down his bedroll. "The harbourmaster says that it snowed a week ago. Same old Isle. Well, captain, where are we going to go first?"

THE GUARD AT the door to the children's room told me that I couldn't go in. I reasoned with him very calmly at first, and then less calmly, and then there was some screaming, and then Regon patted me on the back and told me to take a walk while he sorted things out. I took a walk, hands shoved into my pockets and nerves strung tight. When I got back, Regon and the guard were laughing like old friends. They barely even looked up at me as I passed through the dormitory door.

Well. I bit my lip as I took it all in. Pink marble washbasin and iron-grilled fireplace; row after row of messy bunks; wooden dolls and toy ships, leather balls and spinning tops. It was almost empty—the older children would be with their tutors, of course, at this time of day—but a wet-nurse sat by the hearth, feeding two black-haired babies, one at each breast. Nieces or nephews of mine, no doubt. When I came in, the nurse looked up in confusion, then moved as if to rise and curtsey. I waved her back down.

Something crunched under my right foot, and I lifted my boot to find the broken fragments of a clay pig. Guiltily, I scraped up the pieces and put them on a nearby shelf, next to a child-sized pair of shoes. The toes were badly scuffed, so the owner had to be a child who dragged his feet. I always used to do that on my way to my mathematics lessons.

The memories rose up and choked me.

Your father wants to see you this evening, miss. Scrub up now while I press your good tunic . . . Darren, you can't go to sleep yet. Ceri's going to tell the story about the ghoul that walks the shipyards searching for her missing hand . . . Young lady, for the last time, you will never master trigonometry if you spend every lesson gawping out the window. If you can't pay attention long enough to learn the most basic principles of navigation, then gods help you when you come to command a ship, and gods help Torasan.

Unconsciously, I'd walked to my old bed: fourth along the wall, just to the left of a big shuttered window. It belonged to a boy now; I could tell from the cheesy smell of the blankets. There were chips on the bedpost where he had tested a new pocket-knife against the wood.

The smell of milk and pitchy torches. Sucking sounds, noises of soft contentment, from the sleepy babies.

Was it a nightmare, little miss? Hush, now, hush—nobles of Torasan don't cry. If you wake up your brothers, you know how they'll tease you. I'll stay with you until you go back to sleep if you promise to be good for your tutors tomorrow. Hush, now, little one . . .

"So it's true. You did come back."

The girl in the doorway could have stepped straight out of my memories. I recognized not her, but the bits of her: Rikki's eyes, Fletcher's cheekbones, Alek's chin. A hand-me-down tunic and hose which could well have been Brayan's. An unflattering haircut which left the hair just a little too short to be tied back, exactly like the one I'd worn—and may all the gods forgive me—at age twenty-one.

"Jada?" I asked.

The girl—no, she was full-grown now, though barely—gave me a jerky nod which was almost a bow. "My lady sister."

"Oh, don't start with that crap, get over here!"

She stiffened when I pulled her into a bear hug, so I let go fast. "Sorry. Sorry. I guess you're not a touchy kind of person?"

She smiled, tight-lipped, and stepped back out of reach. "People say I'm frigid."

"Oh, come on. Who said that? Tell me, that I may smite them."

Jada didn't laugh—she eyed me warily, as if she wasn't sure whether I was joking. "Alek used to say it a lot. I think you missed your chance to smite him, unless there's something you haven't told us about the way he died."

"Oh. Um. Yes." With characteristic smoothness, I coughed, then changed the subject. "Can we walk and talk? I was going to have a look at the back harbour."

"The back harbour? I can save you some time—it's the same pile of rocks that it was the day they banished you."

"Well, I have fond memories of those rocks. They're better company than a lot of the people I've met. Help me with the door?"

The back door wasn't locked, but barred with a massive oak beam set into thick brackets. I spat on my hands and got a good grip, but I barely managed to shift it until Jada took hold. Even then it was a strain, but we managed not to drop it on our feet.

"It feels so strange to open it," Jada said, shaking out her hands. "How many times did they threaten to spank us bloody if we unbarred the door without permission?"

"Enough that I'm feeling a twinge in my backside right this moment. But I'm a pirate. I've got the bold and fearless thing going on."

The door opened into a short passage; the passage opened into rock and sky. Two cliffs stood sentry on the sheltered cove where all Torasan children learned to swim and sail. The stone steps down the cliff were older than the Keep itself; you could tell from the way each of them dipped in the centre, the hollows worn into the rock by thousands on thousands of feet.

Jada followed me down the steps, dodging the white splatters gulls had left on the stone. "So you really are a pirate?"

"Yes. Didn't you hear? I haven't exactly been sneaky about it."

"I *heard,* but I figured that you were just spreading rumours. You know, to piss off Father."

"Pissing off a brutal tyrant may sound like a fun time, but it doesn't lead to happiness and cake. I would not have pretended to be a pirate just to yank on Father's ballsack. Even if I had, I would have stopped around the time he sent the tenth assassin. Watch out for that rock, it's wet."

Jada ignored the hand I held out to her and clambered over the rock on her own. "The things people have been saying about you, the things they say you've done . . . it doesn't seem anything like you. Not the Darren I remember."

She sounded maybe a little jealous, maybe a little bitter, maybe a tiny bit impressed. I trod carefully. "You were a very small person when I first went off to sea. People change."

"How much do they change? There's this story that Konrad likes to tell. He says that when you were seven, you asked him how babies were made. So he explained sex, and the thought of it scared you so badly that you cried all night."

"*Most* of the night. Not *all* of the night. Don't exaggerate."

It was good, so good, to see her, and so painful, all at once. Her movements were stiff and awkward, like she had broken glass in every joint, like she wasn't sure where her body had come from or what to do with it. The sight made me want to pounce on her and tussle her until she unclenched. It was a strain to keep my distance.

"Really, though," she said. "You were afraid of everything when you were a kid. Everything from sex to snakes to speaking in public. Now, all of a sudden, you're looting villages and rescuing maidens and you have a ship in your fleet named *Thundercunt*."

My toes curled unhappily inside my boots. I knew that name would come back to bite me. "Now, see, that wasn't planned. Lynn was . . . I mean, *I* was in a screwy sort of mood that day."

"What does that mean?"

"Well, uh, it means that 'I' was on the rag and hadn't slept much, and then 'I' missed dinner and then drank 'my' body weight in spruce beer, and then . . . well, then things got strange."

I didn't elaborate. What had, in fact, happened was that "I" had convinced the crew to dress up an innocent pig that happened to be on board ship, for reasons that are still a mystery to science. It went better than expected, up to the point when "I" tried to add shoes.

"Anyway, there are worse names than *Thundercunt.* It was going to be *Nippledragon, Destroyer of All Testicles* before she . . . before *I* sobered up a bit."

She huffed out a strained half-laugh. "Do you have one called *I Hate My Father And Want Him Dead*?"

"Well. Not quite."

Lynn had, in fact, tried to name a war galley *Darren's Fucking Father Is Driving Me Off My Fucking Tit* one time, after he sent an especially nasty assassin. I wouldn't let her, so we compromised on a rowboat.

By then, Jada and I had reached the dock. It had been repaired since my time—fresh-cut planks lay among the grey weathered boards—but the boat was just the same. It was an old ship's longboat, heavy and clumsy, rigged for sail by inexpert childish hands. You had to feel sorry for the thing. Every inch of it was dented and scratched.

I slid my hand along the rudder and found the smooth indent where hundreds of other hands had gripped the wood. The last time I'd sailed in this bay, I'd almost capsized the boat by holding onto the jib too long in a hard gust of wind. My sisters and brothers ragged me raw for the mistake, but, by snarling a lot and swearing under my breath in a steady stream, I managed not to burst into tears. Our nurses and tutors let us have a fire in the cove that night, and we roasted apples and made ships out of driftwood, setting them afloat with a twist of burning tow on top, so the flames seemed to spring right out of the water.

"Are you crying?" Jada asked.

"No," I said, wiping my eyes with my sleeve. "Look, don't judge me. I know it's just planks and rocks and rope, but this is where we learned to sail. This is where we started to matter."

Jada's lip twitched, and, as usual, I realized my mistake a second too late.

"Crap. Sorry," I said. "I didn't mean—I shouldn't have—oh pissnuggets. That wasn't supposed to be a dig at you, Jada. I don't give a goat's scrotum whether you ever go to sea again. But, see, sailing was the first thing I ever learned to do well. Before that, I was just the kid who was forever tripping over her own big feet. A lot of our tutors never even bothered to learn my name. They just knew me as the family wimp."

"They just called me 'the baby,' so count your blessings." She squinted at the shape of some distant bird—a wandering albatross, probably, judging from the size. "Can I ask a strange question?"

"People rarely ask me any other kind."

"Did you like being one of Father's captains?"

There was a note of challenge in her voice that took me off guard. It was as if, from long experience, she knew not to expect an honest answer. So I gave her one.

"Yes. I did. I mean, once I figured out what I was doing and no longer felt consumed by pants-shitting terror every moment of every day."

"Even though you were serving a—what did you call him? A brutal tyrant."

"I know I was, but it didn't feel that way when I was at sea. There was just my ship, my command, my ocean. I didn't think about Father more than every other week."

"And yet you gave it up—your captaincy, your command, everything—to kiss a peasant girl."

This was becoming an interrogation, but at least she was talking to me. "Well. Can I tell you a secret? Very little planning went into that decision."

"Are you still with the girl?"

"Jess? No. And, word to the wise, just in case you ever meet her: she'll kill you bloodily if you call her a 'girl.'"

Jada squinted at me hard. "So you set your life on fire for this woman, and then you just left her to hook up with someone else?"

"Why do you assume that I hooked up with someone else?"

"It's not really an assumption, since I can count three different hickeys on your neck from where I'm standing."

Oh, damn. I adjusted my tunic collar and lowered my chin. "Doesn't mean anything. They could be bites. I could have been fighting an army of small bitey people, you don't know. Um. Anyway! What about you, are you seeing anyone?"

She turned a blank face towards me. "You know that Konrad's trying to marry me off."

"And we both know that means nothing. Everybody sows their oats."

"If they can get away with it. Konrad's desperate for allies, and I'm the only sibling he's got who's alive and single, which makes me the only piece of marriage meat he has to work with at the moment. He'll be furious if I soil the merchandise before he has the chance to close a sale."

"Yeah. So are you seeing anyone?"

She huffed. "What did I just say?"

"You said a lot of things. But you didn't say, 'No.'"

She laughed at that, in a startled, against-her-will kind of way, and looked at me with slightly more respect. "You're not stupid."

"Don't worry. I'm bound to do something stupid before the day's out. So—is Konrad involving you at all in the search for your husband? Did he let you screen his top ten list? Or ask if you had any dealbreakers? You know—bad breath, violent perversions, boring perversions . . ."

Again, the startled laugh. "You're kidding, right?" She studied me, searchingly. "I know you've been gone for a long time, but have you forgotten how this works? Konrad's lord of the Isle now. He owns my fealty and everything else about me. Why would my lord and master give a singular shit how I feel? Would our father have cared?"

"No, of course not. I just thought that . . . well, I hoped that . . ."

"That Konrad would be different?" She pulled a rotten bit of wood from the waterlogged dock and tossed it into the shallow water, watching it as it sank. "You have to know better than that, pirate queen. If there's one thing we can count on in life, it's that our family is never going to change."

CHAPTER NINE

Lynn

I DON'T SULK. That's a Darren thing. It's not in my repertoire.

So, if it looks like I might be sulking—if I retreat to my cabin, say, and refuse to speak to anyone or come out for lunch—you can take it for granted that there is something else going on. Maybe I'm planning a very violent assassination. Maybe I have decided to give myself seventeen orgasms in a row. Maybe I am burning goats on a small improvised altar as a sacrifice to the gods of hell. But I'm not sulking. Because I don't do that.

"Are you still sulking?" Spinner asked through the cabin door.

I didn't bother to get up from the bunk, or even to raise my head. "Spinner, I don't know how many more ways I can tell you to fuck off."

"Aren't you in charge right now? The captain's ashore, and the first mate, and the quartermaster . . . we're short on important people."

"Latoya's on deck. Go bother her."

"Don't you outrank Latoya?"

That was sort of a complicated question, or, at least, it could be, on a day when I felt like grappling with complications. I wasn't in the mood for complexity right then, so I skipped to the easy answer. "I'm Darren's slave, dumbass. I'm not in the chain of command, I just pass along her orders. I'm pretty much a parrot, except that I have nicer legs, and the ability to clean stuff."

"Right." Spinner drawled the word out skeptically. That was kind of fair, since I had been known to take some, well, liberties, when passing along Darren's commands. Not every time. When I reported something like *The captain says to weigh anchor and head south,* then Darren usually had said that, or something like it, or at the very least she *would* have said it if she'd been thinking clearly. On the other hand, I sometimes came out with things like *The captain says you have to give me the last banana,* or *The captain says you have to help me plan a surprise party for the captain, and the captain says that if you let any of the details slip around the captain, the captain is going to rip your head off and let me wear it as a hat.* In those cases, it was reasonable for people to assume that I was not repeating Darren's words with one hundred percent accuracy.

"All right, fine," Spinner said. "I'll tell you the problem, and you can let me know what 'the captain' thinks we should do about it. But could you open the damn door first?"

"No."

"I can't stand out here screaming. It's bad for my throat."

"Then I invite you to refresh yourself with a tall, cool glass of I don't give a fuck."

"You're being a pissy little brat, you know. Oh, Latoya! Give me a hand here? Lynn's having emotions and she won't open up."

"That so?" A powerful fist hammered at the hatch, the planks almost bowing inwards with the force of it. "Lynn?"

"Oh, don't *you* start." I pulled a fold of blanket over my face.

"I haven't started yet. When I start something, you'll know. Look—I'll give you a fair choice. Would you rather mend your ways, or mend your door?"

Damn it. At that moment, I wanted company about as much as I wanted a mysterious oozing rash on a part of my body the sun never touched, but I also wasn't keen on the idea of Latoya breaking our cabin door, *again*. Darren got squeamish about doing bad horrible things to me when there wasn't a sturdy lock between her and any potential witnesses. I could work around that reluctance, usually, but it required time and effort that could be better spent in other ways.

I rolled off the bunk, unlatched the door, and pulled it open a crack. "All right. I'm listening. You might want to talk fast, though. I have a strange premonition that I might start punching random people in the nads sometime very soon."

Spinner crossed his arms. "You're not going to win any prizes for good manners today."

"Oh, I'm ever so sorry. Talk to me when my mistress isn't playing footsie with a bunch of people who think I'm an animal, and maybe I'll be in a better mood. What's going on?"

"Come on. We'll show you."

Outside, the air was grey and wet with a fine, fine mizzle that wasn't quite fog and wasn't quite rain. It was still enough to make my arms throb. Turning up my shirt collar against the damp, I squinted through the shifting mist at the ship Spinner pointed out to me. It wasn't moored at one of the harbour jetties, but anchored a hundred yards or so offshore. In the dimness, it was just a shadow at first, rocking in the changing tide, until I saw a flash of yellow.

"Oh crap," I muttered, and took the spyglass Spinner held out. The smeary glass brought the plague flags into focus. They were makeshift, bits of rag really, dyed yellow—hopefully with onion skins, and not with the other yellow-type things you can find on board ship. Dozens of the flags were tied all over the ship's rat lines and braces, making it look like the rigging had sprouted dead leaves.

I shut up the spyglass. "What's the disease?"

"Cholera," Spinner said, folding his skinny body forward over the rail. "But here's the fun part. The ship—she's called the *Iris*—just came back from a supply run to Yag Sin Tor. That's the plague port."

" . . .oh, sixteen different kinds of shit."

"Yeah. They were there about a week ago."

"And we were there . . . twelve days ago? Thirteen?"

"We thought you'd want to know."

"You were right."

Spinner arched one fine eyebrow. He had very shapely eyebrows, now that Ariadne plucked them for him. "I'm sorry, would you mind repeating that?"

"Fine. You were right, I was wrong. I forgive you for that, just . . . try not to make a habit of it."

The *Iris* seemed much closer than it had before, now that I knew it was a vat of disease. "You know, if there's one thing that I don't need this month, it's a ship full of sailors shitting their brains out."

"It's not our idea of a good time either," Latoya said, stretching. "We might have lucked out, though. None of our sailors have shown symptoms yet."

"Yet." I counted on my fingers, counted again. "But cholera usually shows up pretty fast. If no one's come down sick yet, chances are no one will. You're right, Latoya—we might be lucky."

Latoya nodded. "You know your cholera."

"We had an outbreak back on Bero when I was . . . I want to say six? Before my mother died, anyway. For weeks on end, she did nothing but rinse out chamber pots."

Spinner's forehead wrinkled. "I thought you didn't remember anything from back then."

"I don't remember much, but trust me, if you live through a cholera outbreak, you don't forget it. Anyway. Can we be sure that no one from the *Iris* snuck onto shore? And when you answer, bear in mind that the universe hates me."

"The harbourmaster says that the quarantine's solid," Spinner said. "And we've been keeping a watch. But we should warn our men anyway—and we might want to limit shore leave as much as we can. Keep most of the crew aboard."

"Maybe." I raked my fingers through my hair. "What do you think, Latoya? Can we do that without rousing the crew to bloody foaming mutiny?"

"Lynn, you know as well as I do—feed them enough beer, and anything's possible."

"That's one option, but we'll be moored here a couple of weeks. I'd like them to be sober at least half the time. Can't we get them to stay put through the force of quiet menace?"

"Worth a try, I guess." Latoya rolled her shoulders, and they went *pop-pop-pop,* like a string of firecrackers. "Let's go have a chat with the crew. See if we can put the fear of god into them."

"Nuts to that. Let's put the fear of death by diarrhea into them. See how that goes. And both of you better remember this. I expect you to tell my mistress later how mature I'm being about this whole thing."

CHAPTER TEN

The Lady Darren of the House of Torasan (Pirate Queen)

"I *DID* WARN you, Ariadne. I told you that Konrad's wife was a rotten musician."

"Yes. You prepared me for a rotten musician. You failed to prepare me for a woman whose lute playing represents an actual threat to world peace. Darren, I would like you to stab her repeatedly before she can trap me again. I am making a formal request."

"All right. I have noted your request that I bloodily destroy my brother's wife, and I will give it all of the consideration that it deserves. Why are you putting on so much rouge?"

"Because we're going to eat in the Great Hall, and it'll be dark there, and you need to use more colour if you want it to be seen in poor light. Science. Do you want me to do your face as well?"

"Allow me to answer that question by screaming non-stop for an hour."

"Just some powder and kohl. I won't paint your lips or anything. It'll look very dignified. Not at all girly. Come here a second."

"Get off. Ariadne. No, I said get *off*. Stoppit. No! Ariadne! *Damn it, woman, I am a very intimidating and terrible pirate and you will not put goop on my face.* Regon! Corto! What do you think you're doing? Get up and destroy her!"

Regon and Corto, the traitors, barely looked up from their game of dice. Since my faithless crew refused to come to my aid, I had to snatch up a pillow and a feather-duster and defend myself. It was a hard-fought battle, but in the end, my tactical brilliance and physical prowess won out over Ariadne's evil cunning, and she dropped, laughing, into a chair.

"You'd better hope that I never turn against you," she said, once she caught her breath. "If I ever need to bring you down, I shall simply sneak up from behind and slip a pink frilly dress over your head. Stripped of your swagger, you will be helpless before me."

She flounced in the chair, rolled her shoulders, and frowned. "*Now* look what you've done. You've gone and stretched my bodice strings."

"Oh, rats. I guess I'll need to sob with remorse and shame all night."

"You should. Well, I'll need someone to tighten these up for me, or I won't be fit to appear in public."

Her eyes skimmed the room and rested thoughtfully on Regon.

"Oh, no you don't." I lunged between her and my first mate before she could swoosh over to him in a swirl of lace. "How many times do I have to say it? My crew is not an all-you-can-eat buffet. You get one at a time."

"You bloody prude. I was just going to ask him to help with my dress— not bend me over a table and have his wicked way with me. If you're not going to let me recruit outside assistance, you'll have to help."

"Fine. Assume the position."

She hopped up, swept over to the bed, and wrapped her arms around one of the posts. "Have you ever done this before?" she asked over her shoulder.

"Sure." I squinted at the bodice laces and set to work unpicking the knots. "It's been a while, though. If you want someone who actually knows what they're doing, we'll have to call a maid."

"A maid, what a lovely idea. If we're lucky, maybe we'll get one who's more than eight years old and only has one black eye. I told you, no servants."

"It's not like I'm crazy about the idea." Every time I turned a corner in the Keep, I expected to see the fawn-eyed girl, with her jug of washwater and her thin frightened face. "But not every servant gets treated the way Lynn did. All right, exhale."

"I . . . know . . . that," Ariadne panted, as I wrenched at her bodice strings. "But still . . . if I had to be a bond servant . . . I'd rather it be on Bero . . . than on Torasan Isle. Not so much . . . penny-pinching. On Bero . . . even our scullery maids . . . got to . . . eat meat . . . every so often. Oh come on, pirate queen, that's not nearly tight enough. Put your back into it, woman!"

"I can't get it any tighter unless I . . . you know."

"Well, do it then. Honestly, do I need to talk you through everything?"

I scowled at her back—waste of a scowl, because she couldn't see it— and planted a foot on her backside to brace myself. "You must have had servants of your own, growing up."

"Yes, of cou-ou-ourse!" The end of the word turned into a squeal as I yanked the bodice strings as tight as they would go. "That's good, Darren, that's better. Tie it off. Not with any fancy sailor knots, if you please; I want to get out of this dress eventually. Servants when I was growing up. Yes. Alma, my old nurse—she dressed me and drew my baths and so on. And the housekeeper would do my rooms out and wait on me a bit."

Regon looked up, crooking a furry eyebrow. "Two old women? Weren't you supposed to have maids or ladies-in-waiting? Girls to catch you when you fainted, or carry your sewing silks?

"I did once. Just the once. Her name was Basia and she was fourteen—I was maybe a year younger. She served me for two months and then I caught my father with his hand up her skirt. So I threw a hideous tantrum, told my parents that Basia snored and smelt of piss, and made them send her back home. I don't know whether it made things any better for her in the long run. There are people everywhere with grabby hands, and perhaps her home was miserable. But at least I didn't have to stand there and watch it happen."

She took a step away from the bed and her knees buckled beneath her. I caught her by the arm before she fell. "What's the matter? Dizzy?"

"Yes. Funnily enough, that will happen when one's lungs get squashed to half their usual size." She detached herself, fanning her face. "What's the plan for tonight? I take it that you want me to work the lady bits and try to get your family to talk to me."

"I'm going to have to ask you never to use the phrase 'lady bits' again, but yes, see what you can find out. Regon—"

He nodded. "I know. Soldiers, kitchen wenches, and page boys. Corto and I'll talk to as many as we can find."

"Thanks, but . . . um. I was hoping that Corto could go check on Lynn."

Corto punched Regon in the arm. "Less than a day," he said, smirking. "You owe me ten bits."

"Funny. Hilarious. Just give her a status report, all right? And see how she is. Please."

He shook his head sadly. "Now, captain, is that any way to ask?"

"Fine. 'Do it, you bastard son of a poxy whore, or I'll see you hung from the yardarm.'"

"Better." He stood and stretched. "I thought for a second that you were losing your touch. Family dinners can have that effect on people."

I SHOULD HAVE felt a great sense of triumph when I paraded into the Great Hall with a beautiful woman on my arm. But it was the wrong woman, and that sort of ruined it.

"Do you have to be quite so clingy?" I hissed at Ariadne.

"I am trying to give the impression that I enjoy touching you," she said through clenched, smiling teeth. "Remember how I'm supposed to be your kept woman? Your personal bit of skin? Stop acting like you're escorting your great-aunt to supper. Pretend you've seen me naked."

"I *have* seen you naked. Your first week aboard ship, remember? When Lynn and I were helping you find some trousers that fit. It was about as erotic as an old man's bath. Besides, why do we want people to think that you're my bit of skin? Why can't we tell them that you're my accountant, or my bodyguard?"

"Darren. We have talked about this. We *want* people to jump to conclusions. They're supposed to file me away in a box labelled 'Stupid useless girl' and then forget that I exist. That way, I'll have space to work."

"Well, I'm not going to grope you at the dinner table."

"I am relieved to hear it. Can we do something a little bit short of a grope, though? For example, you could try not to flinch when I touch you. That would be an excellent start."

"I'll try, all right? Don't expect too much. I've never been all that good at flirting, and now I'm practically married."

"*Practically.*" She pursed her lips. "Now, there's a thought. Didn't you promise that you were going to make an honest woman of my sister?"

"I did! More or less. Well. I tried, anyway. I asked if Lynn wanted to get married and she said, 'Mistress, I just dug a tick out of your backside with my fingernails. Exactly how much more married do you want to be?'"

We had almost reached the high table, where a horde of dark-haired men and women made a solid wall. I took a deep breath. "Brace yourself. We're going in."

THE NEXT HALF-HOUR or so was about as awkward as a social situation could be, considering that no one was naked or on fire.

The men introduced to me as my brothers Gunnar and Talon had sour faces and beer guts. They greeted me with forced, artificial enthusiasm, and couldn't hide their relief when I turned away.

Konrad's heir, his oldest son Karel, was busy talking with a bunch of his cronies. He didn't pause the conversation when I came near, just extended a languid hand for me to kiss. I shook the hand instead, and even that was unpleasant—his skin was damp and soft as a cod's belly.

There were more of Konrad's children, boys and girls who were old enough to sit up to supper, but young enough to think that they had to frown all the time to be taken seriously. They went around looking like they'd been forced to take a long lick of a mule's hind end, and they refused to laugh at anything.

There were throngs of women, sisters-in-law and distant cousins, all of whom looked very prim and proper and upright, except for Konrad's wife. *She* was as drunk as a pisspot, and she started the night off by blinking at me vacantly, asking when I'd grown so fat, and belching in my face. Konrad winced at that, his smooth mask slipping for just an instant. Talon and Gunnar's wives looked almost identical, and both of them were named something that sounded almost but not quite like "Valerie." All they wanted to talk about was clothes. I contributed my personal opinion on the subject—namely, that wearing clothes is generally but not always a good idea—and then couldn't think of anything else to add.

While I was suffering through all this, Jada hung back at the fringes of the room, looking sullen and miserable in a too-small dress of faded yellow which might have been fashionable seven years in the past. Every time I tried to sidle in her direction, Konrad popped up with yet another distant relative or general or priest for me to meet. I bowed and smiled until my face hurt and my tired head spun.

At last, someone herded a boy in front of me who looked far too young to be up so late. He was horribly pimple-pocked, with red splotches carpeting not only his nose and chin, but his neck too, right down to the shirt collar. He'd tried to hide the ones on his forehead by combing down his fringe, but violent yellow-headed lumps glared out between strands of dark hair. He was shortish, but thick around the middle; he was wearing what had to be his only "good" pair of trousers, and a bit of belly flopped over the belt.

Just one glance at him, and I knew he'd have one hell of a time until he went through a growth spurt and learned to stop picking his face. The sight did me good. At a few points that day, I'd been in danger of getting nostalgic. Now I remembered why I'd hated being young.

"Aunt Darren," he said. The word "Aunt" came out in a deep baritone, "Darren" as a squeak. He winced, reddening to the roots of his hair.

Konrad cleared his throat. "Greet her properly, Hark."

The boy flushed even deeper and snapped forward into a bow. He did it so fast, I only just managed to lean out of the way in time to avoid a collision.

"Hark," I repeated, trying to place the name. I thought I recognized it, vaguely. At least it wasn't yet another name that sounded almost but not quite like "Valerie." "Are you one of Konrad's boys?"

"My lord Konrad is my uncle," the boy said, his voice a piping treble. "I have the honour to be Alek of Torasan's oldest son."

Several remarks came to mind about then, but none of them were appropriate for polite company. I swallowed them all down and tried for a sympathetic smile.

"You found my father," the boy said. "You tried to save him."

"Um. Yes. It didn't . . . quite . . . work out, I'm afraid." What to do? Curse? Apologise? Run around the table shrieking? I remembered something I'd once heard a stupid old man say to an orphan and blurted it out before I had time to think. "You must be a great comfort to your mother."

Hark's face became a little blanker. "My lady mother died of consumption two years ago."

I should probably just stop talking completely, I decided. Maybe I could start wearing a gag to formal occasions. I could decorate it with feathers or something, make it kind of chic.

Fortunately, Konrad intervened. "You're a lucky man, Hark, having your aunt here, tonight of all nights. You'll want to pick her brain as much as you can before tomorrow."

"Why? What's so special about . . . ?"

My voice trailed off when I saw what Hark was wearing on his belt: a silver dagger with a hawk's-head crest.

"His maiden voyage begins tomorrow," Konrad said, spelling out what I already knew. "Tomorrow, we send a new captain out in the service of Torasan."

WHEN WE'D ALL taken our seats at the long table for dinner, Ariadne gave me a dig in the side. "Why are you surprised by this?"

"I can't hear you," I said, as I ripped my napkin into little little pieces under the table. "I can't hear anything. My entire being is consumed by the spectacular terribleness of this idea."

"What idea? Putting stupid baby nobles in charge of merchant ships? Of course it's ridiculous, but that's never stopped anyone before."

"But Kila's a war zone now, and every year the seas get worse."

Hark sat, baby-faced and pink with pleasure, in the seat of honour at Konrad's side. I mentally ran through a few of the horrible things I'd seen happen to boys his age, and my stomach shrivelled in disgust.

I slammed my spoon down on the table. "What the hell is Konrad thinking? Couldn't he take two seconds to say, 'You know what, wacky thought, let's maybe *not* throw all our children out into the killing fields.'"

"It's adorable that you can still be that naïve." Ariadne delicately wiped her lips. "Why aren't you eating?"

"All of this talk about dead children isn't doing much for my appetite."

Ariadne clearly didn't have that problem. She was working her way through every dish on the table: lamprey pie, roasted pigeon, onion salad, eggs cooked with apples. Already, her trencher was heaped high with bits and scraps.

Ariadne mumbled something with her mouth full. I shook my head. "Sorry, what?"

She swallowed. "I said, I told you that Torasan had fallen on hard times."

I almost laughed. The table in front of us was groaning with food, an array of dishes dizzying to someone who lived mostly on hardtack and salt beef. True, it wasn't the food I remembered from feast days when I was a child . . .

It wasn't the same food at all, and suddenly I saw the point. Where was the suckling pig, the almond-milk custard, the roast peacock, the capon cooked with rosewater and cinnamon? One of the tureens in front of us held fish stew. Fish stew—the stuff that peasants would eat when they couldn't afford bread. There was a dish of roasted rabbits, half-concealed under thick gravy. Rabbit is meat, but it's a poor man's meat, lean, gamey. The loaves at my elbow were manchet bread, white and fine-grained, but further down the table, below the first salt, the bread was black and coarse.

"You know what this means," Ariadne said. "Even the nobles on Torasan Isle are tightening their belts, so the poor . . ."

"Ariadne, I have wonderful news: You can shut up now." I toyed with a bit of roast mutton and then nudged the trencher away from me. "Maybe, under the circumstances, you could stop stuffing yourself for five consecutive seconds?"

"I'm not stuffing myself," she said, through another huge mouthful. She dropped a barely-touched chicken leg onto her heaping trencher and reached across the table for more bread.

"Well, how about you stop loading your plate with food that you don't want to eat? It could be a nice gesture, if there are commoners starving outside the Keep."

She met my eyes, still chewing. Her face was sort of . . . contemptuously tolerant, if that makes any sense. As if she pitied me, against her own better judgment. "You are really not all that smart, are you?"

"Hey. I can do math and stuff."

"So can Latoya, and she doesn't need someone else to help her bathe and put her trousers on." She wiped greasy fingers on the napkin that hung over her shoulder, and nodded at the musicians' gallery. "Stop pestering me. They're playing your song."

"They're playing what? . . . Oh, bollocks on toast. Oh, son of a sabre-toothed doxy named Gretchen. Oh, *no*."

She was right—it was "The Ballad of Red-Handed Darren." I slid low in my seat. *Hell, hell, hell.*

Now, don't get me wrong. I like it when someone composes an epic song about me just as much as you do, I would think. And when a song celebrating your deeds becomes popular across eight realms and three continents, then you should probably just try to appreciate it, instead of pulling a face and going off to pout in a corner. But gods on high, if one song about me had to spread across the known world, why did it have to be that one? The damn thing goes on forever, and since people keep adding bits to the end, it gets longer with every performance.

Plus, some of the word choices are very questionable. I don't care what anyone says: my name does *not* rhyme with "harem."

I gritted my teeth and suffered through forty-two verses of torment, wishing all the while that I could get up and beat the minstrel into unconsciousness with his own lute without causing some kind of diplomatic incident. When the last wailing strains died away, I joined in the applause, mainly because I was so happy it was over.

There were whispers along the length of the table. A low voice—Konrad's, I thought—said, "Go on, ask her."

"Aunt Darren?" That was Hark, in his place of honour at Konrad's side. "Will you tell us more about your voyages?"

I glanced around the room. They were all listening: priests at the high table, stroking their beards, servants darting sideways glances at me while they topped up the wine cups. Gangling boys and girls ogled open-mouthed. Even Jada showed interest, for maybe the first time all evening. The scene made me flash to a time in the Tavarene desert, when I found a nest of vipers in one of our caravan carts. When I looked in, countless red eyes winked at me from the dark, studying me with hungry fascination.

I blew out a breath. "What do you want to hear about?"

Hark's eyes lit up. "Tell us about your duel to the death against Cathak. When Cathak's men were torturing your best friend down in the hold of his ship, and you could hear him down there all bloody and groaning, and you carved your name in Cathak's chest and then fed him to a kraken . . ."

Damn, again. Why did he have to start there? "That wasn't me."

Hark's forehead wrinkled in confusion. I tried again. "I didn't kill Cathak. I was up in the northeast that month. There was this town, see, and all of their young men and women had died in the war, and we needed to help the survivors get their crops in the ground before the rains. I spent a whole month up to my elbows in manure—"

Hark broke in, clearly not caring about my adventures in the field of agriculture. "You mean that the duel never happened?"

I almost regretted telling him. His round boyish face had gone soft and crushed, as if I had just announced that sunshine didn't exist, or honey candy, or holidays.

"The duel happened," I said. "I wasn't the one who fought it, that's all."

"But then . . . who did?"

"Monmain. One of my captains. His ship, the *Idiot Kid,* ran down Cathak almost by accident during one of his dawn raids, and things sort of developed from there."

"Is Monmain a great swordsman?"

I shrugged one shoulder. "Not really. Fair to middling. For some reason, he's better when he's drunk, except that he loses his sense of direction and you have to sort of prod him towards the enemy."

Hark stared in disbelief. "But then how did Cathak lose? He was a blademaster! One of the best warriors in Kila!"

I shrugged again, using the other shoulder this time for variety. "Even the best warriors in Kila can trip."

"Cathak *tripped?*"

"Cathak tripped. See, when he lunged at Monmain, he didn't notice that a loop of the anchor chain was lying on the deck between them. His foot got caught and the next second, he was lying full length on the deck, spitting blood and teeth. Cathak surged up roaring, but by then Monmain had his mace in position, and he bashed Cathak's brains out. Not very heroic, I guess, but that's how it happened."

Hark's face was getting longer and longer. "What about the kraken?" he asked, a little desperate now.

"Um. Well, Monmain did pitch the body into the water, so maybe it got eaten by something. It was pretty shallow water, though, so probably, uh, minnows or sunfish, rather than a kraken. So . . . not so much eaten. More nibbled on a bit. And before you ask, I don't know whether Monmain carved his name into Cathak's chest. He's usually too laid-back for that kind of thing, but he'd just heard his best friend getting tortured . . . so. You know."

Jada leaned forward across the table, eyes sharp. "What else about the ballad is wrong?"

"What about the ballad is *right?* I haven't done a quarter of the things that people say I've done. How could I? I've only been at this for three years, and I've had to spend some time attending to a few minor details other than piracy, like eating porridge and changing my underpants and oh yes, that little thing called sleeping. And nothing was as dramatic as they make it sound. For example? When I'm about to stab somebody, I don't stop to strike a pose and deliver a ringing speech. It's just never a good idea."

It wasn't sinking in. All the diners at the table looked blank, except for Jada, who now sat arrow-straight, staring at me with intense but opaque eyes.

Hark jumped in again. "Did you murder the mad vizier of Tarsus?"

Verse five. "No. That was Corto, my quartermaster. And it was self-defence, not murder, and the vizier wasn't mad, just an asshole. I guess that 'asshole vizier of Tarsus' doesn't sound quite as poetic, but he really was a raging dick. See, he was supposed to marry—"

"What about the wrestling match in Erudon?"

"That was my bosun, Latoya."

"The time you held up the collapsing temple so the priests could escape?"

"Latoya again."

"The cattle stampede? The stallion breaking? The time when you strangled a bull shark!"

"Latoya, Latoya, Latoya. Let me help you out here. Anything involving a feat of superhuman strength was Latoya. Also anything involving a feat of superhuman mathematical talent, but the math-related stories don't make it into the ballads very often. Which is a shame. You know, she once figured out that—"

Konrad interrupted. "What about the battle with the Sons of Heaven?"

I paused before answering. The constant flow of questions was making me feel testy and crowded, but there was no point in lying.

"All right," I admitted. "That one was me."

The sudden hush at the table was startling. I groped for my cup.

"Is it all true?" Konrad demanded. "All of it? You took a single ship up north, attacked their stronghold, and defeated seven boatloads of heretics, all armed with battle fire?"

"Well . . . yes, pretty much, yes, all that's true. I mean, one of their boats was kinda small, but . . ."

I didn't get to finish. There was an electric hum in the air, excited whispers, buzzing talk. A fat man several seats away pounded on the table, his silver rings clinking. "I knew it!" he proclaimed happily—and boozily; there was a definite whiff about him. "They said it was impossible when we heard about it down here. You know what I said to that? I said *balls*. Nothing's impossible when you have the glory in your blood. Lady, lady, you're a real child of Torasan!"

"That was a compliment, Darren," Ariadne murmured beside me. "Smile, don't wince."

She was right, so I tried to smile—didn't do it very well, but that didn't seem to matter. A rowdy throng of people surrounded me, all of them trying to clap me on the shoulder or wring my hand. It was very friendly, but after a few minutes of sweaty handclasps and wine breath, I began to think that a nice duel to the death would be a better way to spend an evening. It was a relief when Konrad intervened, good-humouredly ordering everyone back to their seats.

"All right, now," he said, leaning back. "Confess. Let's hear all about it."

"Oh . . . heck. You don't really need to hear it, do you? We just sat through an entire ballad, and all."

"That's not the same as hearing it straight from the source. Come on, indulge us. You have to learn to bask in your success."

I glanced at Ariadne, who, so far as I could tell, thought that I spent quite enough time basking. She grimaced, but gave a permissive little wave.

Where to begin? I combed my fingers back through my hair, destroying the coiffure that Ariadne had so carefully arranged, and then, almost at random, said, "I need a war board."

I'd hoped that the request would give me time to think, but the board arrived at the table what seemed like mere seconds later. It wasn't one of the big, elaborate sets that would occupy centre stage in a lord's war room, but a simple pasteboard model, the kind of thing I used when I studied navigation and tactics as a child. The islands of Kila were painted crudely on the base in blobs of green paint. The figurines of ships and soldiers were carved from wood, and stained either dark or light. Some were pocked with teeth marks, showing where bored students had absent-mindedly chewed on them.

I picked up one of the toy soldiers and sighed. That was the first problem, right there. When you're shoving battalions around a war board, one little wooden man is exactly the same as another little wooden man. That's not good enough. To be really useful, the board would have to show you how well each little wooden man was trained, how good a breakfast he'd eaten, whether his clothes were crawling with lice, whether his guts were putrid with dysentery, and whether he trusted the little wooden man at his elbow.

With my index finger, I prodded seven ships into position at the top edge of the board and slid another solitary ship to face them: the *Banshee* soaring into battle. The noise at the table softened to an eager hum.

"I guess you've all heard about the Sons of Heaven," I began. "They were the regular sort of brutes, doing the regular sort of brutish things— raping, pillaging, marauding—except they thought that the gods had told them to do it. So, you know, *divine* raping, *sacred* pillaging, *holy* marauding. I never understood much about their theology, except that they apparently believed that the gods were all horrible dickheads."

I felt for my cup and took a quick swallow. It didn't do much about the dryness in my throat. "They kidnapped some of their recruits, but a lot of boys joined willingly. Hard to blame them. The poor bastards wanted to be holding swords instead of dying on them. Thing was, the Sons of Heaven always put their youngest in the front lines when they expected hard fighting. And when I say young, I mean young: a lot of those boys were nine, ten, eleven. The Sons of Heaven—stupid name—kept their blood up by dosing them with something they called Sun Sweat. Really, it was a little bit of dajiki root in a whole lot of rum. It rotted the life right out of the boys if they drank it too long, because it killed their appetites and it kept them from sleeping. In the short run, though, it made them demons. Dancing, howling little skeletons, with eyes like red glass lamps."

"And that's how you won?" Konrad asked. "Because you were fighting children?"

"No. They had a few boys when I fought them, but even leaving them out of the picture, the grown men outnumbered us six to one. This is what happened. The Sons of Heaven had just knocked over a market town and fled north with their loot. It was winter and they were running straight into the teeth of a storm. They were insane to do it and they must have believed that no one would be insane enough to follow them. But I talked it over with . . . I mean, I thought about it for a while, and eventually we agreed . . . I mean, I decided that it was a risk we had to take. The storm would kill off some of the brutes, but the survivors would sweep south as soon as the weather cleared. Plus, there were the children to think about. Boys who joined the Sons of Heaven never lasted long. So we chased them north to the point of Accra. But before we did that, we prepared our secret weapon."

I paused there to take another drink. I hadn't meant to leave the question hanging, but guests all around the table piped up with guesses. "Battle fire . . . crossbows . . . caltrops . . ."

The people around the table couldn't have been to war. At least, not in winter.

"Poison!" Hark blurted out, his face blotchy red with excitement. "A fast-acting one. Like blackroot or wolfsbane or . . ."

I managed to suppress my snort, but it was a near thing. Hadn't Alek taught his son anything?

"You never use poison for close combat," I said, stating the obvious. "It's too easy to get scratched by your own blade. And battle fire looks impressive, but only a madman would bring it onto a wooden ship."

"So?" Konrad leaned in. "What was your weapon?"

"Hand cream."

There was silence, broken only by a disbelieving titter from a woman swathed in silk and lace, until Hark asked, "*What?*"

"Cream for my sailors' skin. Oh, nothing fancy. It was mainly rendered fat, with a few other things—pine oil, honey—and it smelt like a muck heap in hell, but it did the trick."

"*What* trick?"

"It protected my sailors' hands. Kept them from drying out."

The tone around the table had changed, the carnival air replaced by a suspicious, almost offended hush. Konrad sputtered out a laugh. "This is a joke, isn't it?"

I glanced at the soldiers who flanked the door. Both of them were smiling, faint faraway smiles. *They* knew. But how could I describe it to Konrad? For him, cold was a thing that vanished when you went inside, a detail that gave extra relish to your hot supper and your evening wine. He didn't understand real cold, the ripping tearing kind.

I held out my right hand, letting them all see the roughened skin on my palm. "Sailors' hands are tough, but they aren't made of leather. A few days in the cold and wind can dry out the skin until it cracks. Imagine your skin splitting apart all over your hands, until it feels like you've been raking at yourself with an iron spike. Imagine having hands like that, and hauling on a rope—a rough, tarry rope, studded with crystals of ice. Lose your grip for a second, let the rope slide, and it'll flay your palm to a bloody rag. Then imagine having to take up a sword in that hand, the steel so cold that your own bleeding flesh could freeze to the metal. *Now* does the idea of hand cream make sense?"

Some of the guests shifted in their seats, and Hark looked almost sick as he rubbed his own soft pink fingers. Good. I was tempted to tell him a few more home truths about a sailor's life, the kind of things they don't tell you during the lectures on honour and glory. Like the way scurvy can make your gums swell until they seal over your teeth and black blood oozes from the crevices. Or how, after a few months at sea, the ship's biscuits start to feel light and powdery, and you break them in half to find them furrowed with endless squirming tunnels, maggots and weevils boring into the bread.

But of all the small bodily insults of life at sea, being wet and cold might be the worst. When you're really cold, it's hard to think about anything except not being cold anymore, and all your primal instincts shriek at you to huddle into a ball somewhere away from the wind. When your hands are covered in red-blue sores, cracked and oozing blood and serum, swollen and throbbing with an ache that doesn't lessen even when you're asleep, life isn't pleasant. I learned early in my sea-going career to keep a jar of pig-fat handy to treat chapped hands. Lynn's lard-and-pine-oil concoction was a big improvement, though. The first time I tried it out, I seriously considered proposing marriage—either to Lynn or to the hand cream, I wasn't sure which.

I waited another few seconds to be sure that the message had sunk in properly. Then I helped myself to another dollop of raisin-studded frumenty and continued the story with my mouth half full.

"It was blue cold around Accra that week, the kind of cold that reaches beneath your shirt, closes its fingers around your heart, and grips. Sun so low in the sky that it seemed almost sunk in the ocean. Where the light touched the water, it didn't give heat, just sent clouds of mist rising, thick and grey. It was a terrible place. You heard strange sounds through the mist from every direction. Bells clanging all empty and hopeless, and ropes creaking, as if ghost ships were sailing past.

"We had plenty of food. That was one saving grace. When you're working in the cold, you crave fat more than anything, so we'd stocked masses of salt pork and lard. We served double rations every day we were up north, with fried biscuit and plum duff and as much soup or porridge as anyone could hold. After every meal, when the blood was properly pumping, we all went through the same routine: check your feet for frostbitten patches, wrap them in clean rags, then treat your hands with grease. Lips and ears, too.

"After three days, we caught up with the Sons of Heaven."

Glad to be finished, I plunged my spoon into a fish-and-apple pie and started scooping out the contents. It took me a few moments to realize that people were still staring. I swallowed a barely chewed mouthful. "Um. Then we fought them and we won."

"But what happened?" Hark's voice cracked again in the middle of the question, but he didn't notice. "How did you beat them when you were outnumbered six to one? What did you do?"

"What did *I* do? Killed a couple of people, I guess. I don't suppose I was especially magnificent on the battlefield—my ulcer was giving me hell that day. Anyway, it really doesn't matter what I did after I drew my cutlass. We won the fight before we even caught sight of the Sons of Heaven. There were a lot of them, but they were wrecked. They were hungry, they were limping because their feet were a mess of bloody blisters, and the skin of their hands was split and raw and weeping. We didn't have any of those problems, and we went in and we thrashed them. That's all."

There was a sag in the posture of the people around the table, a sort of letdown, and I wasn't sure whether I should say anything more. To my relief, Ariadne let out a peal of silvery laughter and laid her white hand over Konrad's tanned one.

"My lord Konrad, I'm sure this conversation is fascinating to you and the rest of these clever people, but I really don't understand these things. Could we perhaps discuss something other than military matters? I hear that you killed a wild boar single-handed in the last hunt, and I'm positively dying to hear about it."

For an instant, Konrad looked put out, but he quickly refocused. "Of course, my lady," he said gallantly, and launched into what sounded like a very long tale.

Ariadne, I happened to know, was bored to tears by hunting stories. Her first husband didn't care about much except hunting, hunting dogs, and hunting horses, and during the little time they spent together, he talked about nothing else. For Ariadne, hunting stories ranked as a form of entertainment just below giant wasps and genital warts.

I caught her eye and nodded my thanks. She flicked her fingers—*it's nothing, it's nothing*—then turned back to Konrad with a coy smile and eyes as vacant as a shallow pond.

I HAD TO get away from it, all of the posing and the smiling and the flouncing and the faking, so I kicked my chair back from the table.

The Great Hall was sweltering, packed wall to wall with bodies that reeked of strong sweat and cheap perfume. I stepped outside, but that was no escape. The kitchen fires took up half the courtyard, with at least a dozen cauldrons roiling away on iron tripods. Cooks jostled and bumped into each other as they poured and ladled and stirred. It was all heat and noise and hurry-hurry-hurry, and the cooks cursed the carvers and the carvers screamed at the pot-boys and the pot-boys kicked at passing dogs.

I leaned against the rough-cut logs of the palisade and breathed deep, feeling every moment of that long day in the strain through my back and shoulders.

So why exactly was I doing this, again? It would only take me five minutes to get back to the *Banshee*. In five minutes and five seconds, I could be back in my cabin, with Lynn sitting on my lap to explain exactly how annoyed she was that I was there. She'd chew me out for leaving Ariadne alone at the Keep, but that wouldn't last long and then she'd use her mouth for . . . well. Other things.

Plus, we still had a few jars of the lard-and-pine-oil mix kicking around in the *Banshee's* hold, and, though I wasn't about to explain this to my family, there was more than one use for that stuff.

It would be so easy. I stared at the palisade gate, and my weaker self whimpered and snivelled, begging me to walk away. Mentally, I grabbed my weaker self by the scruff of the neck and gave it a kick. "Shaddup, you."

A servant boy glanced up. "My lady?"

"Oh. Nothing. Nothing."

The boy ducked his head and went back to his task, spit-roasting chickens over a bed of glowing coals. The spits were rusty, and turned slowly in their forks, metal grinding in a painful sort of cadence. In time with the turning spit, the boy hummed a tuneless song. He was barefoot, about seventeen, with hair the colour of old straw. His shirt was mottled with stains from popping grease, and so threadbare that it was almost transparent. I angled my head and counted his ribs.

I didn't remember the servants being so thin when I was growing up. Then again, when I was growing up, there was a lot that I chose not to see.

"Hey," I said, on a sudden impulse.

He fumbled, nearly dropped a chicken, caught it just before it fell in the fire. "My lady?"

"I'm, um, looking for someone that used to work here. She was the washwater girl for the Torasan nursery, when I was a kid. Huge eyes. Thin face. I think her name was . . ."

In the place in my mind where the name should have been, there was nothing but cobwebs and a thin layer of dust.

"You mean Tavia?"

That sounded right. "Yes! Yes, her. Is she still around?"

"No." He wiped his nose with his sleeve. "She fell off a stool in the dairy, a few months back. Cracked her skull open."

Too late for any apologies, then. "Blast it."

He shrugged and returned to his cooking. He was basting the birds, brushing melted butter on the crisp and crackling skin. Starveling boy, golden chickens. What would happen if he pulled a drumstick off for himself? Lynn would know in painful detail, but even I could guess.

"Have you had your supper yet?" I asked.

He looked up, hooded eyes wary. "Not yet, my lady."

"I could get you something from inside. I mean, if you wanted."

There was a quick flash of irritation across his face, but he smothered it. "There's no need, lady. They're already bringing the leavings out, see?"

He nodded to a table by the hall door. Servers were streaming out with half-empty platters and armloads of wooden trenchers—table scraps from the banquet. As quickly as the servers brought out the dishes, others went to work sorting the leftovers. They set aside all of the food that looked more or less decent, like joints of meat with plenty left on the bone, or apple pies only half scooped out. After wrapping the platters carefully in oiled muslin, they carried them back to the pantry, to be served up for breakfast the next day.

Once they'd winnowed out the stuff that still looked edible, what was left on the table was a heap of mashed and broken fragments. There were crusts of bread and fish-heads, bits of bone and gobs of mutton fat, cheese rind and vegetable peel. Servants crowded around the pile of slop, and—I blinked—they were eating it. They turned over the scraps and raked through them, and picked bits out and put them down and picked up others. They stuffed their mouths with soggy wads of bread and fish skin, or they tucked handfuls of the mush into their pockets and down their shirt fronts.

I'd eaten filthy food in my life, and rotten food, and infested food, but something about the raking and the pawing was too much. I took a step back, revolted, and from beside me came a soft snicker. By the time I looked at the kitchen boy, he'd smothered his smile and fixed his eyes on the ground, but there was still a sort of spiteful amusement in his face. *Well, what did you expect?*

Most of the scraps were already gone. How could these people possibly get enough to eat? I hadn't left much more on my own plate than a scrap of pastry and a smear of gravy, and . . . oh, hell, and various other words for hell. Ariadne. Damn it all, Ariadne had known.

"Aunt Darren?"

Hark eased his way between the steaming cauldrons, none-too-subtly hiking up the back of his ill-fitting trousers. "Everyone's asking where you are."

Right. When you were an honoured guest at a banquet, you were supposed to stick around until dessert.

"I'll go back in a second," I said. "I just need to brace myself first."

I took a few deep breaths, and he shifted his weight from foot to foot, waiting for me.

"Everyone keeps telling me that I should beg you for advice," he said. "About my maiden voyage, I mean."

"Do they?" I sighed. "I don't know what I can tell you that would be of any use. There's only one thing I remember from my first week at sea, and that's puking so hard that I thought I was going to turn myself inside out."

His eyes widened. "You got seasick?"

"I hate to be the bearer of bad tidings, Hark, but you will too, pretty definitely. Autumn winds mean high waves. And they don't waste new ships on first voyages—you'll be commanding some wretched old scow with the smell of rotten oysters oozing from every plank. And if you haven't tasted salt pork before—no? Well, that'll be a whole new adventure."

"Right." He nodded, brow furrowed as he tried to look serious and mature. "I can understand that."

"You don't understand anything yet. Do you really want advice? Then here's what you do. First, you have to find the best sailor aboard your ship. You want the man who can steer one-handed through a hurricane, yawning all the while. Find him, then throw yourself on his mercy. Tell him that you're green as grass and ignorant as hell—he'll know that anyway, so it's no good trying to pretend otherwise. Then tell him that you'll run the ship exactly the way he tells you to run it, so long as he doesn't try and fuck with you. Do say fuck. None of your crewmen will even begin to take you seriously until you learn how to swear."

His jaw was dangling somewhere around his naval. "But what then?"

"Then you run the ship exactly the way he tells you to run it, so long as he doesn't try to fuck with you. You'll know if he's trying to fuck with you. If he pulls any crap, then find the second-best sailor and go from there. Other than that, the best tip I can give you is not to take off your trousers during the voyage. Not ever, not *once*. No swimming, no whoring, no sleeping in the nude. Keep your trousers on and your belt buckled and you'll stay halfway dignified."

I paused, suddenly overwhelmed. What advice could carry a chubby little boy safely through a hellscape?

"You don't have to do this, you know," I said haltingly. "I know it's what they expect of you, but Hark . . . things are bad out on the water."

He was hardening now, his face stubborn and mulish. "You seem to cope."

"I've survived. So far. I've been doing this for years, I've won more battles than you've eaten hot dinners, and I'm still scared shitless half the time. And if you're not scared shitless, then you're not paying attention. If you insist on going through with this, then you'd better go to the temple now and light a whole fistful of candles and pray to every god whose name you can remember that the first murder you see won't be your own. The seas are on fire. It's no place for . . . for beginners."

It's no place for children, was what I'd wanted to say, and maybe he knew that, because colour surged to his face. "You think I can't handle it?"

"I know you can't handle it. You're not a captain or a leader *or* a sailor, not yet. During your maiden voyage, your crew carries you—or they don't, and you're screwed. I barely survived my first voyage, and back then, only *most* of the people I met were trying to kill me."

He stepped back, shoulders rigid.

"I regret that you have any reason to think me unworthy of my command, my lady," he said stiffly. "By the grace of the gods, I hope to prove you wrong."

"Oh, bollocks roasting on an open fire—I'm telling you this because I want you to be smarter than I was! If you go through with this, it doesn't prove that you're worthy of your blood, or whatever the hell. It means that you're just as much of a coward as all the rest of us. Hark! Come back here!"

But he was already marching away, head high. For the first time, I understood why Lynn always laughed at me so hard when I tried to act dignified.

Well, I'd tried. Now I'd had enough of guilt and confusion and hollow-cheeked servant boys and self-destructive nephews. It was time to get drunk.

As I headed back to the hall, the boy at the spit began to sing again, in that same tuneless voice. This time, he wasn't the only one. A few of the pot-boys took up the melody, maybe one or two of the cooks, as the song spread across the yard.

I didn't think much of the song. Not that I had the right to an opinion on the subject. Who was I to judge these hungry, grimy people, and the things that they did to get through the day? Still, the song struck me as dismal. It didn't have much of a tune, just a heavy, repetitive kind of beat. And anyway, why in hell would anyone make up a song about killing chickens?

CHAPTER ELEVEN

Lynn

LATOYA SAID, WE'RE going to the tavern on shore. I said, have fun. Don't drink anything with dead things floating in it and don't kill anyone unless it's an emergency or you really, really want to.

Latoya said, you're coming with me. I said, the hell I am. Latoya said, you want to walk to the tavern, or you want me to put you over my shoulder and haul you there? I said, what the hell do you think my mistress is going to do if she sees you carrying me down the gangplank? Latoya said, she'll cry all night, then offer to back out gracefully so the two of us can find true love together. I said, well, exactly.

Latoya said, seriously, you're coming. I said, knock it off. Latoya said, you're coming, put on some damn shoes. I said, I don't have any damn shoes and why are we still talking about this? Latoya said, I mean it, come on. I said No she said Come on I said No she said Come on. I said, Latoya. What. The. Fuck. You know me better than this. Why would I go on shore when there's a perfectly good boat right here? Latoya said, I'm drinking tonight and I want company. Latoya said, I don't give a good goddamn if you hate spending time on dry land; you're coming, even if I have to nail wheels to your ass and drag you along behind me like a wagon. Latoya said, I'm done arguing, you have five seconds to move.

I held out for four seconds. Then I moved. She had a look in her eye that usually led to someone limping around and saying *ow* a lot in a meek and subdued tone of voice.

There was only one tavern in the village. Inside, it was dark and cave-like. The walls were grimed with soot, the dirt floor spongy underfoot with spilled drinks. Latoya ordered supper and four pints of ale, and told the barman to keep the drinks coming as long as we were conscious.

The food was a gritty, salty mash of something hard to identify. Probably boiled peas with a bit of fish oil, and sawdust for bulk. It tasted rancid but it was hot and I hadn't had to cook it, so there was that. I ignored the flavour and worked my way through the bowl spoonful by spoonful. It helped that it was too dim to see what I was eating, especially when bits of something stringy got caught between my teeth. The ale was better, but not by much. I swigged, wiped my mouth, sighed, and hated everything around me.

Before I met Darren, I used to spend a lot of time around taverns, because if you were looking for men who had money and wanted to spend it, that was the place to go. But I rarely went inside. My spot was the front stoop, just outside of the circle of faint firelight that spilled through the doorway. There was usually a cluster of women out there, all ages: girls like me, with matted hair and no fixed address; mothers who couldn't earn enough on the fishing skiffs to feed their children; half-senile wrecks who tried to cover the lines on their faces with a thick coat of plaster or white clay. It was a cutthroat kind of place to work. There were so many women looking to pick up a trick that if you expected to attract attention, you had to be better-looking than anyone else, or cheaper than anyone else, or have fewer limits than anyone else. And I'm not especially good-looking and I was never cheap when I could avoid it.

There were no women around this tavern. Which meant there were no men in the tavern who had the money to spare for a whore.

There was no garbage in town, either, and that was a bad sign too. Garbage means you're in a place that hasn't yet hit bottom. In a really desperate village, no one throws anything away. Anything that you can eat, you eat; anything that you can burn, you burn; anything that will cover skin, you wear; anything else is used as fertilizer or turned into a fishhook. In my wandering days, whenever I entered a new town, I always felt relieved if I could see garbage. That, and rats, because rats meant that there was something around to eat. If nothing else, you could eat the rats.

The beer got worse as I neared the bottom of the cup. I squinted into the murky brew, trying to figure out whether there was a surprise waiting for me down there.

Latoya heaved a sigh over the top of her ale mug, sending puffs of beer foam flying across the table at me.

"Are we going to talk about what's bothering you?" I asked her as I wiped the foam from my face. "I'm ready to listen, but—fair warning—if you expect me to pry it out of you a word at a time, you picked the wrong night."

Latoya mechanically lifted a spoonful of the reeking stew, then wrinkled her nose and let the stuff slop back into the bowl. "This island is a cess pit. Don't see why anyone stays here."

"Latoya, I mean it. I'm not going to nod sympathetically at you for half an hour until you get to the point. You didn't drag me to this tavern so you could complain about being at this tavern. Either spit it out, or let's go do our drinking at home."

"*Sand ape.*"

The muttered words were low and vicious. I spun around, trying to identify the speaker, but nobody was looking in our direction. All of the tavern's greasy patrons had their heads down, bent over their cups of awful beer.

"Who said that?" I demanded, kicking my stool back. "What idiot thought that would be a hilarious thing to say? Come on, let me see your ugly troll face. I've got a knife and two fists and a history of making poor decisions."

Latoya hooked a finger into my belt and yanked me down onto my stool. "Stop that."

I slapped her hand away. "Are we just going to sit here while they spew that filth?"

"It's nothing I haven't heard before. If I wanted their faces smashed, I'd do it myself."

"But I'm not going to smash faces. I'm going to smash testicles, make sure they can't create small terrible children in their image. Future generations of mankind will, on average, be just a tiny bit less awful."

"Lynn, I don't need you to defend my damn virtue. Calm down and have another beer."

Behind us, the muttering continued. "You think that's actually a woman?"

A guffaw. "I think you'd have to shave it if you wanted to know for sure."

"I dunno if shaving it would help. Probably isn't much of a difference between a gorilla and a brown bitch, once you take off the hair."

Against my better judgment, I looked in the direction of the voices. A slouching man grinned at me, licked his thumb, and thrust it in and out of the curled fingers of his other hand. I flicked a fold of my shirt out of the way to show him my long knife, and his grin spread wide, as if I'd done something adorable.

"For gods' sake," I whispered. "Let's get out of here."

Latoya rolled her cup leisurely between her fingers. "I haven't finished drinking yet."

"We could go back to the *Banshee* and dip water out of the bilges and it'd taste better than the beer in this place. Come on, let's just go home. We'll break into my mistress's secret brandy stash and I'll make one of those sticky date puddings you like—"

"I'm the one they're taking shots at. If I can ignore it, you sure as hell can."

She spoke casually, but she'd already shifted her weight, planting her right boot on packed earth. If someone got tired of coarse dirty talk and tried to put a coarse dirty hand on her, he'd walk into an uppercut that would break his jaw into seven pieces. Which would have some repercussions, but would also be hilarious.

I sighed, slouching. "Fine. Fine, but what's the point? Why should we sit here and breathe their poison?"

"What should I do? Go hide in a hole? The world's full of stupid. Can't avoid it all."

"But you can steer clear of the worst parts. Volcanoes? Dungeons? Taverns full of crap-spewing assholes? Those are not my destinations of choice."

Latoya set down her cup with a solid *thunk*. "I don't run, Lynn. Not from dumb peckerwoods like that. They're dirt poor and they spend their days grubbing for food and grovelling at rich men's feet. They spend their nights not having sex ever and calling women sluts because they don't get to screw them. And when they really get depressed, they sniffle and rub their snotty noses and tell themselves, well, at least they weren't born brown-skinned."

"All right, you don't run. But don't you sometimes want to say, 'Fuck these terrible islands and their assortment of terrible people' and go back to Tavar?"

"Sometimes." She rubbed her nose meditatively. "But there are plenty of assholes there, too. I once met a man in a caravan going through the Ughaion Desert—religious kind of knob-head. He spent a whole evening praying that someone would tie me to a stake and, quote, fuck some woman back into me, unquote. Refused to listen to a word I said. So I guess he missed it when I told him that the course he'd charted was at least twenty-five degrees off, and he'd end up going through the widest part of the desert in the hottest part of the year if he didn't let me fix his math. Last time I saw him, he was plodding away from me towards five hundred miles of burning sand. Wonder how that worked out for him."

I grinned. I do love a happy ending. "You should tell Ariadne that story, if you haven't already. She bragged about you constantly while we were in Tavar—she could use some new material."

Latoya smiled, but it looked more like a wince in the dim flickering glow of the rush-lights, and I understood. "You brought me here for a good old-fashioned bitching-about-your-girlfriend session, didn't you?"

She toyed with her cup, sloshing the beer to and fro, which was a much better idea than drinking it. "You know something funny? Ariadne talks more about your mother than she ever talks about her own."

"Why is that funny? Melitta was evil. My mother wasn't, so far as I can recall."

"You really don't remember your mother?"

"No, actually, I decided that my life story wasn't pathetic enough, so I made up the not-remembering-my-mother thing to take it over the top. Fuck's sake, Latoya."

"Nothing? You remember nothing about her?"

"I didn't say that. I've got bits and pieces. Not the ones I would have chosen. Somehow, it was mainly the bad times that stuck."

"Bad times like what?"

"I don't know. Like the time my mother whipped the hell out of me because I dumped a bucket in the wrong place."

She blinked. "Because you dumped a bucket . . ."

"It was a special kind of bucket. It was a special kind of place. What happened was . . . look, who cares? We're talking about you and Ariadne. I'm guessing that when she brings up my mother, she doesn't have bucket-related trauma on her mind."

"No, she talks about visiting the kitchen. Playing with the two of you. Talks about how your mother would always save her a handful of dough to bake. I guess that remembering Elain is how she salvages part of her childhood, finds some memories that she doesn't have to drown. If she couldn't do that, she'd have to hate everything she comes from."

"*I* come from where she comes from."

"Which would be why she's all messed up about you." She tried another spoonful of the stew, gave up, and pushed the bowl away. "What with the guilt and the love and then more guilt. And the whole part where she murdered her mother for you. That hasn't gone away. She's just liquid inside. All contradiction and confusion. Lynn, do you really want her to rule Kila?"

I should have known I couldn't avoid this conversation forever. "Not especially. I want somebody to rule Kila, though. Ariadne's not my first choice, but she'll do fine as long as she has plenty of help."

"Who *is* your first choice?"

"You have to ask? Who's always my first choice when I'm handing out impossible thankless tasks?"

Latoya's eyebrows shot up, but she acknowledged the compliment with a nod. "I'd be the wrong choice. If you install a high queen from Tavar, it'll feel like an invasion, a conquest. That'd feed people a ready-made excuse to revolt. You need a Kilan on the big throne, if you want the isles quiet."

"I know. That's why I haven't brought it up. Trust me, if I could see a way to make it work, I'd be picking out your coronation clothes already. I can't, so Ariadne it is."

Out of reflex, I bounced the spoon in my hands, testing the weight to see whether it would be worth stealing. It wasn't. Cheap tin. "So that's why you're all wound up tonight? You're worried that you and Ariadne don't have a future if she's going to end up ruling Kila?"

"I thought you'd understand."

"I do understand. I just think panicking is kind of premature. It's not as if the end of the war is anywhere on the horizon. We could all be dead tomorrow, so maybe you and my sister should concentrate on having lots and lots of sex, instead of making long-term plans."

"Tell that to your sister. She's already pulling away from me—she just doesn't have the balls to say that's what she's doing. Sometimes we fight about stupid shit, sometimes she acts like I bore her. And the way she flirts with Regon—"

Her voice didn't break or wobble or anything as obvious as that, but she couldn't finish the sentence. I did the only useful thing that there was to do, which was to pour her another drink, and pat her back while she downed it.

"I don't think that she's actually interested in Regon," I said, as I rubbed. "He's just—you know—safer. She thinks that it would be less painful to have him and then lose him."

"I'm not going anywhere."

"Not yet, you aren't. But Ariadne's always getting ahead of herself. Like my mistress. I spend half my time dragging *her* back to the here and now."

The tavern didn't have any windows; the door stood open so that greasy smoke could escape. Chin resting in my cupped hands, I stared out through the gap at the twilight gloaming. It was tempting to picture Darren bursting through the door, yelling, *This was all a terrible mistake! My family is crap! Back to the ship forever!* But I don't like to waste my life in dreams.

Latoya drummed her fingers on the table. "I assign two guards to the captain for every one I put on you. Know why?"

"Is it because, unlike my mistress, I have some rudimentary ability to look after myself?"

She shook her head. "If we lost you, the captain would be wrecked. I don't know whether we could get her on her feet again, but we'd stand a chance, because she'd want to keep fighting. She'd at least want to try. But if we lost the captain . . ."

"You'd lose me too," I said. It wasn't exactly a question.

Latoya flicked her eyebrows to signal agreement. "Sometimes, I like to think I know you well enough to guess where you would go. If the captain got iced, I mean, and you lost your stomach for the fight. But then I figure that it doesn't matter how well I know you, considering how you operate. If the captain dies, you'll disappear, won't you?"

"I won't jump off a cliff, if that's what you mean."

"It isn't. What I mean is, you'll just fade away into the background, won't you? Find somewhere safe—or safer than this—and let life roll over your head. No more hero-making."

"Hell, Latoya, I don't know what I'd do. Sometimes I'm not even sure who I am, one day to another."

I tried the beer again. Still awful, but at least my tongue was going numb.

"Right," I said. "If we're not going to leave, I'd better get another couple of bottles of whatever this is. You almost never bitch about Ariadne, so you must have a lot of gripes saved up. Make a list while I'm at the bar."

CHAPTER TWELVE

The Lady Darren of the House of Torasan (Pirate Queen)

AS THE NIGHT wore on, it grew colder. Servants lit the torches, making orange light lick along the broad beams of the ceiling. The torches did nothing to heat up the cold hall, but they smoked and reeked and made the air taste of cinders. Between that and the uncomfortable stiffness of my new court clothes, I was beginning to feel decidedly peaky. It didn't help that Konrad kept calling for fresh barrels of wine, and the wines were getting darker and stronger by the hour.

Round about midnight, someone poured me a goblet of ferocious plum brandy strong enough to dissolve a brass telescope. I gripped it blearily as I watched the performers cavorting about in front of the high table. Over the course of the evening, we'd had jugglers, magicians, midgets, and a eunuch who sang a rude song about a dairymaid and a baker's boy while wearing a frilly blond wig and very tight pants. Now that everyone at the table was properly pissed, Konrad had brought out the dancing girls. Smooth-skinned and slender-limbed, they were, and every last one was dressed as though she had mislaid her entire wardrobe and had to improvise an outfit in a matter of minutes, using nothing but hair-ribbons and a couple of pins.

Back when I was twenty or so, the sight of those girls would have made my cheeks flame so hard that I would have had to put a tablecloth over my head or go and hide in the outhouse. Now I just watched, absent-mindedly concerned for the red-headed girl in the troupe. She was feeling chilly in her skimpy outfit. I could tell by the state of her . . . well, you know.

A hand clapped against my shoulder, and then Konrad's face was beaming into mine. "Enjoying the show? I ordered them for you specially."

"They're lovely," I said tersely, and took a gulp of brandy. That was a mistake; it nearly stripped the skin from my throat as it scorched its way down.

Konrad's eyes glinted. "Do you want a closer look?"

"I'm fine."

"Don't be shy, now. They certainly aren't."

"Really, Konrad. I'm fine."

"Oh, come on. No need to pretend that you aren't interested. What would you do if I called that red-head up here right now and got her to sit on your lap?"

"I would offer her a hot drink and a woolly blanket. They're going to catch pneumonia if they don't put on something warmer. Honestly, Konrad. I appreciate the thought, and all, but when you throw women at me, it's . . . well, it's kind of creepy."

Konrad turned to me. Too late, I realized that he intended to talk business, right there at the banquet table, while I was still bloated with brandy and rich desserts.

"I'm trying to make a point," he said. "I'm a man of the world, and you're not going to shock me, no matter how unusual your tastes. You don't have to give up women if you want to come home for good."

I blew out a long breath, nervous and relieved and apprehensive all at once. "I was wondering when you were going to get around to that."

"Well, let's stop dancing around the issue. I want to give you a pitch."

The red-head went into a jiggling, convulsive set of movements which made bits of her flop every which way. I wished that she would stop; the clinking of her jewellery was very distracting.

"Fine," I said. "Pitch away."

He settled back in his chair and steepled his fingers. "The Isle is struggling. You know that already. Father all but bankrupted us with his silly little wars. Year by year and season by season, we lost men and ships that we couldn't replace. It was Father's fault, but now it's my problem. My advisors tell me that you're a problem-solver."

I wondered whether Konrad had bothered to find out anything about me on his own, or whether his advisors had done all the research and given him a summary. I rubbed the filigree on my wine cup, noticing the splotches of tarnish that no one had bothered to scour away.

"I can give you a loan, if that's what you need," I said, tracing a decorative metal swirl. "Enough to buy new oxen and seeds before the spring planting. New nets and sails for the fishermen, too. I don't think anyone will ever wipe out the corsairs, but my fleet can drive them back, give you some breathing space."

"That's generous of you, and I appreciate the offer. But Torasan Isle is too far gone for simple remedies. You can't treat a sucking chest wound by draping a handkerchief over it, and I can't save the Isle with a breathing space and a few yokes of oxen. We have to be bold if we're going to rise up again."

"I thought you were going to get to the point."

He smiled at me, reached into his mantle, and took out a silver dagger with a hawk's-head crest. Gently, he set it down on the table between us.

Well, there it was. I drew in a long, shaky breath.

"I don't blame you if you want to make me beg," Konrad said. "Father threw you out like trash. It was cruel of him to do it, but it was also the worst mistake he ever made. Look at everything you've accomplished since he let you go. You renewed people's faith in the nobility—"

I fumbled with my goblet and nearly dropped it. "I did *what?*"

"Darren, think of what you've done. You went into exile naked and friendless, but Father couldn't strip away your bloodright, and look what your blood achieved. You rose from obscurity, from nothingness, by sheer force of will. It's the proof of what they tell us as children, that greatness is born. It's the fire in the soul, the glory in the blood—and it's in everything you do."

"Oh . . . crap." I fidgeted with my doublet sleeves. Spinner had hemmed the cuffs in a double row of chain stitch, complaining all the while that I would never appreciate the effort he was putting in. I'd already stained one cuff with mushroom sauce. He was going to pound me. "Konrad, don't get me wrong, that's nice to hear, but you don't know the full story. I've done some good, I hope, but I didn't do any of it alone."

He brushed that away. "Leaders never work alone. They ignite. They inspire. What matters is that you made it happen. You haven't just given hope to the common people, you've reminded them of what their rulers can and should be."

The dancing girls began a series of flying leaps, bare skin taking up the torchlight, so they almost looked like they were on fire themselves. I shifted my stare to the table. I'd seen enough people burning.

I wondered what Lynn was doing right then. Scrubbing out the galley, maybe—she had been talking about giving it a real down-to-the-wood cleaning. A clean galley meant food that wouldn't make sailors puke, and sailors who weren't puking were less likely to mutiny, or die on an enemy cutlass, or lose control of the ship in a storm. So her evening's work was more likely to benefit the war effort than mine.

One of the dancing girls jiggled up to the table and gave me a coy smile. I smiled back, weakly, before returning my attention to Konrad. "None of that explains why I should swear myself to your service."

"Because someone has to rule, and it can't be you. You can't govern from the deck of a pirate ship. And anyway, would you want to? You work very well as a folk hero, my sister, but as High Lady? I can't picture you putting down rebels or sentencing thieves."

"Why not? Because I'm such a delicate shrinking flower? Hell, Konrad, what do you think pirates *do*? I don't spend my time knitting lace doilies, you know."

He switched tactics. "All right, perhaps. But even if you could live with that part of the job, could you marry? Bear children? Could you be faithful to a husband—at least in public?" He glanced down the table at his wife, who was slumped in her chair snoring, and grimaced. "Of course, every lord in Kila has his concubines, but those relationships can never see daylight. I think you would find it difficult to keep a woman who always had to remember her place, who could never come out of the shadows."

The image that came to mind was of Lynn huddled in that closet in Melitta's room, Lynn too wrecked to even lift her head. *That* was a woman who knew her place, and that was something I never intended to see again.

"You're right," I said. "I'd be a disaster as High Lady and I don't want it anyway. But that doesn't mean I'm going to put you on the throne. I've got another candidate."

"Another candidate? Who would you . . . ah, I see." No flies on Konrad; he didn't need me to spell it out. "Ariadne of Bain?"

"She's got the pedigree, she's got the talent, she's got a universe of brains, and I don't like her enough to feel bad about giving her the worst job in the world."

Konrad frowned and rubbed his chin. "I see some advantages," he said after a few seconds' thought. "But the Lady Ariadne is practically an exile herself, now that her father's cousin rules the House of Bain. She has no lands of her own, no war chest, no council. Do you plan to change that? Will you take back the Bain stronghold on Bero for her?"

"Um. No. No, I will not. I plan to stay alive, you see, and attacking Bero isn't really in line with that goal. I'll set her up somewhere else. And don't ask where; I don't know yet. When the opportunity comes up, I'll take it."

"Very well. Here's the opportunity. Take it." He took a breath. "I'll marry her."

I stared at him, and my ulcer began to throb. I swear, I heard it talking to me in a snivelling kind of whine. "You'll do *what* now?"

"I'll marry her. Say the word, and I'll do it. I'll take her without a dowry and deed her half of all my holdings, and you can swear fealty to us both. I know it sounds like an uneven bargain, but Darren, think. With your fleet and your legend protecting the seas around the Isle, Torasan won't look like prey. We'll be the city on the hill. Once that happens, we can start to come to terms with the smaller houses. Some will want alliances. Some will agree to become vassal states in return for protection. We'd ask them to pay a tithe in men and ships, and your fleet would grow and grow. Don't you see? It's a beginning. You—"

"Just stop, Konrad. Stop!" My head, taking inspiration from my ulcer, throbbed as well. "I'm not going to chart out the conquest of Kila while we're having dessert. You're using lots of big words—and I'm drunk—and Ariadne's maybe in love with someone and maybe trying to seduce someone else—and hell and damnation, you're already married."

This time, he didn't even glance at the pale woman snoring in her chair. "Do you think that matters to either of us? Lassaline and I will both be happier if I set her free and send her back to her father. As for Ariadne's lovers—they're women, I take it? Well, let her bring them along. As long as she's discrete and doesn't give people any reason to talk, she can keep a harem and I won't give a damn. Hell, I'll turn down the bed for them. I told you I'm a man of the world."

I wondered whether Konrad would feel the same way if he knew that one of the potential members of Ariadne's harem was hung like a horse and had stubble on his chin.

My brother was *still* talking. "And then, my children with Ariadne would have a claim to the House of Bain. By the time they come of age, our forces might be strong enough to—"

"Konrad, that can't happen! She's barren."

I regretted the words as soon as I saw him recoil. Down at the far end of the table, Ariadne giggled. Konrad's eyes jerked to her—I think he was astonished that she could still laugh when she was so seriously broken.

Eventually, he mastered himself. "Well. Well, that's certainly . . ."

His voice trailed off. He blew out a breath, shook his head, and started again. "Well, that . . . complicates things. But . . . do you know? It might actually be all right. I have four sons already; my legacy is secure. Perhaps there would even be some advantages. Less domestic drama. Yes. I'll do it. I'll take her."

Ariadne was not my favourite person, but this was too much. "Oh, don't strain yourself. If you want to marry her, then ask her, say her hair looks nice, maybe there could be some flowers involved—but don't expect me to talk her into it. Not if you're going to treat her like damaged goods."

He looked at me in wonderment. "But she *is* damaged goods."

"Oh, go away and put your head in a fish. She bloody isn't."

"Darren, have you thought this through? You plan to make this woman the High Lady of Kila, yes? Well, if she's *barren*"—he almost choked on the word—"then there's only one way that can possibly happen. She'll need to have a *very* understanding husband at her side, one who already has heirs of his own. You know that. You have to know that."

People assume all the time that I know things just because those things are blatantly obvious. All too often, they're wrong.

I scowled, as though he'd offended me terribly by second-guessing my judgment. "Of course I know that, but it's still her choice. I'm not going to put her in a sack and drag her to the altar for you."

"All right. We can talk about that later. But you have your own choice to make." He set his hand over mine. "Sister, please. Take back your title and your name. Come home."

Home. I couldn't hold back a laugh—mind you, I didn't try all that hard. "Maybe I'm not a very big person, but I'm still not quite over that whole part where you banished me."

Konrad pounded the table, and it was my turn to jump. "*Father* banished you! Why should I pay the price for our father's stupidity? Why should Torasan pay?"

He breathed hard, his cheeks a furious red. "It's no good, Darren—you can't spend your whole life hiding from what you are. A phoenix can live among the sparrows, but it can't purge the fire from its veins. Stop denying that you are what you were born to be. Rise up, and take your place at the table."

The dancers had finished their act. Some of the audience clapped, the ones who were still sober enough to understand concepts like "dancers" and "finished." As the dancers headed for the door, my brother Talon leaned over to run his hand up a bare thigh. The girl shivered, but kept a fixed, frozen smile on her face, and walked a little faster.

"At least say you'll think about it," Konrad probed, his wine-flushed face far too close to mine. "Promise me."

"Sure," I said, shoving my chair back, away from the table where there was no place laid for Lynn and never would be. "I'll think about it a whole, whole lot."

AN EMPTY SEAT had opened up next to Ariadne. I collapsed into it and prodded her in the side. "How's it going here?"

"Quiet. I'm winning."

With a flourish, she rattled a dice-cup. Jada sat opposite her, looking sour and defensive and a little desperate, like all the other poor sods I'd seen trying to match Ariadne at koro.

Ariadne flicked her wrist. Two ivory dice bounced from the cup and clattered across the tabletop, coming to rest beside three others. Ariadne wasn't faking the silvery laugh any longer—she full-out cackled when she saw the result.

"House of the crescent moon!" she announced triumphantly. "And you didn't bother to hedge, so I get the full two hundred points and you can choke on it, worm. *Choke* on it, I say. Roll over and expose your belly in total submission."

"Bloody hell," I muttered. "How drunk are you?"

"How drunk?" She hummed to herself, thinking. "On a scale of one to ten, I am, approximately, monkey."

"How much did you drink?"

"That, I do not know. I cannot say. It is a mystery to all of us. But I can say this. There is a very big, very empty bottle of cherry wine over there, and it was full when I got started. All right, Jada darling, your turn."

She slid the dice-cup across the table. Jada contemplated it with a look of loathing, and shoved it back. "Whatever. You win. I give up."

Ariadne swept a small pile of silver coins into her palm while the onlookers groaned in disappointment.

"Do you always forfeit when you're losing?" Ariadne asked, as she arranged her winnings in neat stacks of five coins each. "No wonder you're pathetic at this. How far am I ahead—six hundred points? Even Darren usually does better against me, and her brain is made of marshmallow."

Jada shrugged. She was trying too hard to look like she didn't care, and she wasn't fooling me, so she sure as hell couldn't have been fooling anyone else. "It's just a stupid game."

"Sore loser, are we, buttercup?" Ariadne asked. Her cheeks were pink, pink, pink; her eyes bright with wine and wickedness. "You should work on that."

"Look, you had stupid good luck. Two sunbursts in a row, *and* crescent moon? Fluke."

"Is that so?" Ariadne licked a garnet-red drop of wine from one fingertip. "So I suppose if we played a game without the element of luck, you'd crush me."

"I'm just saying."

"Oh, I heard what you said. Now prove it."

Ariadne collected three cups and arranged them in a row, flipping every other one to make a pattern: upside down, right side up, upside down.

"Now this is very simple," she said. "You make three moves, you flip two cups every time, and when you're done all of the cups should be right side up. Like that."

She made three passes, each time turning over two cups. It took barely an instant, and when she was done, all the cups had their brims turned upwards. With one more quick motion, she flipped the middle cup, resetting the game.

"Your turn," she said. "How closely did you watch? Everybody keep an eye on her—make sure she doesn't cheat."

By now, we had quite an audience, with people all down the table craning their necks to see the game. I had vivid flash of memory—an archery competition when I was twelve, which most of the court came to watch, for lack of anything better to do on a rainy day. I lost spectacularly, and during the banquet that followed, the main topic of conversation was how badly I was going to disgrace Torasan when I was old enough to captain a ship. The general consensus was that the day after leaving the harbour, I'd trip over my feet, fall overboard, and get eaten by a manatee.

I hadn't done the protective-older-sister thing in a long time, but the instinct was still there.

"Listen, to hell with her," I told Jada. "Don't let her bully you. You don't have to play."

For a whole three seconds, I thought she was going to let me rescue her. There was something in her eyes that could easily have flickered into agreement, gratitude, relief. But she looked at the audience, and her face sealed over again.

"I am not an infant in need of your protection, pirate queen," Jada said. She dragged her chair up to the table. "Let's just get this stupid thing over with."

The next few minutes were painful for everyone. Jada flipped cups, paused, stared, started over, stared again, grimaced. I narrowed my eyes at the cups, trying to figure out where she'd gone wrong. Ariadne had started by flipping the middle cup and the one on the right, then the cups on either end . . . hadn't she? But Jada had done exactly the same thing . . . hadn't she? My vision was dissolving in a haze of strong liquor, the scene soft and smeared around the edges.

Jada tried again. She used exactly the same moves Ariadne had shown her, I knew it, I *knew* it, but when she was done, the three cups faced down, not up.

Ariadne shook her head sadly as she reached out with one hand to reset the game. "You do know the difference between up and down, don't you, sweetheart? I didn't think I had to spell that part out for you."

Jada stared at the cups. "It's not possible. It's a trick."

"Of course it's a trick. It's the Beggar's Flip, the oldest trick in the book." Once again, Ariadne's hands moved deftly, flipping cups. "It's transparent. It's infantile. It's the kind of thing I did to pass the time when I was in my cradle. You really haven't figured it out?" She finished the sequence, and once again, the three cups stood with brims upwards.

"Just ignore her, Jada," I said. "She's a bitch and there's no cure known to science. You don't have anything to prove."

Ariadne let out a stinging peal of laughter. "Oh, like hell she doesn't have anything to prove. Jada—darling—this is why your family won't trust you with a ship anymore, isn't it? Because you lack the reasoning skills that the gods bestowed upon the common crumpet? You must have been a disaster as a merchant captain. I bet the other traders slavered when they saw you coming. Brought out all their rotten apples and their moth-eaten wool, and sold you magic beans and hen's teeth."

Jada stared at her empty trencher, teeth clenched.

A few seats away, Gunnar guffawed. "You're not wrong!"

"All right, princess," I said, my last few shreds of patience blowing away with the passing breeze. "Put down the cup. You've had more than enough."

"No. My cup. You can't have it. Stop pawing at me, Darren. Go away. Ye gods, why are you such a wet blanket? Do you hate joy? Is there anything that makes you happy, other than boinking my sister?"

"Oh . . . *sod it,* Ariadne." She'd said it in her brightest, loudest, most penetrating tone, and faces all down the table turned in our direction.

"Because she is, you know," Ariadne went on blithely, to everyone in earshot. "Boinking my sister, I mean. Vigorously. Frequently. I'm a bit surprised that their cabin floor hasn't caved in yet."

Mustering my courage, I managed to look up and scan the room for some helpful person. A captain of the guard stood at attention by the door. He seemed sober enough, and I snapped my fingers to summon him over.

"I know, I know, it's confusing," Ariadne said to Jada, although no one, least of all Jada, had asked. "Everyone thinks I'm an only child. That's because Gwyneth is a bastard half-blood, so, legally speaking, she doesn't exist. She existed enough for my mother to beat the living crap out of her whenever she felt like it, though."

"Can I be of service, my lady?" the guard captain said, leaning down beside me.

"Oh. Uh. Yes. Please see if you can find my man Regon. He's about half a head shorter than me. Scar on his lip, no beard. Ask him to meet me at the main stair?"

"Certainly, lady. Right away."

"Thanks. Your name?"

"We met at the dock. I'm Milo."

"Milo. Buy yourself a drink afterwards."

I flipped him a coin, which he caught with a practised hand before jog-trotting out of the room.

"It's not like I'm worried about her," Ariadne announced to her growing audience. "For one thing? Darren's a cream puff. For another? Gwyn has Darren wrapped around her little finger, and more power to her. The gods alone know how hideously the pirate queen would screw up if my baby sister wasn't there to hold her by the hand. It's just that Gwyneth's always with Darren now. Always. They're always together. It's just that . . ."

Her voice died out, and she leaned over the table, breathing raspily. I took the opportunity to grab her by the shoulders and yoink her up from the chair.

"All right, you're done," I said. "Bollocks and balls, you're a prat when you're drunk."

"Oh, I'm a prat?" Her knees almost buckled when she stood, but she grabbed a fistful of my shirt to steady herself. With her free hand, she slapped me across the face.

"Ow," I said by reflex, though it hadn't hurt. Ariadne had the upper arm strength of vanilla custard compared to most of the women in my life.

"You asshole," she said—she was crying freely now. "They kept us apart all our lives. You couldn't have let me have a year with my sister? One miserable little year before you swallowed her up?"

"All right, you know what?" I panted. She was deadweight, and it was all I could do to keep her from sliding bonelessly to the floor. "If you have to take the piss out of me, could you do it pretty much anywhere other than here?"

There was a soft call—"Captain!"—and when I turned, Regon was waiting at the side door. Gratefully, I lugged Ariadne over and dumped her in his arms. "Start working your way upstairs. If—no, *when* she pukes, try to stay out of the splash zone."

He nodded. "You coming?"

"In a minute."

I expected a lot of wolf-whistles and knowing winks when I went back to the table. Fortunately, a distraction had arrived in the form of more food. Servants passed out little dishes of nuts and olives and anchovies, curd cheese and redcurrants, prunes and medlars. They'd keep bringing snacks of this kind every hour or so until dawn, to fortify everyone for a solid night of drinking.

Jada was playing with a few olives, and didn't look up when I approached, but she stiffened. I told myself firmly that I didn't feel hurt.

"Listen, Ariadne's absolutely bladdered," I said. "She didn't mean anything that she was saying."

Jada crushed an olive between finger and thumb, watching the brine trickle out and drip down her hand. "It doesn't matter."

"Like hell it doesn't matter. She was a total twat and she deserves to be thumped. But she'll apologise to you tomorrow, or I'll hang her out the window by her feet until she rethinks all her life decisions."

I snagged a handful of redcurrants, and was about to go when Jada lifted her head. "So, you do have a new girl."

"Oh. Um. Well, you see . . . there are certain . . . it's sort of . . . yes. All right, yes, yes I do. I'm with Ariadne's younger half-sister. I'd ask you to keep it quiet, but there wouldn't be much point, since Princess Prattlepants just announced it to all the world. I'm sorry I didn't tell you before. It's not that I don't trust you, it's just complicated."

"Why apologise? It's not like people make a habit of telling me things." Her gaze snapped to mine, eyes wide and bloodshot, voice tight and trembling. "Father didn't tell me when he picked out my future husband. I found out by accident months later, when I was going through his mail."

The only thing I found surprising in that story was that our father had remembered Jada's existence for long enough to arrange an engagement in the first place. It did make clear how generally shitty it was to be Jada: the youngest child, the afterthought, overlooked and ignored, the butt of every joke.

I cleared my throat. "Jada—"

"What?"

I meant to pop the big question, there and then. *Did you kill our father? Did you spike his roast chicken with hemlock and watch him froth and writhe on the floor? Because if so, frankly, I don't much care, but Konrad is a different story.*

I don't know why I lost my nerve. It was something about the soft downiness of the back of her neck as she bent over the table. She was so young, still.

Instead, I said, "Jada, do you love it here?"

She gave me a dead, flat, are-you-kidding-me sort of stare, and I went on quickly. "Because if you want another option—well, I don't know if you've heard, but piracy is a growth industry these days."

Her eyebrows went up and up. "You want me to be a pirate?"

"What *I* want doesn't matter. I'm just saying, if the time comes that you need a place to go—whether that's tomorrow or in ten years' time—I'll find a place for you."

Maybe it's because I was drunk, or maybe it was a trick of the light, but it did seem for an instant that her face had softened, as if she was considering it. But then her mouth twisted into one of her brittle smiles, and she gave me a punch on the arm that hurt too much to be purely playful. "How are you going to make good on that promise if you disappear again?"

"I won't disappear. I don't know what's going to happen with—well, all of this." I waved a hand to indicate Konrad, the Great Hall, the Isle in general. "I don't know how much time I'm going to spend at the Keep from now on, and I sure as hell don't know whether I'll swear fealty to Konrad. But I'm not going to disappear from your life. The House of Torasan is a screwed-up family, but I'm still a part of it. That's not the kind of thing that anyone can change."

I expected another snort, but it didn't happen. She reached for her goblet, and, without breaking eye contact, she raised it in salute. "Welcome home, Lady Darren of Torasan."

She drank and set the goblet down. After only a brief moment of hesitation, she reached out to give my hand a quick squeeze. "I'm glad you're here."

CHAPTER THIRTEEN

Lynn

"YOU'RE MESSING WITH me."

"No, it's true."

"Oh, come on. The captain does not *juggle,* you lying shitbird—"

"Not for you, she doesn't. There are skills which my mistress will demonstrate for the benefit and enjoyment of the public, and there are skills which my mistress will demonstrate for *my* benefit and enjoyment—and there's very little overlap between the two lists."

I drained my latest cup of the putrid beer. It still tasted like something that had been left out in a field for three weeks and then strained through a sock, but I'd managed to choke down enough of it to get a buzz. I felt, if not happy, at least anaesthetized, and pleasantly smug.

"You are such a pushy little brat," Latoya said, rolling a coin across the backs of her knuckles. "Remember the day we met? I was there on the dock in Talhim when you and the captain came down the gangplank."

"I have been up and down one hell of a lot of gangplanks. Do you really expect me to remember one specific . . . wait. Was I riding Darren piggyback?"

"Mmm-hmm."

"Damn, I do remember that. She was being really whiny about it."

"You were hanging on to her ears."

"She has big ears. They make good handles. Besides, I had to hang onto something, and I didn't think she'd want me to use her boobs in public. Is that Corto over by the door?"

All through the night, the tavern had been growing more crowded. The last men to arrive had to take their drinks outside, and the barkeep stood in the doorway, arms folded, in case anyone tried to make off with a cup. They were singing out there, stamping their feet in time to the chorus. Corto shouldered his way through clusters of raucous men to our table near the back.

"The locals aren't that friendly, are they?" he asked, dropping onto a stool.

"They are all gigantic dickwads," I said. "Latoya won't let me murder them horribly."

"I don't want you to start a riot while I'm trying to relax. Once we kill this bottle, we can reopen discussions about murdering them horribly." She sloshed a third cup full. "Come on, Corto. Scar your stomach with some of this pisswater and tell us the news from the Keep."

"No news, except the captain's already lonesome. She sent me to see how you were doing, Lynn. Guess I'll tell her that you ran off to party with Latoya the moment she was out of sight."

"You want me to add you to my murder list?" I offered. "I can."

"Pace yourself. It may be a long haul. The captain gets all teary-eyed every time she sees a familiar rock, so I think we're going to be here a while. You don't want to slaughter everyone on the Isle the first night."

"Says *you.*" I put my head down on the table, cheek against its sticky surface. "Stupid island stole my pirate. Everyone on it should die."

The buzz had drained away, leaving a sick, swimming dizziness behind. The smoke from the sputtering rush-lights stung my eyes. I squinched them shut.

"You done for the night, killer?" Latoya's hand ruffled my hair. "I want one last drink before I drag your lightweight ass back home. That work for you?"

"Fine."

I settled my head more comfortably on my folded arms. Above me, Latoya and Corto talked quietly. I didn't bother to follow the conversation, just let myself drift with the rise and fall of their voices.

The whole scene was falling away. The curses and sniggers of the men at the bar, the stench of piss and rotten meat, the tuneless singing outside, all faded. There was just the warmth of my friends on either side of me, the good salt-and-smoke smell of them, the promise of getting home soon. I let myself sink. A warm green wave rolled across my mind, rolled and crested and—*don't you dare fall asleep!*

My eyes shot open. Some kind of shockwave had gone through me, a jolt of sheer panic that rattled my heart around my ribcage. And now I was awake, I was almost frenzied, my body trembling with the same desperate energy that makes you jerk your hand off a red-hot stove.

Some savage instinct, deep in my hindbrain, had ripped into me with sharp little claws of bone, tearing down the curtain of booze and boredom between me and the universe.

Don't fall asleep.

You will die if you fall asleep here.

I straightened up. My lips were painfully dry. I licked them, felt the flakes of skin come away. Every inch of me was tight, stretched, and tingling.

Latoya put a hand on Corto's arm, stopping him mid-sentence. "Lynn—everything all right?"

"No." I looked around. Greasy plumes of smoke trailing from the hearth. Sour-faced men muttering over their ale-cups. What was I missing?

"Lynn . . . ?"

"*Quiet.*"

My eyes were closed when that surge of panic hit, so it couldn't have been something I'd seen. I closed my eyes again, pressed the heels of my hands into the sockets, stopped breathing, stopped thinking, and listened.

Outside the tavern door, they were starting yet another round of the song they'd been singing all night:

> *In the chicken run, under sunset skies,*
> *All the birds goggle up with their bead-black eyes*
> *And they strut in the yard with dainty feet*
> *Too proud to believe they could ever be meat . . .*

They were terrible singers, but they all knew the words. They knew them by heart.

> *. . . See the cockerel preen, see his feathers shine*
> *As he lords it over the ducks and swine.*
> *Lazy and fat, he'll sit and gloat*
> *Till the butcher's hand is around his throat . . .*

I grabbed Corto—got his bad wrist by mistake—ignored his pained yelp. "Have you heard anyone else singing?"

"Lynn, you bitch, I could still lose this arm—"

"*Just answer me.* Have you heard anyone else singing tonight?"

He stared at me, confused. "They're singing all over the village."

> *. . . And the butcher swings, and the hatchet hacks*
> *And the blood drools out like red red wax . . .*

"What song?"

"What do you mean, what song?"

"What song are they singing all over the village? Is it *that* song?"

> *. . . And the earth is pink with the dying sun,*
> *As the chickens follow him one by one . . .*

By now, Latoya was listening too, and understanding flickered across her face in one sudden flash. She stood up without a word, threw a handful of coins down on the table and stalked towards the door. Corto still looked baffled, but he tossed down his drink and hurried after her.

> *. . . And they flap and thrash, and they cackle and squawk*
> *And they peck and they scratch—but a hen's no hawk.*
> *When the sun goes down on the killing day*
> *They'll learn too late that they can't fly away . . .*

A man in a ratty dogskin cap leered up from a crowded table as we passed. It shouldn't have been enough to scare me—*wouldn't* have been enough, on an ordinary day—but a thin bitter voice was in my head now, asking me how I could have forgotten how easy it is to die.

Outside, chilly fog filled the narrow alleys, the damp of it like a long tongue, licking. All around us, invisible in the fog, men were singing. A raucous pack at the end of the street howled the words and stamped in time to the rhythm. A trio of old men sang in thin, quavering voices. A young boy's voice was high and clear, but feverish with emotion, terrible fear or terrible hate.

I caught myself against a post and tried to catch my breath. Latoya touched my shoulder, not saying anything, not needing to—just reminding me that we didn't have a second to waste.

"All right," I said hoarsely. "Corto, we're heading for the ships. Don't catch anyone's attention. Don't look anyone in the eye. And don't run, but walk fast. I've been so stupid, and now it may already be too late."

CHAPTER FOURTEEN

The Lady Darren of the House of Torasan (Pirate Queen)

THE TRIP FROM the Great Hall to our bedroom was unpleasant for everyone involved. Ariadne stopped once to puke behind a tapestry, once to lean out of a window and gulp night air. When we had to climb the stairs, she swayed and stumbled and eventually gave up, plonking down on her backside right in the middle of the flight. Regon and I had to carry her the rest of the way.

By the time we reached our room, I was thoroughly sick of her. I would have cheerfully served her up to a pack of man-eating wolves right then—stuck her on a plate and put little sprigs of parsley around her and everything. I had to settle for dumping her on the floor as soon as we got inside.

It was left to Regon to help her into bed and pull the coverlet over her. She was a mess, gown sodden with sweat around the neck and under the arms, and Regon frowned at her doubtfully. "Are we going to stay awake and watch her?"

"We are not going to stay up and watch her."

"What if she sicks up and chokes on it?"

"Well, I don't know about you, but I'm planning to laugh and point."

I spun around before I yanked off my tunic and trousers, more to hide my fury than to preserve my modesty. Regon had seen me naked countless times, and it wouldn't matter if Ariadne saw, since I would be killing her anyway. Once I'd stripped down to my shirt, I tried to fold my court clothes, made a mess of it, tried again, did even worse. I gave up, sort of rolled the clothes into a ball and kicked them into a corner.

When I turned around to find some place to hang my cutlass belt, Ariadne was sitting up in bed, looking vaguely repentant. "Darren?"

"Princess."

"Would I be right in thinking that I made something of an ass of myself tonight?"

"You would not be wrong."

"I feel that something like an apology should pass my lips."

"Oh, it's far too late for that. Tomorrow at breakfast, while you're nursing the mother of all hangovers, I'm going to march you in front of Jada and you are going to grovel as you have never grovelled before."

"Give her a break, captain," Regon said. "How many times have you got yourself pissed and acted like an idiot?"

"Plenty. When I was a kid. Not lately."

"That time at Madame Lydia's . . ."

"Was an aberration. And besides, I thought we had a gentlemen's agreement that you weren't going to mention it anymore. Here, catch."

I threw a cushion at him. He caught it and tucked it behind Ariadne, then rolled her on her side, as he'd done for me more times than I cared to remember. Ariadne's eyes were closed and her cheeks had gone slack. She snuggled unconsciously into the down comforter.

"Know something?" Regon said. "It was a hell of a relief when you stopped going through that charade every time we stopped at a brothel."

I bristled. "What do you mean, 'charade'?"

"Oh, the whole routine. How you'd pick out the prettiest girl and swagger into a back room as if you were actually going to touch her . . ."

"I did! Before Lynn and I were a thing, I liked scoring some easy sugar just as much as the rest of you."

"Captain. You always brought a book."

He smiled at me over his shoulder—the same easy, understanding smile he'd shown me my first day at sea, when I was forced to ask him whether "starboard" meant left or right. "Don't worry, your secret's safe with me. I'll swear with my hand on my heart that you're the biggest horndog in the western seas, if that's what you want people to think."

"I think my reputation as a horndog is pretty secure, considering how many dancing girls Konrad tried to fling into my lap tonight."

He laughed, then grew solemn. "You're not going to take up arms for your brother, are you?"

I made a rude noise, but when my thoughts caught up with my feelings, I paused. "I don't know. He has some plans which are . . . not completely stupid, I guess. I don't like them, but I'm not going to rule anything out until Lynn and I talk it over."

"Will Lynn hate these plans as much as you do?"

I pictured it. Konrad as the High Lord of Kila. Ariadne as his fawning, tittering bride, never able to be herself except behind closed doors. Me as a Torasan captain and Konrad's sworn vassal, doing my best not to roll my eyes when he gave me a stupid order. It wasn't the worst thing that could happen, but it did not take any mental effort to guess how Lynn will feel.

"She will hate these plans so very much more. Problem is, our end game is to take over Kila . . . and I can't think of a way of doing it that Lynn won't hate. We might have to look for the least bad option."

We laid out our bedrolls on the floor a few feet apart: sheepskins on the bottom against the stone flagstones, then a wool rug and a quilt for each of us. I'd slept in much less comfortable places. Stretched out, head resting on my folded arms, I listened to the logs popping on the low-burning fire.

Regon's voice came through the darkness when I was already half asleep. "Captain?"

"Mmm-hmm?"

"It's kind of nice to see you again."

"You see me every day."

"I mean, *this* you. I was proud, you know, as boy and man, to sail with her ladyship Darren of Torasan, captain in the service of the lord of the Isle. I'd be proud to sail with her again, if that's the way the wind blows."

He fell asleep almost at once after that, and I was left to stare at the ceiling, and try to swallow the lump in my throat.

I WOKE WITH a jolt, opening my eyes to blackness, and found that I was gripping my long knife. I didn't know what had woken me up, but I didn't question it—just rolled sideways and came up in a crouch.

The next second, I knew what had woken me. The door was creaking open, an inch at a time, leather hinges dragging.

I forced myself to stay still. Chances were, this late night intruder was a kitchen girl who wanted to offer me hot spiced milk with honey. Bludgeoning her to death with a table leg would be inappropriate. But my heart kept pounding like a dizzy drum, and an instant's wild thought told me why: No glow of candlelight under the door. I couldn't think of any reason why a kitchen maid would come around distributing snacks in total darkness.

There was a creak of the mattress and a loud snore as Ariadne turned over. With aching slowness, I drew my knife from its sheath.

The door was half open now. Thin fingers, silvery in the moonlight, curled around the edge of the wood. I tensed and lunged.

I was just about airborne when I heard the hissing whisper. "*Mistress!*"

It was too late for me to check my motion, but somehow I managed to change direction mid-leap, crashing into the wall instead of the intruder. The impact knocked the beans out of me, and I blinked away stars as I rammed my knife back into its sheath. "Lynn, what's wrong?"

She slipped inside the room, followed by a larger shadow that moved soundlessly over the flagstones. Latoya, of course. While Latoya was silent, Lynn was breathing in quick gasps, as if she'd been running not long before.

"Get dressed," she said. "And get armed. We need to hurry."

I stooped, groped, and found a bundle of cloth. Hoping that they were my clothes rather than Ariadne's, I set to work inserting limbs into the appropriate holes. "Do we have time for an explanation?"

"Once we're moving. Latoya, what is it?"

Latoya had lifted Ariadne into a more-or-less sitting position on the bed, but her head lolled limply, and even when Latoya gave her a good hard shake, she didn't do more than twitch. Latoya bent, sniffed Ariadne's breath, and then trained an accusing stare on me. "What did you do to her?"

"Torasan cherry wine," I said, jerking on a boot. "It's the great equalizer. Turns everyone into morons, then makes them sleep like the dead."

"She picked a hell of a night to experiment." Latoya scowled down at Ariadne's floppy doll-like form. "How long will you give me to get her conscious?"

Lynn blew out a frustrated breath. "Take five minutes and see what you can do, but after that, we're leaving, even if we have to carry her. Does that work for you?"

"I'll make it work. Any water in here?"

"Jug on top of the washbasin," I said. "Is Regon up?"

"He is now," Regon said from the other side of the room. No noise of hurried dressing. Regon always slept in his clothes. "How did you two make it past the gate guards?"

"That's the point," Lynn said. "There are no guards on the gate."

"The hell you say!"

"The hell I do say. Darren, if you want to kick me, I would support that decision. I made a stupid mistake and we might all end up dead as a result."

"All right, stop torturing yourself," Latoya said. She was bending over Ariadne, slapping her cheeks with a damp rag. "It's no help now. Take a deep breath and get in the game. *There* we go."

Ariadne bucked off the bed, choking, and Latoya gave her back an encouraging pat. "You awake?"

"Hell and damnation," Ariadne stuttered out. "You sadistic bitch, what in the name of gods' little apricots do you think you're . . ."

Latoya put a stop to this by the simple expedient of upturning the jug over Ariadne's head. As she sputtered, Latoya scooped her up, set her on her feet, and threw a blanket around her.

While this was going on, I fumbled my way into my leather gambeson. When I tried to start lacing it up, Lynn batted my hands away and took over. I was glad to let her do it; my fingers were cold.

"Look," I said as she worked. "I know you don't want to get into any long conversations, but while we're just standing around here, maybe you could give me some idea what—"

She jerked a knot tight. "Why didn't Alek give you the name of the traitor?"

"What?"

"Alek. Dying on the beach. Telling you to warn your father about the traitor. Why didn't he give you the name?"

I blinked. "Well, he was . . . I don't know, he was leading up to it."

"Why? To build up the suspense? To add a little dramatic flair? He was dying. His lungs were shredded. With every breath he took, he was tearing his own chest apart. So why did he waffle around talking about *One of us* and *One of our own*? Why not just give you the name?"

"Because . . . well, because . . . ." My tired mind suddenly focused. "Because the name would mean nothing to me. The traitor was somebody I'd never met."

"Exactly. Now, remember, Alek *knew* he had been betrayed. How did he know?"

"Oh crap," I breathed. It was so, so simple. A warship full of badly fed and badly treated sailors, ruled by a casually brutal captain. "It was a mutiny. Alek was stabbed by one of his own men. But my father—"

"Was murdered at the same time, because this wasn't just a mutiny. The peasants of Torasan Isle are rising up. When Latoya and I were in the tavern . . . there's no time for details, but some men were singing—"

"That stupid song about killing chickens?"

"Not just a song. A signal. The song isn't about chickens, Darren."

Pictures flashed in my brain in quick succession: tapestries, weapons, tunics, ceremonial daggers, all emblazoned with the same feathered crest. The symbol of my house. The Torasan hawk.

My stomach clenched into a tight, cold ball. "You think they're coming after my family? Tonight?"

Latoya looked up from shoving Ariadne's feet into a pair of too-large boots. "Have we mentioned that there were no guards on the gate?"

"You mean . . . but they . . . why are we standing here with our thumbs up our asses? We have to bar the gates! Now!"

"It won't make any difference," Lynn said. She gave the laces of my gambeson an extra yank and double-knotted the top, the way I liked it. "The ringleader's already inside the keep."

"How do you know?"

"I heard his name. So did you. I was just too lost in my own stupid head to understand. Remember the last thing Alek said, before his lungs filled with blood? He said, 'Darren, it was my—'. He didn't mean *my sister,* or *my son.* He was trying to say, 'It was Milo.'"

Somehow or other, the room had grown a little brighter. Regon, who stood by the window, silently beckoned us over. Lynn and I joined him, looking down to the courtyard where, just hours before, I'd listened to a hungry servant sing about how much he hated me without understanding a word.

The gates of the Keep were wide open, and the courtyard was packed with people. With a thousand torches casting an orange-red glow, the milling throng looked like a blob of liquid hot metal quivering in a crucible, about to spill, consume, and burn.

I sucked in a long breath of ash-smelling air. "So it's a revolt."

"No." Lynn met my eyes. "It's a revolution."

PART THREE

THE FLIP

CHAPTER FIFTEEN

Lynn

IT WAS DARREN who broke the silence. "Lynn, my sword belt."

It was hanging neatly on a chair. Darren always hung up her sword belt, even on days when she was so tired that she just let her clothes plop to the ground when she undressed.

I brought it to her. She whipped it around her waist, buckled, and adjusted the fit, checking to see that she had a clear draw both for cutlass and main-gauche.

"You all right?" I asked, watching her hands. They were shaking, but no worse than they usually did before a fight.

"I don't know. We should probably talk about it for half an hour before we do anything useful. Yes, that's an excellent plan." She gave a final tug to her belt, then squared her shoulders. "So. Speaking of plans, do we have one of those?"

"I am inclined to go with an old classic. Let's run like hell."

"How? If the rebels took the gates . . ."

"We'll leave the same way that Latoya and I came in. Along this hallway, out the window at the end, jump to the stable roof, shimmy along the ridge beam on our stomachs, climb the battlement to the northwest drum tower, and lower ourselves down the other side. Then we go through the outer wall. In related news, the outer wall has a person-sized hole in it now. It's amazing what you can do with a sledgehammer when you're in a terrible mood. Let's get moving. Latoya should take point . . ."

I had Darren by the arm, drawing her towards the door, but she tore herself free. "Wait a minute."

"We don't have a minute."

"But what about my family?"

Damn, damn, *damn.* I'd hoped to keep Darren moving so quickly that she wouldn't have time to ask that question. I tried to sidestep. "We can talk about that as we go."

"Balls." She took a step backwards. "Don't give me that, Lynn. That's not how you operate. Once we start moving, there won't be any detours. You have a ten-point escape plan engraved in your brain in letters of fire, and there's no way in hell you'll let me improvise."

It was entirely inconvenient how well Darren knew me. I glanced at the window frame, where yellow light from the rebels' torches licked along the stone. I shouldn't have told Darren about the revolt. I should have crawled beneath her covers naked, and asked her in a breathless whispery voice to take me down to the *Banshee* and do unspeakable things to me. She'd have tossed me over one shoulder and started running and we'd have reached the harbour in twenty seconds flat. A little less if she didn't bother to put on her trousers, which was a real possibility if I was breathless and whispery enough.

"I can't just abandon them," Darren said, voice wobbly. "They're pricks, I know, but they still don't deserve to be murdered at the dinner table, and—"

"Darren."

"What?"

"Shut up *now* and follow me."

"No, Lynn, just listen—"

I slapped her hand away. "I will not just listen. I will not follow the twisted paths of your tortured logic and I will not nod at you understandingly and I will *not* continue with this conversation. I am not going to do anything except get out of here, this very minute, and you are going to follow me because *we do not have time for this, Darren.*"

Why, in a room full of people, was I the only one making noise? I raised my eyebrows pointedly at Regon, but he just shrugged and studied the toes of his boots. Ariadne, who was leaning back into the broad curve of Latoya's chest, stared at nothing, mouth agape. Latoya herself looked bored, more than anything.

Were none of them the least little bit interested in staying alive? Or was I the only one who really deep down understood that we weren't immortal?

"I'm not going to turn tail and run when my family needs me the most," Darren said. It might have sounded impressive, if she hadn't grimaced in pain right afterwards, and let out a beery belch. Typical. She'd barely been away from the ship for sixteen hours, and already she'd managed to play merry hell with her stomach ulcer by stuffing herself with cakes and cheese and swilling down strong liquor. Even if there hadn't been a revolution, she would have been in for a rough night. I tried to remember why I'd let her out of my sight in the first place, and didn't come up with an answer that made a lick of sense.

"Thousands of people need you," I said through gritted teeth. "And guess what? They need you to get off of this island alive. They need you to *not* do a heroic swan dive into an inferno, no matter how dashing you think you'd look while doing it."

She flushed purple. "You think this is an ego trip for me, is that it?"

"What did you fail to understand about the words, *I will not continue with this conversation?*"

"My family. What did you fail to understand about *that?* They're my *family!*"

"They're the people who threw you out homeless and penniless because you kissed a girl."

"My father threw me out—"

"And your sisters and brothers stood by and watched it happen, and none of them raised a finger to help you, and it messed you up in ways I'm still trying to fix! Don't kid yourself—they could have helped if they'd given half a damn."

"I thought we didn't have time for a conversation."

"We don't. Let's go."

"*You* go." Fumbling for her cutlass hilt, she headed for the door. "All of you. Take Ariadne and get back to the ship. I'll meet up with you after I—"

"After you what? Get hacked into three thousand pieces for the greater glory of Torasan?" I grabbed for her, caught an elbow, and clung. "You know, I think I'm pretty patient about all your self-destructive bullshit, but I will not let you die for this. Not for this."

Down in the courtyard, new fires blazed. In the sudden hard light, I saw Darren's face turn to steel.

"Latoya," she said. "Grab Lynn and run for the docks."

"Latoya, if you even *think* about grabbing me, I will end you here and now." By now, my voice was shrill enough to cut glass. Serve Darren right if my shrieking made her ears bleed. "Darren, listen to me. No, *listen.* There is nothing you can accomplish here, you can't take down a whole rebel army single-handed—"

"But I can get a few people out."

"Who? Who here is worth the risk?"

I said it without thinking, and realized my mistake a second too late. Darren nodded slowly.

"So that's it," she said. "You don't think they deserve to be saved."

Oh, fuck everything and everyone, twice, backwards, with a rusty spoon and a cantaloupe. "I don't think they deserve *you.*"

"Why not? Because they're a bunch of sadists who torture the peasants just for shits and giggles? Because they have it coming?"

"I didn't say that." I'd thought it, but I hadn't said it. "Since you bring it up, though—this rebellion didn't come out of nowhere. Your father spent his whole reign working out of the 'How to Be a Really Shitty Leader' playbook. Sooner or later, there was bound to be a reckoning. Torasan caused this. Let Torasan pay."

"Why shouldn't I pay?"

"Because you're not one of them."

"Why? Because they banished me? You think that somehow makes me righteous? I would have stayed in my father's service if I'd had the choice. And if I had stayed, do you think I would have gone against him? Fought the tide? Hell, no. I would have said yes-sir-no-sir just like always and I would have followed his orders. I'm no better than my siblings, Lynn, and if they deserve to die tonight—"

"You *are* different, you stupid ass." There was a pressure on my chest and in my throat that barely let me get the words out. "If you don't understand why, I'd be happy to explain it in lots and lots of detail *somewhere far away from here.*"

"Different or not, I'm not innocent! If anyone is blameless here, it's—"

"The children."

Ariadne had pulled herself together. She wobbled two steps forward, still clutching Latoya's arm. "If the rebels take the Keep, will they kill the Torasan children?"

Darren took a shaky breath. I doubt she'd thought of it until that second, but she knew the answer as well as I did.

"Probably," she said. "I think so, yes. That's what happened when Kai of Jiras took the citadel at Yag Sin Tor. Same with the sack of Arraval. It's one of those proud old wartime traditions. Don't leave children alive who might grow up to avenge their parents."

Ariadne turned to me, squinting through her headache, and shrugged. "Well."

"Well *what*?" I snapped.

As if I didn't know what she meant. As if I didn't know that I had just lost the argument.

"Well, I suppose it's high time that we all go to the kitchen and learn how to bake a peach flan—what do you think I mean? We're not going to let these thugs butcher a bunch of babies, surely. Latoya, my love, are you up for a night of heroics?"

Already, there was a rhythmic movement in the shadows, as Latoya, loop by loop, uncoiled her anchor chain. Behind her, Regon twirled an unsheathed knife between his fingers.

I know when I am beaten. I can tell, because when I'm beaten, I get consumed by overwhelming fury that makes me want to go burn down a few mid-sized villages.

"Fine," I spat. "Who's going to take Ariadne back to the ship while the rest of us are busy being unforgivably stupid? Regon?"

Darren glanced into the dark of the hallway. "You should take her, Lynn. I don't want to drag you into something that—"

"With all due respect, Mistress, bite me."

Regon half-raised a hand. "I'll take her."

"The hell you will," Ariadne said. "Nobody will. I may not be much use tonight, but you can't spare someone just to babysit me, and you know it. Let's go."

Worse and worse. "Ariadne, you're liquored to the eyeballs. You can't possibly—"

"Keep up? Yes I can. Because I have to. Simple as that."

"But—"

"I promise I won't get in your way."

"I'm not going to—"

"I'll tell you what you're not going to do. You're not going to stand there and yip objections until the whole Keep is aflame. We don't have time to debate, remember?"

We did not, in fact, have time to debate. Each moment that we stood there bitching at each other, our chances of surviving the night grew fainter. For that reason, and that reason alone, I did not punch first Darren and then Ariadne in their respective faces and screech at them both for their heartbreaking naivety.

Too furious to talk, I spun on my heel and led the way from the room, setting a fast pace through dim stone corridors. Darren must have sent Latoya after me, because she caught me up seconds later, her chain chinking softly as its loose end swung free.

"You were no help at all," I snapped at her. "In case you were wondering."

She shrugged, understanding but unapologetic. "It's not like your sister's wrong."

IT MADE LITTLE to no sense that I was leading the way, since I didn't have a clue where we were headed. Darren figured this out after I'd stalked down two or three hallways. She called a halt, got her bearings, and turned us around. We set off in the opposite direction.

Darren opened doors as we passed them by, checking bedrooms and cursing softly when she found them empty.

"Nobody went to bed except for us," she said. "Everyone else must be downstairs drinking."

"That's why the rebels struck on a banquet night," Regon said. "Have you ever known a noble who would leave a boozer before dawn?"

Ariadne looked up through bleary eyes. "Hey."

"I mean real nobles. You and the captain don't count."

"Well, my brothers picked a hell of a night to play to type." Darren ran a hand through her hair, ruining someone's valiant attempt to comb and style it, leaving it shaggy and windswept once more. "If they were all in the Great Hall when the rebels got through the gates—"

I caught her arm to silence her, and for once, she shut up without demanding an explanation. Seconds later, she nodded, letting me know that she too had heard the approaching footsteps. We drew back into a shadowed alcove just before a small band of men reached the top of the stairs.

They were armed with boat hooks and pikes, not swords. Other than that, they looked like any soldiers who had finished the killing part of a battle and settled down to the fun of looting. One was gnawing on a fat goose leg, grease dribbling down his beard and into his collar. Another was staring glumly into a wine bottle, looking upset and a little offended that it was empty. Their pockets bulged and jangled with coins, which was unfortunate because it caused the usual wardrobe problems. I don't know why men never seem to realize that if they fill their trousers with metal, gravity will take revenge. I can't be the only person in the world who's uninterested in seeing all those hairy bellies and bleached-white buttock cracks.

All their weapons were red-smeared, all their shirt cuffs stained with rust.

"Know what the best part was?" said the man with the goose leg, around a mouthful. "That sound the last bitch made when you finished her. Let's hear it again, Milt."

One of the men—Milt—imitated a girlish scream, followed by a long, drawn-out gurgle. He burst into hysterical giggles before he finished. Beside me, Darren's whole body went rigid. I dug my nails hard into her arm.

"You think we'll find any more chickens up here?" said another voice. "More little squawkers ready for the chop?"

"I think I don't give a damn. We have a chance to work the rooms before the others make it upstairs—"

Another voice, a harsh deep snarl. "I'm not done hunting tonight."

"We've done our share of the killing, Bowden. Now we hunt for treasure. Think of your son. You open the right drawer, he spends his life a rich man. Anyone think these are worth taking?"

There was the sound of ripping cloth, which confused me until I remembered the tapestries that covered the walls.

"It's disgusting," said the snarling man. "Look at them. Scarlet-dyed wool, gold thread. The price of one of these would keep a family in meat for a year."

Darren stirred. "Sumac-dyed wool and gilt paint, actually," she muttered. "Worth about two silver apiece."

I tightened my grip on Darren's arm, squeezing until my nails bit skin. She shut up.

"Going to take one?" asked one of the deep voices.

"No. Too heavy to carry. Coin, that's the thing. We should start tossing the bedrooms. Milt, what in hell do you think you're doing?"

Milt was giggling again. "Now that the tapestries are down, I want to make some artistic improvements."

A rustling sound. I closed my eyes briefly. The dick was untrussing his trousers.

"You're kidding me, you dizzy cockwomble," another looter said. "We have a chance to make our fortunes here, and you want to waste time with this stupid shit?"

"Don't act like you're too good for it," Milt said, still giggling. "Don't you want to wipe your ass on everything the Torasans ever touched?"

"We've no time for this, gobshite. Catch up when you're finished."

Heavy footsteps tramped away down the hall. I dared a peek around the corner. The looter called Milt—skinny, with deep pits in his face from acne scars—had taken a wide stance before a heap of torn-down tapestries, and was rummaging in his trousers. Now he opened the floodgates, swivelling so that his piss sprayed the embroidered cloth from one side to the other.

Darren caught my shoulder and leaned close to whisper in my ear, the words so soft they barely stirred the air. "*Can you take him down without being seen?*"

I didn't bother to answer, because she should not have had to ask. I just unwound the garrotte from my wrist.

Milt was running out of piss. The stream turned into a trickle, then a dribble, then stopped. He bounced a few times, rearranged his trousers, and ambled off down the hall, thumbs in pockets. As I crept out of the alcove to follow him, I matched my steps to his. Milt was wearing sabots—those heavy, wooden-soled shoes that chew your feet to ribbons the first few times you wear them. The wood clattered on the flagstones, drowning out the soft scuffing of my own bare feet.

I got within two steps of him before he sensed something wrong. I'd been trying not to come between him and a window, but you can't keep perfect control over that kind of thing and he must have seen a flicker of shadow where I blocked the moonlight. That could have been bad, but, like the rookie he was, he stopped short and goggled back over his shoulder instead of shouting out or dropping down. That gave me a whole half-second to get the cord around his neck, which was more than I needed.

He was a flailer, and he kicked and he thrashed as soon as he realized what was happening to him. He managed to land one good punch on the side of my head—the garrotte slipped in my sweaty hands and for one panicky moment, I thought he might wrench himself free—but I got a knee against his back and rode him down hard. Another yank on the cord and he went limp.

I sighed, maybe just a tiny bit relieved. Of course, *that* was when Darren raced around the corner and flung herself down on top of Milt. She grabbed a handful of greasy hair and began to bash his head against the floor. She'd done it three times, and the face was wet and sticky, by the time she realized I had things under control, and let it drop.

"I am trying not to be offended," I said, loosening the garrotte and pulling it free. There was a little blood. I stripped it away between two fingers. "I am trying *hard.*"

Darren rolled off of the body. "I don't care whether you're offended. I care whether you stay alive."

"That's very sweet, Mistress. But there's no point sending me out to do a quiet take-down if you're going to gallop noisily to the rescue as sson as I look like I'm in trouble. Oh hell, here they come."

Milt's friends rounded the corner at a run. One of them caught sight of us, threw down his wine bottle, and bolted. Latoya took off after him, blue sparks igniting in the dark as the end of her chain recoiled and bounced from wall to wall.

The others charged at Darren.

There wasn't much suspense about the outcome, not with Darren ablaze with rage, too fired up to doubt or hesitate. She whipped out her blades, the cutlass and the long knife, and used the momentum to spin, feinting past the first man, then lunging fast to the other. With one quick scything dagger-slash, she cut the hamstrings at the back of his thighs. He folded, shrieking, and she spun back to the other man, striking once, twice. Her cutlass hacked through his shoulder down to his rib cage; her dagger ripped a red gully through his throat. The hamstrung man struggled to rise from his knees, but Darren wheeled back on him, and there was a flash of metal, a gurgle and a sigh. We all got one good look at the kneeling looter impaled on Darren's cutlass, the blade going in through the mouth and out through the back of the neck. She pulled it free—it made a long, rasping noise, *snnnnck!*—and the body slumped.

Darren blew out a long breath, and stooped to wipe her blades on the dead man's jacket. "I'm not going to feel good about that later."

"That's a shame. I wonder if there's any way you could have avoided it? Oh, wait."

"Lynn, let's just—let's put a pin in this argument and get back to it some other time."

"You mean, once you think of a way to win it?"

She coughed uncomfortably and looked elsewhere. "Latoya. Did you catch up with him?"

Latoya loped up to us, her breathing calm and even. She made the *all clear* sign, glanced at the bodies, and lifted her eyebrows appreciatively at Darren's handiwork. Darren gave a modest shrug, and the two of them tapped their fists together, because they were, just occasionally, the same kind of idiot.

I stooped to check Milt's pulse before we left. It was thready, but it was there. Honestly, I wasn't sure why I had checked at all. I suppose some people might have felt guilty because he was so young. Me, I just remembered him giggling to himself, and tried to guess the age of the women he'd killed.

THE FIVE OF us fell into a loose formation: Darren and Regon in the lead, Latoya bringing up the rear, Ariadne and I in between.

Ariadne seemed barely awake. She was still wearing her nightgown, although she had shoes on and—for no apparent reason—a silk scarf. She hadn't bothered to put her hair in curlers before going to bed, so her ringlets had come loose into a messy blond frizz.

I reared back and kicked her in the shin. Hard. She tripped, stumbled, almost fell, and tore herself out of her drunken daze. "What the hell was that for?"

"You just had to do it, didn't you?" Darren was getting too far ahead of us. I quickened my pace. "You just had to feed the beast."

"What do you mean, beast?"

"I mean Darren! I mean Darren's oversized, sabre-toothed guilt complex. You just had to feed it red meat. And wherever Darren leads, Regon follows. And Latoya is usually the sensible one, but she can't say no to *you*. So here we all are, being heroes."

"What in the world are you trying to say? Are you—?" She blinked, and ground to a halt. "Lynn, are you mad at me?"

"Look at that. The light dawns. Bleeding shite, what were you thinking? Did you think at all? Did you think for even five seconds before you decided we should all lay down our lives to save Darren's godawful family?"

She stuttered out a disbelieving laugh. "Children. We are talking about children. Babies. I couldn't live with myself if—"

"*You* couldn't live with yourself. Well, I guess we couldn't have that." I rounded on her, anger ticking in every vein. "You know what the difference is between you and Darren? Darren at least knows when she's using people. You? I don't think you even realize. For weeks, you've been holding Latoya at arm's length, but now you want something from her, it's all *darling, sweetheart, would you bleed and fight and die for me?* You know nothing about combat and less than nothing about tactics and you can't tell the difference between a losing situation and a cheese sandwich, but what the hell, right? At least you'll be able to live with yourself. Assuming you survive the night, which is not something I'd bet money on right now."

If I'd said all this to Darren, she would have dissolved all over the floor in a puddle of guilt, and I would have had to somehow assemble her back together again before she could do anything useful. But Ariadne was made of stronger stuff.

"Children," she said again, flatly. "Babies. You'd walk away and leave them to die?"

"We're always leaving babies to die! You haven't figured it out? If we're stopping fires in the east, we're ignoring plagues in the west. If we give twelve loaves of bread to twelve starving children, there's a thirteenth child who gets screwed." Latoya had almost caught us up, so I grabbed Ariadne's wrist and yanked. "Shut up and move."

She moved, but she didn't shut up. "This is not a hypothetical plague island half a world away. There are children at the end of this hallway who could be dead in an hour."

"Us too. Could be dead in an hour. In case you're forgetting."

"Oh . . . *balls,* Gwyneth, what's the matter with you?"

"That's not my name."

"You of all people should want to keep horrible things from happening to children. You of all people!"

She got very shrill at the end, and when I jerked her close to me, the others must have thought I was trying to quiet her down. Just as well. I didn't want anyone interrupting us. I was in no mood to humour well-intentioned people. Not even Darren. Especially not Darren.

"Stop right there," I said. "Stop before you tell me what I should do or should feel or should be. I spent nine years as your mother's plaything. You do not get to tell me what I owe to the universe."

"I spent nine years watching her play with you!" Ariadne tore away, chest heaving. "Do you understand why I can't watch more children suffer?"

"Do you understand how *stupid* it is that you think that's something you can control? You know what? Don't answer that. Don't say anything. Don't talk to me tonight. This is your show, yours and Darren's. Do what you want, but don't expect me to applaud. This is not my war."

I put on speed, outpacing her, and had almost caught up with Darren when we reached a window that opened onto the courtyard.

It was still full of people with torches. Not a great sign. Torches and mobs in close proximity to each other tend to be a bad thing as a rule.

As we watched, a chunk of the glowing mass below us broke off and flowed out the castle gates, towards the docks. It separated into droplets as it spilled, a spray of liquid fire. It would have been pretty if we hadn't known that each glowing drop was an armed man with a torch held high, running for the harbour.

"Bollocking fuck," Darren said softly. "They're going after the ships. If they take the *Banshee* and the *Sod Off*—"

"They won't," I said. "Latoya sent Corto to get the ships underway as soon as we extracted our heads from our asses long enough to figure out what was going on. They're supposed to hug the coast and slip away just far enough to stay out of sight. Corto said there's an anchorage to the northeast—"

"There is. And it's in rowing distance." She blew out a long, relieved breath. "Good thinking."

"Yes, it was good thinking, it was superlative thinking, but that doesn't matter much since *your* thought process seems to be, 'You know what? Survival is overrated. I'm going to try one of those sucking chest wounds I've heard so much about.'"

"I've got no intention of dying tonight."

"Then you're walking in the wrong direction."

"Well, we're almost there," she said, as if that meant anything at all. "Look, we'll find another way out. It's what we do, remember?"

I wondered then what it must be like to have a voice in your head whispering that everything will turn out all right in the end. The voices in my head whisper very different things.

Darren was stalking along so vigorously that she stalked right past the nursery door without seeing it. Regon had to grab her shoulder and turn her around. At the edge of my vision, Ariadne was trying to catch my eye. I ignored her.

Darren jiggled the door handle. Locked.

"Lynn," Darren said—an order—and stepped out of my way.

I couldn't see any light around the edges of the frame, but I put my ear to the door anyway, shut my eyes and listened. There it was, the smothered ripple of sound that meant that the room was full of people trying desperately to keep quiet. There were whispers, a few small sobs, shuffling feet. There was something else too, a strange alien sound amongst all the terror: a lullaby. *Lullay, my dear babe, my dear son, my sweetling; lullay, my liking, the pearl of my heart.*

"They're awake," I reported. "So do they know what's going on?"

"Good question," Darren said, squinting at the door hinges. "I've got an even better one. Where are the guards?"

Latoya had lost patience with questions, good or otherwise. She cracked her knuckles. "Move."

We all flattened against the wall and let her do her thing. Latoya always did have a way with doors. She reared back and delivered a shattering kick to the wood, right below the latch. Planks snapped and splintered and the door lurched open.

Small things scattered when we came in, like mice in a grain bin when someone lifts the lid. Children dove underneath beds and behind curtains, clumped together in the shadows, cowered in corners.

One of them didn't run: a chunky, heavyset boy, dressed only in a nightshirt, who stood in front of the door with a drawn cutlass. His stance was decent—*almost* good enough to make it seem that he knew what he was doing—but the blade was too shiny to have ever been used. Corto, the best of our swordsmen, had a blade so pocked with nicks and burrs that it looked like a star map, and Darren wore out her cutlasses faster than her socks.

Darren didn't even break stride walking up to the kid. He raised his sword—the tip of it trembled—she dealt a quick sharp blow to his forearm, and the sword fell from his suddenly nerveless fingers, clanging on the floor. Darren kicked it away.

The room was lit only by the embers still glowing in the hearth, but even in the dimness, I could see the boy's lower lip quaver. Darren took him by the shoulders and gripped hard.

"Are you here to kill us?" he asked, his voice a thin, high treble.

"What? No. We're here to help. Hark, when did you leave the banquet?"

He drew a shuddery breath. "Right after you left. Uncle—I mean, my lord Konrad—said I needed my sleep. But halfway through the night, our guards woke us up. They were saying . . . things. Mostly to the girls. Awful things. Things that I never heard anyone . . ."

He halted, shivering. Darren gave him a gentle shake. "What happened? Did they hurt anybody?"

He shook his head. "The nurse told them that they had to leave, and they left. I think they were drunk. But they said . . . they said we'd all be dead by morning. They said that the Freemen were coming to cut all our throats."

"Oh, they said that, did they? Probably because they're a bunch of witless, ferret-cocked, jizz-gargling bellends."

Hark choked out a startled laugh at that, which brought some colour back to his cheeks. When Darren pulled his head close to her, he let her do it. She didn't quite hug him, but she held him for a few seconds, and when she let him go, he seemed steadier.

"Anyway, they're wrong," Darren said. "We're going to get you all out the back way, and onto my ship, and then we're going to sail away, and *then* I think we might moon them, just for the hell of it. How's that for a program? Are you all right with that?"

The kid still looked sick, but he managed to breathe, and nodded.

"All right, then. Hurry and put some clothes on, and then—are you the oldest one here? We'll need your help to get the little ones ready . . ."

There were about twenty children, most of them already awake. Red eyes, tear-stained cheeks, snotty noses, but at least they were old enough to walk. I left the others to deal with them while I looked for babies.

There was a long row of cradles against the north wall, simple wooden ones, like crates on legs. Next to that was a shelf of well-worn nappies, and a shallow trough for washing them.

The House of Torasan had quite a production line going here. I peeked over the rims of the cradles. Most were empty, but there were two babies, both with mops of dark hair and chubby cheeks. One was blubbering. The other glared at me with menace in its slitted little eyes, and I glared right back, warning it not to try anything.

"Don't touch them. Don't you touch them!"

A woman lurched out of the shadows. She was stiff with terror, but forced herself forward, between me and the cradles.

I looked her up and down. She was dressed in rough peasant cloth, and had two smeary damp patches on her loose-fitting bodice. "Wet-nurse?"

"Yes." Her teeth were chattering, even the room's stale warmth. "Don't hurt them. Please. Please leave them alone. Even if you kill me for it, I can't let you—"

"I'm not going to hurt them. I just need to check something"

I batted aside the nurse's arm, reached into a cradle, and rifled through the baby's blankets. There was a Torasan hawk-head embroidered clumsily on one corner. I ripped that away with my teeth, leaving the kid in plain wrappings of much-washed linen. The other baby was hawk-free. I left its blankets alone.

That done, I scooped both of the babies out of their cradles and dumped them unceremoniously in the nurse's arms.

"There." I kicked open the door to the nursery. "Get moving."

"Get moving . . . you mean . . . where am I supposed to hide Torasan children?"

"What Torasan children? Those are your babies. Always have been. Take them out of here and disappear."

The nurse still looked terrified, but there was something else in her face now—a quavering kind of hope. She stared at the chubby children fussing in her arms. "Do you mean it?"

"I don't say things I don't mean."

"You won't come back for them?"

"I told you. You're their mother. I have no interest in changing that. Go."

The nurse took a step closer to me. My hand flashed to the knife at my belt, but she just touched my arm with trembling fingers. It might have meant, "Thank you."

She plunged out of the doorway into the dark corridors, a baby in each arm. As soon as she was gone, I hauled the half-shattered door back into its frame. Latoya was awfully good at getting through doors, but on this one occasion, I wished she hadn't broken it down with quite so much enthusiasm.

We'd have to build a barricade. I grabbed a child's bed by one of its rough-hewn wooden posts and dragged it towards the door. It was heavier than it looked, and I strained hard for a minute or more without getting anywhere much before Darren appeared to take the other end. Together, we turned the bed on its side, using the weight to jam the broken door tightly into its frame.

"Quick question here," she said. "Did you just hand my baby nephews over to a complete stranger and send her on her way?"

"I did, yes."

" . . . right. I have immense faith in your judgment, you know I do. So I'm sure there's a good explanation here, and maybe you could reveal it before I panic and go chasing down the hallways after them."

"She's their wet-nurse. Can we brace the door with some of those chests, do you think?"

"Worth a try. Kick a few of them over here. And, all right, you gave the babies to their wet-nurse. How can you be sure she'll take care of them?"

"Why is she breast-feeding Torasan brats?"

"Probably because her own baby died—oh."

"I'm not going to pretend to understand why some women want helpless screaming doughballs in their lives, but apparently it's a pretty common craving. She's been taking care of your nephews since the day they were born. She's invested."

Darren was silent for a moment, helping me to drag a heavy clothespress into position. "What if the babies' real parents survive and want them back?"

"Then we'll deal with it if it comes up. It's not a 'tonight' kind of problem."

Privately, though, I thought that the babies might be better off with a pushy and adoring adopted mother than as products of the Torasan child factory. I looked again at the row of crate-like cradles, and a slow burn pulsed through my chest which had nothing to do with an ulcer. "You deserved so much better than this, you know."

Darren glanced up with a wan half-smile. "Now who's being maudlin?"

"I'm not maudlin. I'm angry. Until you learn how to be angry at your family for all the ways they've screwed you over, I'm going to do it for you. Get used to it."

I threaded a few sticks of firewood into gaps in the barricade, weaving together the chair-backs and bed-frames, and surveyed the result. "I don't think that this thing will hold up to much more than a good sneeze, so please tell me that we're about to go away very fast."

"That is definitely the plan." She looked over her shoulder. "I think we're just about ready."

A door was open at the far end of the room, and the breeze gusting through carried the welcome fish-and-sulphur reek of seaweed. The stocky boy, Hark, now fully dressed, urged the older children through the door, one by one. Regon was nowhere to be seen—he'd probably led the way out. Ariadne had pulled herself together somehow. She was bundling sleepy, squirming toddlers into blankets. When there were five or six blanket-wrapped dumplings, Latoya bent down and picked them all up in one massive armload.

"There are two more little ones, captain," she said, and jerked her head towards the bed where they sat whimpering. "You'll carry them?"

Darren nodded. "You go on ahead. Lynn—we didn't have time for a headcount. Do a last sweep? Make sure we didn't miss anyone?"

"I live to serve, O my mistress. Mostly. When I don't have anything better to do."

"All jokes aside, make it quick? Like you said, we're on a clock here."

"I know. Trust me, I have no desire whatsoever to stick around."

They vanished out into the cold salty air: Latoya with the toddler dumplings, Darren with one small boy in the crook of her arm and another perched on her shoulder. I wanted to follow them so badly that my teeth ached. It was fine, though, I just had to do one quick sweep. It would take no time at all, as long as there were no . . .

"Are you honestly not going to say a word to me for the rest of the night?"

. . . complications. I glared hard at Ariadne. "Go with the others."

"And leave you behind? When a horde of murderers could swoop down on this place any moment? Not likely."

If the nursery did come under attack, Ariadne would be no earthly use to me, but if she couldn't figure that out on her own, what was the good of explaining?

"Have it your way," I said. "We're searching for stragglers. You start in that corner and go clockwise."

I worked around the room in a spiral, looking under and behind every piece of furniture, kicking aside damp blankets and dirty clothes. Everything smelled like cheese and feet.

"Admit it," Ariadne said, as she looked behind a shutter too small to hide anyone. "We made the right choice, coming here."

"When we're back on the *Banshee,* then you get an opinion about that. Not before."

"You just saved those two babies. That means nothing to you?"

"I don't know that I did save them. Maybe I just handed them over to some twisted monster who'll keep them in a box. I *think* I improved their chances of survival, but that's all this is: a game of percentages. Did you hear that?"

"Hear what?"

"Shut up."

I could only just make out the sound—a tiny, choking sob, underneath one of the beds. I dropped flat—yes—there was a small girl cowering under there, her body huddled right against the wall. I made a sweeping grab for her ankle, but my arm was too short by almost a foot.

"What are you doing?" Ariadne hovered, trying to peek under the bed. "Stop that, you'll frighten her. Let me talk to her for a second—"

It was no use; my arm was too short. Spitting hair out of my mouth, I belly-crawled backwards until I could stand, then yanked the bed away from the wall. The girl jerked, leapt to her feet and tried to bolt, but I caught her by her skinny shoulders just in time.

She whined, and tried to pull away. That was fine. I wasn't interested in cuddles. I let go and the child staggered, falling against Ariadne's chest.

Ariadne took possession of the girl, wrapping both arms around her. "Oh, Gwyn—"

"*For the thousandth time,* that's *not* my name."

"I keep forgetting how much you hate children."

"I don't hate children. I don't want them to die, or anything. I want them to be perfectly happy and healthy, somewhere far away from me. Let's get this one out of here."

I could already hear—if I wasn't imagining it—the slapping of shoes against stone. Not the heavy, regular tramp-tramp-tramp of soldiers marching in step, but the broken scuffling beats of men running. Men pushing in front of each other, and falling behind, and ranging out in front, and running, running, running to find us.

"Go," I told Ariadne. "Take the kid out of here. If you argue with me now, I swear I will break your face."

Her mouth tightened, but she hurried the child through the back door. I made one last lap of the room, checking under every bed, inside every nook, behind every hanging curtain. When I was sure it was empty, I caught up the fire shovel by the hearth and plunged it deep into the still-glowing coals. I scattered the red hot embers in and around and over the barricade, then grabbed a cushion and flapped it in wide arcs, fanning the flames until they lapped around the wood and took hold.

Then I ran, blood pounding in my ears and temples. The back door was heavy but well-oiled and I yanked it shut without any trouble. It was dead dark in the passage on the other side, so I worked by touch, finding bolts and latches on the door frame and shooting them home.

When I got clear of the passage, the full moon was overhead, flashing silver on the sheltered bay. The air was tinglingly cold. I took the stairs two at a time until I caught up with Ariadne, then helped her pull the sleepy, stumbling child down the steps. Together, we hurried towards the torch Regon was holding, a bobbling pool of orange light.

"Darren does have a reason for bringing us down here, doesn't she?" I asked, somewhat belatedly. "I mean, we're not just going to build sand castles and hope that nobody notices us, right?"

Ariadne squinted and blew upwards, chasing a sweaty blond ringlet out of her eye. "I think we're escaping from the beach. She said there was a boat."

" . . . *a* boat? As in, one?"

One. I could see it already. One balky, ancient longboat moored at a short pier. Latoya was aboard, straddling two benches. Darren and Regon passed the smaller children to her, one at a time, and she set them down on the thwarts. Clusters of them clung to her legs. She moved carefully, stepping between tiny hands and feet.

Most of the older children managed to clamber aboard without help, but Hark missed his footing, and would have gone into the water headfirst if Regon hadn't grabbed him by the jacket collar.

All but the youngest of the kids seemed to know what they were doing. They found spaces for themselves in the crowded little boat, crouching on the bottom-boards if there wasn't room for them on a bench, and waited without fussing.

That helped, but there were so many of them. With each child that boarded, the boat sunk lower in the water, until it looked like a dent in a glass mirror. When we passed in the last child, a fat and placid girl who was sucking the hem of her shirt, the boat dipped low before it settled. There was a sliver left of freeboard, a few inches at most. Small waves lapped at the side and sent trickles of water over the gunwales.

There was no way the boat could take us all.

Just that minute, Ariadne shuddered, retched, and bent double, hand pressed to her mouth. The raw fishy smell of the seaweed must have got to her; it was pretty ripe. While she was busy with that, I pulled Darren to the end of the dock, rotten boards squelching beneath my bare feet.

"How many more people can we put in the boat?" I asked.

I was pretty sure that the honest answer was "None, oh god oh god, what the hell do you want from me?" But Darren always was a secret optimist. She squinted out at the waves, licked a finger, and checked the wind. "One. Maybe."

"Can we lighten the boat at all?"

"We already unshipped the mast. Took out most of the oars. Unless you want to chop bits out of the hull, or throw a few kids over the side, I don't think we could lose any more weight."

"Latoya's the heaviest. If she got out . . ." I let the words die away, giving up the idea even before Darren shook her head. The boat was so deeply loaded, no ordinary sailor could shift it. Darren and Regon together could strain at the oars until their backs broke without getting any distance. Only Latoya, with her powerful bargeman's arms, stood a chance.

We *could* dump a few of the heavier children. I told myself that Hark kind of looked like a twit. But that would be a non-starter, with Darren around.

"Could we swim?" I asked, knowing the answer already.

"Water's too cold. We'd pass out before clearing the bay. Or we'd panic, and try to climb into the boat, and swamp it. If we try that, nobody's going to make it out."

And we couldn't tunnel and we couldn't turn invisible and we couldn't fly—my brain raced in circles, probing, testing, but hitting walls in every direction.

It wasn't a new thing for me, this certainty that I was about to face something vicious and brutal in a cold dark place, but that didn't give me any comfort. Sooner or later, I was going to outlive my store of luck.

My palms were damp. I dried them against my tunic while my mind went through that familiar adjustment, the world dimming and narrowing until I couldn't see anything but the next step in the road.

"All right," I said. "One more person. You know that has to be you."

"You really think I would save my own skin before yours?"

Bleeding tits, so typical. "I think that every once in a long long while, you manage to stop playing righteous warrior long enough to see sense.

You're the one the rebels want, not me. Nobody's up in the castle screaming for the blood of runaway servant girls."

"Maybe not, but if they capture you, they're not just going to hand you a cupcake and wave you on your way. Gods' teeth! The last time I let you sacrifice yourself for the rest of us, you ended up beaten bloody and locked in Melitta's closet—"

"*I remember what happened last time, Darren.*"

All night long, I'd been fighting the fear, but now it flooded me, acid and blinding yellow, settling in my jaw as a sour ache.

"This isn't about sacrifice," I said, forcing out the words. "It's about what makes sense. You'll be in the deepest shit if you don't escape, so you're escaping, congratulations, *move your pirate arse.*"

Darren reached out to me, but stopped herself just in time. That was a relief. My skin was prickling all over, almost burning.

She said, "If I run—"

"Then I have to stay. We've established that. Get in the boat or I'll get Regon to pitch you off the end of the dock. He'll do it, if I ask."

"That's not what I mean. If I escape, your sister can't."

My heart stood still. My sweet, naïve, noble-born sister with her so-smooth skin and her delusions that the world could be fair and beautiful . . . my sister, having those delusions ripped away from her, once and for all . . . for once in my life, I couldn't think of anything to say.

There was buzzing in my ears and in my head that almost drowned out the sound of Darren talking. "It's all right. Lynn, breathe, it's all right."

"You are such a damn liar." I could only get air in short gasps. That burning smell was back again.

"No, listen. We're going to send your sister to safety. You and I are going to stay together, because that's what we do. And, together, we will find a way out of this. Are you listening to me? Breathe."

I breathed, shallowly. She nodded with approval. "Are you with me?"

I stuttered out a laugh, choked on it, and forced myself to breathe again. "Asshole. You still need to ask?"

Instead of answering, she reached for my face. I flinched backwards but managed to check the motion, letting her pick something from the corner of my eye with gentle fingers.

"Eyelash," she explained, and flicked the short hair away. "And no, I don't need to ask. Isn't that strange? Go get rid of the princess so that you and I can get some real work done."

Down at the end of the dock, Ariadne straightened, wiping her mouth. "What's the hold-up?" she asked, voice shaky. "Aren't we going?"

Darren gave me another encouraging nod. I somehow managed to steady myself.

"Of course we're going, you dozy pillock," I said. "We've been waiting on your puking ass. Hop on the boat. You're next."

It sounded good—brisk, casual. No sign that when I said *You're next,* I meant *You're last.* But my sister never was a fool. She looked at me with suspicion, then with dawning realization, and the blood sprang into her cheeks.

"No," she said fiercely. "No!"

This was just too much. "Why is everyone trying to argue with me tonight? When are people going to realize that I'm always right about everything? Get in the damn boat."

"And leave you here?"

"Just for now," I said through my teeth. "We'll catch up."

"You're lying!"

"Yes, well, you're ugly. Get *in*, Ariadne!"

She took two stumbling steps forward, and gods, did she look a mess now, with her nightgown slicked sweatily against her back and breasts, and her hair flying free in wild tendrils. "Gwyneth, I don't care how much you hate me right now—"

"Oh, here we go. Yes, please do dissolve into weepy hysterics; that'll fix everything."

"—I am not going to stand aside and watch you get broken!" By now, she was screaming. "Not this time. Not again!"

"You don't have to watch!" Cold wind off the ocean sliced through the linen of my tunic. Revolution or no revolution, I wanted to get away from the water and find some place warmer. "I don't *want* you to watch. Whatever happens next, I don't want you to be here!"

Ariadne shook her head, her pinched face almost a skull in the grey moonlight. She was gripping at her scarf in her distress, twisting it between her fingers, knuckles pale as old bone. "You've been through enough. It's enough, Lynn! I won't let it happen again! I *can't*!"

"I'll be fine! I'm nobody! You're the noble, you're the true-born, you're the one with the target painted on her back—"

She took one step closer. "But you're my baby sister."

There was a blur of motion.

It was funny. I should have recognized the manoeuvre—I'd done it so often myself—but like most of my victims, I hesitated for just a second as the silk scarf whipped over my head. Another instant and I did understand, and I was clutching at the scarf with both hands, trying to pull the noose free, to clear my airway. Too late. Ten heartbeats after Ariadne's makeshift garrotte tightened around my neck, my legs gave way, and the blackness rose to meet me.

CHAPTER SIXTEEN

The Lady Darren of the House of Torasan (Pirate Queen)

I THINK THERE must have been something strange in the water on Bero, where Lynn and Ariadne grew up, because I swear, those two thought twice as fast and moved twice as fast as anyone else. Lynn hit the ground unconscious before I even had time to say, "Wait a minute."

Ariadne loosened the scarf, straightened up, and shot a glare at me that felt like a punch between the eyes. "Lynn takes the last spot in the boat. Any objections?"

Objections or no objections, there was no point in discussing it. Lynn's eyelids were already fluttering—she wouldn't be unconscious for long—but she'd wake up woozy and dazed. She wouldn't be able to walk in that state, and piggybacking a girl through enemy lines isn't as easy as you might imagine.

But Latoya surged to her feet, making the boat roll dangerously. "No!"

Ariadne didn't respond, just turned that piercing stare of hers towards Regon and me. "Get her in."

No time for second thoughts or long goodbyes. I grabbed Lynn's shoulders, Regon took her ankles; we heaved her up and swung her twice and tossed her into the lifeboat. She landed with a *plop* and rolled into the bilges.

Latoya was trying to claw her way back to dry land, but she ran into trouble. The Torasan children—who had, apparently, decided that Latoya was the one thing in the world they could depend on—clung to her. They formed clumps, grabbing at her legs, her boots, her hands. She could have brushed them off like so many breadcrumbs, but instead she teetered in place, afraid of breaking tiny fingers if she ripped herself loose.

Meanwhile, Ariadne had reached the boat's painter. She clawed at the knotted rope, undoing the cleat hitch that fastened the boat to the dock. There was a soft splash as the rope's free end hit the water.

The boat drifted from the dock. Latoya, still weighed down by clumps of children, stood atop a thwart, face a mask of horror. "Why? *Why?*"

"Get them out!" Ariadne shrieked at her. There were tears in her eyes, but they didn't fall. "Get my sister away from here! Get the children away from here! You're the only one who can do it—don't you *dare* disappoint me!"

That reached Latoya. She staggered back, dropped onto the bench, and, after one last look at Ariadne, took hold of the oars. Her first pull barely moved the boat at all, just stirred the waters. On her next stroke, she thrust the oars deep, and then strained until it seemed like either her arms or the oars had to break. Wood planks bowed and creaked, and Latoya gasped, but slowly, painfully, the oars broke the water, and the boat bobbed towards the open ocean. Latoya whipped the oars around and pulled again. Again. Again. The longboat was moving—sluggishly at first, then with greater momentum, faster, faster, and, finally, fast enough to churn up foam around the bow.

Latoya was dragging that massive weight through the sea with sheer brawn and willpower. Ariadne was right—no one else could have done it.

That didn't make Ariadne's stunt any less suicidal or rash, but give credit where it's due. She had just, very possibly, saved the lives of the two people she loved most on the planet. That was a pretty good night's work, considering that she was unarmed and hungover.

Regon cleared his throat. "Not to spoil the moment, but does anyone else hear pounding?"

ONE MAN, ONE pirate queen, one princess. A bare dock, a pebbled shore. Death behind us, and killing cold in front. And a distant drumming from the stairway, as someone rammed something heavy against the barred nursery door.

Ariadne wiped her eyes. "What now?"

"Now you and I get to pay for our drinks," I said.

I couldn't reassure her. On an Isle in revolt, a noblewoman was in much more danger than a runaway servant, just as Lynn had said. Still . . . still . . . I couldn't help but think that Ariadne had made the right choice when she forced Lynn to take her place in the longboat. Our class, Ariadne's and mine, had sowed the seeds of this revolt and it was only fair that the two of us should stay to reap the harvest. All noble houses are trading houses, and the first rule of trading is this: At the end of the day, the books have to balance.

Above us, at the top of the stone stairway, the pounding went on. The tempo of the blows had slowed, but it was more deliberate, now, more steady, the rebels finding their rhythm as they smashed away at the iron-bound door.

"Could we climb the cliffs, maybe?" Regon asked.

"I doubt it." Most things on the Isle seemed smaller to me now than they did when I was a child, but not the sheer granite slabs that framed the cove. "Fletcher tried, when he was about thirteen. He fell from halfway up and hit his head on a rock."

"Huh." Regon glanced at me, curious in spite of everything. "Is that how he went wrong?"

"We think so. Unless he was just born wrong, which, with my family, isn't an outlandish theory."

"When you say *wrong* . . ." Ariadne let the sentence trail away.

It wasn't something we were supposed to talk about, but who cared anymore? "I mean that he developed a habit of cutting things up."

"What kind of things?"

"Mainly animals. Sometimes women. Anyone have an idea other than the cliffs?"

Regon hefted the torch high and we all looked around us: sheer rocks and dark water. Pebbles, sand, beach grass.

"Should we try to swim?" Ariadne asked, voice thin and high. "It wouldn't give us much of a chance, I know, but not much is better than none."

Regon shook his head. "You've got it backwards. A cold sea will kill you surer than a blade, every time."

"What about a blade with a crazy person swinging it? What about a hundred blades with crazy people swinging all of them?"

"Regon's right," I said. "You can't fight the sea—or outrun it, or surrender to it. Given a choice, I'd always take the hundred maniacs. Douse the torch, Regon. Let's not make this too easy for them."

Light arced overhead, then vanished with a splash and a hiss as the torch hit the water and sank. Blinking away orange sparks and haloes, I ripped my cutlass loose from its sheath.

"I'll see what I can do to keep them busy," I said. "You two stay close to the cliffs, in the shadows, and as soon as you've got a clear path to the stairs, run like bunnies. Try to blend in with the rebels somehow—maybe wave some torches and curse my name. Get back to Lynn, if you can. Tell her that I . . . uh . . . you know what? Never mind. It's fine. She'll know. Also, she'll be pissed. Try to stay out of garrotte range while you're telling her."

Regon breathed slowly, but didn't speak. I was talking nonsense—they'd never reach the stairs—and I knew it and so did he. But what else could I say? *Right, well, I guess that's it; how about a rousing pirate song while we wait?*

From the top of the stairs: a dull *crack*, then a dry splintering, and muffled shouts. The oaken planks and iron braces of the door had begun to split.

Ariadne squared her shoulders. "Someone give me a knife."

I hesitated. "Are you sure?"

"Am I *sure*? Why wouldn't I want to pull a weapon on these child-murdering shits?"

"Because you might hurt them."

"Which would kind of be the point, you stupid pirate!"

"Three minutes, Ariadne. That's all you've got. In three minutes, or maybe less, those child-murdering shits will be able to do whatever they like to you. Do you really want to spend that time making them angrier?"

"So drop your cutlass! Hell, let's tie each other up before they get here. Let's greet the bloodthirsty rebels bound and kneeling. Would that be a winning strategy, in your books?"

"There *is* no winning strategy here. If you haven't dealt with that yet, do it fast." I yanked a spare dagger from my boot and slapped the hilt into Ariadne's hand. "Eyes, throat, or groin. Don't bother trying for the heart. Stab until your knuckles meet skin, then twist."

More splintering cracks from above. Pale yellow light spilled through the broken door onto the surrounding stone. As soon as the light appeared, it fragmented. Dark shapes piled on each other, boiling and seething as they surged through the gap. The rebels flooded down the steps, their shadows thrown huge and stark against the cliff. The forms of them blurred together until the mass of men was a great shadowy beast running the whole length of the stairway. Spines of pitchforks and pikes; horns of fire.

Fuck, shit, bugger and balls, this was going to be ugly and could we just *not?* I was terribly sleepy and, more than anything, I wanted to go back to bed.

The tide of men reached the bottom of the stairway, pooled there, then rushed forwards.

I licked my lips and tried to think of something to say that wasn't too terribly inane. The only thing that popped into mind was "Here we go," which didn't seem like quite the thing.

I swore a few times instead. You can almost always find a cuss word appropriate to your situation. Here, I went with that good reliable standby, "Crap."

Then I charged.

I crashed into the front line of rebels. It broke and spilled around me, a wave on a rock, but bodies pressed close, trapping me, gripping me, before I could swing my cutlass even once. I stumbled, and the packed crowd blotted out the sky. And then they had me.

THEY WEREN'T GENTLE.

The people in the crowd all fought to touch me, which might have been agreeable under other circumstances and which, under these circumstances, was not. At all.

Hard hands tore at my clothing, stripping away my coat and boots, belt and scabbard, purse and dagger and silver ear-cuff. A grinning man with no teeth ripped out a hank of my hair and thrust it up for all to see, howling in delight. One of them—fat-fingered, stone-faced—got a hand up my shirt and grabbed a fistful of what he found there. Others just spat on me.

I guess you'd expect me to fight at a time like that. Struggle, thrash, roar, bite, punch heads. But I went limp as a rag doll in their hands, and I didn't make a noise. There were too many of them, milling around me in a swarming mound, maggots on a corpse. There were so many of them, and they were so *fucking* strong. Worse even than the touching was the sheer hatred rippling out of them, the venom in their taunts and their blows and their gropes and their spit. It's exhausting, you know, to be hated with such total intensity, and it left me shaky and numb.

Once, just once, I caught sight of Ariadne through the throng. Two men had her by the wrists, two more by the throat, a host more by shreds and rags of her tattered night-dress. Her face looked nothing like you would expect. Not teary or frightened or even angry. She had a look of fixed, furrow-browed concentration, as if she was very close to solving a riddle that she'd been puzzling over for years.

> *And the butcher swings, and the hatchet hacks,*
> *And the blood drools out like red red wax,*
> *And the earth is pink with the dying sun,*
> *As the chickens follow him one by one . . .*

KONRAD HAD SAID, *You can't spend your whole life hiding.* But I'd had a pretty good run, hadn't I? Somehow I'd managed to convince everyone that I was a captain, a warrior, a leader—hell, a *hero.* The most pathetic part was, I'd managed to fool myself too.

No more. As they dragged me back through the empty nursery, I was brought back to myself, for what seemed like the first time in years. This was who I was, this shambling, clumsy woman, with shaggy hair and jutting elbows, eyes stupid with panic, tripping over her own feet. This was who I had always been, and I never should have forgotten.

They kicked me down a stairway and then another. I tried to shield my head with my hands as bits of me bounced off hard surfaces, but my torso hit the sharp edge of a stair with a dull meaty *crunch*. All the breath left my lungs in a violent *huh* and I fought for air. Twenty hands dragged me to my feet again.

The doors to the Great Hall swung open in front of us, the room cruelly bright with a hundred torches. I saw what was inside not as one single picture, but as a series of jagged flashes, reflections in the shards of a broken bottle. There was the high table, overturned, surrounded by smashed goblets and trenchers. The floor, its flagstones smeared with blood and crushed fruit. Hordes of rebels eating, gorging themselves on platters of meat and white bread, swilling cherry wine so fast that it ran down their necks.

And then the bodies. A woman's corpse, sprawled across a chair, clothing in shreds, loose threads hanging where someone had ripped away the expensive lace trim. A heap of young men in a corner, stacked up like cordwood, with one white arm hanging free of the pile. I recognized the rings of pink jade that Konrad's oldest son Karel had been wearing at dinner.

And then there were two large, dark-haired men—they'd both been stabbed in the back, so they must have tried to run, but they hadn't made it anywhere near the door. I was too numb to feel much, even when I saw the dead men's faces. Gunnar was on the left, Talon was on the right. Four blue-grey eyes, open and staring at mine.

Ariadne and Regon were behind me, yanked and kicked along in my wake. The rebels dragged all three of us past my brothers' bodies, past leering men with mouthfuls of rotten teeth, all the way to the dais where the throne sat. That's when I saw what was left of Konrad.

"Oh, *hell*," Ariadne sobbed from behind me, and retched.

I only recognized Konrad by the gold buttons on his shirt-cuffs. The rest of him—face, neck, torso, limbs—was a black, ruined, half-liquid mess. They had doused his whole body in boiling pitch. Spikes driven through his wrists and ankles had held him to the throne during his murder, and, judging from the hideous wounds caused by his efforts to wrench himself loose, he hadn't died quick.

Scattered across the blackened body was a mass of white chicken feathers, some of them half-buried in tar, some drifting free.

"His eyes," Ariadne choked out. "Did you see his eyes?"

"Don't look, lady," Regon said. He leaned forward against the arms that held him to block her view. "Just don't look."

The hall doors swung open. There were two more rebels, both with drawn swords, and in between them . . .

"*Jada!*"

My little sister stood two heads shorter than the man on her right. Both men together could have picked her up and pitched her over a barn roof. In spite of my panic and pain, the sight of her sent a jolt of lightning through me. I bucked mightily, flailing in my captors' hands, kicking and biting at anything I could reach until I ripped my way clear.

"Jada, run! Go, get moving, I'll hold them off—"

I lurched towards her, dodging between benches and corpses, all the while groping blindly for some kind of weapon. A dagger, a brick, a salad fork—anything. "Jada! *Move!* Don't just stand there—get a grip! The balls, Jada! Kick them in the balls!"

A blow from someone's burly fist sent me down to my knees. Then there was cold steel kissing my throat and someone's hot breath in my ear, hissing, "This is how it ends for you, bitch, here and now—"

His forearm muscles bunched and the blade began to slide, but a voice cut the air, screaming, "*No!*"

The knife moved away. I blinked upwards to find Jada in front of me, staring down. No wounds on her yet. I tried again. "Jada, *run.*"

A smile flickered across her face.

Then came the kick.

It clipped me on the cheekbone, and my vision burst into burning points of light. When the first blaze of agony dimmed, Jada was crouching beside me, face inches from mine. "You don't talk to me, dog. Not ever."

Laughing hoots came from the rebels as Jada rose to her feet. I stared at her, unbelieving—her eyes narrowed and she kicked at me again. Her aim was off that time, and I managed to catch the blow on my uninjured shoulder. But the truth of the thing was sinking home.

So. On the plus side, Jada was in no immediate danger of being burned to death by an angry mob. On the minus side, what the fuckety fuck fuck fuck?

While I reeled, someone grabbed my arms and lashed my wrists together in front of me. I didn't fight it, couldn't fight it. My chest was shrieking with pain, no matter how shallow I tried to keep my breaths. Two broken ribs, I thought. No, three.

Another rebel hovered close. He was grizzled, his lean face daubed with charcoal, chicken feathers threaded through holes in his jacket.

"I'll keep her from talking," he said. His voice was scraped and raspy, as if he'd spent the whole night screaming. He probably had. "I'll open up a thousand mouths all over her, and none of them'll say a word."

Everybody in the room seemed to feel pretty good about this idea, judging from all the shouts of approval, so it was a surprise when Jada snapped, "Not yet."

Chicken-feather-jacket man bared his teeth. "We swore we'd purge the Isle clean of the Torasan scum! Smoke out the vermin, rip off their stinking hides!"

Howls of agreement met this, but Jada raised her voice over them. "*Milo wants this one*! You heard him! This one's his! Once he's finished with her, you can have her hide. I'll tie her down for you and make the first cuts. But until then, hands off!"

Jada's deep tone was identical to the one I used when I was trying to get people to take me seriously. In spite of everything, I almost laughed. *She are boss.*

"Excuse me," Ariadne cut in. She'd regained her composure, somehow, even though a man with no teeth was holding her in an iron grip, a billhook quivering near her throat. "You all do know that Jada is a Lady of Torasan herself, right? One of those wicked little chickens you're so cranky about? I just thought I'd mention it. Since nobody else was bringing it up."

Jada wheeled on Ariadne. "Quiet, dog."

"'Quiet, dog'," Ariadne repeated, thoughtfully. "Oh, that was really witty. That was just inspired. Do you come up with these clever remarks yourself, or does someone else write your material?"

Jada advanced on her, the skin under her right eye twitching. Just like when I'd met her back in the nursery the previous morning, her whole body was tight and tense. I'd thought then that she was scared. I knew better now. Every line of her was rigid with fury and hate.

"Do you know how many people here would jump at the chance to kill you with their bare hands?" she asked.

"I could ask you the same question. How did you convince these charmers to let you join their club? Did you promise that you would make yourself useful? If so—do you really think they'll keep you around once your usefulness ends?"

Jada snatched a long knife from her belt. It wasn't the blunt silver dagger of a Torasan captain, but a fisherman's fillet knife, wicked sharp and hook-pointed.

Ariadne managed a rusty laugh. "Oh, sweetheart. It's so easy to get under your skin. You should work on that, if you plan to stay in politics. It's not all wacky hijinks like betraying your family and getting them murdered. It's hard work."

Jada inhaled. "When the time comes, bitch, I will gut you myself."

"*All* by yourself? My, my, what a big girl you're getting to be."

Regon hissed a warning, but too late. Jada, face flaming, nodded at the man who held Ariadne; he grinned and shoved her hard. She stumbled forwards, straight into Jada's path, and Jada's dagger-pommel smashed into her face. Ariadne cried out—she had nerve, but she'd never had a chance to learn how to deal with pain. Jada dealt out more blows, now with an open hand, smacking Ariadne's face from side to side, until she finally sputtered, "All right, stop it, *all right!*"

Jada halted and inspected her handiwork. Ariadne's jaw was already swelling, her bottom lip split open and bloody. With her knife point, Jada caught a stray strand of Ariadne's hair and flicked it out of the way, then drew the blade lightly down Ariadne's face, past the corner of her eye and the side of her nose. Ariadne flinched—almost cringed—at the touch, and my stomach turned inside out.

"Jada, stop," I said—my voice wobbled, I couldn't help that. "Stop it. Please. You don't have to go any further. She gets it. She'll be quiet."

"Maybe I don't want her to be quiet yet." Slowly, Jada traced a line across Ariadne's throat with the tip of her knife. "Maybe I want her to spend some time begging for the chance to be quiet. Or maybe I want her to make some interesting noises."

The tension stretched agonizingly, then slackened when Jada thrust her knife back into its sheath. With a deliberate swipe, she wiped her sweaty, bloody hand on the front of Ariadne's nightdress. "We'll finish this later. Don't go anywhere."

THEY DRAGGED THE three of us—Ariadne, Regon, and me—into a line facing Konrad's blackened corpse. One by one, they kicked us to our knees.

"You have to stop it," I whispered at Ariadne, not trying to hide the desperation. "Don't piss them off. *Please* don't piss them off. What in hell am I going to tell your sister if you get yourself killed?"

Ariadne kept her eyes fixed on the flagstones in front of her, where the blood and spit dripping from her swollen lips were pooling into a murky puddle. "Don't worry about that, captain. I'm pretty sure you won't have to tell Gwyneth anything."

A wave of excitement licked through the crowd. Shouts became cheers; hands pounded together in wild applause, and the cheering became a chant: "*MI-LO! MI-LO! MI-LO!*"

And there he was: Milo, captain of the guard, a tall, muscular figure, loping towards the throne with an easy, unhurried stride. He walked like a man heading home at the end of a tiring day, in spite of the bloody crust that covered each of his arms past the elbow.

Milo mounted the dais, then turned. He said nothing, ordered nothing, but the sweep of his gaze calmed the room. The crowd fell silent.

Once he had everyone's full attention, he nudged the foot of the throne with his boot. "Someone get rid of this trash."

It was no surprise that they jumped to obey him. If I hadn't been on my knees with a soldier at my back, *I* might have jumped to obey him. His voice wasn't very loud, but there was a calm assurance in it that was somehow more compelling than a shout.

Rebels came forward with crowbars and pried the throne loose from its place on the dais, tossing it down the steps. Konrad's corpse came loose from the throne as it bounced down. Something broke off of it in the fall—a burnt, blackened arm.

They brought up a simple wooden chair for Milo, placing it where the throne used to stand. Seating himself, he pulled off his helmet to expose his bare face. I sucked in a breath when I saw what the helmet had covered until that moment: hooked nose, jutting cheekbones, and a short crop of dark hair, coarse as a horse's mane.

Well. That explained a thing or two.

His eyes scanned the crowd and rested on me. He smiled. I'd never before seen a smile that looked like a razor, like just the touch of it could cut.

"Darren, so good to see you," he said. Leaning back, he dug into his belt pouch. "I was hoping that we'd run into each other so I could give this back. Naturally I appreciate the gesture, but I've decided that I'm going to buy my own drinks from now on."

He pulled out the copper coin I'd given him only a few hours before and tossed it to me with a lazy flick of the wrist. It *tink-tink-tinked* across the stone floor and juddered to a stop by my knee.

"Why don't we—?" My voice caught in my throat. I coughed and tried again. "Why don't we cut to the chase here? I take it that you're my brother."

A hard rap on my head made my ears ring, and Jada's voice hissed, "You're nothing to him, you piece of shit."

"Now, now," Milo said, his voice calm and distant. "It's only natural for her to be curious. And no, Darren, I'm not your brother. My father wasn't Stribos, he was—"

"Uncle Saxon," I finished for him. I could see the resemblance now. Something about the jaw. "So we're cousins."

"Well, that's not quite true, is it? Bastards don't count as real children. That's what we were always told."

We. My stomach gave a sharp twist, as my head flooded with pictures of my father chasing skirts, groping thighs, and pulling girls onto his lap. And Uncle Saxon hadn't been much better, from what little I remembered. *Of course* I had a horde of bastard brothers and sisters and cousins that I'd never bothered to ask about and no one had bothered to mention.

"How many of you are there?" I asked. "How many bastards?"

He smiled again, distantly. "Just think for a minute. For three hundred years, the House of Torasan has raided and robbed and violated the people of the Isle. Every young lord with a prick has taken his fill from among the servant girls. For every pure line of Torasan succession, there are a thousand muddy tributaries. You probably share blood with half the people in this room. Stribos knew that, even if you didn't. He thought it was funny. He liked to yell 'Bastard!' while his soldiers were drilling, to see how many of us would jump."

"Konrad wasn't Stribos," I said. My bound hands were shaking—whether from pain or shock or rage, I wasn't sure. "He wasn't Alek, or Fletcher—he wasn't a tyrant or a maniac or a brute. He cared about the Isle; he knew that people were hurting. He wanted to make things *better*, you murdering wankstain—"

"Better?" Milo said. "Oh, no doubt. I've known plenty of men like Konrad, men determined to be better than their fathers. Instead of throwing you a scrap of mouldy bread when you're starving, they'll throw you two scraps. Steal an apple, and they'll give you five lashes with the rawhide, not ten. And they always act so hurt when you're not grateful."

He looked out to the crowd, eyes burning. "We decided we weren't going to beg on bended knee for the little mercies that Konrad of Torasan was willing to show us. What do you say, Freemen of the Isle?"

The roar of agreement made the rafters quiver.

"And I wouldn't throw around words like *murder*, Darren." *Darren,* he said, but his attention was all on the mob. He was speechifying, working the room. "Today, those of us here avenged old Varro, hung two years ago yesterday for hiding his son from the press gangs. We avenged Tomm the wheelwright, who lost a hand for daring to strike that animal Alek in the face. We avenged a thousand men over ten generations who were worked to death on Torasan warships. *What do you say, Freemen of the Isle?*"

Another roar, but Jada's voice—piercing, frenzied—rang out above them all.

And Milo leaned forwards in his chair, turning his attention towards her. "Jada."

She came to attention like a pointer dog, trembling with eager energy.

"Jada, you were born a parasite, and they tried to make you think you'd never be anything more. But you killed two slave drivers with your own hands—the first when you gave Stribos the last cup of wine he'd ever drink, the second when you baptized your blade in Gunnar's back. Any regrets?"

Jada lifted her chin. "No more than when I crush a cockroach underfoot."

"That's what I thought. And in helping us cleanse the Isle, you've cleansed your own soul, at last." He crooked a finger. "Come up here to me."

She mounted the steps to the dais, and the sight nearly made me vomit. It had been strange and painful to watch Jada playing the bully, her face lit up with cruel childish glee as she drew her knife point down Ariadne's cheek. It was worse to watch her simpering at Milo. Her face glowed with a stupid sort of awe and wonder that bordered on worship.

"Oh, you have got to be kidding," Ariadne muttered. Then, louder, "You think you're in love with him? He's using you, idiot!"

Milo's eyes flicked up briefly. He spoke, not to Ariadne, but to Jada. "Is this the one you told me about?"

Jada cast us a look of smug triumph, like a child who'd tattled on a misbehaving sibling. *I told Teacher what you said, and now you're going to get it.* "That's the one."

"Are you listening? You're nothing but marriage meat to him!" Ariadne struggled upwards, and got about halfway to her feet before the rebel behind her shoved her back down to her knees. She winced, but didn't stop. "He *knows* that every nobleman in a thousand miles will come down on Torasan Isle like a hammer, once they find out it's been taken over by a bastard with ideas above his station. He *knows* that he has to marry a true-born if he's going to have any vague chance of holding the throne. That's all that matters to him, so forget whatever sweet nothings he's whispered in your ear. He doesn't give a shit about you, Jada!"

I tensed, ready for Jada to fly down the steps and smack Ariadne's head clean off her shoulders. Jada didn't move, though, just looked down at Ariadne with supreme contempt.

"You know nothing about him, filth," she said.

Ariadne almost screamed in frustration. "Oh, for goodness's sake—I'm trying to save your life. Don't be a stupid brat, just because I embarrassed you at the dinner table!"

Milo ran gentle fingers along the side of Jada's jaw, turning her face towards him. They kissed. At least, I think that's what they were doing. Jada went at it so vigorously that she could have been mining for gold in his back molars. After a few seconds, Milo extricated himself.

"Mouthy little thing, isn't she?" he murmured. "Could you do me a favour and take care of that?"

Jada glowed. "Anything for the Master of the Free Isle."

She slid off of Milo's lap—she'd ended up there, somehow, while she was plumbing his tonsils—and rose to her full height. There she stood, naked knife in one hand, staring down from on high at Ariadne, as a roomful of armed men watched in reverent silence. I watched her taste the moment, and like the taste.

"Take her outside and have her whipped," Jada said. "Maybe that'll teach her how much her opinion is worth."

The rebels howled their approval and eagerness, and I wondered how many of them were personally familiar with the whipping post that stood just outside the palisade. Ariadne breathed slowly. Then, once again, she tried to rise to her feet. This time, her guards let her do it. Calmly, methodically, she smoothed out the skirt of her nightgown.

Out of pure panic and instinct, I grabbed her sleeve. I couldn't stop this, I knew that, but how could I just let her walk away?

She pulled her arm free. "It's fine, Darren."

"How the hell is it fine?" I whispered. I'd seen so many servants and bondsmen sagging against the whipping post, while the rawhide carved their backs into flapping rags. My skin was tanned almost to leather by sun and salt water, but I knew I couldn't cope with that kind of pain. Ariadne was all soft curves and smooth surfaces, and I didn't see how she could survive.

Maybe she didn't see either, because she tried to smile and couldn't. "All right, it's not fine. But I can take this. Gwyneth took worse. Don't judge me if I make lots of stupid noises."

"Flaming shite, of course not." I racked my brain, trying to remember everything I'd heard about flogging, everything that could possibly help her. "Lean back after every stroke, don't let yourself slump against the post. Don't turn your head sideways. Um—"

"Don't hold your breath," Regon put in, quietly, tiredly. "You'll want to. Don't."

Ariadne nodded, teeth chattering. "I'll see you on the other side, you two."

Somehow, she managed to stay on her feet as they led her from the hall, though she stumbled more than once. Jada followed them out, smacking her knife-hilt against her palm, and whistling the chicken song under her breath.

"So," Milo said briskly. "While Jada takes out the trash, let's deal with the larger issue. What am I going to do with you, Darren?"

I WENT FOR him. It was stupid, of course, but I was so very tired of listening to Milo talk. I thought that maybe if I tore his nose off and threw it out a window, he might say something that was more worth listening to—something along the lines of, *Oh gods, the pain, the pain.*

After he'd knocked me down a couple of times, I stopped getting back up, and just hunched on the dais steps, trying to remember how to breathe. The air was thick and tasted like iron bees.

Far away, I heard Regon's voice, saying things like *Captain Captain Captain* and *Get up* and *Breathe through it.* Regon type things, comforting things—the same kind of reassurances he'd been giving me since I marched onto the *Glory of the Isles* in a state of blind terror at age fourteen.

"Red-Handed Darren," Milo said. "Pirate queen, defender of the helpless. Pride of Torasan Isle, and the peasants' white-hot hope. Isn't it a joke, how reputations are made? You know, Darren, I once heard a shepherd say—and he was dead serious—that you understood the plight of the common man because you knew how it felt to be hungry. This because you once ran low on rations during an overland haul and had to tighten your belt for a couple of months. A couple of months of hunger in a lifetime of gorging yourself at the royal trough, and suddenly you're the people's champion."

"I'm not—" I started, but the toe of his boot caught me right in the pit of the stomach. I barely recognized my own gasping sob.

"Now I don't want you to worry," he said, still in that calm, conversational tone. "This isn't your last night on earth. I have some plans for you that I think you'll find interesting. You're going to relive your glory days. Who knows? Maybe you'll end up understanding the plight of the common man even better than you did before."

Well, that wasn't at all ominous. I rummaged around in my head for a menacing and impressive reply that I could deliver while curled in fetal position on the floor. Came up empty, but Regon was there in the pinch.

"If you hurt her," he said, "if you put a single stinking hand on her, then people from here to the Bay of Accra will curse your name until the sea drains dry."

"Do you lick the boots of every noble you come across, or just hers?" Milo asked, a nasty edge in his voice. "Just hers, right? I know your type. You're a one woman dog."

"You think you can shame me for following her?" Regon spat on the floor. He must have managed to work up a fair amount of spit, because it made an emphatic *splat*. "I don't know how long you've been planning this shit. But all the time you've been smarming around the Isle, working up the courage to slaughter unarmed women, my captain's been on the seas fighting the real fight."

I balled my bound hands into fists underneath me and pushed up until I could see something other than floor. Regon's boots. Milo's boots. Two shadows across the flagstones.

"Fighting the real fight," Milo said. "You mean, her own people threw her away when she turned out to be a sexual pervert, so she decided, what the hell? Might as well side with the commoners. Hell of a comfy way to fight the system, piracy. She gets all the glory of being the peasants' champion and never has to scrub a single floor."

That wasn't fair. I *had* tried. Lynn always complained that I missed too many spots.

Regon grunted. "All right, you fetid sack of goat scrotums, go ahead and shit on her motives. She's still saving lives, and you're still a butcher. And don't give me that crap about justice. You're hardly the first bastard son of a noble to whip the peasants to a lather and send them out to cut down their liege lords. It always ends the same way. The other lords strike back with a great mailed fist, and then farmland's salted and villages are burned, and women and children are starving in the streets. I've heard this song before. So go ahead. Preach yourself blue in the face, and promise your followers castles in the clouds and feasts of sugar candy. You aren't going to get them anything but dead, and they'll realize that sooner than you think."

Was it just me, or did Milo not have a ready response to that? I groped in a random direction, found something steady to hold, and managed to totter up to my feet.

"You're a loyal bitch," Milo said to Regon at last. "Does Darren take you from behind, when she's bored with her little slave girl?"

"Don't you fucking talk about Lynn," I snarled. It was a pretty good snarl, but since I was still hunched over my aching ribs, most of the effect was probably lost.

"Lynn," he repeated. He rolled the name around his mouth, and I cursed myself for giving it to him, letting him touch it and mangle it. "That mouthy little blond called her something different—but what the hell, right? Maybe you don't know her name. Maybe you assign her a new one every day. *Muffin. Slut. Fido.*"

Incandescent with rage, I opened my mouth, but Regon got there first. "You really are a pig of a man, aren't you?"

"And you let a woman lead you around by your prick," Milo said, his voice becoming even nastier, somehow. "Why is that? You think she can help you now?"

Regon spat again. This time, the grey gobbet landed on the toe of one of Milo's hobnailed boots. "You're not worth arguing with, you sad little boy, and you're boring me. Just get on with it."

Get on with what? My brain must have been numbed almost to crawling pace with exhaustion and pain, because even when Milo drew his sword, I didn't understand.

Regon was saying Regon-things again, like *It's all right, captain* and *It was worth it,* and the words buzzed fitfully around my head, connecting with nothing. I looked at the sword and I looked at Regon.

"No," I said, brain snapping back to life. "Don't you hurt him, leave him alone—"

"I'm not going to hurt him," Milo said. "I'm going to put him out of his misery. When you cut his balls off, you made one hell of a clean job of it."

"Sad little boy," Regon said again. "Sad little boy lives in terror of meeting a woman smarter than he is. Sad little boy holds his dick with both hands when he talks to a girl, in case it starts to come loose."

Milo's face didn't show that the jibe had landed, but his knuckles whitened on his sword-hilt, and he hefted his blade.

"*No!*" I gasped. "Milo—No! Leave him alone! Do it to me! I'm the one you're after! Milo, me! Me, me, me, me, *me!*"

"Me, me, me," Milo repeated. "That's always the way of it with you nobles, isn't it?"

The blade flashed out.

For a second, I thought Milo had missed. Regon still stood upright, though his head was bent at an unnatural angle. But then came the blood, streaming from the left side of Regon's neck like a red carpet unrolling, down his shoulder and arm. Maybe the sword was dull, or maybe Milo's sword arm wasn't as strong as he fancied it, because the blow had only taken Regon's head off halfway.

There was no such mistake with the second strike. Regon's body crumpled to the flagstones. A fraction of a second later, so did his head. The grey eyes, in a suddenly ashen face, were still wide open, and staring.

Too late—far too late—I surged at my captors, howling, flailing, not even caring what Milo was going to do to me if only I could punch a few of those perfect teeth out. Hard hands grabbed me and pulled me backwards. Someone dealt a clout to my skull that took me down, and then they all closed in with fists and boots.

Very dimly, through the blows that rocked me, I could hear noise from outside the courtyard: the cracking of a whip. Ariadne didn't last even one stroke before she started screaming.

PART FOUR

BASTARDS

CHAPTER SEVENTEEN

Lynn

I THINK THAT Milo's messenger expected me to cry, or something. Joke was on him. I never did that in front of men.

I stared down at Regon's body where it lay on the *Banshee's* deck, taking in the details, one by one. The body was still dressed in shirt and breeches, but it was barefoot, so someone must have stolen his boots. The stump of his neck was ragged, as if his head had been hacked off, rather than sliced. His head lay alongside the body, its skin the colour of week-old biscuits, tinged with olive green.

Flies were buzzing around the nostrils. I knelt to brush them away. The deck of the *Banshee* rocked beneath us: a strong wind, what would have been a good running wind, if we had the option of running away.

I breathed in, breathed out, and read Milo's letter again.

Dear Lynn:

I can already tell that the two of us have much in common.

That being the case, I feel like I should begin with some kind of pleasantry, something like "I wish we'd met under different circumstances." But neither of us is the type to beat around the bush. So. Here's what I have to say, in the bluntest words possible.

I need money. You have money. I have your sister and your lover. You don't want them dead.

You are going to pay me ten thousand gold royals. You will do this fast, because until you do it, Darren won't eat. She'll last a little while—I hear that she has some practice when it comes to going hungry—but it would be inadvisable to dawdle.

You will bring the gold straight to the lighthouse at the southernmost tip of the Isle. You will not approach any other part of the island, including the main dock. If I see a red sail within ten miles of the harbour, then your sister will die screaming.

Once you have delivered the money, we will discuss terms for the release of your people.

I trust that you will govern yourself accordingly.

Yours faithfully,
Milo
Master of the Free Isle

I crumpled the letter in one fist and looked up at the messenger. He was starting to look nervous, which meant that he wasn't entirely stupid. He'd been smirking when he first clambered onto the *Banshee's* deck. No longer. Maybe he'd seen murder in my face. Maybe he'd seen it in Spinner's.

Spinner. He was beside me, staring at Regon's body, his eyes stone, his face stone. I didn't touch his hand, or show any other sign of gentleness. Better to focus on the banal aftermath of a murder: the cleaning up.

"We need to sew him into his hammock before the funeral," I said. "Can you cope, or should I ask someone else to handle it?"

"Piss off."

Roughly translated, that meant, "If you think I am going to let anyone other than me do this one last thing for Regon, you are batshit crazy, and if anyone else tries to touch him, I will break their fingers like breadsticks."

So I stepped out of his way, and he headed for the forecastle to fetch Regon's hammock. Once he'd sewed the body into its shroud, we'd give Regon to the ocean, where his parents and twin brother and at least eleven cousins were already at rest. I hoped that Spinner, at least, would find some comfort in that thought, even if I couldn't.

Everyone has a well of strength right down in the deepest part of their soul, a place too deep for doubt or confusion to reach. It's raw, that strength, and it's harsh and it's elemental, and it's what sustains you when everything else is ripped away. Some people, like Darren, have fire down there, but people like me have ice, and the more desperate we are, the colder and harder we turn.

As I returned my attention to Milo's messenger, I felt the change happening, a rime of frost settling all over my skin.

"Start again," I said. "Tell me again exactly what Milo wants from me. And while you're doing that, a word to the wise? There are a whole lot of people on this ship who want to hurt you. If you can't wipe that smile off your face, I might let them. Hell, I might help them heat up the irons and find the hungriest rats. I'm hardly an angel to begin with, and you've caught me on a very bad day."

ABOUT TWELVE HOURS went by between the moment when Ariadne choked me senseless on the shore, and the moment when Milo's messenger arrived at the *Banshee* with Regon's body. I can't claim that they were the worst twelve hours of my life, but still, I'd rather douche with lye than relive them.

Here's how that twelve hours went.

First five minutes: Still unconscious. The only good part of the night.

Next five minutes: Splinters of awareness, shreds of the world coming back. Rushing wind, creaking oars; hard drops of briny spray hitting my tongue and teeth. I must have known, even in my stupor, that something had just gone terribly wrong, because disconnected words kept tumbling through my brain: *Ariadne. Idiot. Stupid damn nobles. Oh shit.*

Next half hour: Woke up, wished I hadn't. Head not just pounding but pulsing with pain, the ache a thick sticky liquid that throbbed in my veins and coated my eyes. Sat on a thwart, gripping my head in both hands, in the middle of a mob of small children. Tried not to notice the children crying, whining, puking, or pissing. Failed, miserably.

Tried equally hard not to notice that Latoya was talking to me. I managed this for a while, because her remarks weren't all that interesting—pretty much just *Lynn do you hear me Lynn talk to me Lynn snap the hell out of it Lynn*, over and over and over. But she kept getting louder and louder and then she sent one of the kids over to poke me in the ribs. I did a quick calculation and decided that it would take more effort to keep ignoring her than it would to answer.

I asked, "What the hell is it, Latoya?"

Silence. I squinted at her through the haze of wan moonlight and mist.

She was . . . well, no, she wasn't crying, not exactly. She was taking short gulpy breaths and hissing the air out through her teeth. For a normal human being, that would have been a sign of extreme exhaustion. But Latoya was a person who considered a ten mile run to be just a warm-up for a fifty mile run, and who thought a fifty mile run was a warm-up for another fifty mile run, this time uphill while carrying a sandbag on each shoulder.

She was off her game, and that meant the situation was seven steps beyond bad.

Imagine being out for a swim and feeling a sharp tug on your leg, just below the knee. Then the water begins to turn warm and red all around you, and a dark shape is moving in the depths beneath, as you realize that you can't feel your right foot anymore. That's the kind of fear and panic that sluiced through me that second as I remembered what had happened that night. We'd already lost so much, and it had only just begun.

FOR THE HOUR after that, I was no use at all. I spent the time dwelling on a few obvious and unhelpful thoughts, like how my head hurt like hell, and how Darren might already be dead, and how maybe it had been a mistake to take just about everyone that I loved in the world and assemble them all on one pirate ship.

At last, Latoya told me to take the rudder. Or, more accurately, she told me for the thousandth time to take the rudder, and I was too tired to keep on ignoring her. My head throbbed worse than ever when I opened my eyes to the streaky dawn light, so I steered blind, jerking the tiller whenever Latoya yelled a direction.

But Latoya was rowing, so her back was to the boat's bow, so she couldn't see where we were headed unless she twisted right around. So she kept telling me to open my eyes, and I kept growling at her in answer. She lost patience for maybe the first time ever and reached over to shake my arm, and I bit her. And then there was a certain amount of swearing on both sides.

"Pull yourself together, Lynn," Latoya said, once we ran out of curses. "I do not have time to babysit you while you fall apart. If you get in my way when I'm trying to fix this, I will get you out of the way, fast."

She was so tightly wound, just an anguished knot of pain and terror. Maybe, I thought, that meant I shouldn't take her threats seriously. Maybe, I thought, it meant that I really, really should.

AFTER A FEW thousand years on the cramped longboat, we found the *Banshee*, or the *Banshee* found us. One or the other. I wasn't coherent enough to care about little details like that. There was a lot of shouting back and forth, and a lot of ropes being thrown around. Somehow, I ended up on deck, with Spinner leaning over me, sponging the salt from my mouth with a wet rag.

The first word out of his mouth was, "Regon?"

"I don't know," I said, sitting up gingerly and wincing at the sunlight. "Ariadne had herself a good binge on stupid juice and decided it would be fun to get us all killed. Then she thought she might as well double down on the stupid, so she took Latoya and me out of play."

"Latoya told me. Do you know what happened to Regon?"

"All I know is that as of right now, Regon's the only one on Isle who has a working brain."

"The captain's there too."

"I stand by my assessment. Darren's playing hero right now. You know how she gets. Where's Latoya? We need to huddle and think of a way to unfuck this turd of a situation."

"Latoya's arming up. There are sails heading our way from the southwest. Could be coming from the Isle." He pointed to two square white blots sitting on the horizon. "Latoya wants to be ready for violence when they get here, in case they have plans other than giving us all great big hugs. I think she's missing the obvious explanation, though . . . it could be the captain and Regon, couldn't it?"

The hope in his voice was painful to hear. I pressed his shoulder, and we waited together for bad news.

"ONCE AGAIN," I said to Milo's messenger. "The fuckwit you call your leader—"

"The Master of the Free Isle—"

"Whatever. He wants me to bring him ten thousand gold royals . . . and then what happens?"

"Then he releases your people. He explained all this in his letter. I thought you could read."

"He didn't say he'd release them. He said that he would think about it. He's not going to give me any kind of guarantee?"

"If you don't like it, you can always piss off in the other direction. Go spend some time getting hammered at the Freemarket. Buy a monkey. But you're not going to, are you?"

I was tempted to bluff, to say something along the lines of, *You know what? That's a splendid idea. Tell Darren goodbye for me; I'm off to the monkey store.* But there on the deck beside me was Regon's corpse, proof that Milo was the sort of man it wasn't safe to test.

"Oh, you're not leaving?" The messenger smirked. "Well, then, you have your orders. Go on, little girl. Fetch."

It's pathetic when some stupid amateur pretends to be in control of a situation, not realizing that he's in far over his head.

"Can I ask a quick question before I scamper off?" I said. "Why does Milo want you dead?"

His smirk didn't go away, not exactly, but it wavered. "What are you talking about?"

"Oh, come on. He sent you here to deliver the body of a murdered man to a bunch of people who loved him. You really think he expected you to come back?"

He paused. I could almost hear the phrase *Oh crap* rolling around his mind, like a marble in an empty bowl. "He trusts me—"

"He sent you to near-certain death to deliver a letter. Someone who does that to you is probably not your best friend in the whole wide world. If you want to get anywhere in politics, you have to learn to pick up on these subtle social cues." I raised my voice. "Bind this man and take him below."

At least ten pirates perked up—they'd been waiting for a chance to do something violent—and tramped forwards.

"No, wait!" the messenger blurted, sweaty palms upraised. "I'm an emissary, you can't harm me—"

"Says who?"

"You're breaking parlay!"

"Yes, I suppose I am. And you're a commoner who took up arms against your liege. Go ahead and tell some lord's court what I did. See which of us gets whipped to death first." I snapped my fingers. "Get him out of my sight."

"Should we kill him now?" one helpful sailor asked.

"No. I'll need to talk to him again. But feel free to make him extremely uncomfortable. Drop him on his head a few times. Insert spiky things into places where spiky things should not be. Get inventive."

They dragged him off, with a fair degree of enthusiasm. That meant that I didn't have to look at his stupid sneering face anymore, which was nice, but it also meant I had no excuse to keep avoiding Latoya.

She was up on the quarterdeck, doing a pretty fair impression of a volcano about to explode. You know that point when there's no visible lava, but the earth swells and cracks and strains, and steam hisses up through the fissures.

I headed for the steps up to the quarterdeck, because apparently I'd turned into one of those idiots who walk towards volcanic eruptions. Before I reached the stairs, a pudgy hand gripped my shoulder.

The next thing I knew, I had a boy in a wristlock, twisting his arm until he yelped. It was the kid called Hark, tears standing in his eyes as he teetered there on tiptoe. I checked for weapons, found none, and let him go.

"Why did you do that?" Hark said, hurt. He retrieved his hand and cradled it.

"Do you make a habit of touching highly strung, heavily armed people? If so, maybe rethink. It's going to get you into trouble one day."

"I need to ask you something."

"This is not the time to ask me for favours. My love of humankind is at an all-time low, and believe me, that is saying something."

"But this is important." He was bright-eyed and flushed, like a healthy baby. "I'm Alek's oldest son. If my lord uncle Konrad is dead, and Karel is dead . . . well, Konrad's other sons haven't come of age yet. Don't you see?"

"Don't see, don't care."

"I'm next in the line of succession." He was leaning towards me in his eagerness, and his breath smelt of wet bread. "I am the lord of Torasan!"

"Oh, like tits you are."

He gaped. "Aren't you listening? I'm the rightful heir. You want to rescue my aunt Darren, don't you? If you help me retake the Isle, then I can—"

"You can . . . what? You can eat pie while we do all the actual work?"

"I'm the true lord of the Isle," he repeated, slower this time. "Without me, you can't—"

"Bollocks on toast. You're not very good at reading the room, are you? Listen, Hark: you think you're lord of Torasan. The shitgibbons who took over the Isle think you're demon spawn. And me? I think you're a kid on a boat."

The deck beneath us rolled as we crested over a wave. I barely noticed the gentle sloping, but Hark went staggering sideways, first to starboard, and then to port as we righted. His eyebrows furrowed, his shoulders hunched, and a shudder went through his whole body, knees to shoulders.

I sighed, grabbed him by the back of his shirt, and ran him over to the leeward side of the ship. It was self-interest, not kindness. If he made a mess on the deck, I would have to clean it up and I was not. In. The. Mood.

I got him draped over the side just before he was disastrously sick, then left him to it. For at least a few hours, he'd have better things to worry about than the line of succession.

"SO," I SAID to Latoya, as I stepped up to the quarterdeck. "Probably time to come up with a brilliant plan."

"You think?" She let go of the railing to wipe her face, and it left a crimson handprint behind. Both her hands were a mess of tattered skin and bloody bruises, after the long night of rowing. "You sure you don't want to have another nap first? Maybe a snack?"

Oh, fucknuts. "You want an apology? I'm sorry that I wasn't at my best after my sister strangled me until I passed out."

"She did it to save you."

"I know that."

"As if you were the one who needed saving." She stared off at some fixed point on the horizon, the way Darren did when she was trying very hard not to explosively lose her shit. "If Ariadne's still alive, she's hanging by a thread."

"I know. So's Darren. I doubt they'll set her free even if we pay the ransom. She's too valuable—"

Latoya smashed her fist down on the rail with a shattering *crack,* and wood splinters flew.

I jumped. I challenge you not to jump when someone of Latoya's size starts breaking things near your head. It was her voice that scared me most, though—the rawness of it, every nerve exposed, just like her flayed and bloody hands.

"Darren, Darren, Darren," she said. "How about we talk about your sister? Can we do that for half a minute before we talk about the woman they're *not* going to kill?"

"You think Darren isn't in danger?" I asked, slow and unbelieving. "They're starving Darren. Did you miss that minor detail?"

"But they won't kill her. You said it yourself, she's too valuable. Ariadne? She's nothing to them. She might as well be a paper butterfly. If she talks too loud, if she makes trouble, if they want to send a message, if they get nervous, if some stupid fleshbag wants to prove his manhood—"

"I know."

"They could kill her for fun. They could get screaming drunk and throw her out a window."

"I *know*."

"So forget the ransom! They might slit her throat as soon as they get it. We need to go in and get her."

"You know we can't do that. Like you said, they'd kill Ariadne at the drop of a very small hat. What do you think happens if we send a bunch of red-sailed ships swooping down on the island?"

Belatedly, it occurred to me to wonder whether red sails had been the best choice for Darren's ships. They were good for making an impression. Less good if you wanted to go, well, anywhere, without being obvious about it.

"I'm not planning to march up to the front gate blowing a trumpet," Latoya said through her teeth. "We go in dark and quiet, the way we broke into Bero. Remember that? Remember how the captain and Regon and I invaded Bero, armed with a couple of knives and a rock in a stocking, to bust you out of a cage in Melitta's closet?"

On an ordinary day, the mention of Melitta's name would have turned me to liquid. Not this time.

"I remember Bero," I said tightly. "Trust me, the things that happened to me on Bero were not the kind of things that one forgets. Now, do you remember how that whole rescue operation went down? Because, let's face it, it was not Darren's finest hour as a tactician. Remember how her plan was, literally, to jump in the ocean a few miles offshore, and then kind of hope for the best?"

"It worked."

"Yes, it worked—because Ariadne came and found your sodden carcasses on the beach and found a way to get you inside the castle. If she hadn't been there to help, then the three of you would still be staring at the outer gates and scratching yourselves, and I would still be—"

A pulse of blind panic went through me, and I stuttered to a halt. I had to bite the inside of my mouth until I tasted wet copper before I could keep going.

"None of us should have escaped at all," I said. "It was the purest luck that we made it out—sheer angel farts. We can't count on a miracle this time."

"So what do you want?" Latoya asked wildly. "You want a signed letter from Milo, promising that he'll lie down and surrender as soon as we reach the keep? What'll it take to make this rescue worth your time?"

When I was a kid, I had to learn to eat anger. Choke it. Smother it. It wasn't safe for me to be a real person, with a real person's feelings. But then I met this pirate queen and began cheerfully venting all of my frustration at her. After a year or so of that, I lost the knack of strangling my feelings until they went limp and silent.

So it took a few seconds of hard breathing before I could muster a reply.

"You know damn well that I would burn the world down for Darren," I said. "She may be the only reason I haven't burned it down *yet*. I will walk through hell for her, but I'll do it when I have a real chance of bringing her out the other side. Not before."

"So you'll sacrifice Ariadne?" Latoya demanded. "We're not talking about some Torasan brat now. This is your sister. Your *sister*, the woman who loves you more than her skin and her soul. You're going to leave her in the meat grinder while you figure out how to give Darren her best chance?"

"What the hell is wrong with you?" There was a *something* in her eyes that I'd never seen there before, and I didn't know what it was but it frightened me all the same. "We're going to go after them both. Obviously we're going to go after them both!"

"Once *you* decide. Once *you* give the word. And you think your sister should take her chances until *you're* ready to lift a finger."

"Oh, shitlumps on a jam-smeared badger, are you serious?" I was sort of screaming by then. "Latoya, we *don't have a plan*. If you're so desperate to bleed for Ariadne, go ahead and slit your wrists on the aftcastle. But it won't do *shit* to save her, and it *won't* make her love you back!"

I heard the *crack* before I saw her hand fly—and then I was running, skittering backwards, half-falling half-jumping down the stairs to the maindeck. It was only when I was down there—once I'd taken stock for a bewildered, heart-pounding second—that I realized what had happened. She'd punched the railing again. Hard enough, this time, to send a sizable chunk of it crashing down into the sea. Hard enough to slash or tear something on her injured hand, so a stream of red curled around her wrist and drip-drip-dripped on the toes of her sea-boots.

She stared at me, panting.

"You think I'd hit you?" she said. "Really?"

"It's just instinct," I said. But I kept backing up.

"All this time. Everything we've been through. And you still don't trust me."

My heel hit the railing of the ship's side. I couldn't retreat any more.

"You don't trust anyone, except for Darren," Latoya said, answering her own question. "In your broken little brain, it's still the two of you against all the world. And no one else matters, not really, at the end of the day."

The crew. Where was the crew? I darted a glance sideways and—yes. There they were, a silent but fascinated audience, watching.

Waiting?

"You never face anything," Latoya said. "You dodge. You duck. You go around. It's all you know how to do. And when it's time to stand, you're nowhere. Even if it's your sister's neck in the noose."

I spread my arms wide. "Are we really going to stand here and argue about who loves Ariadne more?"

"I don't care whether you love her or not. What the hell does it matter whether you love her, if you won't fight for her?"

"You want proof that I'll fight for her? For both of them? I will not *let* you get them killed. So back off before I take you down."

Had I really just said that? The part of my brain that dealt with the business of survival sent an urgent message to the part that controlled my speech, asking whether I had in fact just challenged Latoya, and if so, *why the fuck.*

Someone—one of the newer recruits, I thought—tittered nervously. Latoya didn't smile. Nowhere close. And for once, I wondered if it was a good thing that she knew better than to underestimate me. Her right hand bunched into a fist, and relaxed again.

"Latoya, Lynn," Corto said, his voice wavering and uncertain. "If this goes on, the men are going to end up mighty confused."

"No one's getting confused." Latoya's eyes didn't move from me. "Lynn's had a hard night. She's going to go to her cabin and lie down for a while. Right?"

"Oh, yeah. That sounds nifty." My garrotte, as always, was tied loosely around my wrist. I dug a forefinger under the cord, ready to pull it free. "If I do that, is the cabin door going to stay open behind me? Or is it somehow mysteriously going to end up locked and barred?"

"No one's going to lock you up." Latoya started down the steps to the maindeck, each step a heavy tread that I could feel as a tremor in the deck-planks. "Not if you stay out of my way."

"Well, here's the problem: I'm not very good at staying where I'm put. And one more problem: I can't let you get in *my* way, either."

Silence hung in the cold, still air. Somebody coughed. Everyone was listening.

"You really want to do this?" Latoya asked, with utter calm. "Go toe to toe with me?"

She hadn't reached for a weapon, but it wasn't as if she needed one to knock me flat. Mentally, I measured the distance between me and Corto. He wasn't far, I could maybe make it behind the protection of his sword arm before Latoya could grab me, but then, would he be willing to draw steel on Latoya? Bloody hell, would I?

"You know I don't want to do this," I said.

"So don't." She adjusted her stance, shifting weight to her back foot. "Stand down. Let me handle this. Don't force the situation. Don't make the crew take sides. Because if it comes to that, Lynn, if you start a civil war—who the hell do you think is going to win it?"

I pictured what the crewmen of the *Banshee* were seeing that second, as Latoya and I squared off. On one side, a seven-foot musclewoman and master marlinspike sailor, with fists like chunks of granite and a mind like steel wire; on the other side, a short, skinny, barefoot girl, armed with a glorified piece of string. It should have been obvious which way the crew would swing, except . . . except . . .

"You forget," I said. I tapped my shoulder, the one with the storm-petrel tattoo—the same mark that was emblazoned on Darren's flag, and Darren's seal, and Darren's best surcoat, and Darren's secret brandy flask, the one I had stolen from her and thrown over the side of the ship just the day before. Everything she owned.

"I belong to the pirate queen," I said. "I don't speak for myself. Her will is my will and her voice is my voice and *anyone loyal to her* will follow my orders!"

I was almost screaming when I finished, and my head swam with vertigo and my eyeballs ached as though my head was coming apart. Which was only right, because the world was coming apart. Because this was going to happen, me against Latoya, and it couldn't happen but it had to happen and if it happened, I had to win.

Latoya's mouth twitched. "You really think that'll work?"

It had damn well better work, considering how long this had been my emergency plan, and how much effort I'd put into it. I didn't say that part out loud.

"All right," Latoya said quietly, and again, "all right. Corto, Sal. Take her and tie her up. Put her down in the hold. We can drop her off with Jess as soon as—"

"*All hands,*" I roared. When you're smaller, you have to be louder. "All hands, in wing formation, prepare to advance on my mark."

"—And I guess you'd better gag her," Latoya finished. "This is fucking stupid, Lynn."

"This is doing what it takes." I tugged the garrotte loose from my wrist and ran its slippery length through my fingers. "And I do what it takes, whatever it takes. Always have."

"We have that in common." She blew out a long, resigned breath. "All right. Corto, make sure to pin her legs. You know how she likes to go for the heel stomp."

"Mark!" I yelled. *"All hands, forward!"*

There was the familiar ripple along Latoya's neck and shoulders as her muscles tightened, preparing for a lunge. She was tired—that was something—and her hands were torn up too badly for her to hold a weapon with any ease. So she was, maybe, only eighty percent as dangerous as usual. So attacking her wouldn't be *pure* suicide. Still pretty close.

I wanted desperately to see what the sailors behind me were doing, but there was no point in turning to look. The talking was over, and I couldn't fight or fuck or trick my way out of this, not this time. It all came down to whether the crew would rally to me. It was up to them, now, and as Latoya began her forward charge, as the power of her footfalls made the decks thunder, I could only wait to see what they would do.

CHAPTER EIGHTEEN

Darren of the House of Torasan (Prisoner)

I WAS CONSCIOUS when they threw me in the cell—just—but it was some time before I was alert enough to get up and explore the space with outstretched hands.

It was just a cell. A stone box, about six feet by six feet. It was windowless; a faint line of torchlight trickled in beneath the barred door, but not enough to see by. A bucket in one corner oozed a foul smell into the room.

The bucket was heavy iron. I thought maybe I could use it to smash the skull of the first person to come through the door, until my groping hands felt the chain that secured it to a ring-bolt in the wall. The bastards were one step ahead of me.

There was a pile of straw in another corner. Bedding. A soft scritch-scratching noise from the pile told me that it was crawling with fleas. I fumbled my way into another corner and sat on the bare stone.

That was it. That was all I could do. And that's when I began to lose it.

If you're lucky, you get one person in your life like Regon, a person who never blames you for anything and so never needs an apology, a person who knows you so well that you can never surprise or disappoint him. If you do have a friend like that, then try not to let him get murdered, because if you lose him, I promise you this: You will never get another.

Even on that first day, I felt the loss like a missing limb. Raw with grief and fury, I pounded the floor until my fists were chunks of bleeding meat. *Why* had I brought him with me on a suicide mission, *why* had he decided to follow me in the first place, *why* hadn't I done something to save him . . . ?

All right, announced a calm voice from the back of my head. *That's quite enough of that.*

It sounded like Lynn. So much so that I could picture her sitting there in the darkness beside me, with that look of grave, slightly sad concentration.

What would Lynn say if she was there? Well, that was obvious: she'd say, "Take a nap."

And I'd answer: "Those sons of bitches murdered Regon, and you expect me to sleep?"

And she would say: "You're in a box. You can't do anything useful right now. Take a nap. Save your energy for when it matters."

Save my energy—yes. They weren't planning to feed me. I was hungry already. I would be hungrier soon. I had to slow the starvation process as much as I could, and that meant doing my best impression of a vegetable.

I wedged myself in the corner, did some deep breathing, and closed my eyes.

That was my first nap as Milo's captive. Between the grief, the shock, the rage, and the hunger, it was not a very relaxing one.

LATER—HOW MUCH later, it was impossible to say—a sort of cat-flap at the bottom of the door rattled, and an unseen hand shoved a bowl inside.

I lurched my way over to it and inspected it by touch. My fingertips found cool water. I drank off the entire bowl before I realized what I was doing, and cursed my own stupidity. Had that been a day's supply of water? A week's supply?

Well, there was nothing I could do about it now. I retreated back into my corner, and dozed fitfully until I had to get up to use the bucket. I had been avoiding this, but I couldn't put it off forever. The stink in the cell became twice as bad. I pulled my shirt up over my nose before I went to sleep again.

HUNGER STARTS AS pain: stabbing pain, cramping pain. A scraping sensation, as though your stomach is a gourd and the soft inside is being scooped out spoonful by spoonful. As time goes on, the pain gives way to dizziness and nausea. Your gastric juices bubble up and sear your throat. Your heart begins to pound so hard that your brain seems to bounce inside your skull.

How long had I been in the starvation cell? They had delivered water three times—that was all I knew.

"You have to think about something other than food," my imaginary Lynn said to me. She was wearing the sheer white tunic and the copper bangles that she usually only put on for special occasions. My birthday, for example. And the day before my birthday, because, as I've remarked, I'm not a patient person.

"What am I supposed to think about?" I asked. "It's not like there are any dancing girls or flute players in here."

Imaginary Lynn smirked. "Trust you to be thinking about dancing girls at a time like this."

"I'm just saying, there's nothing here to distract me."

"You could wank. That would distract you."

"I find it hard to communicate just exactly how much I am not in a sexy mood."

"Well, *that* we can fix. Should I strip, or do you want to fantasize about the dancing girls instead?"

"I don't remember what the dancing girls looked like. I barely even noticed them."

"Congratulations, Mistress. You almost managed to say that convincingly."

In some dim corner of my brain, I knew I was carrying on a conversation with myself. There was probably a spy just outside the door, snickering and playing with himself as he listened. I was past giving a damn.

"Do *you* dance?" I asked imaginary Lynn.

I had never asked the real Lynn this question, so I had to make up the answer.

"Ariadne tried to teach me once," imaginary Lynn said. "But we didn't have music. The way I hear it, music helps."

"Want to try it some time?"

"Depends. Is it as much fun as the dancing you can do with trousers off?"

At this interesting juncture, the conversation was cut short. There was a grating sound—metal on metal—and the cell door banged open.

I stared up listlessly as two soldiers tramped in, wheeling a large, stinking barrel. What was a hero supposed to do at a time like this? Bounce up and knock their skulls together, I supposed. Even the thought exhausted me. I didn't move.

They paid me no attention as they emptied my slop-bucket into the larger barrel. It took all of twenty seconds, and they left as soon as they were finished.

I waited for the door to slam shut again so that imaginary Lynn and I could continue where we'd left off. Instead, a tall thin figure appeared in doorway, holding a guttering rush-light. She stepped inside, and the door scraped shut behind her.

She seemed to be one of the castle cooks, judging from the grease-stained apron, but her face, with its pox-scarred forehead, wasn't one I recognized.

My voice came out as a croak. "Who'd you piss off?"

"I didn't piss off anyone," she said. "They'll let me out when I knock."

"Oh," I said. "That's nice."

Silence. Something rustled in the bed of straw. Bigger than a flea. Cockroach, maybe.

"Well?" she finally snapped. "You're the one who came looking for me."

I stared at her in tired confusion. I didn't have the energy, or the brainpower, to ask what the hell she meant. But that was when I noticed her eyes. They were deep-set in that wrinkled, scarred, unlovely face, but in the faint glow of the rush-light, I could see their colour: a pale, pale shade of brown. I'd only seen eyes that colour once before, and they'd been wide and liquid, like those of a startled fawn.

"Tavia?" I whispered.

WE STARED AT each other for long enough for the rush-light to burn down to half its length.

At first glance, Tavia seemed middle-aged, her face and hands wrinkled and spotted from years of hard work. Only the skin of her neck, still smooth and fair, showed that she was a few years younger than I was.

"So," Tavia said at last. "You wanted to talk?"

I took a shuddering breath. "The boy at the spits told me you were dead."

She laughed coarsely. "You marched into the kitchen and asked for me by name. He didn't know whether you wanted to beat me for burning your supper, give me to your men as a present, or throw me off the tower roof. He covered for me."

Clever servants talking their way around the gormless noble. Classic. Lynn would have done it better, though—she'd have made up some bloody and interesting death for Tavia, something involving mad cows. Or carnivorous plants.

"I guess you're working for Milo now," I said.

She smoothed her apron. "I'm cooking for him. And his men. If that's what it means to work for someone, then I guess I am."

"And are things better for you now?" I was groping for words. "For you and for . . . people like you?"

Tavia shrugged. "Cooking's still cooking. Onions still stink. Boiling water's still hot. Nothing changes that, no matter who's sitting in the big chair. Some things are better now. Some may be worse. I'll tell you this, though. No one down below stairs is mourning your father. Or your brothers. Or Torasan House. *Or* you. That's your truth and that's for you to live with."

I nodded. "That's fair. But a lot of people died so that Milo could sit in the big chair instead of my brother. It would be nice to know that he actually fixed a problem or two. People aren't moved to revolution by the battle cry, 'Things'll pretty much stay the same!'"

She shrugged again, clearly uninterested. "Why were you looking for me?"

"I was . . . oh, crap." It seemed a little bit pointless now. "I wanted to apologize."

"For what?"

Well, I hadn't imagined it this way, but this was the moment, I supposed. I raised my chin and straightened out my filthy shirt.

"For hitting you," I said. "I'm so sorry for the times that I hit you. It makes me sick to think about it. I don't have any excuses. I'm just sorry. That's all."

She studied me in response, eyes unreadable. "Did you apologise to the others?"

I don't know what I'd expected, but this wasn't it. "What do you mean, the others?"

"The other serving girls you slapped around." The flame of the rush-light was flickering low, so just the barest glint of dull orange light played on Tavia's grim smile. "You don't remember, do you?"

Through a rising wave of shame and nausea, I tried to search my memory. "I . . ."

Tavia reached back and struck her fist against the door, twice. It grated open, and she turned to go, glancing back at the last moment.

"All of us were afraid of all of you," she said. "You weren't as bad as some of the others, though, for whatever that's worth."

The door swung shut behind her and the dark closed in. My knees buckled and I didn't fight it—just let myself collapse against the wall and buried my head in my hands.

Once I'd cried myself out, more or less, and wiped my face on a dirty sleeve, I opened my eyes to darkness and pictured Lynn again. She was sitting cross-legged in front of me, her hands pressed on my knees, her expression all tenderness.

"Let's say I survive this," I said to the vision. "Can I ever do enough to make up for what my family's already done?"

Imaginary Lynn didn't have an answer for this, because I didn't have an answer. Instead, she stroked my shoulders, in what would have been a comforting caress, if I'd only been able to feel it.

Softly, I asked, "What now?"

"Go back to sleep," imaginary Lynn said. "I know it's not what you want to hear, but there's really nothing else that you can do."

"Nothing?"

"Nothing. I'm sorry."

She touched my shoulder. "If you need an added incentive, Darren . . . you're beginning to starve now, so the dreams are going to get *very* good."

I DON'T RECOMMEND starving yourself just so you can experience hunger dreams, but you would not believe how good they can get.

Lying there on the bare stone floor, I heard impossibly wonderful strains of music and tasted every delicious food I'd ever craved. Those fried cakes Jess used to make in the summer, full of tart dried cherries, topped with cream and a drizzle of honey. Succulent cuts of lamb from a market in Tavar, chargrilled on one side, dripping savoury juice from the other, with a smear of crushed garlic. The little speckled trout that Lynn would lard with a thick slice of bacon and roast to crisp and crackling brown . . .

And then Lynn was there herself, all wicked smile and gentle hands. Her skin was unblemished, her scars healed, her demons banished. She was twelve inches taller and a whole world gladder, with nothing in her past that she needed to wish away. When she touched me in those dreams, I felt it, the weight and the heat of her, her want and her need and the unfeigned joy she took in me. The soft ripple of her laughter and the warmth of her breath on my face.

The problem was that the better the dreams got, the worse my waking hours became. By now, I had so little padding on my bones that their hard edges ground painfully against the floor. Finally, I admitted defeat and crawled over to that pile of straw. I felt the first stinging punctures of flea bites before I sunk back into my stupor.

The civil war was over. No, the war had never happened. All the pain and terror had fizzled away, like dew in strong sunlight. The *Banshee* was flying through bright blue waters, the foam creaming around the bow, Regon's sure hand on the helm. The people of Kila crowded on the shores of the isles to watch us pass, and was that . . . ? Yes! They were screaming my name, in joy and in gratitude. They lifted up the children so they could see me better, and the children clapped their hands in glee. Lynn's eyes were aflame with her pride in me, because I'd *done* it, I'd *done* it, I'd . . .

I woke again and my arms and legs were riddled with bloody scrapes. I'd been scratching my flea bites in my sleep and now I scratched them harder. My stomach was a hollow bag, sucked empty. The dizziness took over and the room began to whirl.

You are better, Darren, because you were born to be better. You can deny your birthright, but you can't strip the glory from your blood. You're a phoenix among sparrows, and fire runs in your veins, so rise up and take your place at the table . . .

At the table, at the table . . . I choked out a high-pitched laugh and bit my own fist.

"Lynn," I whispered. "Oh, Lynn."

"I'm right here." Imaginary Lynn stooped down beside me and checked my ragged pulse. For once, she looked genuinely worried. "Can you stand?"

I shut my eyes against the spinning of the room. "I'd rather not."

It was a very vivid dream. Imaginary Lynn's hand was warm and solid on my wrist, and her voice sounded just like the real thing. "I'd carry you if I could, Darren, but that's unlikely to go well. So could you try?"

"All right."

Somehow I got both feet on the floor, and pushed. I didn't put much effort into it, I just wanted to show that I was trying, but imaginary Lynn got my arm around her neck and gave a heave. My head spun as she wrenched me upright, and I would have fallen straight down again if she hadn't leaned me against a wall, wedging her body against mine.

"Damn," she muttered. "Damn, damn, and damn."

Frustrated, she brushed her hair back with her free hand, exposing a small knotted scar at the base of her neck. I stared at it.

"New plan," Lynn said. "I'll have to try and drag you."

"Lynn."

"What?"

Though my jaw was trembling, I got the words out. "Do you dance?"

One pale eyebrow went up. "At spear point, do you mean, or just for the hell of it?"

Imaginary Lynn had never said that before. The Lynn in front of me had mussed hair and a sweat-stained shirt, and looked as if she hadn't slept for a week.

"Oh gods," I breathed, understanding at last. "It's you."

"If you were expecting someone else, I may get cranky."

The cell door stood open and two guards waited just outside. Still propping me up against the wall, Lynn turned to glare at them. "Well?" she snapped. "Were you two bastards planning on helping, or are you just here to enjoy the scenery?"

For one moment, I let myself believe that it was Latoya and Spinner out there. Somehow Lynn had infiltrated the castle, she'd smuggled my most loyal sailors inside, and now the three of them would spirit me down to the harbour and away before Milo knew what was happening.

But the guards were both rebels, Freemen. I recognized them, one from his harelip and the other by a mottled red-and-grey beard; they were two of the men who had dragged me down to the starvation cell on the night of Regon's murder. If help was coming, it wasn't here yet.

"You surrendered yourself to Milo," I whispered to Lynn.

"I was out of options."

"You shouldn't have—"

"Mistress, hush."

I hushed—not because I lacked strong opinions on the matter of Lynn's surrender, but because I'd run out of strength. It took everything I had just to lean against the wall, with Lynn propping me up like a third leg. Dimly, I heard her speaking with the guards: first arguing, then persuading, and finally begging, until at last one of them stepped into the cell and threw me over his shoulder.

There was a hallway, then another hallway, then a few stone steps. At a low door reinforced with iron straps, the guard swung me down like a sack of oats. Lynn immediately wormed her way under my shoulder, steadying me before I dropped.

The door swung open into a small stone room, probably a storage chamber. A little light filtered in through a barred window-slit. As Lynn and I staggered inside, a woman rose from a stool by the window. It was Ariadne—Ariadne in a servant's tunic of lumpy grey homespun, her eyes impossibly large in her face.

"Help me," Lynn said, breathless. "We need to get her on the bed."

The bed was just a plank shelf with a sack of straw for the mattress, but it was as good as anything I'd ever had on board ship. Ariadne and Lynn hauled me over to it, my feet bouncing over the bumps in the floor.

My eyes slipped shut of their own accord as soon as I was horizontal. For an instant, a hand cupped my cheek, and then it slipped away.

"Take care of her while I'm gone," I heard Lynn saying. "Get her to eat something, if you can. I'll be back as soon as—well. I'll be back."

"Will you?" Ariadne asked numbly. "Milo's been in a foul mood all day and when he's like this—"

"*I'll be fine.* Don't dwell on it. Think about something else. The time we went night swimming together down south, and the plankton was all glowing bright blue, like stars underwater. Or—better yet—think of how violently I'm going to kill Jada, as soon as I have the chance."

Ariadne laughed, high-pitched and tinged with hysteria. "Get in line!"

The voices moved farther away. The door creaked open, creaked shut, and, with a scraping sound, a bolt slid home.

I opened my eyes. Ariadne stood by a small table. There was food there—I could see cheese and apples—and Ariadne was busy murdering a plum. With efficient strokes, she tore the fruit into weeping red gobbets, laying each on a cloth, one by one.

"Fruit juice first," she said. "If you keep it down, then we'll try a little dry bread. We can't rush things, or you'll vomit, and that'll make you even weaker."

I licked my lips with a tongue that felt like dry leather. "How long . . ."

". . . have they been starving you? Fifteen days, less a few hours. It was night when they took you away. It's late afternoon right now."

Fifteen days. The last thing I'd eaten was that handful of redcurrants at the end of the banquet, the night of the revolution. It was sickening to remember how much food I'd left untouched on the table.

Ariadne squeezed the cloth, and purple-red juice trickled musically into a tin cup. When the cup was half-full, she knelt down beside the cot and helped me lift my head. "I'll hold it. You just swallow."

The sweetness of it was blinding, like a club to the skull. The acid stung a thousand tiny cuts and sores inside my mouth which, until that moment, I had barely noticed. But the worst part was when the liquid hit my wasted stomach. It washed away that comfortable numbness in my midsection. All of the hunger pains hit again with new force. The nausea, too.

"That's enough," I gasped, pulling back. "Enough."

Ariadne rested the cup on her lap. "I'll give you a minute. But you're going to drink the whole thing before I let you go to sleep."

"Damn it. Regon was right that time he called you a budding sadist."

Ariadne flinched, and I felt a dull ache that had nothing to do with hunger.

"I'm so sorry, Darren," Ariadne said, a tremble in her voice that didn't belong there.

"Not as sorry as I am." I stared stonily at the wall until I could trust myself to talk without crying. "Give me the damn juice."

She held the cup, and I forced myself to sip and swallow. It hurt, *fuck* it hurt. As though I was feeling hunger for the first time.

But pirates don't whimper, beg for mercy, and hide under the bed, much as we might want to on certain occasions. I gulped until the cup was empty, then shoved it away.

"Well done." She squeezed my hand. "I'll see about that bread."

The bread was back on the little table with the cheese and fruit. Ariadne limped across the room to get it, her right leg almost buckling with each step.

I somehow managed to lift my head. "Ariadne. I forgot. Your back. Are you all right?"

"What?" she said, confused. Then, dully, "Oh. You mean the whipping. My back is fine. I'm fine."

I doubted *that*. "Don't play iron man. Are you badly hurt?"

"Darren."

"What?"

Ariadne was tearing viciously at the loaf of black bread. "What is the point of asking me that question, considering that you can do exactly jack shit about it?"

She was standing full in the light now, exposing the details I'd missed at first. Her long hair was gone, cut off ragged with a dull blade. Her eyes were puffy and swollen. A red weal crossed her shoulder, so fresh and raw that it looked like a slash of red paint.

"Jada?" I asked weakly.

"Yes." Ariadne was being much rougher with the bread than necessary. Maybe she was pretending it was Jada's face. "She'll send for me before very long. She likes to parade me around. Apparently it's good for morale. This room, it's like a toy shelf. It's where she puts me when she doesn't want to play."

"Play?"

Ariadne stared down at her hands, jaw muscles locked tight. "The good news is, she only keeps me with her for a few hours at a time. My lady gets bored easily. Also, Milo gets sick of seeing my, quote, stupid smug bitch face, unquote. Did you know that I have a face that can make an honest man puke from across a crowded room? Apparently such is the case."

"Sod it." I massaged my temples, trying to concentrate. "All right. Tell me everything that's happened since the night of the revolution. I need to know whether Milo's grip on power is secure, I need to know what he's planning, I need to know how the gibbering bollocks Lynn ended up back on the Isle—"

"You should ask what I told him."

"What?"

"You want to know what you missed? You'd better start by asking exactly how thoroughly I spilled my craven guts while you were otherwise occupied. Shall I spare you any suspense? I told him everything, Darren. The places where you've buried gold over the past five months? I gave him an exhaustively annotated map. The names of all your ships and their approximate positions? I told him everything I could think of and a whole lot more I had to guess. Your weaknesses? I gibbered out Gwyneth's name before they even finished asking the question. *Gwyneth's* weaknesses?"

She turned to me, her eyes glassy and fierce, but her lower lip trembling. "You would think that I could at least keep my fat mouth shut about Gwyn, wouldn't you. And I did hold out for a while. Almost ten whole minutes. After that, I got extremely talkative. Here's your bread."

I took the bit of dry black crust and stared at it, feeling put-upon in that way you do when someone needs comfort and you haven't got any to give. I took a stab anyway, mostly out of reflex. "It's no shame to give up information under torture. Everyone has a breaking point."

"Oh, no doubt. But I have a feeling that some people don't break until *after* the torture begins. Whereas I, after a small amount of quality time with my lady Jada, started to spew facts like a geyser each time she cast a sharp look in my direction. Eat your damn bread, Darren. I'm not going to spoon-feed you."

I fumbled it up to my mouth and gnawed at a corner experimentally. Rock hard. I snapped off a small bit and tucked it into a corner of my mouth to let it soften.

Ariadne sat by the cot, fingers knotted together, face twisted up like a wet dishrag. And I have never in my life known what to say to a crying woman, but I can recognize pure self-loathing when I see it.

"You can't blame yourself," I said, with the little energy I had left. "I mean it. It's not your fault."

She bit her hand hard before she answered.

"*It's not your fault,*" she repeated, in a mocking sing-song. "In other words, you don't expect me to act like a vaguely competent human being. Which, I suppose, proves that you're an intelligent woman after all, because it turns out that I'm a useless collaborating cunt."

I sighed. "Don't call yourself—"

"Gwyneth is with Milo right now, Darren, and he knows everything about her that there is to know, and *I did that.* Go ahead and tell me that it's not my fault. I'll laugh in your stupid pirate face."

A moment of silence.

"Lynn can take care of herself," I said, mainly to see whether it would sound any more convincing if I said it out loud.

Ariadne snorted, with the utmost scorn. But she'd screamed herself dry. Now she sat on the little stool and curled into a ball, legs tucked underneath her.

"You still haven't answered my question. How did Lynn end up on the Isle?"

"She surrendered." That dead, defeated tone again. "Didn't she tell you?"

"She mentioned it. She didn't say—"

"Why she did it? What her strategy is? She doesn't have one."

I snorted. "Lynn? Lynn thinks that you're never fully dressed without a five-year plan and accompanying budget. She's got something up her sleeve. She's more likely to show up for violence without her trousers and her left kidney than without a plan."

Ariadne didn't rise to this. Not even the faintest glimmer of a smile. "Well, she had her trousers when she showed up, and her kidneys, so far as I can tell, but she didn't have anything else. She came to the Isle alone, and when they brought her to the throne room—"

"Wait. Alone?"

"—they brought her in and she told Milo that she didn't have anything to offer him, but that she'd do whatever he asked as long as—"

"*Alone?*"

"Shut up. She came here alone, she begged Milo to feed you, she promised she would do whatever he asked as long as he fed you, and it was all very tragic and awful and pathetic and I got to stand there and watch the whole thing because, apparently, that's what I do."

Her voice seethed with self-hatred, and I barely knew what was going on, but again I said, "Ariadne, it's not your fault."

"*Not my fault?*" A horrible, pained laugh. "It's exactly my fault, Darren, don't you see? Latoya mutinied. She took your *Banshee,* and she took your crew. That's why Lynn had to come after you on her own. And I'm sorry, Darren. Because Latoya did it for me. She turned on Lynn for me. And I have no idea why she believed that I could possibly, possibly be worth it."

CHAPTER NINETEEN

Lynn

MILO HAD TAKEN over the bedroom that once belonged to Stribos. It was hung in red drapes, and the woodwork was mahogany, with ebony inlay. Pretentious and sleazy all at once. It would have been cheaper and easier to just hang a sign in the room that said *I am a huge self-important wanker*, and leave it at that. The effect would have been about the same.

When they brought me in, Milo was busy at his desk, writing. He didn't look up at the creak of the opening door. The guards left silently. For some time, the only sound was his reed pen scratch-scratching over the paper. At last, he set down the pen, reached for a decanter, and poured himself a glass of wine.

"Take your clothes off," he said.

Balls, I thought, and pulled off my shirt. Folded it. Set it on the ground. While I was still loosening the laces of my trousers, Milo leaned back in his chair, one finger upright. "Wait."

I waited, stripped to the waist, while Milo took his time sipping his drink. It's an old trick, making someone get naked before you question them, but even if you know it's coming, there's no real counter-play. You can blunt the force of it a bit by obeying the command to strip as soon as it's given. That way, you give your interrogator one less excuse to bash you on the head, and you take away the satisfaction he'd get from watching you cringe and dither. That doesn't make you any less naked, though.

Plus, it was cold. It's always cold, in castles. I stared at my bare arms, watching the skin prickle and the goosebumps rise.

At last, Milo set down his wine-cup. "I gave some very specific instructions. You weren't supposed to show up here empty-handed."

"No," I said. "I was supposed to pick up a gigantic sack of treasure and haul it to your door. It turned out that a bunch of heavily-armed pirates had other ideas about how I was going to spend my time."

Now he turned around. He had bright blue eyes, Milo did, like little bits of the sky were stuck in his face.

"Explain," he said. "Start from the beginning, the night you escaped the Keep. And Lynn—I'm not going to get bored, so try not to leave out any little details."

I nodded, and launched into the story: how we smuggled the Torasan children out to the back dock, how Ariadne forced me into the escape boat, how we received Milo's message the next morning with his ultimatum. And then what came after: how Latoya and I had a serious difference of opinion, which led first to a lot of yelling and then to a certain amount of violence, as the crew picked their sides.

"Latoya got most of them," I said, tiredly. "It turns out that when you're trying to corral confused sailor-boys into your corner, it helps to be seven feet tall and have muscles like steel potatoes. But I did some shrieking and biting and managed to assemble a crew of eight or nine men. Enough to man the *Sod Off*."

"The *Sod Off*?" Milo asked, interrupting for the first time.

"It's a sloop. One of our smallest ships. Latoya took the *Banshee*. I haven't figured out how to explain that to Darren yet. There will probably be some crying."

"And then you just went your separate ways?"

"Not exactly. Both of us were trying to hit the treasure caches first."

"Why did you go after the treasure?"

"I wanted to get enough money to pay the ransom, obviously. I don't know what Latoya had in mind. Maybe she wants to hire mercenaries before she attacks the Isle? I cleaned out a few of the caches before Latoya could get there—the *Sod Off* is a speedy little beast—but Latoya caught up in the end. She took the gold I'd managed to gather. Held me upside down by my ankles, more or less, and smacked me until the coins came jangling out. And I guess I'd really pissed her off, because she took the *Sod Off* and the rest of my sailors, too. She let me have one of the *Banshee's* rowboats, though. Because she's all heart."

I stopped to let out a long, jaw-cracking yawn. It had been a long two weeks and sleep had not been on the priority list.

"Anyway. When I lost the *Sod Off* and the money and the rest of my men, that left me without any choices. By then, you'd been starving Darren for ten days. I didn't have time for anything clever, and I only had one thing to bargain with . . . so." I gestured at myself. "So. It took me a few days to get here, but I made it. That's all."

He leaned back, studying me with those bright blue eyes, and said one word. "Again."

I went through the whole thing again. When I was done, he told me to tell it again, which I did, and then a fourth time. Maybe he hoped it would wear me out, standing still and talking for so long. He should have known better. Anyone who's ever been a servant in a great house knows how to stand motionless for hours on end without fainting. The trick is to keep your knees very, very slightly bent.

So I stood, and I talked, and I wondered. The children of castle servants start working when they're five or six. What was Milo's first job? Turning the spits in the kitchen, maybe, or carrying water to the harvesters, or picking up chips by the woodpile for tinder. If he was a pretty child, then maybe he served as drink-boy in the Great Hall, waiting at the lord's elbow during meals with a pitcher of wine. However he had begun his career, it would have involved a lot of standing around.

I'd finished the fourth run-through of the story and was starting on the fifth when Milo gestured for me to stop. "You know what surprises me? I do believe that part of what you're saying is the truth."

I blew out a long, exhausted breath. "You can believe what you want, Milo. I'm too tired to lie."

"Well, you'll have to find some energy somehow. Get the rest of those clothes off."

Fuck, bollocks, fuck. I loosened the laces of my trousers and drawers, let them fall, and stepped out of them. Milo turned back to his papers, looking over a long column of figures as though he found them much more interesting than a naked woman. "So. Even with Darren's life on the line, you failed to bring me anything that I asked for."

"I did my best," I said, not bothering to hide my frustration. "Can we consider the circumstances? I was up against a pirate crew of fifty men, led by Latoya. Have you ever met Latoya? She can fold pewter plates into little toy ducks, using only two fingers, and occasionally her tongue. What was I supposed to do, grab a hammer and squash her flat?"

"I'm not asking for excuses. I'm asking why I should let Darren live if I'm not going to get any return on my investment."

"Oh, please. You're going to keep her alive for exactly the same reason that you didn't kill her along with her brothers—because she's worth more to you than a solid gold dolphin. She's the damn pirate queen. Half of Kila reveres her; the other half is at least a little nervous about pissing her off. She's a legend and a hero, and now, thanks to you, she's also the oldest trueborn Torasan left alive. You're not going to throw away an asset like that."

"If you're so sure of that, why did you come crawling to the Keep to beg me not to starve her to death?"

He thought he was so stinking clever. Maybe he even was, a bit. "Let me rephrase. You would be an idiot to kill her, but people act like idiots all the time. Consider me the voice of reason."

"Is that what you are to Darren?"

"I'm a lot of things to Darren."

"So I hear." He flicked his eyes over me—and there was no interest or excitement in them, just cool calculation. "Get on the bed."

There it was. I couldn't say I was surprised, even if I'd hoped, however stupidly, that things wouldn't go in this direction. If there was anything strange about the whole scenario, it was that Milo planned to do this to me, whom he didn't hate, instead of Darren, whom he did. But then again, deeply as Milo despised Darren, he seemed to think of her as a sort of honorary man. Just another captured soldier. And in the deranged etiquette of war, one does not rape a fellow soldier. One rapes the soldier's wife.

I sat on the edge of the bed and scooted backwards, keeping him in view. It was hard not to think about all the other women and boys, in their dozens and their hundreds, who must have sat on this bed, staring up at the dark-red draperies, as they waited for Stribos to finish his wine.

I stared up at the ceiling. Oaken beams.

"You have nothing to prove, you know," I said. "I know that you can do this to me. Darren knows that she can't protect me. You don't have to go through with it, just to . . . to make a point."

A soft *click* as he set down his goblet.

"Where are they now?" he asked. "The plate-folding giant and Darren's band of merry misfits? Where did they go?"

"I don't know."

"Didn't they talk about their plans?"

"Not in front of me. They're not stupid."

A minute of silence, during which I counted all the rafter-joists in the ceiling. Then Milo's voice again. "I know you're lying."

"Have it your way," I said tiredly. Truth be told, if the atmosphere had been a little less charged, I could have fallen asleep right there. I can handle a rowboat when I must, but it wears me out, and making the trip to Torasan Isle had just about flattened me.

"Lynn, don't shut down." His voice was softer, now—almost encouraging. "I don't *want* to treat you like an enemy, but my men will insist on getting answers from you. The more you come clean, the more I can try to help you. If you hold back . . ."

"Let me save both of us some time," I interrupted, rolling over onto my elbow. "This is the part of the conversation where you insist that I'm lying, and I insist that I'm not, and you make veiled threats to turn me over to your men for torture if I don't come clean. And for the record, Milo—I am useless when it comes to dealing with pain. If your Freemen put me in thumbscrews or beat the soles of my feet, then I'll confess to anything they suggest. I'll confess that I murdered the last High Lord and took your mother's virginity and had carnal relations with a badger. I'll confess to any damn thing and I'll keep going for hours and, when I'm finished, none of you will have any idea what to believe. Every little grain of truth is going to be drowned in the sludge of don't-hurt-me-I'll-say-anything. So, when you're making decisions tonight, bear that in mind."

Milo shook his head, smiling a vague smile that didn't reach his blue-blue eyes.

"You're too dangerous for me to let you live, and too valuable for me to kill you," he said. "So what am I going to do with you?"

I lay back down on the must-smelling mattress. In a way, I almost wished he'd get on with it. "You're going to rape me, apparently."

I wasn't looking at him at that moment—so whatever the strange thing was that I noticed, it can't have been something that I saw. Nor something that I heard, because he made no sound. Best I can describe, it was a sort of ripple in the air. A sudden tension, as if someone had plucked at an invisible bowstring.

Ever so casually, I rolled to face Milo. He was knocking back the dregs of his wine, but the tendons down his neck stood out from the skin, like drawn cables.

Well, now. Well, well, well. So Milo didn't like the word. It was a small thing, a tiny thing, but maybe it gave me a chance. I settled back and stared at the ceiling again, not thinking, barely breathing, but bringing myself to the moment, disciplining myself to be nowhere but here and now.

When Milo finally sat down on the bed, back facing me, he had taken off his trousers, but not his shirt or stockings. He had the wine flagon in one hand, and his cup in the other.

"Do you want some?" he asked. "It might make it easier."

It never had before. On the other hand, it would give me a little more time.

"Sure," I said, and took the cup he passed over. "Is this the cherry stuff I've heard so much about?"

"It is." He sloshed around the wine that remained in the flagon—it sounded almost full; he couldn't have drunk much—and swigged straight from the neck. "I'd never even tasted it until a couple of weeks ago. Now I'm trying to figure out what all the fuss is about. It smells like spoiled fruit and tastes like perfume. Try it yourself."

It spoke volumes about Milo, his character and his blind spots, that he expected me, at a moment like this, to pay any attention to the taste of wine. Under the circumstances, though, it would have been a tactical error for me to roll my eyes. Instead, I took a sip, made a big deal of swishing it around my mouth, and then frowned.

"I see your point. Any chance of trading this in for beer?"

He laughed. It was the first human sound he'd made since I stepped into the room. "I haven't got any beer on hand, and I'm not going to make a kitchen run dressed this way." His hands moved up to the lacings of his shirt, then fell away again. "You know, I still think it's possible that the two of us could reach an understanding. I'm not so naïve as to expect Darren to forgive and forget. You and I, though—we're both bastards. Little bits of our fathers' discarded seed, people who come from nothing."

"We come from our mothers."

He shrugged. "We come from our mothers, who had nothing and were nothing. I don't need to explain any of this to you, do I? We're like two strangers who grew up in the same town. You should understand better than anyone why I had to break Torasan."

"Oh, I understand *why*," I said. "I just disagree with your methods."

He shrugged. "It was ugly. That's what happens when you put victims in the same room as their torturers and pass out a few knives. Stribos and Alek, and that whole miserable family . . . they spent their worthless lives tormenting people like us. Then the big wheel spun and they got theirs. You can't deny the justice of it. I fight fire with fire."

"Do you? I fight fire with water, myself, but what do I know?" The wine really did smell like fruity varnish. I set the cup down on the nightstand. "If you want to reach an understanding with me, then raping me is not the way to start."

That not-quite-flinch again. Not a sound, not a motion, just a sort of tightening, like the feel of the air before a storm.

Still, he looked me straight between the eyes. "You belong to Darren."

"Yes."

"Any chance that'll change?"

"No. Not that it matters, because you'd never trust me if I did switch sides. I'd try that play if it had any slim prayer of working—but unfortunately for me, you are not a stupid man."

"No," he echoed. "So here we are. You're Darren's whore, and an ally of Torasan, and a prisoner of war. Don't expect too much."

He moved his hands down and he fumbled with his clothing. The candlelight guttered; a fat brown moth was flitting around the flame. It drifted forwards, danced up, then dove. There was a hiss and a flicker and a smell of burnt dust. I watched the papery wings char and shrivel inwards until Milo reached over and pinched the candle out.

Darkness and the burnt dust smell. It was a relief that Milo couldn't see me anymore, but now it would be even harder to try to read him.

Maybe there was no point in trying to change the night's direction. Maybe the thing I'd seen as a flinch was just Milo shivering in the chilly air. Maybe I shouldn't fight the tide this time, but just let it carry me, wash me out to a wide and barren place beyond feeling.

His weight settled on the mattress. I closed my eyes tightly.

Now. Either do it now, or go inside yourself and go dark and small and stop thinking until it's all over.

I licked my dry lips, and went to work. "Milo, I know this isn't a negotiation or anything, but if you're going to rape me, there's something I have to ask you."

The mattress ticking rustled—that was him, moving—and maybe he was about to reach for me, but I'd started now and what the hell. "It's like this. When I was eight, my father gave me to his wife. Pretty much as a present? I'm not positive why he did it, but I think he was sick of her screaming at him, and he hoped that she could take out her frustration on me instead. Plus, he had to keep me in line. You see, he was going to breed me so that I could give him grandchildren, and he needed to make sure that I didn't get ideas above my station, or wander out of reach."

He made a noise deep in his throat, and I couldn't tell what it was or what it meant, but at least he wasn't touching me yet. "I know all this."

"You know that part, from Ariadne, but you don't know what came next, because Ariadne wasn't there. I ran away. Did you ever try to run? Don't answer that. It wasn't fun, because . . . I don't need to explain why it wasn't fun, do I? I had no money and I had no one to help me and I had no place to go, so, not fun. Not many of those outrageous luxuries like food and clothing. Lots of bad-smelling men who thought that there wouldn't be any consequences if they messed with me—and they were right, of course."

He was so close now that I could feel the warmth of his skin, but he still wasn't touching me.

"So I used sex a lot," I said. With my fingers, I traced the contours of an old scar on my wrist, concentrating on the rubbery feel of it instead of the memories. "At least, I used it a lot the first year, before I found a place to stay. Sometimes it was just a transaction—you know, pull somebody's dick for a loaf of bread. Sometimes it was the best way I could think of to calm someone down. And sometimes I figured that it was going to happen one way or another, so better to give it up than to get beaten first. I kind of got numb to it after a while, but I never stopped being scared. When you're naked in the dark, with someone else's breath in your face, you can feel death hanging in the air all around you. I used to wonder what they'd do to my body afterwards. Leave it where it was? Kick some dirt over it? Who was it, by the way?"

He didn't answer right away—he had to catch up. "Who was what?"

"Who was it that got raped? It must have been someone important to you, since you cringe every time you hear the word. Was it your mother? Your sister, your brother? Who?"

Milo said nothing. I hadn't expected him to answer, not out loud, but I'd hoped for *some* kind of sign. No luck.

"It doesn't really matter which," I said, before the silence became too overpowering. "It could have been all of them, for all I know. But I think there was one time, one rape, that sticks in your memory, one that matters more than any other. If I knew about that time, I'd understand you better, Milo. Especially if you were the one it happened to. Or the one who did it."

Damn. Too far. I knew I'd gone too far, even before I felt him move. The blow took me right on the solar plexus—not as hard as it could have been, but so sharp and sudden that I didn't know whether I'd been punched or stabbed. Then he had me by the throat.

Fast, angry breaths above me, hot on my face. An iron grip, sandpapery with callous. I grabbed his wrists—couldn't help myself—but didn't dig in my nails.

"I'm not going to fight you," I said, working the words out one at a time against the pressure of his hand. "Calm down. Please calm down."

No answer. I wasn't getting through to him anymore, oh gods, I'd miscalculated, I'd lost my chance with him, and now—

He jerked my head and shoulders up off the mattress, then slammed me back down, knocking the wind out of me.

"*Please,*" I repeated, as soon as I caught my breath. "Milo. Please. You don't need to frighten me, I'm there already."

His face loomed close, a darker patch in the dark room. "If you have a request, spit it out."

Bitter bile filled my mouth and I struggled to swallow. I didn't have to ask, I didn't have to keep talking, I could shut the world out and let my body go through the motions—oh hell, I didn't want to go through the motions.

I forced my eyes open.

"It's like this," I said. "Nobody in my position would want a kid, but I have a real hang-up on the subject. On balance, I'm probably more afraid of dying than of getting pregnant, but it's a close call. So here's the request. More of an offer, really. It's the same offer I make every time this happens. Leave my cunt alone while you're raping me, and I'll do anything else that you want. *Anything.* And yes, I will beg."

On balance, it was good that he didn't respond right away, but my stomach still turned over and over as the seconds passed. I'd see this through if I had to, but suddenly I wasn't sure whether I could do it without throwing up. Maybe I should go ahead and puke; that might make Milo kick me out of bed. Or maybe it would turn him on. I didn't know him well enough to tell which.

After a few eternities of waiting, Milo leaned back in bed. I couldn't see him, but the headboard creaked.

"You're dangerous," he said, mostly to himself. "You are so damn dangerous."

"Why?" My voice rasped; only then did I notice how dry my mouth had become. "Because you don't want to rape me?"

"Just . . . stop that." His hand made a fist in the blankets. "Do you even understand what we wanted to accomplish here?"

"You wanted to take the Isle. You've done that."

"We wanted to give people their lives back. Did you ever meet Alek? The brother of the woman you call your mistress."

I sighed, trying to switch mental tracks without losing my grip on myself. "I met him. Didn't have a chance to engage him in any deep conversations, he was too busy dying, but yes, we did meet. Why?"

"Well. When Alek came back from his maiden voyage, his father Stribos gave him four gifts: a horse and a girl and a boy and a whip. A horse to ride, a girl to bed, a boy to beat—or maybe to bed; how the hell should I know—and a whip to use on the other three. That's the kind of viciousness that's been bleeding into the soil of the Isle for generations, the kind of cruelty—"

"Milo. Alek is *dead*. Stribos is *dead*. You killed them very and extremely dead. You can't make them any more dead by raping me—or by torturing my sister."

"She's had the barest taste of what the average cabin boy or scullery girl has to suffer."

"She's terrified every second of every day. Even if you weren't doing anything else to her, that would be enough." I sat up. "You think I'm dangerous? Then get rid of me. Give me my sister. Give me my mistress. Give us a boat and let us go. That'll be the end of it."

"I had your captain kneel before me on flagstones washed black with her brothers' blood. You think she won't look for payback?"

"I'll talk her out of it."

"You really think you could do that?"

"*Yes.* Gods of hell, yes. Of course, yes. It wouldn't even be difficult. This is what I *do.* Milo, I know you don't want me as an enemy. End this here. Let us go."

"Let you go," he repeated. "Let go of the pirate queen, master of the richest fleet in the south seas, the oldest unmarried Torasan heir. Let all of that go—and watch and wait as all the minor houses from here to Cromm Tuach band together to rip my men to shreds and put the Isle back in chains."

"They might not."

"Don't pretend to be stupid. It's not a good look on you. You think all the pureblood lords will put up with a bastard usurper?"

"Sure, as long as they have an excuse to look the other way." I paused. What the hell. "Darren killed Lord Iason of Bero, and I stuck a commoner on the throne in his place. You don't hear anyone griping about that, do you?"

A pause. I'd surprised him. "That's a lie. The throne was taken by Iason's cousin—"

"That's the cover story I made up. It's a wafer-thin cover story made out of spider webs and moonshine, but people are mostly sort of stupid, so it's worked so far. Milo, in all honesty, I do not give a bucket of warm salt piss what you do here. You can turn the entire Isle into a gigantic compost heap, for all I care, as long as you let go of the people I love."

"And if I don't?"

I was breathing too hard, too fast; it made my heart race. I reached up to my throat and massaged the big artery, rubbing until I felt the pace of my pulse slacken.

"Oh, you know the answer to that," I said. "People like you and me, we have only one way to win a battle. People like Darren, like Latoya, like Corto, they can mess around with disabling shots and non-lethal blows. Not me. My first strike has to end the fight, because if I miss, I won't get a second chance. So don't expect me to be reasonable, or honourable, or even pretend to fight fair. I don't work that way, any more than you do."

My eyes had adjusted now to the dark, more or less, so I saw his head tilted sideways, as he studied me. "I could just kill you now."

"You could."

"So why shouldn't I?"

"I mean, Darren will go berserk. Good luck having a civilized conversation with her after she sees my corpse. She'll tear your throat out with her teeth, or she'll keep trying to until you put her down. Other than that, killing me sounds like a dandy plan." I took a huge but calculated risk. "I'm going to get off the bed for a second, do you mind?"

He didn't say anything. I scooted forwards until I could climb off the end of the bed. There was still a little water in the washbasin jug. I poured a cup, rinsed my mouth and spat, swilling away the taste of bile as well as the sharp, tannic after bite of the cherry wine. I poured another cup, drank it slowly—he still hadn't moved. I set down the cup and reached for my clothes.

He didn't stop me. Didn't speak, didn't move. I unfolded the clothes, shook them out. Still nothing. I didn't hurry, just worked my way through the bundle, pulling on my linen drawers, shirt, trousers, and jerkin, double-knotting all the laces.

Moment of truth. If he was going to force me to strip again, this would be the time. I watched, as he swung his legs off the bed and got up. He came nearer, nearer—and bent to grab his trousers off the floor. I released a breath I hadn't known I was holding.

"You're going to want me as a friend," he said, fastening his heavy belt. "Darren is going to want me as a friend. You're right that there are reasons to keep her alive, but not everyone appreciates that the way you and I do. My Freemen are simple people, people who pray to the gods of the tide and hope for the coming of the Master of Storms. They don't understand the political realities. All they understand is that Darren is one of the tyrants that brutalized them, and they're baying for her blood. If it wasn't for me, she'd already be dead."

"Are you expecting me to say 'Thank you'?" I asked, after a pause that seemed to invite it.

He raised an eyebrow. "It wouldn't hurt."

"Thank you," I said, only I made it sound more like *Fuck you*. I'd had a certain amount of practice at doing that.

He laughed instead of lashing out, then grew solemn.

"Lynn, it's time for you to adjust to the reality that you're not in control here. Darren spoils you, anyone can see that—so I suppose, at this point in your life, you're used to getting your way. But I don't keep pets and I don't play favourites. You can't wrap me around your finger."

He stepped closer to me and my heart gave a lurch, but he just tipped my chin up so I had to look at him.

"Here's what I can promise, though. If Darren cooperates, if she brings her fleet under my command, then I'll do my best to make sure that she goes on breathing. I may even be able to keep both of you fairly comfortable, if you do as you're told. Decent rooms. Decent food. I'll even allow the two of you some privacy for, ah, intimate visits, within reason."

Privacy within reason, sure. That probably meant a closed door with Milo peeping through the keyhole. "What about my sister?"

He puffed out an impatient breath. "You'd better hope that the lovesick giant doesn't do anything stupid, like showing up here with a battle fleet. Because if she does, I'm going to ask Jada to think of all kinds of creative ways to make your sister wish she was never born. That's all."

"Look, I did my best to stop Latoya. I *told* her that attacking the Isle would only make things worse. It's not Ariadne's fault if—"

"Oh, do people only suffer for the things that are their fault? I wish somebody had told me. Lynn. Your sister once got ease and leisure that she didn't deserve, and now she'll get pain that maybe she doesn't deserve either. That's justice—or what has to pass for it, in the world we live in."

He returned to the desk, relit his candle from a smouldering bit of touchwood, and scanned some kind of list of trade goods, every inch a Very Serious Man with Very Serious Things to Do. As if I'd distracted him by demanding that he interrogate, strip, and menace me, and he'd indulged me, out of the goodness of his heart.

"If we're done, can I go back to Darren?" I asked. "Please?"

Seconds ticked away—the asshole *did* like making me wait—but at last, he lifted his eyes to the door.

"Sentry!" he called.

Hobnailed boots tramped along the other side of the wall, and the door creaked open. Milo jerked his head towards it. "The guard will take you to her cell. Go on and tell her all about how badly you've been treated. Tell her that I'm such a brutal tyrant that I didn't lay a finger on you tonight."

"Again—you want me to say thank you?"

"Again—it wouldn't hurt."

"Milo, you decided, *eventually*, not to rape me. You're going to have to do better than that, if you want us to be best friends."

With a frustrated sigh, he lifted his eyes from the ledger. "And *you're* going to have to learn to show gratitude, if you want more favours from me."

I can't claim that what I did next was smart, but I'd swallowed my feelings enough for one night.

I reached out and knocked over the candle. Molten wax splashed, and Milo's papers caught light in a satisfying *floof* of flame. He yelped, lurching backwards.

"Want to put that out?" I asked helpfully. "You'd better throw some fire at it. I hear that works."

And I was out the door before he could do me any more favours.

CHAPTER TWENTY

Darren of the House of Torasan (Prisoner)

WHILE I WAS sleeping, soldiers came for Ariadne. The scraping of the door woke me, but I didn't open my eyes. I didn't know what I could say to her, and I didn't know what she could say back.

I slept more deeply then, and didn't wake until the straw mattress rustled and an arm encircled me from behind. Thin arm. Skinny wrist. Lynn.

"Hey," I whispered into darkness.

"Hey," she whispered back. "Did you eat?"

"I ate. Lynn . . . ?"

For once, she didn't ask me to make the question any more explicit. She just planted a quick, firm kiss on my shoulder.

"He didn't touch me," she said. "He changed his mind."

"How long before he changes his mind again?"

"Let's not borrow trouble. I talked him out of it once. Maybe I can do it the next time, if there is a next time."

She combed her fingers through my matted hair, trying to sort out the tangles, but her hands stilled, and she swore beneath her breath. The damn fleas. They were like a fiery, stinging net wrapped tight around me, one that I couldn't scrape or beat loose.

"Sorry," I whispered. "They're all over me."

"Why are you apologizing? Just roll over and let me get at them."

I rolled over as far as I could—she had to help—and felt Lynn's deft fingers brushing my skin as she began the long and gruesome task of picking the little bloodsuckers from my hair and clothing, crushing each one between her nails.

Lynn, who knew about abuse and helplessness from the bitter inside, had given up her world to join me in captivity. And now, after gods only knew how long a day, she was picking the fleas from my stinking body, one at a time.

"You know, Lynn," I muttered into the straw mattress, "you don't have to tell me a thing."

Lynn flicked a crushed bug away. "Well, you don't either."

THEY PUT ME on trial the next day. I pretty much slept through it.

I didn't plan to do that. I didn't plan, period. Lynn roused me before dawn and bullied me into choking down a meal of dry bread and pulped apple. She got most of the food into me, but my abused stomach fought to hurl it straight back out. Everything between my breastbone and groin was a gurgling bag of pain, a tidal pool in an ocean made of acid. I curled into myself and bit my fist and swallowed over and over, trying to keep the tide from rising. Lynn held onto my big toe—one of the few parts of me that didn't hurt—and said nothing, but squeezed hard each time I groaned.

That was the state of things when we heard approaching footsteps and a rattle of chains.

"Crap," I said into the crook of my arm. "I'm going to need you to help me up."

"I could do that," Lynn said. "Or you could stay on the bed like a non-crazy person."

"*Or* you could help me up, because somebody's coming and like hell I'm going to be on my back when they arrive."

"You do realize that none of your sailors are here at the moment? Nobody to impress with your macho posturing. You don't have to play butcher-than-thou."

Despite the complaints, Lynn wormed her way underneath my arm and lifted me. By the time the door opened, I was up. Wobbling, but up. I even managed a pretty good scowl. Neither of the guards seemed intimidated, or even interested. One grabbed me by the shoulders, and the other slapped manacles on my wrists with all of the interest and engagement of a man combing his hair.

Lynn, none too pleased at these proceedings to begin with, lost her head when the guard stooped to chain my ankles as well.

"What's the point of this?" she snapped. "What are you afraid of? She can barely stand! You think she's going to *kick* the fortress down?"

The guard at my feet grunted as the fetters snapped shut. "Orders."

"Don't be too hard on them, Lynn," I said. "Some people are just helpless without orders. I bet these two need Milo to follow along when they go to take a shit, so he can tell them when to wipe, and how hard."

It was, I realized too late, a mistake to insult a man who was so perfectly placed to throw an uppercut. The punch came all the way from the floor and took me straight on the point of the chin. Fortunately, the guard had lousy technique—asshole didn't know what to do with his feet *at all*—or I would have gone to my trial with a cracked jaw and a mouthful of broken teeth. As it was, I saw whole galaxies of falling stars, and all but crushed Lynn when she dove to catch me.

"Idiot," she said in my ear. "This is not the time."

"I know it's not," I said, and spat stringy red. "But you have to admit, it was kind of funny."

THERE HAD BEEN changes made in the Great Hall. The throne was gone, and so was the raised dais where the high table used to stand. Milo's simple wooden chair rested on the same level as everyone else's. Subtle.

For me, there was a little barred pen like a pigsty in the middle of the room. Less subtle.

They probably meant for me to stand in the pen, looking all forlorn and sniffly as I gripped the bars. Lynn had other ideas. She plopped down to the floor, arranged herself cross-legged, and raised an eyebrow at me meaningfully.

Well, honestly, why the hell not? I sat down beside her.

Milo read out the charges against me. I don't remember exactly what they were. I was accused of at least a couple of murders, I think, plus various acts of torture, theft, and high treason. Near the end, he threw in a few counts of bestiality and public drunkenness—just for the hell of it, so far as I could see. The phrase Milo kept throwing around was *crimes against the gods, crimes against man, crimes against nature.* He could have cut through the bullshit and said, *You're a giiiiiiiiirl, and I think you're icky,* since that was what he was really getting at.

While he rambled, I let my eyes roam the crowd. At first, I was playing spot-the-bastard, wondering whether every man in the crowd with darkish hair or a hooked nose was a distant relative of mine. Before long, though, I got interested in the people themselves. The hall was packed, not just with rebels armed to their broken teeth, but with commoners in their everyday clothes, cooks and farmers and fisherman. And not all of them seemed thrilled to be at my trial. There were divisions in the crowd, little groups and huddles; here and there, a pale and anxious face. You know how every time a bunch of friends goes out drinking, there's always one spoilsport who spends the whole time worrying about the bar tab.

I was trying to find Talia in the mob when Lynn's feather-light hand traced a path down my face from forehead to chin. "You should sleep, you know."

"Sleep?"

"Yes, sleep. It is a thing that humans do if they want to stay functional. Can you think of a better use of your time right now?"

This was one of those strange floating moments that came up from time to time in my life with Lynn, when I suddenly wondered whether I knew the rules of reality as well as I'd believed. "Lynn, I'm on trial. If they find me guilty, then they'll probably insert lots of sharp objects into me and light them on fire. Don't you think I should pay attention?"

"Is there really any suspense about how the trial's going to turn out? They can handle it without you. And anyway, I'll fill you in later. Go to sleep." She patted her thigh.

Feeling stupid, and probably looking stupider, I scooted down until I was lying half-curled with my head on her lap. The pen was too cramped for me to stretch out my legs—which made it just like our bunk back on the *Banshee*, except the chains were on me for a change.

I thought maybe I'd rest for a second, just to stop Lynn from fussing, but as soon as my eyes closed, I was out. Properly out, dead to the world. Even though I'd spent most of the previous two weeks lying down, I'd slept only in short snatches filled with violently coloured dreams that felt more like madness. This time, with Lynn's warmth beside me, I slept deep and soft, and the whole world went away.

After some time—don't ask me how long—I woke to an ear-splitting roar.

I opened one eye. The rebels were yelling, shouts of approval and cruel glee. I caught a few words here and there—mainly *kill* and *the* and *Torasan* and *bitch,* in that order.

Craning my head around, I crooked a questioning eyebrow at Lynn.

"Milo just found you guilty," she said.

"Oh," I said, and fell asleep again.

Before long, there was another round of shouting. I didn't bother to open my eyes, but poked Lynn in the side, and she spoke in a tight, thin tone. "Milo just sentenced you to death."

"Oh," I repeated, and yawned and snuggled up against her.

This time, I didn't have the chance to fall all the way under. Once more, the Great Hall rang with shouting, but this time, it was jangled, discordant, cries of protest and confusion.

"He's not going to execute you yet," Lynn said, as I opened my eyes crankily. "He said that you might be useful to the cause, so he's going to keep you around until he can figure out whether you're—how did he put it?—teachable."

"Interesting decision." I scrubbed at my sandy eyes and slapped my cheeks, trying to wake up. "Sounds like a good way to piss off everyone who wants me dead *and* everyone who doesn't."

Milo's mouth was flapping open and shut, but whatever he was saying got lost in the roar of the crowd. Most of the rebels, it seemed, were not on board with Milo's domestication project.

"There's been a change in the weather," I told Lynn. "The night Milo took the Keep, all his Freemen were slobberingly loyal."

Lynn shrugged. "Well. He's been lord of the Isle for two whole weeks. Plenty of time to start disappointing people."

"Fact."

In my experience, being in charge means disappointing everyone pretty much constantly. Hard to keep a hero's halo when you're deciding on a daily basis who has to clean the shitter.

I would not weep for Milo if someone happened to hack his head off and beat his internal organs into slurry . . . but if he lost control, that might be the end of the road for me. The screaming, frothing people in the room had all kinds of plans for my future, and none of their plans involved a tea party.

Lynn caught my elbow. "Hang on—he's going to try something."

Up at the head of the Hall, Milo stood in a huddle with two of his lieutenants, talking tersely. Giving directions. When Milo stepped back, the other two jogged from the room. Seconds later, they were back, followed by Ariadne, who shambled along with her eyes fixed on the floor, and Jada, who looked as if all her birthdays had just come at once.

Jada had a new toy, a thin rattan cane of the kind schoolmasters sometimes use. I winced at the sight. One of my nastier math tutors was a believer in canes. It hurt several orders of magnitude worse than being spanked with a bunch of reeds, and the sting didn't go away for days.

Ariadne watched the cane warily, wearily, as Jada flexed it between her hands. It was too noisy for me to hear Jada, but I could read her lips: *Down. Now.*

Ariadne would have gone down on her own, I think, but either she moved too slowly, or she wasn't allowed to avoid punishment just by obeying. With a lunge, Jada grabbed her by a handful of her close-cropped hair, and threw her at the floor. Ariadne went down and stayed down, crouching on her knees and knuckles, and trembling.

"Freemen!" Milo called, and this time his voice cut through the noise in the room. "Freemen, I hear you. That thing"—he pointed at me—"that thing is everything we're fighting to wipe off the face of the world, and she deserves to be cut down where she stands."

I was sitting. That didn't seem to matter to him.

"But I have to fight the urge," he said. "For the sake of the Isle, and for every one of you. If we keep her caged, we have a better chance of living free. That's the only reason I haven't nailed her pelt up on my wall yet. But in the meantime, let me prove to you that I know what to do with parasites."

He nodded to Jada, who snapped into motion. The cane whistled through the air, crashing into Ariadne's collarbone. She gasped, but the cheering drowned it out.

Lynn, beside me, had gone very still. "Tell me again how Jada was always a good kid?"

"She was, damn it." I watched, helpless, as Jada dealt out another savage, cutting blow. She was smiling with clenched teeth as she did it, and her pupils were blown so wide, they looked like black stones. What the hell had happened to her?

As if she'd heard my thoughts, Jada's head snapped in our direction. "You. Come up here."

I shifted, but she was pointing at Lynn. "Yes, you, the Torasan whore. Come up here and we'll see whether we can find you some honest work."

"I think, on the whole, that I don't like your sister," Lynn said, in a quiet, measured voice. "I may have to do something about that."

"Like what?"

"I don't know. Something. I'm still working on that part." She darted a look at me, apologetic for once. "It may end up being something kind of stupid."

"Do what you have to do. I'll understand."

"Even if it's the kind of stupid that could make us both dead?"

"Especially then. I mean, come on. This is supposed to be a partnership, and I've been doing all of the stupid-that-could-make-us-both-dead for years. You need to step up and do your share."

Lynn huffed out a tired laugh and clambered over the bars of the pen. It seemed to take her a long, long time to walk to the front of the hall, while some of the onlookers snickered, and some looked sick. All that weary while, Ariadne stayed where she was, curled on the ground, head bowed. I rocked back and forth, willing her to stand. She should have had enough strength for that, at least.

Lynn stopped six feet away from Jada. "Well?"

"We all know you love taking orders." Jada stalked forward, closing the distance between them. "So here's one. Make her bleed." She pointed the tip of the rattan cane at Ariadne.

Lynn showed no surprise, and I felt none. We'd both seen it coming. It was only Ariadne who flinched, slumping even lower to the ground. Shaky breaths, trembling.

"Do you need the help?" Lynn said. "Looks like you can handle it on your own."

"I know, I know, but it'll be educational." Jada drew the tip of the cane down Ariadne's back, and watched her shudder. "The poor little chicken hasn't figured all this out. She still thinks that this can't be happening to her. Still waiting for a hero to break down the door. We need to get her focused on reality."

"This isn't necessary," Ariadne said tightly. Cracked voice, through cracked lips. Her eyes never left the floor. "I'm going to do what you say."

Jada considered her, letting the cane slide between her fingers, then lashed out. One vicious slice. Ariadne convulsed, and a new whip-weal bloomed on her cheek, the same shade of red as watered wine. Jada grabbed her by the neck and yanked her upwards, and only then did Ariadne try to stand upright. Her bare feet scrabbled on the stone.

Jada pulled her in close, mouth next to Ariadne's ear, as though she was going to whisper a secret, but the words were loud enough for the whole room to hear. "Oh, I know you are."

With a quick shove, she sent the princess staggering; one kick, two kicks, and Ariadne fell back to her knees. There was a belch of laughter from the crowd, though I saw one woman in the audience close her eyes tight. Ariadne crouched low, and her head shook slowly to and fro; *I can't do it, I can't I can't I can't.*

Lynn didn't look at her sister, though they were only inches apart. When Jada tossed the cane at her, she caught it deftly.

"I don't need to spell things out for you, do I?" Jada asked. "Take the skin off her back. Do it like you mean it. Do it well enough and I won't make you do it over again—or send her back to the whipping post to have the job done right. Do it or she'll spend the next week screaming curses at you for not doing it. Is there any confusion at all about what you're about to do?"

Lynn said nothing, and now even the watching crowd was quiet, waiting.

The waiting was too much for Ariadne, who choked out, "For the love of all the gods, Gwyneth, just do it!"

She'd mistaken Lynn's stillness for hesitation. I knew better, and Ariadne should have, too. Lynn had already decided on her course of action, and was taking a second to work out all the angles before she followed through.

Lynn breathed in, held it, and raised the cane. Jada grinned savagely, and Lynn returned the smile. She was still smiling when she opened her mouth and, with neither hurry nor hesitation, thrust the tip of the cane down her own throat.

I have never had to dodge a spray of vomit myself—a record which, gods willing, I hope to keep intact—but I don't think Jada handled it very well. She did manage to turn her face, but the reeking spray still caught her head on, splattering her from cheeks to knees. Before she had time to do more than gasp, Lynn pounced. Still retching, Lynn thrust her hands into the mess on Jada's shirt, smearing it over Jada's face, into her mouth and eyes. Jada lost all sense of control, shrieking and spitting. Lynn made full use of the opening, hooking an ankle around Jada's leg and taking her down hard onto the bare flagstones.

Lynn squatted down beside her, raked a vomit-smeared hand through Jada's hair, and forced her chin up. "You see that?"

"That" was Milo, who was bent over as if racked with terrible cramps. But he wasn't in pain—he was laughing, his whole body shaking with laughter, gripping the arms of his chair in a useless attempt to keep quiet.

"He doesn't love you," Lynn said. "You knew that, of course. But he doesn't respect you either. Is that part a surprise?"

Jada came out of her paralysis, flailing, kicking, punching. I'm sure she was doing her best to make Lynn dead, but it was hard to take her seriously, that moment. With her face screwed up in a wet purple scrunch, she looked like a toddler mid-tantrum.

Which was appropriate, since that was pretty much how she was acting. A stern sisterly talking-to was in order.

I banged my manacles on the bars. "Lynn, shove her over here!"

Lynn glanced at me, nodded, and aimed a kick at Jada's head that made her scrabble backwards across the floor. Milo wasn't laughing anymore, but he seemed almost gleeful, a hard glitter in his eyes. When one of the Freemen started forward, Milo waved him back.

Jada managed to wrench herself to her feet, but in the process, she took her eyes off of Lynn—always a mistake. Lynn lashed out with the cane, swinging it up and down rather than left and right. We used to call that "the bacon-slicer" when our tutors did it to us, and it hurts like a particularly unpleasant hell. Jada clutched at her ear, blood oozing between her fingers, and flinched back when Lynn raised the cane again. I'd been waiting, measuring the distance between us. One careless step brought Jada in range.

An open message to the peoples of the world: If you want to get bonked on the head real hard, then get yourself a prisoner, put some wrist shackles on her, and stumble into her reach. I don't know offhand why you would want to get bonked on the head real hard, but I am not one to judge people's hobbies.

I balled my fists together and swung. The metal cuffs smashed against Jada's temple, and when she staggered, I threw an arm around her neck and dragged her back against the bars.

An experienced brawler would have grabbed my fingers and bent them backwards until either they broke or I had to let go. Jada just shrieked and kicked. I put a stop to that by squeezing her throat, increasing the pressure until the shrieking turned into gurgling. Then I gave a little extra squeeze, just to be sure I had her attention.

"You'd better listen to me, Jada—are you listening? You really should be listening because you'll be dead in less than a month if you don't get smart."

"You piece of shit," she gasped, almost sobbing with fury. "Filthy pig. Coward. Liar—"

"Sure. Plus, I'm reliably informed that I'm a pervert, and also I snore. Forget about my personal failings. Start thinking survival. Don't you get that you're walking on fire? If Milo didn't need a Torasan wife to have a claim on the throne, he'd have killed you already—"

She thrashed against my grip. "Stop lying. Stop lying, you're lying, stop it!"

"You know this already. You're just too chickenshit to look truth in the face. You're his useful idiot, not his girlfriend, and your usefulness is going to run out." Milo had finally signalled his Freemen, and they were almost on us. I yanked Jada's head back until my mouth brushed her ear. "Think, Jada. For once, think. I'm more valuable to Milo than you are, and he doesn't need us both."

I let her go before the Freemen reached us and backed away, hands upraised. Jada reeled, swaying, purple-red blotches covering her face.

"Get them out of here," she choked out. I figured that her throat was a bit sore, and grieved not. "Get them out of my sight, take them all away!"

Someone took Ariadne by the shoulders and bundled her through the nearest doorway. Lynn was in a less docile mood. The first man to grab her got a gouging thumb in his eye, and limped off howling. The other rebels didn't make the mistake of attacking one by one. They all piled on at once, and Lynn vanished underneath the heap.

To hell with self-preservation, to hell with keeping my head down. I took three quick breaths and threw myself against the bars of the pen. Once. Twice. My ribs screamed, but the fence cracked, and one wall toppled. I scuttled towards Lynn, dragging the chains behind me, dragging a length of fence along with the chains.

By now, they had her upright, holding on to her by the arms and the hair and the neck and I couldn't make them take their stinking hands off of her, so I put my hands on her too.

I touched her shoulders and I touched her face and framed her cheeks with my hands and leaned into her and against her. In the middle of that screaming crowd, in a room still charred black with my family's ashes, I kissed her with a fierceness that would have been pathetic if she hadn't been kissing back the same way. I pressed close, covering as much of her as I could, and grinned into the kiss when I felt her right hand moving. *Clever girl. Clever, clever girl.*

They yanked her away from me, before the kiss had gone on nearly long enough, and more hands clamped onto me when I tried to follow.

She twisted in their grip, trying to look back. "Darren, I'm sorry."

"Don't you dare," I told her, and kept telling her, getting louder and louder as they pulled her away. "Don't you dare be sorry. Give the bastards hell!"

But I don't know how much she heard before they dragged her out of sight.

CHAPTER TWENTY-ONE

Lynn

THEY THREW ARIADNE in the cell first, then me. The door slammed shut, cutting out the light, as I scrambled back onto my feet.

"What are you doing?" Ariadne whispered.

"Just getting my bearings." The room was clean-swept and empty. I found the door and wrenched at the handle—yes, locked. Not that I'd expected otherwise, but it's best to try the simplest solution before getting fancy.

"Lynn, stop that and sit down!"

"Why?" I stooped and squinted through the dimness at the door fastener, trying to figure out whether it was a warded lock or just a latch.

"They'll hear us, they'll come in here, you'll only make it worse—"

"Well, I hate to break it to you, but I've already made it worse. Jada won't forgive me for throwing up on her if I sit quietly in a corner for a while." I shook the door hard, and the hinges rattled.

"Stop it!" The words tore out of her, hoarse and desperate. "They'll beat us! They'll beat us!"

"They sure will, if you keep making noises."

Her mouth snapped shut so fast that her teeth grated together. She was learning.

I left it at that. No point in trying to comfort her. All the platitudes in the world don't mean much when you're locked in a bare cell, waiting for a woman with a whip to decide exactly how much she wants you to hurt.

Leaning back against the door—I couldn't stop anyone from coming in, but I could make sure of a few seconds' warning—I ran my fingers along the hem of my shirt. Milo's men had searched me when they first brought me into the Keep, but they hadn't stripped me, the damn amateurs.

When I found the stiff spot in the fabric, I bit away the hemming thread, poked two fingers into the hole, and drew out my garrotte. I wound it around my right wrist, where it belonged, and felt a bit better.

"Come over here," I said.

"I don't want a hug."

"Good, because I'm fresh out of those. Get over here. Please."

She would have argued if she'd had more energy. As it was, she shuffled towards me. Once she sounded close enough to touch, I patted around until I found her arm, passed her the knife, and wrapped her fingers around the hilt.

She almost dropped it. "What's this?"

"I hope that's not a serious question, because I know for a fact that you've seen a knife before."

"Where the hell did you get a knife?"

"Darren. She lurched over to kiss me before the Freemen dragged me out of the hall—"

"Oh gods, that idiot . . ."

"No, this was a strictly practical kiss. She squashed herself against me so that nobody could see what I was doing with my hands. While everyone was watching us suck each other's faces, I reached backwards to a guard's belt and groped around until I found something hard. Which could have been very awkward, if the hard thing had been something other than a knife, but it was, in fact, a knife. Take it."

"What am I supposed to do with it?"

"Keep it on you, just in case. Things are about to get hairy. Milo's struggling to keep control, and if he slips, then the Freemen could do something stupid."

"You mean they might kill us."

Actually, I meant that they might kill *her*, but there was no need to go into that level of detail. "Yes. So hang onto the knife, and if worst comes to worst—"

"If worst comes to worst . . . what? What do you expect me to do if some hulking thug tries to cut my throat? Challenge him to single combat? If they want me dead, I'm dead!"

The shrillness in her voice could have been terror or fury, but either way, it was exhausting. For just a second, I let my head loll back against the door. This would be so much easier if Darren and I didn't have any deadweight to carry.

"That's not true," I said, with an effort. "As long as you're alive, there are things you can do to try to stay that way. If someone attacks you, then pick a body part of theirs and do your best to rip it off."

"You really think—"

"Shut up and listen. This is the important part. Once you start fighting, you can't stop until everyone around you is friendly or dead. You can't stab twice and then cringe away and hope for the best. In a fight, the first person to stop hitting loses, so keep hitting, no matter what. If they break your arm, use the other. If they break both of your arms, kick. But whatever you do—"

Metal crashed against the wall in a shower of sparks. She'd thrown the knife.

"No wonder he likes you," she said, voice raspy and trembling. "You even sound like him."

"What are you talking about?"

No answer to that, just heavy breathing, and the rustle of cloth as she let herself slide to the floor. Then she said, "You know, Gwyneth, when you were with my mother—"

"When I was 'with' your mother?" The dam in my head broke and icy water rushed through. "I wasn't dating her, you know. She was my jailer!"

"When you were with my mother, no matter how bad it got, at least you were never disposable. You knew she couldn't kill you."

"No. I really didn't."

I listened to her shuddering breaths in the darkness. She was barely a foot away from me, but the space between us had substance and weight.

"Do you actually want to play the who-had-it-worse game?" I said at last. "That won't end well, but if you have to get it off your chest—"

"I know who had it worse," she said, biting the words off one by one. "I've never been confused about that."

Well, good. I ran my forefinger up and down the rough wood grain of the door.

"But it doesn't matter. Maybe what I'm going through is just a pale shadow of what you've lived—hell, maybe it looks like paradise to you. But I still can't take it. You hear me? I *can't*."

"You are taking it. This is what it means to take it. The pain happens, and you live through it because you don't have any choice. I don't have some magical way of coping. If I did, I'd let you know. But this is all there is."

More silence. When she did speak again, it was muffled, as if she was curled into a ball, with her head on her knees.

"I'm sorry if I disappointed you," she said.

We didn't speak for the next few hours.

"AREN'T YOU GOING to ask me about Latoya?"

It was well into the evening, judging from the chill in the air. The silence between Ariadne and me had gone from annoying to ridiculous. She still hadn't lifted her head.

"What's to ask?" she said dully. "Latoya mutinied. Now we're both here. End of short, stupid story."

"She mutinied because she wanted to save you."

"Yes, that detail did not escape me. Thanks for the reminder that I can't even fall in love without screwing you over."

Well. That was new information.

"So you do love her," I said. "I've wondered."

She let out a dull little cough of a laugh. "Have you ever tried *not* loving Latoya? It is a frustrating enterprise. She's steadfastness and kindness and strength and patience and . . . just everything good. Plus, have you seen her? Especially the legs. Gods on high, the *legs*."

"So why . . ."

I let my voice trail off before I asked the obvious question—something along the lines of "Why, in the name of every last god, have you been shoving her away from you with a stick?" There wouldn't be an answer that made a lick of sense. If there was one thing that Ariadne and Darren shared, it was a talent for making simple things complicated.

Instead, I said, "If the three of us are ever in the same room again, I'm going to toss both of you in a large wooden crate, drill a few air holes, and nail down the lid. Once you've sorted yourselves out, I'll send Darren along with a pry bar."

I thought she was ignoring me until I saw her shoulders shaking, her hand pressed against her mouth. Didn't she ever run out of tears?

I tried again, just for something to do. "You know, I'm fairly sure that Latoya would break this island in half for you. I'm not saying that's enough, or that it's the only thing that matters. But it's true."

She sniffed, wetly.

"Does it help at all?" I pressed. "To know that she's out there?"

Ariadne wiped her nose on her palm, then wiped her palm against the floor. She spoke in a voice that sounded like the puff of air that escapes when you press on a dead man's chest.

"The night that Jada sent me out to be whipped—well, the first time—I didn't believe it would actually happen. Not because I thought you and Latoya would storm the palisade in the nick of time and snatch me away. I just couldn't imagine the whip. Not really. Not in connection with my own back. Not until they had me up against the post, and my face was to the wood, and the wood had this reek of sour sweat from a hundred people's terror—I won't talk about that part, you know what a whipping post smells like. The point is, my body got the message, that bad things really were about to happen to it, and my heart began to go like the clappers and the blood was shrieking through my veins, steam hot. And I thought, I have to keep breathing. Regon told me that, it was the last thing he told me—I have to concentrate on something else so I can keep breathing. So, I watched the horizon. The whipping post is outside the palisade, there's a view of the horizon, and I looked past the post and out to sea."

She leaned back against the wall, eyes half-shut, as if in a trance. "I wasn't sure which way I was looking, because there were clouds blotting out the stars, but I thought it was maybe north and I knew the *Banshee* was to the north of the island somewhere. And there was a light. Not a star, redder and ruddier than that, and I thought, or I guessed or I imagined, that it was lantern-light. That it was the ship. And I said to myself, Latoya's out there. She's safe and she's free, and for some reason, gods know why, she cares for me, and if there's anything on earth she can do for me, she'll do it."

"And did that help?"

"No. Not at all. It seemed like a cruel sort of joke after a bit. Once they'd started, I mean. I was staring at the light, at the horizon, and the light jumped with each stroke of the whip. And she was out there, maybe, but that couldn't be as real as the pain. Before long, I couldn't see or think anymore. But later—the third night, or maybe the fourth—when Jada was done with me for the day and I was lying on that stinking cot, trying to convince myself that I wasn't actually dying—I realized, that's what I must have looked like to you. Back when you were my mother's favourite victim, and I floated by in the evenings to try to cheer you up. Me with my lilac gowns and my poetry. That's what I must have looked like to you then—a distant light, almost lost on the horizon."

A short pause.

"Are you done?" I asked—rather politely, I thought, under the circumstances. "Or is there more very important self-pity that has to happen?"

Her head lolled forwards. She breathed hard.

"Stop wallowing, Ariadne. Those years with Melitta? They were hell, and now they're over. And you won't make anything better by going into a guilt spiral. The last thing I need is for you to pull yet another stupid useless bullshit act of self-sacrifice."

"If you haven't noticed, I'm still a bit busy with my last stupid bullshit act of self-sacrifice." She pounded the floor with a balled fist. "Which, *by the way,* would be a damn sight less useless if you hadn't surrendered yourself to Milo!"

"You should have left the island when I told you to go—"

"And you should never have come back! Gwyn, do you have the faintest idea of everything that I've given up to try to make sure that you could have a life?"

"You want me to thank you for the thousandth time? Or do I have to go further than that? Should I get down and grovel for a bit?"

"I have never asked you to grovel! I just don't want you to waste it! You know, all those years after you ran away from home, when I didn't have a clue where you were, when I spent half my time sick with worry about you—I told myself, over and over and over, that you could take care of yourself. I thought, if nothing else, you knew how to survive. But all of a sudden, you're spending all your time in war zones and . . . and giving yourself up to a murderer just for the hell of it—"

"Sure. If, by 'for the hell of it,' you mean 'to stop them from starving Darren to death.'"

"Darren. Of course, Darren. Because you love to lecture other people about not taking pointless risks, but if Darren's in trouble, all bets are off. Because of *course* you should gamble your life over and over and over again for a pirate with an inferiority complex who likes to tie you to a bed."

There were footsteps down the hall, but I barely paid attention. A skinny vein in my forehead was ticking with a steady pulse.

"I know part of you misses the time when you were everything to me," I said. "But I don't. So you'll have to find a way to cope, because I'm not that child anymore."

She wasn't listening. Face rigid, she stared at the door. "They're coming."

"I know. I hear them." I shook myself, trying to reorient. "Get the knife."

"I'm not touching that thing! Do you know what they'll do if they find it on me?"

She was on her feet again, wringing her hands, and I was torn between wanting to shake her hard and wanting to hold on and never let go.

"This could be it," she said, brokenly. "Tell me you don't hate me."

"I don't hate you. I could never hate you. Come here, quick."

I still wasn't in a hugging sort of mood but you don't always get to choose when goodbyes happen. I gathered her in, her teary face hot and wet against my shirt.

"You could though," she mumbled into my shoulder. "You would hate me if you knew, I know that you'd hate me if you knew . . ."

The door smashed inwards to reveal Jada. She grabbed Ariadne by the neck, ripping her away from me, and dragged her up until she was forced to stand teetering on tiptoe.

"Have you been keeping secrets from me, pet?" Jada asked. "Not smart."

"I'm sorry," Ariadne said, without hesitation. "I don't know what I did, but I'm sure I'm sorry—"

"Get her out of here," Milo said, stomping through the doorway. "Get her out of my sight and make her shut up. If I have to see that useless little bitch again today, I don't want to hear anything from her except silence or screaming."

"I can make that happen for you, Master of the Free Isle." Jada's lips curled up in a poisonous smile. "Do you want to watch?"

"Jada, this is not the time for one of your stupid games."

She blinked, looking absurdly hurt. "I'm just trying to help."

"So take her away. You can amuse yourself however you want once you're out of here, but for the love of all the gods, don't bother me when I am trying to *work*!"

Jada pressed her lips together, sullen, but she managed to incline her head in a more or less respectful nod. Then she dealt a quick, vicious kick to the back of Ariadne's ankles. "You heard the man, pumpkin. He wants you to learn how to be quiet. Let's go practice."

She steered Ariadne out the door with one forefinger pressed to the back of her neck. As I watched them go, I made a mental map of Jada's arteries, and imagined slitting them open lengthways, one by one.

Then I turned my attention to Milo, and found that those blue-blue eyes of his were like bits of paint in an old fresco: flat and cold.

"Did you say some prayers last night?" he asked.

"Never do. I was badly brought up."

"This would be a good time to learn how to pray." He jabbed a finger towards the door. "You think your sister's having a hard time? I can make it so much worse. The markets in Sohanchi pay double for blondes, and they don't much care whether they're virgins."

Something had happened. He'd been on edge earlier, but not off balance. Was he . . . scared?

"What's going on?" I whispered.

"Don't pretend you don't know."

"I don't have a clue. That's why I'm asking."

"All right, Lynn. I'll play it your way." He stepped closer. "The lovesick giant just arrived on the Isle."

My heart skipped several beats. "Latoya's here?"

"Not in the Keep. She didn't get anywhere close. And let me make it perfectly clear—if she *had* reached the gate, I would have had your pirate *and* your sister hung from the rafters and skinned. Just as a matter of principle. I warned you what would happen if—"

"Milo. Milo, listen to me." My pulse was racing so fast that it buzzed in my ears. "I told Latoya not to attack, not to do anything stupid—Milo, I *begged* her. Please don't take it out on Ariadne. Milo, please—"

He slapped me hard across the face, and I took the subtle hint and stopped talking. While he gathered his thoughts, I waggled my jaw. Not broken. Just felt that way.

"Follow me," he said at last. "We're going to have a long talk, and you're not going to enjoy it. But if it's any consolation to you, your mistress is going to enjoy it a whole lot less."

CHAPTER TWENTY-TWO

Darren of the House of Torasan (Prisoner)

I WAS DONE playing nice. As six Freemen dragged me from the Great Hall, I expressed some strong and persuasive objections, with my fists. Also my elbows, and my heels, and the knobbly part of my skull. Once I ran out of juice, I let fly with some really blistering insults that I'd thought up for Lynn's father and never had a chance to use on him.

They threw me back in the storeroom where I'd woken up with Lynn that morning. There was still half a loaf of dry black bread left on the table, which was one point in the room's favour, but Lynn wasn't there, which was fifty points against. I kicked the door for a while; once I was too dizzy to stay on my feet, I flumped down on the cot and fumed.

It was the clanging of the warning bell that brought me back to my feet. Instinct. Back in my day, children on the Isle learned before they were out of diapers to leap into action when the bell rang to signal a corsair attack. Even kids too small to fight could make themselves useful filling fire-buckets and carrying bundles of arrows.

But what if the warning bell was a good omen this time? What if it meant that Latoya was storming the gates of the keep?

If she managed to take the city, then, mutiny or no, she wouldn't just leave me in a cell to rot. I was almost eighty-five percent sure of that.

I was still puzzling out what I thought about the mutiny business. On the whole, though, it felt like the time when I tried dragon fish, and Latoya sprinted the whole length of the ship to whack the first piece out of my mouth before I started to chew. In other words, I was confused, embarrassed, and bruised, but I had no fair reason to complain. Latoya and I had both known for a very long time which of us would make the better captain.

On the other hand, Latoya had set Lynn adrift in a rowboat. For that, she deserved a punch up the bracket, or two or three or twenty. However many punches I could land, really. Which would not be many, unless she bent over or gave me enough time to go and find a stepladder.

Regon would never have betrayed me. Given how things turned out for him, maybe he should have considered it.

I waited, guts churning with a sour mix of impatience and dread, as the alarm bell clanged and clanged. When it broke off, I endured the long stretch of silence that followed.

The door finally opened while I was wondering whether I should try to build some kind of booby-trap out of stale bread and my own trousers. Freemen flooded the room, formed up around me, and quick-marched me to what used to be Konrad's study.

Milo sat glowering in Konrad's old armchair, a drawn cutlass resting on his knees. A familiar cutlass. *My* cutlass. The impossible jerk had my cutlass, and that hoisted my fury to new heights. No, there wasn't anything special about it, yes, it could be replaced, but still, you don't mess with a pirate's cutlass. It is just not fucking done.

Of course, it is also just not fucking done to mess with a pirate's slave girl, and Milo had managed to miss that memo, too. Lynn stood at attention in front of Milo's chair, and as I stepped into the room, she shot me a warning look.

I decided to take the warning as more of a suggestion than an order, and ignored both it and Milo. Instead, I snapped my fingers. "Lynn. Report."

She showed a touch of exasperation. "Right now? Really?"

"Yes, really. I need to know what's going on and *this* asshole can't tell a story straight. He just launches into a speech every time he opens his mouth. That's how you can tell he's in politics, instead of a decent and respectable career like piracy."

"You don't always have the best sense of timing, you know."

"I have an excellent sense of timing. It's the rest of the world that's wrong. Report."

"The things I do for my marriage," Lynn muttered beneath her breath. Almost unconsciously, she rolled her shoulders and clasped her hands behind her back. "It's about an hour after high tide and the weather is cool with a chance of scattered showers. Latoya has just attacked the Isle. Judging from what I overheard while Milo was frogmarching me in here, she had two ships with her—maybe a hundred swords. Milo's forces managed to beat her back from the Keep, and she retreated inland. Milo should be happy about this, but he is not. I speculate that this is because Latoya both terrifies him and makes him feel uncomfortable things in his undershorts which he does not care to admit. Plus, he's probably nervous because he's only ruled the Isle for two weeks and he's already started to run low on beer."

"Really? Goodness. It's such a sloppy mistake to run out of beer in the middle of a campaign."

I glanced at Milo sidelong. His face was composed, more or less, but his eyes were all thunderclouds and murder, from which I deduced that he wasn't having the best day. "So, does Milo still have his Freemen in line, or are they getting anxious about their future in his administration? Anxious about their career prospects. Anxious about their life expectancies. Either, really."

Lynn rocked her head back and forth. "From what I can tell, things are at a gentle simmer right now—they've yet to boil over. But with food stocks getting so low, he may have to start rationing bread and salt soon, and when that happens, his subjects are going to get awfully cranky. Maybe they'll rebel."

"The rebels are going to rebel? That's a stunner. Still, I'm sure that Milo has some bright idea to boost his people's morale."

"Well, he's a fight-fire-with-fire man, so he might try burning all their houses down. That will for sure go just great."

Milo stirred. His thumb ran lightly down the blade of my cutlass, and a hair-thin line of red appeared where skin had touched metal. "If you had a single grain's worth of sense, Darren of Torasan, you'd fall on your face right now, and beg for my mercy."

I shrugged. "I'm not very good at that, the begging. If you want to go first, show me how it's done, then—"

It was like a whip-crack when Milo moved, rearing out of the chair to press my own cutlass against my throat.

"Well, now," I said. "This is getting interesting."

"All right," Lynn said, palms up in surrender. "Let's calm down. We're not—"

The cutlass flashed forwards. There was a lick of sensation along my neck, like a cold wire had been laid on it, and then a burning wire alongside that. I gasped, sort of, and Lynn shrieked, almost, and then something was trickling down my collarbone. I brought a hand up gingerly—I had the delirious feeling that my head might topple off if I prodded too hard. It turned out to be just a cut, a shallow one, but bleeding juicily. Just as well that the shirt I was wearing was already a lost cause.

"Shut your mouth," Milo said, the words slow and deliberate.

"Not going to happen, you son of a—you know what? I'm not even going to call you a son of a bitch. Your mother was probably lovely. You're the jerk son of a lovely person, that's what *you* are."

"I said *shut your mouth!*" Milo's pretence of calm cracked like a thin plaster veneer, as something in his mind spilled, ignited, and flamed. "You stupid cunt, what does it take to make you be quiet?"

"Yeah, you like your women quiet, don't you? You're in for a lot of disappointment if you keep me around."

"Milo, wait," Lynn said. She edged forward, trying to angle herself between us. "Darren's impossible when she's cranky. Let me get a hot meal into her, and she'll be a whole different person."

He wheeled on her. "I think you're confused about what's happening here."

"I'm trying to—"

"How this works is that she does what I say, and *maybe* I don't gut her like a salmon."

"I'm just saying—"

"Don't say anything. Get down." He jabbed the cutlass at the floor. "Get down on your knees and put your hands behind your head."

Lynn's eyes flicked over to me. Not asking permission, but assessing my mood, wanting to see how I would take it.

Not well. That was how I took it. Not well at all. "Lynn, ignore him."

Milo cursed beneath his breath. "Down, *now*."

"Do not do a thing for that diseased piece of smegma. Unless you happen to feel like kicking his bollocks right through his body so they bounce off the opposite wall. In which case, carry on."

"Lynn, you have ten seconds before I start cutting. Unless you want your mistress to pay in blood for your mistakes, get on your knees."

"Oh, you daft wanker. Lynn knows how to assign blame and she knows better than to take on guilt she hasn't earned. You just—"

Lynn snapped. "Darren, *shut up!*"

I shut up.

She'd used The Voice, you see. When she took that tone in our bedroom, I levitated straight off of her, no matter what stage of the proceedings we'd reached.

Lynn knelt and clasped her hands behind her head. Just like that. "I wish you wouldn't always make such a big deal out of this kind of thing."

HERE'S THE THING: I'd just spent the better part of two weeks chatting with an imaginary Lynn, and it wasn't easy to shed the habit.

As Milo stalked back over to the desk and massaged his temples, imaginary Lynn and I had a brief but intense conversation. I said *Honestly what the piss* and she said *Trust me* and I said *I do* and she said *Well then* and I said *You can't just give in to bullies, it emboldens them; every time you jump over the stick, he'll raise the stick higher* and she said *What a good point Darren, I didn't think of that, you're right of course.*

And then the whole illusory scene fizzled and fell away, because even in my agitation, I knew that imaginary Lynn was falling out of sync with the real thing.

Milo cleared his throat, and I tensed.

"The black giant fled inland," he said. "So, a simple question. Does she know about the hill fort?"

"How the festering knob should I know?"

Lynn raised herself up on her knees. "Darren."

The Voice, again. I hoped to hell that Lynn knew what she was doing. "Yes, Latoya knows about the hill fort. She knows about every military asset on the Isle. I don't hide things from my people."

"One hundred men, in the hill fort," he muttered. He rapped his fingers on the table and moved his lips silently as he calculated. "Well, she can't hold it long."

"Says *you.* Listen, Latoya is a master at fending off siege. A couple of months ago, she didn't want to surrender the last piece of cake to me, but she wasn't hungry, so she just held it out of my reach the whole day. The *whole* day. Even when she was taking a nap. If Latoya gets her men into the fort, then you won't get her out of it in less than a year."

"What's to stop me from starving her out?"

"She'll have brought rations with her."

"They landed five or six barrels. That's all they took inland. One cart's worth."

That was . . . not as many barrels as I had expected. That was not enough barrels. "All right, fine, call it three months, but still. That's all Latoya needs to rip you an exciting assortment of new assholes. She'll hole up on the ridge until something distracts you. The moment you're looking the other way, she'll storm down here and tie your legs around your neck in a pretty, pretty bow."

"And you think that's good news for you?" Milo's voice was ice, iron, granite. "Let me make something perfectly clear: there will be no rescue. Even if the sand ape comes back, even if by some miracle she breaches the gate, I'll cut your throat six times over before she can reach you."

"Latoya's not here for me, asswipe. Haven't you been paying attention?"

"You think I'm joking?" The skin under his eyes twitched, the sclera a vivid pink where a blood vessel had blown. "If I can't hold the Isle, I can still cleanse it—kill every last parasite that got fat sucking us dry. And I swear to you, Darren of Torasan: I will rip your lungs from your chest before I let you breathe free air again."

"Oh, for the love of syphilised scrotums, Milo, do you ever stop making speeches? We get it. You're going to kill me. That doesn't change the fact that you are most exuberantly and overwhelmingly and *delightfully* fucked."

He narrowed his eyes at me, calculating, like a tanner trying to estimate the exact amount of leather he could get off a cow's carcass. "You're never going to be the least bit of use to me, are you?"

No, was what I intended to say. *No, Milo, no matter what wet dreams you are entertaining on the subject, I am not going to be your tame monkey. Not when I have a chance of going out as righteously as Regon did. So go ahead and lop my head off and kick it down main street. Lynn will find a way to survive, she always does, and Latoya will be a better pirate queen than ever I was, anyway.*

What I actually said was, "N—"

That was as far as I got before Lynn clawed her way across the floor, scuttling and clambering on hands and knees, and grabbed Milo by the ankles.

"Milo, Milo, Milo, stop," she said, the words spilling out, rushing out. "Stop right now before you make the biggest mistake of your life."

He kicked her off of him. "Are you going to tell me again how valuable Darren could be?"

"Yes. Exactly."

"She isn't worth a damn if she won't do as she's told, and she never, ever will. She's just the kind of arrogant cunt who'd rather die than compromise and—hell." He snorted. "Look, she's nodding as I say all this."

"No, she's not."

"She *is*. Look."

Lynn looked. Sighed. "Mistress, not helping."

I stopped nodding. "Well, he isn't wrong."

She made a guttural sound of frustration and returned her attention to Milo. "You know what the problem is here? You've started to think small. Killing Darren, just for the satisfaction of wiping out one last Torasan before you're wiped out yourself—that's not how a winner thinks. That's not how the Master of the Free Isle thinks."

Oh, she was good, was my Lynn. Fired up as he was with hatred and suspicion, Milo hesitated. That didn't make it any easier for me to hear her working on him, using that familiar wheedling, coaxing tone.

"So how does the Master of the Free Isle think?" Milo asked.

"That's easy." Lynn rocked back on her heels. "The Master of the Isle thinks long term. He's planning how to win the war, not how to survive the day, and he doesn't waste assets when they fall into his lap. He wants to use Darren, not stab her for a quick thrill."

"So how does the Master of the Isle convince a stubborn pirate to obey?"

Lynn laughed. Hand on my heart, I swear to every god, she laughed.

"How do you still not understand this?" she asked. "You don't have to convince Darren of anything. You have to convince *me*."

Seconds crawled by, as Milo stared.

"Explain," he said.

"I don't know how much clearer I can make this." She scrubbed at her eyes with a balled-up fist. "Convince me that you'll let us live, and I'll make Darren toe your stupid fucking line."

"You really believe you can do that."

"Yes," Lynn said, tightly. "She'll do anything that I tell her to do, all right? I can make her do whatever you want."

"Well, now." He smirked at me, with the same half-hidden glee that Jada had worn when she sentenced Ariadne to the whipping post. "Does it hurt that she just went ahead and said it out loud?"

Despite the fraught atmosphere, I indulged in a good long eye-roll. *Of course* it wasn't a revelation or a torment to hear out loud what I'd always known, that Lynn was the one who held the reins in our relationship. Yes, I'd tied her to all manner of things and had her in all manner of ways and made her say things that tickled my ego to its darkest and deepest roots. Yes, she would kneel and bow and bend at my command, and act out scenes from fantasies that I wouldn't admit to having when I was sober. But none of it would have happened if Lynn hadn't known bone-deep, soul-deep, that I would fling myself to the far side of the room the instant she whispered, "Stop."

But then, it was supposed to work the other way around, too.

"Lynn," I whispered. "What are you doing?"

She cast me the briefest glance, looking harassed. "This is the only way, Darren."

"Please don't—"

"I made her a pirate queen," she said to Milo, without waiting for me to finish. "You want me to make her a freedom fighter? You want her to parrot all of your kill-the-parasites crap and give it back to you double? Become a flag that your rebels can rally around? I can do that."

"And what if I decide to marry her?"

Lynn flinched. "I—"

"Oh, come on. You sounded so confident a second ago." Milo tapped Lynn under the chin, forcing her face up. "She is the oldest unmarried Torasan heir, as you keep reminding me. What if the Master of the Free Isle decides the best way to keep power is to hold his nose and marry the bitch? Can you make her say the right things at the altar, and act demure in public, and spread her legs when she's told?"

"*Lynn!*" I yelled, desperate now, but she didn't turn. Her attention was fixed on Milo, and she looked him full in the face when she said, "As long as you don't care whether she likes it."

Now, I can't possibly describe my feelings at that moment, but if you want to replicate them for yourself, you can do the following: Stick a bunch of razor blades into your ear, and then thrash your head wildly from side to side for half an hour.

Milo stepped back, looking wary and pleased all at once, like someone who'd just received an unexpected present and had yet to unwrap it. "Stand up," he said, and, as Lynn stumbled to her feet, "What about the ape?"

"What about her? Latoya's here for my sister. Give her Ariadne, and she'll go."

A flash of suspicion. "Sounds awfully convenient."

Lynn released a soft, exhausted sigh. "If it makes you feel better, you can threaten to starve Darren for a few more weeks or throw me into boiling jam if I'm lying. Doesn't matter. It's true. Tell Latoya that you'll give Ariadne back to her if she leaves. She'll leave. Keep your end of the bargain, and you won't have any more trouble with her."

"She'll leave you and Darren behind?"

"Yes. She won't be happy about it, but she's picked her side and she's good at prioritizing."

"What about her men?"

"Her men are Darren's men. They're following Latoya now because she's a masterful presence, but if Darren tells them to join your rebellion, a lot of them will do it. Same with the rest of the fleet, if we can find them."

"Even though the *Banshee's* men decided to follow the giant instead of you?"

Lynn shrugged one thin shoulder. "I'm not Darren. If there's one thing we can all be sure of in this life, it is that."

Milo stepped over to his desk and straightened a bunch of papers that didn't need straightening. "Well. You raise some interesting points. I'll give it some thought and tell you my decision. In the meantime, I'll have you taken back to your cells."

"Wait," Lynn said, and licked her lips. "Could you give me some time to talk with her first? Five minutes, that's all."

He crooked an eyebrow at her, and she exhaled. "Please . . . my lord."

I almost gagged. Milo looked surprised, but he couldn't hide the flicker of satisfaction. "Five minutes," he said, and stepped outside the door.

Lynn all but raced across the room. Just before she reached me, she hesitated, as if she wasn't sure what kind of reception she was going to get. Her eyes were wide and shiny, which was as close as she ever came to crying in my presence.

I opened my arms and Lynn hurled herself into them, nuzzling into my filthy shirt.

"I'm sorry," she choked. "But he was ready to kill you. I didn't have any other play."

"Hey. Do we apologise when we save each other's lives, now? When did that become a thing?"

"All right. New rule. We apologise when one of us promises to manipulate the other one into a lifetime of abject servitude."

"Speaking of lifetimes of servitude—bet you feel pretty silly *now* for letting me capture and enslave you."

She pinched me hard. "Don't be an idiot."

"But just think! If you had stayed in that fishing village where I found you, who know what dizzying heights you might have climbed? By now, you could be the owner of your very own mud hut. Or half a mud hut. Or, well, some mud."

She took hold of the front of my shirt with both hands, where she would have gripped me by the lapels if I'd been wearing my pirate coat, and looked up at me gravely. "I just sold you as marriage meat to the man who murdered your family, and you're trying to make *me* feel better?"

"You didn't sell me." I'd come to my senses, now that the first rush of panic had dimmed. "Lynn, I trust you."

She tensed. "What's that supposed to mean?"

"Well." There was no sign of a shadow in the crack under the door, but I lowered my voice anyway. "I know you didn't mean what you were saying. Whatever your long game is, just keep working it. I'm ready to hold up my end, as soon as you're ready to tell me the plan."

Her face fell. Figuratively and literally, because she let it drop against my chest, and rolled it to and fro. "Oh, bloody hell."

"Hey. Don't worry. I'm not interrogating you. I know you have your reasons to keep me in the dark."

With a look of deep concentration, she fiddled with my shirt, smoothing out a crease here and adjusting a loose thread there. As if it was one of my best coats instead of a stinking rag; as if we were home on the *Banshee*, and she was getting me ready to appear in public without embarrassing us both.

"You know something?" she said. "Sometimes you are such an innocent that it's just agony."

"Like I said, I trust you. I know there's a reason you're not telling me the plan."

"There's nothing to tell," she said, as if explaining to a five-year-old that fairies didn't exist. "We ran out of luck, and we lost, and this is the end of the line."

"Don't say that. We always—"

"We always what? Find another way? Darren—you think that every time you jump fearlessly out of a window, someone's going to arrange for you to land on a mattress. But I live in a world where gravity exists and blades cut skin and the wrong people die sometimes. The Master of Storms is not going to walk out of the waves and kill all our enemies with lightning bolts." She pulled back, studying me with near desperation. "Do you understand?"

"I . . . I understand that you're afraid."

"Sometimes I have to be afraid enough for both of us, Mistress." She detached herself, took a step away. "I can't let you die. It's that simple."

The door opened again. Milo glanced inside and meaningfully cleared his throat; Lynn nodded. "I'm coming."

She only turned back once, after she'd allowed Milo to take her by the arm.

"I've never been a hero, Darren," she said. "I wish like hell that people would try to remember that."

PART FIVE

MY MOTHER TAUGHT ME WAR

CHAPTER TWENTY-THREE

Lynn

I WAS PRODDED awake with the butt-end of a spear. The grass around me was damp with both dew and rain, and lightning crackled across a dull grey sky.

"Get up," the soldier said. "Milo wants you."

I nodded, yawning. No point in being an asshole to him. He hadn't kicked me or used the sharp end of the spear for prodding purposes, which alone meant that he was one of the more polite of Milo's Freemen. "Can I tell Darren?"

"If you do it fast." He moved a few steps away.

Ariadne, on my left side, was still dead to the world, but when I rolled over to Darren, I found her awake. Her eyes were closed, but I could tell from her tight-pinched lips. Darren wasn't so good at keeping her mouth shut when she was asleep. There was almost always some drooling.

I smoothed her shaggy hair back from her forehead. "Mistress."

"They just let us go to sleep," she muttered, cranky as she always was before breakfast. "Don't tell me it's already time for walkies."

"No. No more walking. We're not going any closer to the fort. Milo wants a big buffer zone during the negotiations, in case Latoya gets impatient and sends out a raiding party."

Darren looked up at that, eyes open and hopeful, and a knife twisted sharply in my guts. "Stop that. Latoya is not going to rescue us. Not you and me. Please don't make me tell you that again, because it's not getting any easier."

I licked the ball of my thumb and wiped a smudge of mud from her cheek. At least I could do *that* much. "I have to go and let Milo talk at me. I'll be back as soon as—Darren. Stop fiddling with that thing."

"That thing" was the fetter on her right ankle, the other end of which had been looped around a tree and fastened with a heavy padlock. I'd poked rags into strategic places to keep the metal from rubbing all the skin off her leg, but Darren kept dislodging the cloth when she squirmed.

Darren stopped mid-fiddle and reluctantly drew her hand back. "It itches."

"I don't care if it itches. Leave it alone. And don't think that you can start messing with it again as soon as I'm out of sight, either. I'll know."

I hated leaving her and Ariadne alone, especially in such an exposed part of the camp, where armed Freemen kept prowling past in search of the latrines. I couldn't very well tell Milo to get stuffed, though. When you take the king's coin, you kiss the king's ass, and Milo was paying for a full-access pass to me and all my ass-kissing talents.

Milo's tent was pitched on a hill, probably so he could survey the rest of the camp at a glance. From his vantage point, you could look downslope in either direction: west to a cluster of supply wagons and skinny mules, east to a flat plain scattered with the tents of the Freeman army. Beyond that was a dirt wagon-road that wandered up towards the mountains, and at its top, barely visible in a shroud of fog, reared the dull grey timbers of the hill-fort.

Milo sat on a stump just outside his tent's open flap, flanked by two disturbing specimens of manhood. One had an honest-to-goodness ear tied to his belt. The other one held a braided hank of dark, coarse hair that he would not stop fondling. Souvenirs from the massacre, I guessed. I was careful not to get too close.

"You wanted me?" I asked Milo. I didn't add "my lord." Better to save that for an emergency.

"Your giant wouldn't come outside the fort walls to talk," he said, squinting down at a map. "She just stood on the ramparts and shouted down at our messenger. Explain."

"What's there to explain? She doesn't want to give up the high ground."

He grunted. "I don't like talking on unequal terms."

"Who cares, as long you get what you want? She agreed to deal for Ariadne, didn't she?"

"So she *says*. I'm not giving her anything while she's still holed up behind fifteen-foot walls and an iron portcullis."

"Tell her that, then," I said, with as much patience as I could muster on three and a half hours of sleep. (The army had marched for most of the night.) "Tell her that you won't negotiate until she meets you on level ground. You have the hostage. That's all the advantage you need."

"Maybe. But what if she still won't get serious?"

He already knew the answer to that. He just wanted to know whether I'd say it, like a good little turncoat. I very deliberately took my feelings by the throat and squeezed until they stopped twitching.

"If Latoya won't get serious, then you parade Ariadne up and down in front of the hill-fort until you have everyone's attention, and then tie her to a tree and set Jada loose. Latoya will be ready to deal as soon as she hears screaming."

A smile hovered right at the corner of his lips. "And you would be fine with that, would you?"

"I want my sister off the Isle and away from the nutter you have babysitting her. If she has to catch a few more bruises for that to happen, fine."

Speak of a nutter, and she shall appear. Jada, sour-faced and sleepy-eyed, pawed her way out of the tent, her shirt drooping off of one bare shoulder. Her mood took a dive when she saw me—her face got more sour, by a good couple of lemons' worth—but she pretended not to notice my existence. "Milo, love, can't we just get this over with? Shove the little slut into her ape-woman's arms and tell them to *go*. We can be on our way back to the Keep by noon if we—"

"If we hurry. And risk making sloppy mistakes. You have a lot to learn about strategy—my love." He gave her hand a half-hearted pat before returning his attention to me. "Lynn. I want your recommendations on how to manage the handover without any nasty surprises."

"Well—"

"And, Lynn—I'm sure I don't need to remind you of this, but just in case. There's still time for all kinds of ugly things to happen to your sister before we send her back to her giant. So don't try to get cute with me."

"I won't," I said, stiffly. Did he really think I was stupid enough to screw him over right at this moment, when he was holding every card? Maybe he was a paranoiac like my father. "All right, let's discuss timing."

I laid out a fairly detailed plan of action for him, which involved getting all of Latoya's troops to leave the islands, in groups of ten, a couple of hours apart, before he handed over Ariadne. Milo listened, but he squinted at me suspiciously when I was finished. "That'll take the better part of a day."

"But it means that you'll never be within arm's reach of Latoya until she's stripped of all her back-up. You stay in control the whole time."

"What if her men double back to attack the Keep after they leave the hill-fort?"

"That's why we're splitting them up, so they won't have a chance to coordinate. Anyway, you left almost three hundred men back at the Keep with Gryff. If he can't hold the walls for a couple of days, he's not trying."

He sucked his teeth. "I don't know."

"Fine. Ignore me. But if you won't listen, don't blame me if the situation turns to shit. Latoya *will* feed you a bucket of tent pegs if she gets a chance. You can't give her one."

"If you're playing games with me—"

"I know what'll happen if I play games with you."

"I'm just giving you fair warning. This is not the time to piss me off. Jada's going to need a new hobby once the princess is gone, and she doesn't care for you much. Isn't that right, Jada?" He sat upright, annoyed. "Where is she?"

"She wandered off while we were talking."

"Where did she go?"

"I didn't look to see. I don't care where she goes. Unless she wanders into a pit of fire and pain and cannibal sharks, in which case I want a seat with a good view. When are you planning to kill her, by the way?"

"That's an awfully personal question."

He smiled when he said this, though, and there was a kind of teasing intimacy in it, like he didn't mind that I knew. Our little secret. I pressed on. "Any chance of doing it sooner than planned? You don't need Jada anymore. You have Darren for your tame Torasan wife, you have me to keep her honest. You can go ahead and get rid of the crazy one."

"Nice try." Still with the smile. "But we need a little bit more of a relationship of trust before I'm ready to make that commitment. Ah—here she comes. You'd better mind your manners. Jada's talents may be limited, but she never forgets an insult."

THE REST OF the day was a long, dull slog. Messengers came back and forth, terms were negotiated and re-negotiated, Milo pestered me with endless questions, and Jada stared at me with cold malevolence whenever Milo was looking the other way.

There was one break, around noon, when trails of smoke spooled into the sky from cook-fires near the supply wagons. A sallow-looking woman in a grease-spotted skirt came over to deliver pannikins of soup. I asked Milo if I could check on Darren and my sister while he was eating, and he pretended to agree and then "changed his mind" as soon as I'd walked a few feet away. My own fault, really, for failing to predict the bait-and-switch.

After a lot of dickering back and forth, Latoya agreed to send her men off the Isle in ten-man groups, but it soon became clear that there wasn't time to complete the process before dark. Milo's brain boiled over with impatience, and he all but slapped Jada when she tried to wipe a bit of spilled soup from his neck.

An hour past sunset, the sallow woman came by again with hunks of bread and cheese. I called Milo "my lord" five or six times during dinner, keeping it up until his mood softened. *Then* I tried again.

"Can I *please* go back to Darren and my sister for the night?" I asked. "It's too dark to do the exchange now. We might as well get some sleep.

And Darren's less likely to act up when I'm with her. I'm her security blanket."

"Or her chew toy." He waited just long enough to make it clear that he could say "No" if he wanted. "Fine. Take her over to them, Jada."

Jada's idea of escort duty involved a lot of pinching. I didn't really feel the pinches, but I made little desperate yelping noises anyway. People tend to be easier to manage when you let them have the occasional win.

The moon had topped the trees, giving a soft ghostly light to the clearing where I'd left Darren and Ariadne that morning. I relaxed a little when I saw them—one body, two bodies, both of them still breathing—and barely rolled my eyes when Jada produced a chain and ordered me to hold out my foot.

"You did some good crawling today," she said, fastening the lock. "You have a real talent for it. What's next? Are you going to get on your knees for Milo? Lick his boots clean?"

"If he wants me on my knees, I'm sure he'll let me know," I said. "Your nieces and nephews are fine, by the way. In case you were wondering."

"You think I give a shit about those little bloodsuckers?"

"No, but I enjoy the thought that one of them might grow up to kill you."

She wanted to hit me—I saw her hands twitch—but either she was scared of angering Milo or she didn't want to be away from him any longer. Instead, she spun on her heel and stomped off into the dark. I let out a long breath, trying to rid myself of the day, and jumped a full yard in the air when cold fingers closed on my arm.

"Sorry," Darren said. "Just me. I can't believe I forgot to ask about the Torasan children. Do you know where they are?"

"I don't know specifics. They were still on the *Banshee* when I left it. But Latoya will have hidden them somewhere safe."

"How do you know?"

"Because she's *Latoya*." I jerked my head towards my sister. "How is she?"

Darren winced. That was enough of an answer. I scooted over to the hillock where Ariadne sat cross-legged, head in her hands. A lump of dark bread lay by her knee, untouched.

So my working day still wasn't over. Typical.

"Do I have to remind you how food works?" I asked. "It goes in your mouth. Unless it's a carrot or a cucumber or *maybe* a summer squash, and you're satisfying a different kind of appetite."

She raised her head, and looked at me blankly, like I was a page of writing in a language she could never hope to learn. Finally, she held the bread out. "You should eat this."

"I've had mine."

"I'm getting rescued tomorrow—or I'm getting my throat cut, if things go wrong. Either way, you need it more."

"Milo's not going to starve me. He needs me alive."

"So did my parents, and we all know how that went."

Her voice wobbled, and I wanted to scream. Did she think that if she shoved enough food into my mouth, my twelve-year-old self would somehow taste it?

"Anyway," she said, picking at the crust of the bread with thin white fingers. "We should talk, you and I, before tomorrow."

"All right. One second . . . Darren, could you leave us alone for a little while?"

Darren raised her eyebrows. Glanced at the chain that bound her to the tree. Raised her eyebrows some more.

"I'm not asking you to take a walk. Roll over and cover your ears."

She did it, huffing, and I returned my attention to Ariadne. "What do you want to talk about?"

Oh, hell, emotions were happening. She'd curled tightly into herself, and was rocking back and forth.

"I have to tell you something," she said. "In case this is the last time we see each other, which is looking increasingly—"

"It's not going to be the last time we see each other."

"You don't know that."

"Call it a goal."

"Lynn, I have to ask you to forgive me."

Was that all? That was easy. "All right, I forgive you. Eat your dinner, and I'll forgive you twice."

"You can't forgive me until you know what I did."

"Sure I can. Call it a general amnesty. Here's the bread. Open up."

She slapped my arm away, and I almost lost the bread. "Would you listen, for the love of every last god?"

I sighed. This whole thing seemed like a deathbed confession, and I didn't want to encourage those kind of morbid thoughts, but I didn't want her to get over-excited, either. "Fine," I surrendered. "Tell me."

She put one cold hand on each of my cheeks, holding my face still. She used to do that when she said goodnight to me, back when we were children.

In a voice that sounded like something breaking, she whispered, "You were supposed to be mine."

"Oh," I said, pretending that this made sense.

"That was what our father meant to happen. You weren't supposed to go to my mother. He wanted you to be *my* servant."

"Oh," I said in a rather different tone.

"And when I told him 'No'—this was when you were seven, I guess, or thereabouts—your mother came to me and she asked me to change my mind. She . . . she almost begged me, Lynn. But I wouldn't do it."

"Why not?"

I only asked to keep the conversation going, but Ariadne took it as if it was the rebuke she had been dreading all her life. Her face crumpled, like a fresh handkerchief wadded up in someone's fist, and she took in a shuddering gasp of air.

"I told your mother that I wanted you to be my sister, not my property. I said that, and her eyes just went flat. Not angry. More . . . desperate. And she said something like, 'My lady, she's going to be *someone's* property. You do know that, don't you?' And then she waited, and I . . .'"

I didn't want to hear the full conversation, repeated line by line in Ariadne's shaky, gulping voice. "It doesn't matter," I said, trying to cut her off. "Melitta would never have let you keep me."

"She might have," she said. Passion spent, she just sounded tired. "If it meant that you were kept out of her sight, and she never had to acknowledge that you existed."

Well. Maybe.

"I was a fool," Ariadne said. There was the dead flat voice again. "I was a selfish little idiot."

"You were just a child," I said, and not for her sake, either. Suddenly, I needed that to be true. "You didn't know what was going to happen."

Ariadne's face contorted again, as though she was about to scream. She squeezed her eyes shut. "But I did, Lynn. Your mother told me. She sat me down on a wine cask, turned around, and took off her shirt. Then she told me the story behind every last scar. Hers weren't quite as impressive as yours, but they were bad enough, and all the exciting ones were my mother's work. Long streaks the colour of wine, where she'd been beaten with some kind of a rod."

Fireplace poker, I thought.

"And tiny scars, crescent-shaped, on her shoulders. Know what made those? My father's fingernails. That was the day when he caught up with her in a dark room. The day you were conceived. Your mother told me all about it, Lynn. She told me everything. Everything! Then, as she was tying her shirt back on, she said, 'You won't hurt her, my lady. At the end of the day, that'll have to be enough.'"

"Then—why did you say no?"

It was a mistake to ask, I knew that, it was just going to push her over the edge, but I couldn't stop myself. Ariadne hunched into herself as if the question was a blow.

"Your mother, Lynn, she hated my mother so much. The hate hung around her that day, like smoke over a fire, black and choking. And I just thought . . . if you were my servant, I would try to be kind to you, plan to be kind to you, but you would still be cleaning up after me day after day after day, and you would come to hate me in the end."

". . . I probably would have."

Ariadne looked me square in the face. "But I should have taken you anyway. Shouldn't I?"

"I . . . don't know." My tongue felt numb, and too big for my mouth. "This is a lot of new information. I'm going to need some time."

"You don't have time. This is our last night. If you need to slap me or yell at me or eat my spleen, this is the only chance you're going to get." She pulled back, her eyes searching my face frantically. "Say *something.*"

"I don't know what to say. You can't land something like this on me and expect a written analysis of my feelings all of thirty seconds later. If you wanted a quicker answer, then you could have told me literally any time before this moment . . . No. Ariadne, no. Stop that. Don't you fucking cry!"

She was doing the stuttering-gulpy-breathing thing that meant a full breakdown was imminent. I had her by the shoulders, ready to shake her until she either pulled herself together or shattered into a million pieces, when a quiet cough interrupted us.

"That's enough, I think," Darren said. She'd propped herself up on one elbow, and was raking leaves from her hair. "Sorry to pull rank, but I ought to take point on this."

"I can handle it."

"I know you can," she said, diplomatically ignoring both my maniacal tone, and my death grip on Ariadne's shoulders. "But it's not your responsibility, and you're tired. Go to sleep, Lynn. That's an order."

If I thought about arguing with her, the impulse lasted all of an instant. Ariadne's revelation had sent a sort of tidal wave of emotion crashing through me, and my mental landscape was the shore after the tide receded: a mass of debris, smashed planks and bits of rope and stoved-in casks and beached fish gasping for air. Too much mess for me to cope, especially when I was so exhausted that my thoughts were all dissolving into a sickly slime of yellow-green.

I wanted to sleep, not to try to wrestle Ariadne back to a state of sanity. And—you probably have figured this out about me by now, but just in case—I get a kick out of being ordered to do things that I desperately want to do anyway.

I switched places with Darren, letting her scoot closer to Ariadne while I moved away as far as the chain would allow. At Darren's pointed look, I rolled over and wedged my fingers in my ears, but I unplugged my ears as soon as she wasn't paying attention. If Darren didn't want me eavesdropping on her, then she should have fallen in love with someone less nosy, so it was really her own fault.

For the first few minutes, Ariadne just snuffled, and Darren murmured soft, meaningless words.

At length, Ariadne sniffed thickly, and someone—Darren—ripped up a handful of dry grass. "Here. Blow your nose."

There was scuffling and sniffling and blowing and more ripping, as Ariadne worked her way through half of the surrounding vegetation in her quest to clear her face of snot and tears.

"Gods, I'm disgusting," Ariadne muttered at last. "If I ever get a chance to take a bath again, I'm going to boil myself raw. You don't have to stay awake to babysit me, Darren. I'll muddle my way through to the morning somehow."

"Sure. Since you're up, though, I do have a question I'd like to ask."

A tense pause. "What?"

"The Beggar's Flip. How the flippety fuck does that thing work?"

"*That?* Darren, that's just a stupid party trick."

"All right, it's a stupid trick, but I still can't figure it out and it's driving me out of the soft spongy remnants of my mind. So—if you please?"

"Well—all right, I suppose. We don't have any cups."

"We have rocks." Three pebbles clinked as Darren set them down in a row. "I'm marking the tops with mud. There we go. Yet another feat of pirate ingenuity. I deserve a raise. As soon as I figure out who's paying me, I'm going to ask for one. Now school me, princess."

"It really is stupid. Here. This is how you set up the cups at the beginning of the game . . ."

There was a soft scuffing noise. I pictured how Ariadne was positioning the pebbles: upside down, right side up, upside down.

"But then, when you reset it and invite someone else to try, you set them up this way." A few clicks as Ariadne shifted rocks: right side up, upside down, right side up. "So when your mark tries the same moves . . ."

Darren let out a yelp of real indignation. "Oh, come on!"

"I *told* you it was stupid. It works best when you use it against people who are really pissed drunk, or—"

"Or people like me? Is this your polite way of calling me a raging thickhead?"

"Darren. No. I was going to say, it works on children. I was completely mystified when . . . when Elain first showed it to me."

Darren pretended not to notice the hitch in Ariadne's voice when she said my mother's name. "Elain taught you the trick?"

"Eventually. She tortured me with it first. See, I'd upset Gwyneth— Lynn, I mean. We'd been running races up and down the buttery, the two of us, and I kept winning. Longer legs. I got cocky and bragged a bit and Lynn got sore and went off crying. Once she was gone, Elain said that she wanted to teach me a game. We played over and over—must have been twenty times or more—but I couldn't figure out the trick. So *I* got sore and went off crying, and life was a misery until Elain finally explained it, a couple of weeks later. Afterwards, I cried some more, and said she'd cheated. And she shrugged, and said, 'I started the right way, and you didn't. Whether that's cheating is something you have to decide.'"

Darren laughed quietly. "Cheeky."

"Elain had a talent for putting me in my place, which few people are able to do." A sniff, and then, "That's not true anymore, I guess. Almost everyone on this island has seen me cringing and cowering all over hell's half acre. So if anyone ever wants to put me in my place in the future, they can just copy Jada's techniques."

It was a cold night, but even so, the mention of Jada's name seemed to chill the air. Ariadne sniffed hard, and Darren sighed into the silence. "I know you don't want to hear this, but—"

"Don't say something kind and banal and meaningless. I can't bear it."

"I have to say it, because it's true. It's not your fault that Jada tortured you, and it's not your fault that you were human enough to break."

"*Shut up. I mean it.* Do you not understand how it *burns* when you say things like that?" She wasn't crying yet, but her voice was half-choked. She'd start again any second.

"You know what the worst thing is?" she asked. "Jada broke me, but that just exposed all the rot and the weakness that was already there, beneath the gilt. I already knew it was there; I've known it forever. I can't even remember the last time I liked myself, or felt proud of anything I've done. And now Latoya's sold out you and Lynn for me, and Darren, *I know* she loves you both. How long is it going to take her to figure out that saving me wasn't worth the price she paid? How am I ever going to look her in the face?"

"Stand on a box? On your tip-toes, if necessary."

After a frozen second, there was the sound of a well-deserved slap.

"Ow," Darren said. "Sorry. Sorry. I'm not laughing at you, I swear. But, see, I've been where you are now. I know how it works. You sit alone in the dark and take out your soul and look it over. You see a rotten patch, and you try to cut it out, and then you see another one, and you go after that too. And you cut and you cut and you cut, and by the time you're done, you can't remember what you were trying to save, or whether there was even a 'you' to begin with."

Ariadne sniffed thickly. Cloth rustled—she was wiping her nose on her sleeve. "Maybe we're not worth saving. Look where we come from, both of us, the way we were raised. You think we weren't warped and twisted by that?"

"Maybe." Another pause. "You know, ships are built of warped wood. You have to bend the planks to make them fit the frame."

" . . . Are we seriously going to talk about shipbuilding right now?"

"We could. Why not? It's interesting. I cut my teeth in the timber trade—used to work the wagon routes up and down the Screaming Peaks. You learn things. Say you need a mast for your ship. Then it's a pine tree you want, as tall as possible, without a speck of decay. But let's say you're making a longbow. The best longbows come from yew trees that are rotten on one side. The other side, the good one, has to hold the tree's full weight, so the wood there gets denser and stronger. Of course, for a longbow, the wood needs to be dead straight. But say you're making a wheel hub. Then you want elm, with a twisted grain, all knotted and burled, so the hub won't split in half when you drill holes for the spokes."

"Darren."

"Yes?"

"Is there a reason for you to tell me all this that makes even a tiny little bit of sense?"

"Oh, hell. I don't even know." Darren rolled over on her back. "I'm probably just rambling. I'm sleepy, is the thing, and my blasted ankle itches and I'm not allowed to scratch it and I haven't had nearly enough dinner. Maybe I'm talking total rubbish. But do you want to know something funny? My old girlfriend, Jess, she's a better human being than I am, in almost all the ways that matter. But she'd be a lousy pirate."

Ariadne shivered, making the leaves around her rustle. With a grunt, Darren sat up.

"Come over here," she said. "We should at least try to sleep. You and I can share our blankets—it'll be a few hours before Lynn's ready to be touched. And . . . Ariadne? You and Latoya are going to have to hash things out between you, but can I give you one piece of advice? Don't push her away because you've decided, all on your own, that she's too good for you. I have both been there and done that, and it's never a good idea."

I DOZED FOR a while, but when I woke to the sound of my own chattering teeth, I rolled over to join the others. Darren and Ariadne were sleeping back to back. I burrowed in beside Darren, and pulled her arm around me.

She woke about halfway, enough to let out a soft questioning snuffle. I patted her hand. "Just me. Go back to sleep."

She nuzzled into the nape of my neck, and there it was, her warm breath against my skin. I'd kept her breathing. Whatever else I'd done or failed to do, I'd kept her breathing, for one more day.

"Here's the thing, O my mistress," I said, and I didn't really care whether she heard me; it just needed to be said. "I could say 'You're my world,' and I'd mean it, but that doesn't go far enough. There wasn't a world in existence that I wanted to be a part of until we built one together. And I can't lose that. So, you know. How far would I go to protect you? Pretty damn far. I hate that I took your power away, but I'm not sorry I did it."

Darren kissed the back of my neck, then reached up to stroke my hair. It was the kind of leisurely, possessive touch that always left me hungry and aching—at least, when I wasn't lying on stony, freezing ground with my sister a few inches away.

"Will you promise me something?" she asked.

"Probably. I should ask for more details before I commit myself, but let's face it—yeah, probably. Considering what parts of you I've licked, it's a bit too late for me to start setting boundaries."

"No. It's never too late."

Serious voice. Crap. I squirmed around to bring us face to face. "You know that was a joke, right?"

"I know. But maybe don't joke about that part of us. That's what I want you to promise." She ran her hand along my jaw, traced my ear. "No matter what happens tomorrow, or the day after that, or the day after *that*, no matter how far away they keep us from each other, no matter what they force us to do or say—we decide, the two of us, what we are to each other and what happens between us. Our world is the one we make together. They can control everything else, but this—"

I caught her hand, kissed it, and pressed it to my chest so she could feel the beat.

"I promise," I said. "No matter what happens. I swear it, Darren. But since we *are* together tonight . . ."

"Yes?"

"Stop thinking, for once in your life. Just shut up, and come over here, and kiss me properly."

"The things I do for my marriage," she muttered, and leaned forward.

CHAPTER TWENTY-FOUR

Darren of the House of Torasan (Prisoner)

DAWN IN THE hill-country.

It was raining again. Not a downpour, but a drizzle hard enough to keep the blankets damp and chilly. Lynn started shivering, and couldn't stop.

"I don't know why the damp is bothering me so much," she said through chattering teeth. "When we're at sea, I spend half my time soaking wet."

"Wet with salt water, though. Fresh water always feels colder than salt."

"You just let that innuendo sail right over your head, didn't you?"

"I know. Sorry. I guess I'm a little off my game this morning."

"Yeah." She huddled into my side and tugged one of my arms around her. "I can't think why."

There was very little movement in the soldiers' camp. Maybe, with the cold and the wet, the men were reluctant to leave their bedrolls, or maybe, with the sky so dark, they didn't even know it was morning. At the bottom of the ridge, the Freemen's tents stood as if deserted, grey canvas flapping in the wind.

For a brief, shining moment, I allowed myself to fantasize that Milo's entire army was gone—that Latoya had invaded the camp during the night, and smashed all the Freemen's heads into mushy pancakes, and kicked Milo into the mouth of a giant shark on the way out.

Then a soldier stumbled blearily from a tent, tired and squinty-eyed, but definitely with a head of non-pancake shape. He scratched himself, then lowered his trousers to squat.

Yet another fantasy destroyed by a pile of crap.

In all the chilly camp, there was only one fire alight. Of fucking course, it was in front of Milo's tent, and Milo sat by it, sipping from a cup that steamed. A silent woman in servant's garb toiled to and fro, stoking the fire with handfuls of twigs and leaves.

Was this how revolution worked? One fiery burst of desperate hope and violence before everyone fell back into the same old shitty routine? Man on a big chair, ruling. Women at his feet, serving. Maybe Milo wouldn't force Lynn to empty his chamber pots, but her degradation and humiliation in his service would be as bad as anything she'd suffered under Melitta.

Maybe worse, because he would force her to hurt me. That was one thing she'd been spared as a kid.

As for what would happen to me, in Milo's service . . . I wasn't quite ready to think about that, I decided.

Jada sloshed towards us through the mud puddles. "All right, princess, on your feet. We have to gift wrap you for delivery."

I've never been the parenting type, but I felt a flutter of almost maternal anxiety as I waited to see how Ariadne would cope. Not that badly, as it turned out. She stood up without comment and matter-of-factly presented her hands, wrists together.

"There's something you should both know," she said to me and Lynn while Jada bound her hands, pulling the knots tight with savage little jerks. "I'm going to come back here for you. I don't know how I'll do it and I don't know how long it'll take, but I won't leave you here."

Jada seized Ariadne's face and twisted it towards her. "Found your voice again, did you, chicken?"

"Yes." For the first time in days, Ariadne managed to meet Jada's eyes without flinching. "I have."

"Feeling brave again, now that you're on your way home? I guess it's only natural. But just so you know . . ." Jada leaned in, and scratched lightly at Ariadne's throat with one pointed nail. "If you ever come back here, your voice is the first thing that I'm going to take away from you."

"I know you're scared," Ariadne said, with barely a pause. "You're in over your head and the water keeps on rising. So stop posturing already, and ask Darren to save your ignorant, vindictive, petty, selfish ass. She's such a bleeding heart that she just might do it."

"I won't," Lynn put in helpfully. "I hate you."

Jada's eyes narrowed, but she had no time to respond before Milo joined us, still nursing his steaming drink.

"The men are late getting up," he said. "Go give them a good kick, Jada."

"Why not make one of them do it?" She nudged Lynn with the toe of her muddy boot. "Aren't they supposed to be working for their keep?"

"Oh, they will. But until the black giant is off the Isle, I don't want the two of them wandering around off-leash."

"But—"

"Now, woman."

Jada pressed her thin lips together and stalked down the hill towards the soldiers' tents, casting a death glare back at Lynn over one shoulder.

Milo chuckled. "Ah, Lynn. That girl is going to do her best to make things hot for you, once she doesn't have your sister around for entertainment."

Lynn shrugged. "Emphasis on *do her best*. I think we all know she's outclassed. Milo?"

"What?"

"You never did tell me about your mother."

At the bottom of the slope, Jada pulled a tent flap aside and poked in her head. A second later, she recoiled, looking revolted. Silly girl. If she'd only asked, I could have told her that while it's tricky to knock before you go inside a tent, it's still a good idea. Back when I worked the caravan routes, I used to bash a couple of rocks together before I walked in on any of my men. It was self-preservation as much as politeness. People have many, many ways to masturbate and very, very few of them are fun to watch.

"My mother," Milo repeated. "She was nobody. I told you that."

"Was she nobody to you, really? Come on, you can't think of a single thing she taught you?"

Jada stooped down by another tent, but this time, the tent flap was flung aside before she had a chance to touch it, and soldier staggered into the open air.

Jada screamed. I didn't blame her. He looked like a living corpse. Chalk-white skin, dry and shrivelled. Dark eyes sunk deep in the skull-like face. His shirt was foul with greenish slime—vomit, maybe?—and his pants were around his ankles. Milo let out a sharp, shocked exhale.

"So I guess I'll talk about my mother, then," Lynn said conversationally. "I don't remember much, but from what I've heard, she believed in a lot of the old peasant remedies. Like putting mouldy bread on wounds instead of boiling oil. And raw cabbage as a cure for bleeding gums."

Jada looked about wildly, seized the canvas of another tent, and ripped it free from its pegs. The four men inside didn't even blink up at the light. They lay writhing weakly in their twisted blankets, the dirt around them sludgy with some liquid foulness that I didn't want to see up close.

"What's going on?" Milo whispered. "What the hell is going on?"

"Cholera," Ariadne said, with unhesitating confidence. She glanced at Lynn.

"Cholera," Lynn confirmed. "That was one of my mother's stranger ideas. We had an outbreak on Bero when I was six or so. My father's physicians and apothecaries blamed it on bad air wafting uphill from the slums—in the end, they burned down half the village. My mother was not a physician or an apothecary, though, and she clung to an old superstitious notion about what caused the disease. Can you guess?"

Down at the foot of the hill, Jada's flight instinct had kicked in. She hurried away from the tents, but another corpse-faced man stumbled into her path. She shrieked, kicking at him.

"My mother," Lynn said, "thought that cholera spread when human muck got into the drinking water."

The army camp looked less like a ghost town and more like a nightmare as more and more men crawled out of the tents. At least half of them were shrivelled, cadaver-like shapes, lurching and groaning; the rest were goggle-eyed with shock and disgust. Unconsciously, I'd been ignoring the reek in the damp air. It's hard to survive as a sailor if you can't ignore horrible stenches. Now I let myself notice how truly foul it had become, like an outhouse that backed on to a swine farm in hell. The whole lower camp had to be awash in puke and shit.

"Want to know how strongly she believed it?" Lynn went on. "She gave me a very memorable whipping right in the middle of the outbreak, because I emptied a waste bucket in the wrong place. I was supposed to lug it out to a drainage ditch, see, but I didn't want to carry it that far, so I poured it out in the middens, near the castle well. My mother wasn't very happy about that, and after she whipped me, neither was I. On the bright side, it made me a lot more careful about where I pour out chamber pots. At least, until today."

"You," Milo breathed. "You little bitch, what the fuck did you do?"

"Well, I can't take all the credit. It was a team effort."

"The giant. You and the giant—"

"Her name is Latoya. And, yes. We have our differences, the two of us, but there's no one I'd rather have at my back when I'm visiting a plague port. Yag Sin Tor is putrid with cholera at the moment, did you hear? We made a quick stop there and picked up a bucket of that which cholera patients produce in large runny quantities. Then we used it to spike a couple of barrels of beer."

Lynn waved a hand at the road that stretched between the hill-fort and the Keep. "The plan was for Latoya to leave the barrels in the road, apparently abandoned, about half a mile from the fortress. Now, your men aren't stupid, so they probably tested the beer for poison once they found it lying around. Sopped a piece of bread in it and fed it to a hound, something like that. But that must have been the extent of their safety precautions before they got their drink on. Don't blame them. It was really good beer."

Milo's teeth were bared and his chest was heaving.

"Your men didn't tell you that they'd found and guzzled a bunch of random road beer, did they?" Lynn asked with gentle sadness. "Poor communication. It's a killer."

From the far side of the camp, a horn pealed. This confused the fuck out of me, because we didn't have any hunting horns on the *Banshee* that I could recall. Then I asked myself whether Lynn was the kind of person who, while planning a rescue, would stop to pick up a hunting horn just for the damn drama of the thing, and the question answered itself.

"It's an attack, you cunts!" Milo screamed at his men, eyes bulging. "Get into formation!"

The men in camp, the ones who weren't on the ground retching with their trousers half-down, scrambled for helmets, clubs, and spears. They were confused, and groggy, and they kept tripping over prone bodies as they rushed about. Still, there were a fair number of them. Enough to put down a righteously pissed-off Latoya, and however many pirates had snuck back onto the Isle during the night? My sleep-addled brain wrestled with the complex mathematics involved and was only able to reach one conclusion: At best, it would be close.

This thought was enough to spur me to action. I yanked and cursed at the rain-slick shackle on my ankle, then the chain, and then the tree. It wouldn't move, I couldn't move, I couldn't help, I couldn't get to them, unless . . . hang on. Maybe if I broke the bones in my foot . . .

I raked frantically through the leaf litter around me in search of a biggish rock, but Lynn grabbed my hands and squeezed. "Mistress, just wait."

The horn rang out again, a clear pure note in the mountain air. On the other side of the camp, forms appeared in the mist. One seven-foot shape strode in front of the rest, swinging a length of heavy chain in slow, lazy circles.

Latoya was wearing some kind of intricate vest, and though I'd never seen it on her before, it looked familiar. I figured out why after a couple of seconds of squinting: it had enjoyed a previous career as my best blue coat. Somebody had cut the sleeves off, and used the spare cloth to widen the garment until it fit Latoya's muscular trunk. The same somebody had embroidered the vest with a pattern of roiling clouds and thunderheads in mauve and deep purple, shot through with threads of silver.

And I didn't know whether I was hallucinating or just seeing clearly for the first time, but when Latoya threw out her arm to whip that chain forward, it really did look like she was throwing a bolt of lightning.

"The Master of Storms!" someone shouted, high and wavering.

One of the Freemen nerved himself and bull-rushed Latoya with a burbling howl. She caught his mace arm on the down swing, bent it back until it creaked, and hurled him away. He flew three clear yards and crashed into a tree nose first. Several nearby soldiers exchanged nervous glances, dropped their weapons, and echoed the cry. "The Master of Storms!"

"Oh, you cheeky devil," I said to Lynn, wonderingly.

Her eyes danced. "I told you people would go for that."

Jada panted her way up the hill towards us, swaying and gasping. "Milo, you have to get out of here!"

"In a minute." He'd gone cold again, his voice level and hard. "Go to the wagon. Get a rope."

She reached out a trembling hand to his face. "My love—"

"Woman, do as I say!"

Jada dashed off, while Milo wheeled, braced, and dealt a vicious kick to Lynn's stomach. "You lying little bitch, I'll gut you."

"Oh, I think very the fuck not," I said, and flopped my body over Lynn's. Inelegant, maybe, but it was the best I could do. "You better start running before Latoya gets here, you shitbird, or she'll fold you up until you fit in a very small snuff box."

Jada dashed back, coil of hemp rope in hand. "I have it."

"Good," Milo said. "Tie two nooses."

He turned burning eyes on Lynn. "I warned you. There will be no rescue. Not for your parasite sister, not for your Torasan pimp. Did you think that I was bluffing?"

She was still shivering, now from the pain of his kick as well as the cold, but she looked up at calmly through messy bangs. "I knew you weren't. That's why I killed you."

Jada's hands froze in the act of tying a slipknot. Milo snorted. "You really think—"

"Check your cup."

His drinking mug sat on a stump where he'd abandoned it, still topped with a plume of pleasant-smelling steam. Milo stared, then nudged the cup with his boot until it tipped. Thin golden liquid trickled out, followed by thicker, darker dregs.

"Blackroot," Lynn said. "It was my father's favourite poison. No smell, no taste. Takes a while to kick in, but that's why I've been talking at you at such ridiculous length. I think you should be past the point of no return by now. If you want to make yourself vomit, be my guest. It won't help, but you should do whatever you like with your last few minutes."

He stared, uncomprehending, unbelieving, but a spasm ripped through his whole body, racking it neck to ankles, and his confusion turned to panic. He thrust his finger down his throat—retched, spat, retched again.

"But I didn't let you touch my cup," he said between heaves. "You never touched it."

"I didn't personally, no. You know, I've never been very good at delegating, but I'm trying to work on that."

Jada let a half-formed noose drop from her shaking hands, and ripped her hook-pointed knife loose from her belt instead. With a strangled cry, she hurled herself towards Lynn, and I braced for the impact, but someone else got there first.

Barely half an hour before, I'd watched as a silent servant-woman carried fuel for Milo's fire. Now, that same servant sailed out of nowhere, long skirts billowing. As Jada blundered forward, the servant dropped into a low crouch and then sprang up, a quick driving motion with all the punch and snap of an uppercut.

A head-butt is not a complicated move, but executed correctly, it's a thing of beauty. The servant's skull met Jada's throat with a meaty-sounding squelch. She stumbled backwards, clutching at her neck, gasping and croaking, tripped over Milo, and went down hard.

I understood, then. I'd taught him that move myself, so he'd always have a trick in reserve if he got jumped by some cocky asshole in a market town.

"Nicely done," I said. "And much appreciated, Spinner."

"THANKS, CAPTAIN," SPINNER said, ever so casual. He pulled off the woman's headscarf he'd been wearing and ran his fingers through his hair. "Lynn, you all right?"

"Just dandy," Lynn said. "Get the key to the chains. It's around his neck."

Milo was crouched on his hands and knees now, still hacking and spitting, shoulders jerking as his body convulsed. Very deliberately, Spinner stepped on both his hands before leaning over to rip the key loose.

He tossed it to Lynn, who went to work. Her shackles came off easily, and so did Ariadne's, but the lock on mine must have rusted tight. Lynn cursed at it under her breath, wiggling the key, while I stood there looking gormless and feeling unwanted. "What can I do?"

"Um. I don't know." Lynn hammered at the key in exasperation. "Inspire the troops."

"How?"

"I don't know. Say something piratical."

"Avast, ye swabs!" I yelled at nobody in particular. No one seemed to notice.

"I don't think that helped," I said.

"It was beautiful, darling, you're being very useful," Lynn said absent-mindedly. With a grunt of triumph, she wrenched the rusty shackle loose. "There. Now, if you could give me one second—"

She whipped the garrotte from her sleeve, and I winced. "Lynn."

"What?"

"Do not murder Jada to death."

"Why not?"

It was a cold-blooded question, but maybe a reasonable one. Ariadne, beside me, stood transfixed, one hand crushed against her open mouth, and her eyes, once again, glassy with tears. But, well. I wasn't Lynn and she wasn't me, and we had different ways of fighting our wars.

"Because I'm asking," I said. "And I'll say please if I really have to. Just tie her up for now."

"Oh, fine," Lynn muttered testily. With rather a poor grace, she used her foot to roll Jada over onto her stomach and looped the garrotte around her elbows.

"If you were anyone else's sister," Lynn said. "*Anyone* else's . . ."

She let the sentence trail off while she pulled the garrotte tight and knotted it firmly. "There. Now stay down, you little coward. If you give me any grief, then I may do something very fatal to you completely by accident. Darren would scold me later, but you'd be too dead to appreciate that."

Meanwhile, Milo was crawling, his face a blue-white rictus mask, reaching out with splayed fingers for the knife Jada had dropped. Spinner hiked up his skirts and kicked the knife away. "We're not done, you and I."

It was Spinner's normal quiet voice, but there was icy strength all through him, straining in his sinews.

"So," Spinner said. "You remember the man you killed the night you took over? The one you delivered to the *Banshee* in two separate pieces?"

Milo stared up, eyes wide and blind with agony and confusion, his lips moving soundlessly.

There was a tug on my sleeve. "Come on," Lynn said. "We should let them have some space."

We straggled down the hill, my arm around Lynn's shoulders, her free arm on Ariadne's waist. Behind us, Spinner kept talking in that soft and deadly tone.

"Some people might say that he wouldn't want this," Spinner said. "And it's true, he wasn't a vengeance kind of person. I don't think he ever hated anyone in his life. But there's the thing—if you kill all the people like him, you end up surrounded by the people like me. Tell you what, though. I'll make this quick, if you can tell me his name."

IT WASN'T UNTIL days later, when the dust had finally settled, that I found time to punch Lynn in the arm and say, "See? I knew you had a plan."

"You want a shiny prize? Of course I had a plan."

"Although—not your best one ever, to tell you the truth? I don't think you're allowed to give me any more grief about how shitty my plan was when we rescued you from Bero."

"What? Your plan was shitty. My plan was not. Cosmic justice demands that I continue to give you grief."

"Really? Don't you think you left a lot up to chance?"

"Lies. Lies and slander. The plan was a little complicated, but that was so we didn't have to take any chances. We had a lot of back-up options and fail safes built in. You should see the chart I made. It is colour-coded. It is glorious."

"So there never was a mutiny?"

"Well. Latoya and I did come close to blows, the day after you and Ariadne got taken. We were both exhausted and scared, so we lost our minds and screamed at each other for a while. Not our finest hour, I know. Fortunately, Spinner came up from belowdecks just as things were getting stupid. He went and fetched the hose, and sprayed us both until we couldn't do anything but gasp and squelch. He asked us what precisely the fuck we were thinking, acting like assholes right in front of Regon's body, and . . . yeah. Latoya and I managed to agree that our mutual assholishness wasn't helping the situation. We didn't exactly hug it out, not then, but we pulled ourselves together. Took a nap. Had a bowl of porridge and a long drink, and sat down for a council of war once we were human again."

"But then why fake a mutiny?"

"It protected Ariadne. If Milo thought that I was in charge of the fleet, then Ariadne was expendable—he already had you as a hostage. But if Latoya and I were on opposite sides, then he needed you both alive. Ariadne became the only card he had to play against Latoya."

"Clever."

"Latoya and I have been known to be clever from time to time. I'm sorry we had to leave you in the hunger cell for so long, but we had to stall for a while, so the commoners on the Isle could work through their emotions and start to have some sober second thoughts."

"About Milo?"

"And about mass murder. Plus, we knew that Milo would start to lose his grip on the Freemen once he ran low on meat and good wine. And we needed time to drop off your nieces and nephews with Holly and Jess, and we had to collect supplies for the next stage of the operation."

"You mean you had to go get a giant barrel of cholera shit."

"That. When we'd stalled about as long as we could, I made a big noisy song and dance of my surrender, to keep Milo occupied while Spinner made his way into the Keep. You'll have to ask him about the specifics, but you know how good he is at being invisible."

"And he knows the Isle—he grew up here."

"Yes, that helped. Apparently, he has a former boyfriend at the Keep, who is maybe not so much a former boyfriend anymore. With Spinner in position, we had a fallback in case I couldn't keep control of the situation once Latoya invaded. But I managed all right. And then we just had to wait for things to play out. We had the cholera outbreak to whittle down Milo's forces and make them want to surrender, and the Master of Storms to give them someone they'd be willing to surrender to, and we had Spinner lurking around with a vial of blackroot in his pocket, waiting to make Milo dead as soon as his usefulness ran out. And here we are. Now tell me that my plan was excellent, or I'll poke you."

"It was adequate, I guess. Ow. All right, fine, the plan was good. But did you have to keep Ariadne and me completely in the dark?"

"Mistress. High up on the list of Things Not To Do When You Have a Plan—maybe even at the number one spot—is 'Talk about the plan lots and lots when your enemies might overhear.' It was bad enough that you kept being so relentlessly optimistic. I mean, your blind faith in me was touching, but—"

"It wasn't blind faith."

"Mistress . . ."

"It was a *little* bit blind faith. But only a little. As soon as you showed up, I knew that you didn't come to the Isle alone. So I knew you weren't telling me everything, and it stood to reason that—"

"How did you know that I didn't come to the Isle alone?"

It was rare for me to see something that Lynn had missed. I sat back smugly, basking in the moment, until she poked me again.

"Ow. *Ow.* All right. You arrived in a rowboat. Now, you may have powers beyond mortal understanding—but you're really, really short. There was no way you could have handled both of the oars in any of our rowboats. You couldn't possibly have reached."

"Huh." Annoyance flickered across Lynn's face. "I guess that was a bit of a weak point in the story. Good thing Milo missed it."

"But I didn't miss it, because I'm a genius and the best pirate ever. Tell me I'm the best pirate ever."

"If you're going to make that claim, you'd better be prepared to prove it. Think you can shiver both of my timbers before suppertime?"

"Yarr," I said happily.

And matters kind of progressed from there.

BUT THAT WAS all in the future. On the day of the battle, I understood very little about what was going on, but we weren't dead and Lynn seemed pleased with herself, so I wasn't about to complain.

In what was left of the soldiers' camp, the resistance had thinned out to the most hardcore Freemen, the ones with chicken feathers adorning their jackets and helmets. These stood back-to-back in a tight circle as Latoya's troops closed in, ready for a brutal and bloody last stand. But there were only a handful of them. Nearly all of Milo's soldiers lay groaning in muddy pools of their own waste, or had thrown their weapons down when they saw Latoya walk out of the mist.

This, I realized, was going to be a bitch to explain to people. It was hard enough to tell the story of our battle against the Sons of Heaven, and how we won it with porridge and hand cream. Now people were going to ask how I defeated Milo's troops, and I'd have to say, "Shit and religion."

Noises had been coming for a while from the top of the hill. At last, there was a dull crunch and a drawn-out gurgle. Seconds later, Spinner joined us on the slope, wiping his dagger on the hem of his skirt.

"Did he remember Regon's name?" I asked.

"He did not."

Spinner didn't volunteer any more information, but he passed me the bundle he'd been carrying under his arm: my cutlass, with its belt and scabbard. It was a bit damp and sticky in places, but Spinner had thoughtfully wiped off the worst of the blood.

"Lynn?" I said, raising my arms. "If you please."

"Of course, Mistress."

She fastened the belt around me, while I steadied myself on her shoulder. Now that the crisis was over, the past few weeks of pain and hunger and fear were catching up to me, all at once. My knees wobbled and my vision blurred.

"Do you need me for anything?" I asked, squinting at Lynn through one eye. "Because, if it's all the same to you, I think I'd rather like to pass out."

"In just one second." Lynn drew the cutlass for me—oh, that comforting steely ring; I'd missed it—and pressed the hilt into my hand. "Our troops still have some work to do today and they've been worried about you, so first, give me one good roar."

I figured I had just about enough left in me for that, so I coughed to clear my throat, punched the cutlass high in the air, inhaled until my lungs burned, and let it all out in one long howl. The distant cliffs caught the sound and whipped it back, until the hills themselves seemed to be screaming.

Down below, Latoya raised a fist high in salute, grinning, and the pirates cheered. Good enough.

"Now," I said. "May I please pass out?"

She was already clearing a space, kicking pebbles and twigs out of the way. "Be my guest."

I'd never checked out of a battle before in exactly this way, but I knew Lynn and Latoya could handle things without me. So, with vast relief, I let myself drop face forward onto the soft earth, and the shadows closed together blissfully over my head.

CHAPTER TWENTY-FIVE

Lynn

I WOULD HAVE liked to pass out myself, but someone had to do the cleaning up.

It took about ten minutes for Latoya and her troops to finish off the last of the Freemen, ten minutes that Ariadne spent standing stock-still, eyes glued to Latoya as she whirled and slashed and pounded. I myself was tired both of standing and of sitting in the dirt, so I sat on Darren instead. She'd fallen on her stomach, luckily, so her buttocks made a raised seat, and it was easy to keep an eye on her that way.

When the last unfriendly face had been punched, and the last unfriendly testicle smashed into testicle jam, Latoya hurled down her sticky chain and raced over to us. Ariadne raised herself up on her toes and lowered herself again, like someone getting ready to jump off a cliff, and changing their mind at the last second.

Latoya ground to a halt a foot away. "Uh," she began, with eloquence rivalling that which Darren displayed at stressful moments.

Ariadne had no such difficulty. She spread her arms. "Seriously? Seriously?"

"Um," Latoya said this time.

"I'm so angry that I can't even decide who to murder. You made me believe that you betrayed my baby sister!"

Latoya closed her eyes briefly, and she let out a sigh of pure exasperation. "Because it was the best play we had after you decided to martyr yourself."

"That was my choice."

"And coming after you was mine. I've chosen you so many times and in so many ways, Ariadne. Now you have to decide whether this is what *you* want, too."

"Well, of bloody *course* I want you!" Ariadne screamed into the wind. "But how can I do that to you? You know what it'll mean to live your life with me. It would mean choosing this bloody country and its bloody people and this bloody, *bloody* war—"

"I already chose those things—"

"But why? *Why?*"

"You chose them!"

"Yes, well, I'm an *idiot*!"

"Maybe I am too. Or maybe it's because I like solving problems, or maybe Darren infected me, or maybe I want to do something that's never been done before. Whatever the reason—no, look at me—I'm not afraid of what a life with you would mean. Not as long as you're choosing me, too. Are you listening?"

"I . . . I . . ." Ariadne put a hand up to her head, and blinked hard, swaying. Latoya's eyes widened with worry, but Ariadne shook off the moment of dizziness.

"I want to continue this conversation," she said, in something close to her normal tone. "But not this very minute. You see, I think I'm on the point of having a bit of a breakdown, and if you don't mind, I'd like you to hold me for the next ten hours."

Latoya blinked. "Oh."

"Is that all right?"

"Of course."

I can be polite, from time to time, in situations where it doesn't take much of an effort, so I looked away when Ariadne launched herself into Latoya's arms. I still heard them—the heavy breathing, Latoya's husky voice murmuring, "I was so scared for you," and Ariadne's voice in answer, repeating, "I'm here, I'm here, I'm here."

At least I didn't have to lock them in a crate together, I thought, patting Darren's thigh as she stirred underneath me. I already had more than enough to do.

THE NEXT WEEK passed in a blur of dispatch-sending and bandage-rolling and firewood-gathering. Miniature disasters bloomed on every side, and had to be stomped out before they grew to full size.

Ten or so of the Freemen who had surrendered to us tried to unsurrender the next day, then re-surrendered when Latoya demonstrated her ability to bend swords into novelty cock rings. The sick men called Ariadne an angel when she brought them clean water from the well in the hill-fort, and kept clutching at the hem of her dress. It rained, snowed, and rained some more. A rabid-looking squirrel found its way into the middle of the camp. The messengers from Torasan Keep were hostile at first, then cautious, then curious, and then swung back to hostile for no apparent reason.

It was just one thing after another in a sort of conga line of frustration. Darren, through it all, was so loving and patient with me that I finally had to bite her ear and chew semi-hard until she was forced to grab me and hold me still. Once she figured out what I was asking her to do, she did it, with as much pirate queen swagger as I ever could have wished. All the restless itchy terribleness of the world's never ending demands went away when I was pinned to our bedroll, with Darren's weight and breath above me, keeping me down.

The world came back the next day, because the sun has this exasperating habit of rising each dawn. Fortunately, Darren ordered me to stay in our tent all morning—once I'd given her a series of pointed hints to that effect—and that gave me enough time to level out again.

Three days and a cross-island march later, we were back at the Keep for peace talks.

There was an odd selection of people on the rebels' side of the bargaining table. Gryff, the lieutenant whom Milo had left in charge of the Keep, had shown a bit too much interest in a seven-year-old page boy. As a result, a bunch of kitchen servants got together and encouraged him to take a swan-dive off the castle walls. Encouraged him pretty hard, I must say. He splattered into so many bits at the bottom that it took a whole month of rainstorms to get rid of all the stains.

After Gryff made his dive, a ragtag bunch of strong personalities had taken charge in his place. There was a drover, and a dockmaster, and a cook named Tavia that Darren couldn't quite look in the eye.

It was the drover, a man named Kelman, who bent over the table in the first hour of negotiations and said, "There's one thing you have to accept. Darren of Torasan will not be lady of the Isle."

And Darren, who wanted to rule the Isle rather less than she wanted to wear trousers with inward-facing spikes on the crotch, managed to summon a shocked expression. "You must admit that I'm the rightful heir."

All by herself, Darren did this. Without any encouragement from me. Without so much as a nudge or a poke. Which proves, once again, that nobody is unteachable, as long as you're willing to put in the time.

Latoya jumped in. "You're going to have to give way on this one, pirate queen. Torasan's legacy can't be redeemed. Your house has to end here, or there'll never be peace."

"That's what we say," Kelman agreed, and a mighty argument erupted, Darren shouting and protesting on one side of the table, Latoya pounding her fist on the other.

And I twisted around and pressed my face against Darren's trousers to hide the smug smile that I couldn't suppress. Sometimes, things just work out.

We'd spent hours preparing for the negotiation the night before, charting out eight or ten ways that Latoya could emerge as the spokesman of the rebels without being too obvious about it. Then Latoya and I came up with five or six more ideas after the others went to sleep. Even so, we hadn't been really happy with any of the options. They'd been sketchy, relying on guesses and estimates, full of if-this-then-that contingencies.

No need for any of that now. Darren and Latoya could dominate the table for hours, as Darren demanded the throne and Latoya shouted her down. By the time Darren finally, reluctantly gave way, Latoya would be positioned as the loudest voice among the rebels, which was right where she needed to be, for the next stage. Negotiations are much smoother when you control both sides.

And all with minimal work on my part. Hell, I could probably take a nap.

I didn't nap, though, because it was too entertaining to watch the two of them going at it. Darren wasn't used to Latoya yelling at her, sneering at her, and discussing her personal flaws in brutal detail. It made for some quite genuine frustration on Darren's part, which, in turn, caused Darren to be extra shouty and obnoxious. Lots of fun.

After a few hours of this, a bell clanged down in the harbour. Darren went rigid; so did Kelman, and Spinner, and—I scanned the crowd quickly—yes, everyone who had grown up on the Isle. Only outsiders like Latoya and I were in the dark.

"Corsairs," Darren said. She gave my shoulder a squeeze and stood up, ripping her cutlass from its sheath. That was sort of silly, since she would have to sprint to the harbour and climb onto a ship before she could get in stabbing range of a corsair, and it would be awkward to do all that with sword in hand. It looked good, though, so it was still a reasonable decision, from a piracy perspective. "Quick break for violence?"

Latoya shrugged. "I need to stretch my legs, anyway."

And they headed out together because they were *still*, occasionally, the same kind of idiot.

While Darren played conquering hero, I kept up my work in the council room, flitting between groups of people, now listening, now suggesting, now diving behind a pillar to compare notes with Spinner. I got so engrossed that it seemed minutes before she was back.

Darren stalked through the hall, sweaty but uninjured, and tossed her bloody cutlass down on the council table as she went—a nice touch. Just before she reached the far door, she snapped her fingers in my direction. "Girl, attend me."

I scrambled to follow her to the storage room we'd appropriated as a base of operations. "How did it go?" I asked, as soon as the door swung shut behind us.

"Fine. Corto's sword arm is back in form. He did the slashy-slashy-make-them-all-die thing. I just watched his back." Darren nodded towards the council chamber. "Do you think that our friends in there are ready for the next step?"

"I think so. Spinner and I have been warming them up for you. Question is, are you ready, Ariadne?"

Ariadne had been waiting in the storage room for most of the day, alternately pacing and chewing her nails down to the nub, fussing with her clothes and re-doing her makeup. She must have gone through six or seven different faces before she settled on light powder, faint blue shadows around the eyes, and a hollow in each cheek. It was a haunted, unsettling look, but it gave her a solemnity that was worlds away from her old costume of lace, frills, and titters.

"Am I ready?" Ariadne repeated. "Well, that depends. You think anybody'll notice if I throw up and then run away screaming? Or if I scream and then run away throwing up?"

"You won't."

"You don't know that. The things that I've done here . . . the things that these people have seen me do . . ."

Her voice cracked on that, her breath quickening. It was all so fresh and raw for her still, and I wondered all over again whether this was really the right move.

I took hold of her hands before she could rub her eyes and destroy her makeup all over again. "You don't *have* to do this. We can find somebody else."

"Lynn, stop," said Darren, of all people. It was surprise, more than anything, that made me shut up. "Ariadne, listen. She's right. You don't have to do this. You can say no. But I'm asking you to do it, because in a decade of searching, I won't find anyone better. The job needs you. It needs *everything* that you are."

Was it my imagination, or did Ariadne stand a little straighter at those words? She moistened her lips. "You'll be there?"

"Every moment. For crowd control, and whatever else you need, up to and including snack delivery." Darren carefully plucked a piece of lint from the shoulder of Ariadne's dress, and flicked it away. "Not that you'll need us. You're a force of nature and you've terrified me since the day we met, and I know with every speck of my soul that you can do this goddamn thing. So give them hell, princess."

"You bloody pirates and your smooth talk," Ariadne said, after a few seconds in which I didn't breathe at all. "Fine. But you've promised me snacks, and they'd better be excellent. If you try to foist me off with carrot sticks, murder will be committed."

"I think that's entirely fair."

BACK AT THE council table, Ariadne sat very tall, very straight. She didn't fidget, and her face was cool and composed, but she was breathing much too fast.

Latoya, on the rebels' side of the table, cut right to the chase with her first question. "Why should these people let you rule their island?"

"I'd do it well," Ariadne said, without a pause, but without a whole lot of conviction, either. "I know how to administer a state. I understand trade and fiscal policy and military strategy."

"So we should make you a queen because you've read a lot of books?"

Yes—that was the right tone, that edge of scorn and condescension. It stiffened Ariadne's spine, made her eyes flare and her chin jut out.

"I know how to do the job," she said. "I once negotiated a sixteen-part treaty with the House of Tours and entertained thirteen lords for supper on the same day. I can make a balance sheet sit up straight and sing hallelujah."

"So what would you do if, say . . ."

Latoya shot off a question, a complicated one that involved flour prices and barley blight, and Ariadne answered. Latoya asked another, this time about defending a long border with inadequate troops, and Ariadne answered. By now, the other people at the table were getting interested. Kelman asked about conscription and Tavia asked about meat imports, and Ariadne answered and answered and answered again. She didn't always have a perfect solution, and when she didn't, she admitted it, but she weighed each problem, took it apart into bite-sized pieces, and suggested a way over or under or through.

She wasn't shaking anymore.

After an hour or so, the rebels ran out of questions. Latoya shot me a quick glance, and I nodded. Time for the tricky part.

"All right, you know how to govern," Latoya said. "But someone else could learn. Why should these people put your faith in you? Why should they let you send their children to war? How do they know that you won't turn into another Stribos, or Milo? Why will you be any different?"

Ariadne's eyes sought out mine, and held them, as she gathered her courage. We'd planned for this, practised it, but even so . . .

She swallowed hard, gripped the edge of the table, and finally said the words out loud. "I'm barren."

There wasn't the uproar that I'd half-expected, but there was instant unease, bodies shifting in their chairs.

"I know," she said, before anyone could talk. "Blood is rank and blood is right and blood is bloody everything, and in the eyes of every other Kilan noble, I'm a broken useless woman, unfit to rule so much as a tea trolley. And that's exactly why you want me ruling you. You need a guarantee that things won't go straight back to business as usual once I'm on the throne? This is the best you're going to get. The rest of the ruling class will never accept me, and if I adopt an heir, they'll never accept him or her. Whatever happens, I'll have to fight all my life for the right to exist, and the right to pass on my crown. If I'm going to rule in Kila, I have to change Kila. I don't have another choice."

That was the end of her prepared speech, the one she'd practised in a mirror the night before, while I rubbed her shoulders and muttered encouragement. But she wasn't quite done.

"I've been messed up a long time," Ariadne said. "Like most of you, I suspect. But I'm done with hiding my damage. I'm going to hone it and polish it and sharpen it and send it off to war, and with it, I will fight for you. For us. I'll fight for all of us."

THAT WAS THE end of the job interview, but not the end of the conversation. There was more talk after that, and more, and more, and bleeding hell, more, about everything from the punishment for theft to the price of salt. So much talk that Latoya scooted her chair close to Ariadne so that they could hold hands under the table, and Darren took me out of the room for half an hour to commit some crimes against god, man, and nature. But we all refocused for the last item on the agenda, which was the re-naming of Torasan Isle.

Darren was very quiet during this, though she didn't protest. I stroked her leg while other people made their proposals. I really wanted to suggest "Thundercunt," because, though I knew it wouldn't win, it was bound to liven up the debate. I managed to quell the urge, though.

It was Kelman who suggested calling the Isle the "Stormrock." It sounded ridiculous to me, but most of the people in the room seemed happy with it. It wasn't important. I let it pass.

THE FIRST TIME I offered to deal with Jada, Darren refused very politely. The second time she was less polite, the third time she was positively sarcastic, and the tenth time, she was too frustrated even to speak, and just made gurgling noises. We argued for approximately forever before she agreed to at least let me in the room.

Jada didn't bother to get up from her stool when we came in. (She had a stool in her cell—and a cot, and a bucket. All the conveniences. Darren had insisted.) Her breakfast tray was at her feet, empty except for crumbs and spilt tea. For a little while, Jada had refused to eat and her meal trays came back to the kitchen untouched, but you need willpower to play that game, and she didn't last long.

Darren closed the door, leaned against the door. She wasn't quite as angry as I would have liked. More bewildered, and sad, and even a bit fond.

Jada spoke before long. Of course the little coward didn't have the stones to wait out the silence. "Are you going to ask why I did it, pirate queen?"

Spite in the words, a prickle of venom, but Darren didn't blink. "How's your head?"

"I won't die before you have a chance to execute me," Jada said, picking at the skin around a thumbnail. "That's what you're worried about, right?"

"You're not going to be executed."

The breath left Jada's lungs in a sudden hard pant, a sign of relief that she couldn't quite hide. When she looked up, her eyes were bright and glassy with unshed tears. "You murdered Milo. Why spare me?"

Darren sighed. "Jada—"

"You murdered him!" And now the tears were flowing, as Jada's face twisted up with ugly anguish. "There's never been anyone like him, there never will be again. He saw all the horror around us that no one else could see, and he dared to take the world by the throat and shake it and choke it until the rest of us could see it too. He took the stupid preening pigs who were set to rule over us and he made them crawl and he made them cower. There are a thousand fat greasy nobles gloating over his death today who don't deserve to lick his boots clean. And you killed—"

"It was me, actually." I raised my hand. "Spinner helped, but I definitely got the killing process started. Rather enjoyed it. Would do it again."

Darren pinched the bridge of her nose. "Lynn, didn't you promise to keep your opinions to yourself during this heart-to-heart?"

"Yes, but I didn't really mean it, so it doesn't count. Jada, you vicious little idiot—you do realize that Milo had nothing but contempt for you?"

"Maybe I deserved it," Jada flung back. "Maybe we all deserved contempt from a man like him. You'll never understand why—"

"I do understand," Darren said—tired now, as well as sad. "You sat alone in the dark and took out your soul and looked it over, and whenever you saw a rotten patch, you tried to cut it out. Maybe you wouldn't have cut so much if you'd been a little less lonely. Maybe you wouldn't have cut so much if you'd been a little bit braver. But as it was, you cut and you cut and there wasn't much left of you when you finished. You left a big hole, and Milo poured in and filled it. And that was that."

She put a heavy hand on my shoulder, and I shifted my weight to support her. I hadn't had a chance yet to bully her into eating lunch.

"I'm leaving now," Darren said. "You'll be leaving soon, too. Maybe, one day, we'll be able to talk to each other again. But if that happens, it won't be for a long time, I don't think. You need to figure out who you are, and whether you want to be something more than Milo's creature. And if you do come back from that, it's going to hurt like hell. I couldn't keep you from that pain if I wanted to. I don't even know if I want to. I think I probably don't."

There seemed nothing else to say after that, and anyway, Jada had lost interest. She slumped in the corner of the cell, tears streaming, and gnawed at a bloody hangnail. Darren rapped twice on the door.

Outside the cell, Jess stood waiting, a solid reassuring presence in her tunic of nut-hull brown. She fell into step beside us as we headed down the hall.

"I'm not making any promises," she said. "That is one damaged girl."

"I'm not asking for promises. You know what I'm asking for?" Darren squeaked to a sudden stop. "Cows. I want Jada to spend at least the next five years up to her elbows in cow shit. I want her to shovel mountains of the stuff."

"And as I told you, Holly and I can make that happen. But that doesn't mean she's going to *change*. Just don't get your hopes too high, that's all I'm saying."

"Right." Darren stared at the toes of her boots. "I'm grateful, you know."

"Yes, yes. I should be horribly insulted. Your sister is an accomplice to mass murder, and how are you punishing her? You're sending her off to spend time with me."

"Her punishment is being banished to cow shit purgatory, as you know perfectly well—and can you please stop taking the piss out of me for two consecutive seconds? I'm serious."

Jess smoothed her hands down her long split tunic, flicking away an invisible speck of dust. "Our relationship, such as it is, consists of me taking the piss out of you. It's a little late to renegotiate."

"Oh, for the love of crumpets." Darren turned imploring eyes at the ceiling. "Will you just let me thank you for once?"

"For what?"

"For always being there when I needed you. Even after I dumped you by sneaking out of the house in the middle of the night. When I think of everything that you've done for me—when I try to imagine what would have happened if you'd been even a little less kind—"

"Oh, shut up," Jess snapped, though her eyes glistened. "Are you fishing for compliments? Fine, then. You are, in many special ways, an asshole, but damn it all, you care so much and you try so hard. So I don't mind having your back. I never did. Now, begone. Ariadne wants to see you before the coronation."

They managed to get through something that was halfway between a handshake and a hug before Darren hurried off, and then I politely pretended not to notice while Jess blew her nose and wiped her eyes.

"I forgot to ask," she said, tucking her handkerchief away. "Are Holly and I supposed to send updates about the murder baby? If Jada discovers the remnants of her soul, or if she falls off the wagon and starts to kill kittens with her teeth, do you want us to keep Darren in the loop?"

"You'll keep me in the loop. I'll decide what my mistress needs to know."

"Yes, I figured." She tucked her hands into the opposite sleeves and gave me a long, level stare. "Are both of you all right?"

"Sometimes. For certain definitions of 'all right.' Or did you mean now, specifically? Because we're not all right just at the moment, no."

Darren had woken up halfway through the previous night and spent an hour sitting at the edge of our bunk, just staring. I'd been awake already, so I watched, and eventually held her, but I couldn't take her nightmares away, any more than she could take mine.

"Holly wants to see you," Jess said.

"And I want to see her. Maybe we'll be able to swing by the secret harbour soon, for a visit."

"For an afternoon. Or, at most, a day. And then you'll be back at sea." She sighed. "We both know that Darren's martyr complex will drive her forward until she drops, but that doesn't mean you have to keep pace with her. I wish you would slow down once in a while, Lynn."

"I can't. Sometimes, I wish that I could . . . but, well, I'm useful this way. And I just can't."

This didn't seem to cheer her up much, so I gave her hand a reassuring pat. "On the plus side, now I've met Darren's family, so I don't have that hanging over my head anymore."

AND SO, AT high tide on New Year's Day, as all the world knows, Ariadne was crowned High Lady of Kila.

That "High Lady" part was aspirational in the extreme, since her realm was limited to the Stormrock and a mile of sea offshore, but we had to think big. Besides, we were pretty sure that we'd make gains soon, what with Darren's fleet and our connections to Bero, and we didn't want to have to arrange a whole other coronation six months down the line.

We didn't have an actual crown, a problem we'd only recognized the night before, so Spinner improvised something at the last minute with copper wire and grey seed pearls. It did the trick, though it fell apart shortly afterwards, if I remember right.

We also didn't have a priest, so Latoya did the crowning. She was in full Master of Storms regalia, with embroidered vest and wrist bands. A coiled anchor chain hung over her shoulder, scoured until it gleamed silver-bright.

I lurked behind a pillar at the back of the Great Hall and watched the pageantry. Ariadne bowed her head, Latoya set the pearl-and-copper chaplet into place. The sun cooperated, for once, and streamed through the window arches just at the right moment, bathing everything gold. Cheers, clapping, all of that.

Darren marched forward in boots I'd polished to a mirror shine that morning, and went down to one knee in front of them. In a firm, clear voice, she swore to bear arms for the High Lady and the Master of Storms, to serve them with all her strength and all her wit and all her soul, until the fall of their house or the end of the world.

"You could be up there, you know," Spinner murmured, from his place beside me. "They didn't ask you to hide in the shadows."

"I know. But I like the shadows, and I'm not the only one." I poked him in the ribs. "I heard a rumour that Ariadne offered somebody a job as her spymaster."

"Well. Not all of us are so in love with the seafaring life that we want to give big wet kisses to every ship we meet. And Gilbert, my old flame, the one who helped me sneak into the Keep? He's aged pretty well. Bit of a paunch, but it suits him. What the hell are they doing up there?"

Latoya stepped to the edge of the dais and cleared her throat. She glanced at Ariadne, and the two of them did a bit of the talking-with-their-eyes thing that Darren and I could manage on our better days. *Are you sure? Yes I'm sure. Are you really sure? For gods' sake, woman, get on with it.*

"All hail Ariadne, High Lady of Kila!" Latoya roared—and it really was a roar; it put Darren's best to shame. "All hail Ariadne of the House of Elain!"

"Elain," Spinner muttered. "Isn't that—?"

"My mother's name," I finished for him. Oh, that cheeky so-and-so. I'd wondered in an idle way whether Ariadne would rule in the name of her own house, or come up with some other alternative, but this . . .

Latoya wasn't done. After a pause to let the clapping die down, she took hold of Darren's shoulder. "All hail Darren of the House of Elain!"

The clapping was more scattered that time, but Spinner joined in it. "Do you have any idea what they're up to?" he asked.

There was no time to answer, because Darren cleared her throat. "All hail Latoya of the House of Elain!" And she started the applause when no one else would.

"Well, it's official," Spinner said. "They're all cracked in the head."

I rubbed my chest. I was aching there for some reason that made no sense at all. Now was a silly time to get emotional.

Spinner sighed and gave my arm a squeeze. "Your romantic life is entirely too complicated. I'm going to stick to hairy men with sexy paunches. Now—the captain's coming, so I'd better go look busy."

He slipped into the milling crowd just as Darren reached me. She was looking entirely too pleased with herself, so I had to smack her a few times.

"What exactly was that?" I flicked her nose. "What was that meant to accomplish?"

She rubbed her nose, but the smugness didn't dim. "Had to send a message, didn't we? A sign of a new beginning."

"A new house?"

"A new kind of house. A house made up of people who choose it, rather than being born to it. Is that such a terrible idea?"

"No." I smacked her again anyway, just because. "I should have been consulted about the name, though. *Sod Off* would have been a brilliant house name. It rolls from the tongue."

"Too bad you blew it on a ship, then."

"But seriously, why name the house after my mother?"

"Who else? This is really your mother's victory. Isn't this what she planned?"

" . . . how do you know what she planned?"

"I know her daughter. And I recognize the tactics." Darren linked her arm in mine, which I'm almost sure was a chivalrous gesture and not an attempt to forestall further smacking. "Your mother spent every moment she could with a lonely princess, teaching her about love and guilt and abuse and devotion. You're going to tell me that there wasn't a plan behind that? Your mother couldn't protect you on your own, so she set out to create a person who could. She always planned for Ariadne to grow up into someone who would change the world for you."

My eyeballs got a bit hot, and I quickly squinted off into the distance—which, strangely enough, had gone misty. Somehow or other, we'd left the castle, Darren's arm in mine as she guided me down the path. "Where are we going?"

"Back to the *Banshee*. It's all settled. Ariadne and Latoya and the rest will join us there tonight for dinner—Jess said she'd cook. But after dinner, I think we should get underway. I don't want to sleep on this damn rock another night, and we shouldn't waste the full moon."

What she didn't say, what we both knew, was that the nightmares would matter less once we were at sea. Back on the *Banshee*, where we alone decided the limits of what was possible, we could run from our demons and stay at home together, fight for the old world and invent a new one, all at the same time.

Dream a world with me, build a world with me, change the world with me, rule the world with me. It's much the same thing, in the end.

"Wind from the west," said the pirate queen. "If it keeps up like this, I bet we can outrun the rain."

EPILOGUE

FIVE YEARS LATER

THE GALE OVER the Stormrock was whipping its way to a howling crescendo when the *Banshee* made port halfway through the night. Spinner, keeping vigil at the castle gatehouse, put another log on the fire while he waited. Twenty minutes later came the expected knock at the gatehouse door, and Darren staggered inside with Lynn on her back.

Spinner inspected them gravely. "Should I ask?"

"I lost a bet," Darren said, bouncing on her toes to adjust her grip. "Lynn, you're going to get off when we reach the stairs, right?"

"And deprive you of the opportunity to grunt and strain and look sweaty and muscular in public?" Lynn clucked her tongue. "Come on, Mistress. I'm not that cruel."

"If I'd won—"

"Against me? At koro? Please."

"Just out of curiosity, captain, what did you stand to win?" Spinner asked. "There must have been something pretty special on the table for you to go up against Lynn at koro, of all things."

Darren glowered. Lynn smirked. "You know her birthday's coming up in three weeks?"

"Of course."

"Let's just say that there's something she really doesn't want to wait three weeks for. Where's your boss?"

At that moment, Ariadne came bursting into the gatehouse at full speed, barefoot, clad in a violet silk bathrobe. The thin folds of the robe fluttered as she ran, exposing a dangerous amount of thigh when she took the corners. At one point, she tripped on a flagstone and fell headlong, but she bounced up again without seeming to notice her skinned knees. Her eyes were wide and panicky, and, for no apparent reason, she was clutching a sandwich.

"I told you we'd make it," Lynn said. "How's Latoya holding up?"

Ariadne nodded frantically. "*I THINK SHE'S FINE?*"

Lynn winced. "Does there need to be screaming?"

"*I'M SORRY!*" Ariadne yelled. "*I'M A LITTLE BIT EMOTIONAL!*"

She clutched her throat and shook her head, as if adjusting, then continued in a hoarse whisper. "Latoya's contractions are about ten minutes apart. It'll be a while before she's ready to start pushing. I mean, I think? I haven't done this in years, so what do I know, really? Maybe she'll get sick of waiting and she'll sort of clench, and the baby'll pop out and go flying. Is that a thing that happens? Can babies survive being flung across the room? Maybe I should close the window. Put down some pillows?" She stared blankly at the sandwich in her hand. "How long have I been holding this?"

"Let me take that, princess," Darren said. She freed a hand and reached over. "Drop it. Drop it, I said. Ariadne, let go."

It took a bit of grappling and a slap or two, but Darren managed to pry the wadded clump of cheese and bread out of Ariadne's clenched fist. "Has someone been trying to get you to eat?"

Ariadne scrubbed at her face. "I suppose so. People keep telling me things. You have to go to bed, my lady. You have to get dressed, my lady. You have to get out of Latoya's face before she goes into a howling rage, my lady. Everyone is so bossy this week."

"When did you last eat?" Darren asked patiently.

"Um. I'm fairly sure I had lunch yesterday. When was yesterday?"

"I'm so glad that the High Lady of Kila is facing this challenge with her usual equipoise." Lynn slid down from Darren's back. "I'll make you dinner."

"*THE MOTHER OF MY CHILD IS IN LABOUR—*"

"Volume, Ariadne."

"The mother of my child is in labour," Ariadne whispered, starting again. "And you want me to go suck down soup?"

"The mother of your child won't thank you if you faint from malnutrition the identical second that she needs you to change a diaper. Darren . . . ?"

"I'm on it. Come on, princess—let's keep Latoya company while Lynn raids the kitchen. You can teach me how to destroy Lynn at koro, the next time I challenge her."

"For the last time, Darren, I may be a miracle worker, but even *I* have my limits."

Lynn waited until their bickering voices disappeared down the hall before she flicked a glance at Spinner. "Walk with me?"

"Of course."

"We should make it quick. I promised Darren I wouldn't work today."

"Just as well. There's not much to report. That splinter group of the Sons of Heaven is still making noise in the north, but Monmain's keeping an eye on things. Someone finally knocked out that slaving operation in the Bay of Souls—"

"I know. We were there."

"I figured. The last time I heard 'Red-Handed Darren', there were six new verses."

"Oh, I've heard those. Or, well, bits of them. Darren screeches and hides under the nearest tablecloth whenever anyone starts up that song, so I miss things. I don't know what she's complaining about. I thought it was kind of clever of them to rhyme 'bosom fun' and 'chosen one.' Any letters?"

"One from Hark. He'll finish his apprenticeship with that pastry cook next month, and he wants to take out the captain and get her drunker than drunk. And, uh, one more. Jada wrote."

Lynn quickened her pace. "Did she really."

"Say the word, and both her letter and the faint perfume of bitch that hangs around it will disappear down a hole in the universe."

She hesitated, but barely. "It's not my business to keep Darren from hoping. Even if I sometimes wish that she'd do it a little less. After all, that's why I picked her in the first place."

The kitchens were still warm from the last baking of bread the day before. Lynn busied herself slicing pears into a pie dish while Spinner wrestled a sleepy cat onto his lap.

" 'Red-Handed Darren' isn't the only thing they're singing in the taverns these days," he said, tickling the cat under its ginger-furred chin. "Twice this week, or maybe more, I've heard a song about a little black bird that flies before the storm. She never tires and she never makes landfall, and she can turn cowards into warriors and queens with the touch of her wing."

"Ariadne," Lynn muttered. "She always thinks she's being so bloody subtle when she's writing poetry. Just tell me she's not planning to name her kid Gwyneth, or I'll go ahead and commit regicide by pie."

"Latoya chose the name. It's going to be Nico. I can't speak much Tavarene, but, apparently, it means—"

"Sort of 'suddenly' and 'wonderful' at the same time."

"How did you know that?"

"I heard it once and it stuck in my mind—it reminded me of when I met Darren, so I guess that's why. Hey. No. Don't get emotional on me now. There's going to be more than enough of that today. Let me tell you what my mistress and I have planned for the Bay of Souls. It's going to change everything."

Benny Lawrence lives in Toronto, Canada, where she works as a lawyer while wondering just when in hell she grew up. Occasionally, she dons elaborate hats and sallies out after dark to solve crimes. There being no crimes lying around for her to solve, she mooches off home and eats cookies instead. She enjoys dead languages, not-dead cats, fizzy drinks, preparing for the apocalypse, and board games. She has been told that she takes her board games much too seriously. On a literature front, she is obsessed with mysteries, science fiction, and fantasy books, as long as they involve snappy dialogue and females who can deliver it.

www.ingramcontent.com/pod-product-compliance
Lightning Source LLC
Chambersburg PA
CBHW030341020726
47493CB00003B/625